I0665807

DESTINY REVISITED

Eleanor Tremayne

Copyright © 2017 Eleanor Tremayne

All rights reserved. No part of this book may be reproduced or transmitted in any form or by any means, electronic or mechanical, including photocopying, recording or by any information storage and retrieval system without permission in writing from the publisher.

Published by *Scotoma Books Publishing*
ISBN: 978-0-692-89331-9
Card Catalogue Number: 2017908198
Destiny Revisited/ Eleanor Tremayne
Digital distribution | *Scotoma Books Publishing, 2017.*
Paperback | *Scotoma Books Publishing,* 2017

DEDICATION

To my grandson, Nicklaus Tremayne. May you always have control over your own destiny.

Thank you to my granddaughter, Victoria Tremayne for contributing the original surrealistic eye on *The Tybee Lighthouse.*

CHAPTER 1

Like a moth attracted to fire,
Yesterday's memories are
Laced with lethal visions that
Invade our dreams,
Invade our lives,
Invade our piece of mind.
Impossible to flee,
Impossible to relive,
They prey, on the scabs,
That surround our heart,
Like an interloper,
Who hunts relentlessly
For a new host to inhabit.
We are invincible, yet vulnerable.
Defying all logic.

- Gabriella Girard

Boston - February, 2001

Ashes to ashes, dust to dust; All lie down around the Mulberry bush London Bridges falling down; heavy rain, heals all pain.

Last week, attorney, Andrew Young, notified me of Jake's passing.

"This must come as quite a shock to you Mrs. Blair. Jake shared with me his special relationship with you. I hope you don't mind. He was my friend, as well as client," He said on the phone.

It has been almost thirty-four years since Jake and I last spoke. Yet, rarely did a day pass that I wasn't reminded of him.

"Mrs. Blair, are you still with me?" The voice on the other end of the phone was asking.

The uncomfortable silent pause lasted longer than I realized.

"Yes, Mr. Young, I am here. Thank you for taking the time to personally notify me of this sad news," I said, quietly.

"It was one of Jake's last wishes that I find you and request that you attend his eulogy next week in Boston. If you agree, I will make all the arrangements," Mr. Young concluded.

Perhaps it was a moment of insanity, or merely grief, but I agreed to attend. Once the date and time was confirmed, I began to mentally prepare myself for what I thought would finally be closure to thirty-three years of premeditated mourning.

What happened was unexpected. I am not certain that I can even now explain how surrealistic it felt to be surrounded by strangers, and yet totally alone. It was not how I expected love to end; and in reality, it never did.

Immediately the aroma of burnt oranges, filling the Boston chapel, is reminiscent of that deserted Savannah barn, where all of this started. On those cold January mornings, when Jake and I would wake in the loft, I would smell the oranges being smudged in the orchards. It was a simple happiness, that I could never rekindle

Outside, a thin sheet of ice formed on the windows. We would watch shadows dancing in the dense fog, wrapped in each other's arms until the sun would coax us to start the day. The loft was our safe place.

Eventually, other teens, searching for a sanctuary, away from snoopy parents, would discover the barn, but, it would always hold our special memories.

Sitting here, now in grief, it is easy to return to another time. A time when James Dean was our hero. We all related to his rebellion. It was the same as ours. Soon it became a lifestyle that we all embraced.

The old deserted barn is where I have now escaped. We are drinking cold beer, smoking weed, safe in our love nests, listening all night to "wicked" MUSIC. But, mostly it is where we can be free.

"How did we allow all of this to change, Jake?" I ask silently.

That was the sixties. A time to challenge the establishment. Elvis Presley created a fusion of country music and Rhythm and Blues that this new generation immediately adopted.

Then came the British Invasion. The Rolling Stones, The Who and The Beatles contributed their version of rock 'n' roll. These bands not only changed music forever, it challenged contemporary thinking.

Despite racial discrimination and protests, Barry Gordy's Motown, had us "dancing in the streets" while we burnt our bras.

I wept for Natalie Wood in "Splendor in the Grass." And, thought I was Sandra Dee, when Moon Doggy kisses her in the surfing movie, "Gidget". It was a time to laugh and cry and live every moment with no regrets.

By 1969, when Woodstock originated in the Catskills, near White Lake, New York, it became more than a three-day music festival or peace event. For us, it was a pilgrimage in search of the Holy Grail. Perhaps even more. It redefined the American Dream for a new generation.

The best and worst of times were at our doorsteps. With the assassination of President Kennedy, followed by young boys being shipped off to the Vietnam war and the lynching of black protesters in Selma; there was a somber sense of reality.

Even in my hometown, Savannah, Georgia, the ugly head of racial inequality was dominant.

Now, four decades later, here I am, sitting in a pew, lit by candlelight, staring dramatically at adorned purple wreaths,

7

with satin bows and ribbons, reserved traditionally for weddings.

No celebration today, my mind snaps back. It is at this moment that I am reminded of a passage *that we chose not to take, towards a door we never opened, into a dead rose garden, that remains empty. Nevertheless, I know that my words can still echo, those thoughts in your mind, Jake, even beyond the grave.*

At the altar, there is a large oak framed portrait. It is a handsome young Marine, in full dress uniform with medals on his chest. It is obvious that this is an outdated picture.

Like a magnet, my eyes focus on the words Semper Fidel. The Latin translation means, "Always Faithful ".

Any Marine will tell you that this phrase is nonnegotiable. Absolute! Sometime, in the near future, I would learn how important Semper Fi meant to Jake.

Opposite, the Marine portrait, also framed, and the same size as the first one, is a more recent photo of Jake with, his wife Isabella. What stands out, is how their eyes are focused on some unknown object. They are sitting together, but seem so far apart. *Or, once again, is this my own personal bias?*

It is only now that I realize that there is no casket. In its place is an ornate urn, on a pedestal with a spotlight shining directly above it. Instantly I think that this is a definite replica of "Ode on a Grecian Urn", immortalized by John Keats. Jake and I read that poem together in high school.

We talked about those famous lines *" All yea need to know is that Beauty is truth, truth is beauty."* But, what fascinated Jake, was how the male lover, pursuing his maiden, is always within fingertips from reaching her.

Now, I am sitting here at Jake's memorial service, acknowledging finally how that TRUTH destroyed my life.

The Minister, at lasts speaks, but I vaguely hear him. Jake's final request, he explains, is to have his ashes spread throughout the ocean, at Tybee Beach near the Lighthouse. That "Beauty" that I loved so much, is now gone forever. Then, like a cymbal resonating in my brain, it occurs to me that the Minister has just said, Tybee Beach.

Jake has chosen "our" beach near Savannah, as his final resting place. This is where we walked for hours; where we spent early autumn nights wrapped in a blanket watching the bonfire lighting up the dark sky. The same beach where we skinny dipped in the moonlight during summer nights. It was where we made our plans for the future. Where Jake taught me how to surf; Where I lost my virginity and learned how to love hopelessly.

Now the music begins to play. Some unrecognizable dirge. I am not here. My body is, but my spirit has transformed into that URN on the altar. It has now become my own personal "Ode on a Grecian Urn". Jake and I are the ones now, whom are *"in mad pursuit," in "wild ecstasy". Sweet melodies are no longer heard because they are sweeter than our "pipes", that play on.*

We have become frozen in time. No matter how very close he moves to me. Our time has passed and only here, now, has it been momentarily captured. *But do not grieve, my mind shouts, you will never fade away, forever wilt thou love, eternally, forever, remain.*

Then the minister begins to lead the traditional ceremony of the dead. People stand and follow a script that will never be staged. I force myself from this cataclysmic trance. My head is now pounding. I have heard NOTHING.

At last it is over. I remain seated, waiting for everyone to leave, before I finally get up. I want to stand perfectly still. Once I move from this very spot, everything becomes reality.

Slowly, I begin to inch closer to the urn, for just one more final view. My breathing has suddenly stopped. My tears are smearing my makeup. Breathing will not bring him back. He will never brush away these tears again, or kiss my lips. Ashes to ashes; dust to dust.

A hand that feels like ice, touches my shoulder. It is Isabella.

"Gabriella. We have never formally met. I am, Isabella Jake's wife."

9

I sense that it gives her great satisfaction to point out the obvious, to me. The tone of her voice, is strained. She is uncomfortable.

On the floor, next to the railing, behind the altar is a cardboard box, neatly taped.

"Jake requested me to personally deliver these objects to you."

Isabella, reaches down, and hands the container directly to me without saying another word. Before I can respond, she is walking away, and I am left holding the box.

Once I realize that she has left, I now recognize what this is. It is the same box that I gave Jake on New Year's Eve in 1967, the very last time we ever met. Our final embrace.

Now someone has labeled it, with a Bold Black marker, **"Death Box".**

In my arms, it feels like death. But, then again, I have been carrying Death with me for a very long time.

Isabella got what she wanted; Jake's name, and his remains, for a short time in that urn. Tomorrow the sun will come up as usual, and set in the evening, but I will no longer care.

It will take me two years before I discover what this **"Death Box"** contains.

All I know, is that at this moment, it holds the best three years of my life, that no one has ever been able to replace.

CHAPTER 2

Release the moon from bondage,
Call the savage dogs,
Foaming at the mouth.
Call the sucking vultures,
With their burning poison.
Then watch them bleed.

The fools will no longer play
With the souls that wander.
Not until the moon,
Turns its back on the earth.
                    -Gabriella Girard

August, 1963 Savannah, Georgia
Gabby and Jake

Like a baker who patiently waits for the yeast to rise, Savannah Georgia, my hometown, during the 1960's, was experiencing its own mini revolution. Growing up in the south, there was not only segregation, but, also civil disobedience.

Then there were the Militant Black Revolutionaries, like the Black Panthers, who were not satisfied with the NAACP's (National Association for the Advancement of Colored People) civilized agenda.

Huey P. Newton became the National leader of the Black Panther Party that argued that their agenda was not violent, but to empower their race through self-defense and education. The Panthers were fighting for the same equal rights that the NAACP supported, but more aggressively.

In 1962, eight downtown lunch counters in Savannah, became the target. Demonstrators, following Dr. Martin Luther King's strategies, refused to leave the indoor restaurants and outdoor entrances, until the owners agreed to desegregate the properties.

They also demanded that black employees be respected. No longer would it be tolerated for them to be referred to as "boy" or "girl."

It would be my generation that would challenge inequality, support women's rights, invent rock 'n 'roll, protest the Vietnam war, and reject traditional relationship values.

We would also be known for our LSD and marijuana, often referred to as "Mary Jane". These became our drugs of choice. All of these altering changes, mixed together in a cocktail shaker, created some lively libations. This new era, sometimes referred to as the Age of Aquarius, would determine many of our future choices.

For me, Gabriella Girard, often known as Gabby, the summer of 1963 would change my life forever. I was going to be a freshman at Savannah High School. Most importantly, high school meant, more independence, less supervision, freedom to date, freedom to drive, and freedom to stay out past curfew.

All of us heard those enchanting sirens, tempting us to "run wild", "stop in the name of love," hang on to "Sloopy", or, "Love me Tender", jump in "The Ring of Fire" and of course, "I wanna Hold Your Hand".

Then came harsh reality. If junior high school was the breeding ground for social encounters, now would be the time to create pods where those social butterflies would land and claim their property.

What was even more dangerous was the queen bees with their obedient drones. They would reside on the outer circles of the hive waiting for an unsuspecting fly to approach.

And, those who were moths or even mosquitoes were just plain annoying. They were the true outcasts that everyone ignored; the Untouchables of the high school social order.

In my case, it was not a matter of being rejected, it was a matter of circumstances. Jake Chevalier, three years my senior, football quarterback, and way out of my league, somehow managed to create for me, my own isolated pod.

A few weeks before school officially started, a small group of naive freshman girls, including me, decided to check out the local teen club. That was when I first laid my eyes on Jake Chevalier.

Surrounded by an entourage of Jocks, Jake, lead the way. All were dressed alike. White T-shirts, tight Levi jeans, and a sense of confidence that filled the air. They were on a discovery mission, not hunting. I almost expected to hear the disc jockey announce that "the Studs have arrived."

Jake was definitely intimidating, but from a distance, I could safely imagine what he would be like, close and personal. The Jocks only stayed for a very short time. Enough to make a lasting impression, and then they were gone.

It was not until the following Monday night, when, I least expected it, that the Studs returned. Our drill team was practicing the halftime routine for Friday night's football game with the marching band. The band director, Mr. Adams, chose the grass plot, adjacent to the football field for our routine.

While trying to follow instructions from our Drill Team advisor, Miss Davis, Molly, my best friend, began to whisper that, the football team was huddling on the sidelines.

What I noticed was, Jake dripping in sweat, wearing a cut off football jersey and drinking ice water from a large plastic jug. He was sitting alone on the hood of his 1955 blue and white Chevy Bel Air. As his eyes met mine. I turned away, trying not to be obvious.

"Gabby, that is Jake Chevalier staring at you, Savannah High School quarterback. He is signaling that he wants to talk to YOU GABBY. You can't just ignore him girlfriend..." Molly was relentless.

But, by this time nothing was making any sense. She continued to give me a play by play commentary, while I refused to look back.

"Oh my gosh Gabby..."

Without looking up I asked her, "what was 'gosh'?"

"Well, now half the football starting lineup is standing by Jake staring at all of us."

Just as I was about to look up, I heard Miss Davis' voice, amplified from the bullhorn, instructing us to march toward her off the field.

Summer in Savannah is brutal. Most of us were wearing short shorts, and midriff shirts that barely covered more than a bikini.

"Listen up Ladies. That means you too Bridget."

Miss Davis seemed to always pick on Bridget who was considered the official blonde airhead in our group.

"Anyone coming to practice dressed inappropriately will be sent home immediately. You notice those bobble heads over there?" She was pointing directly at Jake and his crew.

By this time, they were making catcalls, whistling and blowing kisses to all of us.

"Those Neanderthals horny hornets are here to check out the "fresh meat". That would be you, ladies. And when you dress like you are at the beach instead of drill team practice, those hornets could end up stinging you. Do we all understand what I mean?"

We all began to giggle. This only made her angrier. Next, she walked over to Jake and his teammates.

"Gentleman... I use that term loosely. It is time to move on. If you are here again, I will be forced to talk to your coach. Is my English clear enough for you?" Miss Davis said.

In unison they replied, like a trained group of seals.

"Yes Miss Davis. We love you Miss Davis." They all watched her walk back to the field to dismiss us.

That is when I noticed Jake coming directly toward me . I was sure that he was headed in Bridget's direction, which would have made much more sense. She always got noticed, with her long, natural platinum blonde hair and plunging necklines.

But, no, Jake was standing right in front of me. I stood up from the grass and he was towering over me, by at least eight inches.

"Hi, my name is Jake Chevalier. I just wanted to apologize for all those guys disrupting your practice." He reached out and held my hand. I could barely say my name.

"Glad to meet you...I'm..., I'm, Gabriel... I mean ... Gabby." I felt so ridiculous.

But, in fact, Jake was the only real guy who ever noticed me. In junior high school, all the boys were playing sports or hanging out with their buddies. There were some girls, like Bridget, who everyone noticed, but not me.

"I know who you are Gabby. How about we grab a burger and Coke and get to know each other better?" He was still holding my hand.

When I looked back at Molly. She was giving me, the go ahead signal.

"I will cover for you Gabby. Go have a good time." I looked back at her, bewildered, but still following Jake, who was holding my hand tightly.

As I was being led to the car I began to panic. What could we possibly have in common? I guess, you could say that we shared the football field, and that was a stretch. But, then what?

There was also this age difference. Three years. Might as well be a lifetime. Even if, by some miracle, we ended up liking each other, which I could never imagine why someone like Jake would ever fall for me, my parents would never allow it. I was just learning to fly, and he had been around the world and back.

So why was I walking over to his car right now? Every fiber in my body was warning me to turn around and ignore this man. Then he opened the driver's side of the car to let me in.

"Oh, but Jake I don't know how to drive yet," I said.

"I know you don't know how to drive GABBY. You can just scoot right next to me and I will do all the driving. Is that okay with you?" Jake replied, smiling.

I felt like a total moron. Of course, he didn't expect me to drive. I moved as far over as I could. Then Jake got in.

"Are you scared of me Gabby? I rarely bite on the first date. Will you please sit next to me?" He asked, politely.

Strike two. If this is a test on how cool I am, I am failing miserably. I moved over next to him, reluctantly. Now what stupid thing will I say next?

"Are you hungry? I thought we could stop by Wilkes. I am always starving after football. How about it?" Jake continued.

Being that this is the only time I have ever been alone with the opposite sex I was not sure what to expect. Was I supposed to pay for my own meal? This was getting really confusing and making me nervous.

I finally decided to be safe and just be cautious.

"That's fine, but I will just have a Coke. I didn't bring much money with me," I said seriously.

Jake started laughing.

"Oh Gabby. Where have you been all of my life." He put his hand on my knee gently. I didn't feel threatened or uncomfortable. It actually, made me feel secure.

"This is our first date. I will buy you whatever you want. I mean within the limits of my twenty dollars." Jake had just called this a date. I liked the sound of that.

For about two hours, we talked about everything in our lives. What high school was like; Favorite music groups, football, baseball, things that scared us, and what we hoped to do after high school.

"You must be a genius Gabby. You are signed up for honors English literature. I barely passed my basic English class," Jake confessed.

"I am no genius, Jake. Literature just happens to come easy for me. I love reading and writing. But, ask me to solve an equation and my brain freezes."

I was beginning to relax now. Talking was not that bad, at least here in public.

Back in the car alone, it was slightly different. I was way out of my element. Being with Jake, right now, was the closest that I had ever been to a boy. Being an only child meant I didn't even have a limited amount of knowledge about what was expected when you are alone with the opposite sex. But, what I never imagined, was this very natural desire to remain close to Jake.

While he was driving me home, we continued talking about how we would be spending the last few days of summer, what the rest of the week would be like and how hard it was going to be getting up in the mornings once school started.

Right before we got to my house, Jake pulled in to a vacant lot. He turned off the lights and engine. He reached across and held my hand.

"Gabby, I know that I am older than you, but eventually that won't even matter. I hope you enjoyed spending time with me tonight?" He said softly.

I looked into his crystal blue eyes, that just invited me to jump in and never regret or think about the future.

"I did have a wonderful time with you. But, I won't lie. I am a little concerned about how to act around you. We have so very little in common. And I know so little about..."

He stopped me from finishing my thoughts by drawing me close to him. I felt his mouth pressed next to mine. His lips opened and my tongue was greeted with his.

There was a gentle forcefulness that made me slightly tremble. We continued for an unknown amount of time. Neither one of us wanted it to end.

At last, it was Jake that pulled away and looked directly at me.

"I have to see you tomorrow. And the next day, and the next day, and the next..."

I was beyond the moon. Nothing ever before or ever again would make me feel complete.

"You know that my parents will never allow this," I waited for him to respond.

"I don't want to see your parents Gabby. I want and MUST see you again. You trust me, don't you?" His voice was whispering.

"Yes. I do trust you. I do not know why, but I do. And I will work it out, somehow," I said, giving him a quick kiss goodbye.

Back in the house, inside my bedroom, I opened my collection poems by TS Eliot, "The Love Song of J Alfred Prufrock". *Watching the evening spread out against the sky, I too am a patient etherized upon a table/ Should I, after tea and cakes and ices/ Have the strength to force the moment to its crisis.*

Jake never intentionally became my Svengali. His only motivation, I am certain, was to love and protect me. But, there were just too many odds against us from the beginning.

Staying away from each other after that first night was impossible. To avoid any parental objections, we had mutually agreed to avoid all public demonstration of affection on campus. Both of us knew that the school counselor would object and inform our parents if there was any suspicion.

Several months later, after dinner, a movie and a very hot make out session, at the deserted barn that we frequented, Jake began to fear that people on campus were recognizing that we were a couple.

"Maybe we should just come up with some smoke screens Gabby. You know like a camouflage. "Jake suggested.

He was always concerned that if someone realized how much time we spent alone together that my reputation would be in danger. But, what I did not expect was for him to do anything without my knowledge.

The next day, on campus, I noticed a cheerleader wearing Jake's letterman jacket and hanging on him at the school cafeteria. When Grant Gibbs, Jake's best friend, handed me a note, I threw it in the trash, without even reading it.

I refused to accept *the excuses that one can make; the reasons why he and I should not be in love, or to begin measuring my life in and out with coffee spoons; that is not life at all.*

After refusing to see Jake for two days, he showed up early, outside of my last class of the day. He was wearing his Letterman Jacket.

Nothing was ever mentioned again about that incident. But, by this time everyone knew that we were together exclusively. There were only a few people that seemed to object.

One afternoon, after football conditioning, Grant approached Jake.

"We need to have a little heart-to-heart. An honest conversation. I will be the first to admit that Gabby is hot, but man...she's only fourteen; like in jail bait," Grant said.

Grant was trying to be diplomatic, but Jake was getting tired of all the negative vibe.

"Grant, how many times do I have to tell you, Gabby and I are not having sex," Jake said emphatically.

"At this point it really doesn't matter, bro. Everyone thinks you have her cherry," Grant answered without even thinking.

Jake grabbed Grant by the neck and slammed him against the gym lockers.

"You ever say that about Gabby again I will pound your face into the ground." Jake was adamant about everyone showing me respect.

But, there was no denying, that it was rare for a steady relationship to last more than a few months. By that time the *gossip mongers begin to fix you in a formulated condition, where your body begins to be pinned to the wall of disgrace,* where everyone takes turns pulling you apart.

What was developing between us now, was more than a teenage crush. Maybe in part because of the age difference. In the early sixties, pre-birth control era, it was risky to become sexually active. Those who took the chance, often found themselves pregnant.

Heavy petting was as far as most couples ventured. After that they would move on to another *set of arms, bracelet, white and bare, filling the air with a new perfume, while walking the narrow streets watching the smoke rise from the pipes of lonely men.* TS Eliot

The longer Jake and I remained a couple, the more chance there was that we would be another Savannah High School statistic. So, we tried not to disturb the universe and *ask for time to make a hundred visions and revisions of our lives.* TS Eliot

Instead, we took one day at a time and lasted three years together. We redefined the meaning of love. It was a love that would reach beyond the grave.

Spending time alone together was never tiring. There were long walks that somehow lead us to places like the Bonaventure Cemetery. We would explore the historical tombstones and sit for hours planning our future in a place where life had ended.

Other times we would find ourselves on River Street just drifting in and out of the tourist shops or sharing some clam chowder on the wharf. It really never mattered where we went, we always found something that drew us closer together.

Then we found Tybee Island. It was always there of course, but we never spent time there together before. It was only eighteen miles from Savannah. The perfect retreat, especially in the fall and winter.

In the summer, it was insanely crowded. Mostly because of the Tybee Jubilee, Island parades, beach barbecues, and even clam races. During these times, Jake and I easily faded into the background.

September through February we would gather drift wood, wool blankets, ice chest, flashlight and Jake's guitar and head right to the edge of the beach.

On special occasions, when there was something romantic playing, I would beg Jake to take me to the downtown cinema. One evening after watching "Breakfast at Tiffany's", Jake, told me that the song "Moon River" was written by Henry Mancini, who lived right here in Savannah.

"Gabby, did you know Black River, is the very same one that runs past the deserted barn ...our, barn?"

I wasn't exactly ignoring him, but I was still crying after watching the character Holly Golightly walk away from Paul, who really loved her.

"Gabby... Baby, are you okay. I just wanted to tell you that we have our own Moon River. And, you are my Holly Go lightly," Jake said, wiping away my tears.

"I am definitely impressed Jake. I had never heard that before," I answered, genuinely surprised.

"You remind me of Holly in that movie. Just, don't get any ideas about running off like she did.... promise me," he says, seriously.

I reached across the cinema seat, once I knew everyone had left, and kissed him, playfully.

"There will never be anything that could take me away from you, Jake Chevalier. Not even death itself," I said, without any doubt in my mind.

CHAPTER 3

Like oxygen,
I inhale
the scent of love,
that carries me beyond death's
other Kingdom.
This is the land where the
Apocalypse begins.
Without warning the stone
Images raise the dead.
Voices from the grave, disguise
themselves, as doves singing,
And the shooting star,
eclipses
the sun,
Leaving only haunted
shadows as
Memories,
Walking alone once more
At an hour when my voice
dries out,
And my soul shrivels into dust.
                              - Gabriella Girard

Gabby and Jake
1964-1965

Summer in Savannah; my favorite time of year. People complain, " it is too hot, too humid and that the No-see-ums, biting midges, are everywhere" .

All I care about is that Jake and I, have now officially been together for one year. He is finally a senior. We have learned to fly under the radar. Parents and Counselors no longer seem to care.

Ironically, it is our closest friends, like Molly McGee and Grant Gibbs, that are still worried that we are headed into the eye of a deadly tornado.

This is partly, due to the fact that we have moved beyond the hand holding stage. But, intercourse is still off limits.

It is never Jake who complains, it is always me that wants to go further. Jake always stops, just before he enters, refusing to take any chances.

"Why, Jake? Why do you always stop making love to me? Is it because you don't think I will please you? Is that what it is?" I ask relentlessly.

This becomes the main issue that we argue about. And every time it is the same response.

"Don't be ridiculous Gabby. If you trust me, I mean really trust me, you need to be patient. The first time, for you and me must be memorable," he says again.

Jake is holding my face between his two hands. He kisses the top of my fore head. I move away annoyed.

"I'm not a child Jake. We lay here in the loft naked, our bodies touching and I can feel you getting hard...and then you pull away," I say, obviously irritated.

By this time, I am in tears. That is when Jake holds me tight and it becomes serious.

"I never want to lose you Gabby. If anything happens...you know, like I get you pregnant ... I need to be able to take care of you. Please, let's not argue over this," he says emphatically. As always, I acquiesce .

At last, I resolve that the summer of 1964 will be my Gap year. That is in terms of sex. Jake is so happy that I am not nagging him, that he finally teaches me how to surf at Tybee beach. I am there nearly every day. While Jake is working as a lifeguard, earning extra money, I hit the waves.

Next to spending time with Jake, surfing becomes my obsession. That is, until one day I lose control of the board. Up in the air I see it fly, nearly hitting me head. I get caught in the riptide and Jake ends up pulling me out of the ocean. I look like a wet urchin with seaweed tangled in my hair. That ends my days of surfing. At least for a while.

In the evenings, when I am able to escape, for "all-nighters", the deserted barn with the ideal loft, provides a decent amount of privacy. Even when other couples are around, we still manage to respect each other's space. It is one of the early stages of communal living.

Jake and I, not only make intimate memories in that barn, we spend hours listening to music and planning our future. We both know we want to leave Savannah, as soon as possible, and see the world together.

"When we get to Paris, at the Eiffel Tower, just as the sun is about to set... I will be on one bended knee..." Jake demonstrates exactly what his plan is. "I will propose to you in front of the world." He waits for me to respond.

Being in a playful mood, I stroll over to the open window that looks over the orange groves.

"I miss not smelling the burnt orange peels ...you know, during the smelting season." Jake looks at me like I am crazy.

"Did you hear what I said Gabby? I am asking you to marry me... I mean not now. In Paris....and, you are talking about the smell of oranges?"

I walk over to him, and in my best Scarlet O'Hara pose, and in an exaggerated Southern drawl, say, "Well, Mr. Chevalier I would be honored to be your wife, but you are just too damned old for me."

Before I can say another word, Jake has me by my legs, pulling me down to the floor next to him. Rolling in the hay, we are laughing, playing, until Jake suddenly stops.

"Seriously, Gabby...you will say yes, won't you?"

I look directly in his eyes and for just a slight second he reminds me of a young boy who is lost. I brush the straw out of his hair and in almost a whisper say, "Jake, you are

24

the love of my life, the oxygen I breathe, the blood that runs through my veins. Without you, life is meaningless."

His embrace is almost too tight, as if he lets go, I will evaporate into thin air. His kisses are now intoxicating. This is it. My mind is hovering above my body. *Tonight, I know we will make love.*

But, then Jake gains his composure. It is an enchanting moment, but it soon passes. The flame that we have lit with a mere match will smolder, turning into an inferno.

Soon after our evening in the loft, Jake and I agree that our best defense against the gossip mongers, is to be more open with our relationship, not less.

Since Jake is graduating in June, the library is our new meeting spot. The plan is, he will get a football scholarship to Alabama University, and in two years, I will follow him. Since I struggle in math and Jake needs tutoring in British Literature, the library "dates" are also very practical.

It is during one of these library meetings that Jake experiences an epiphany that will change our relationship. He is studying the short story, "Portrait of an Artist as a Young Man", by an Irish novelist, James Joyce. Since I am in an accelerated Honors class, it just happens to be the same assignment that I have.

Joyce's psychological approach fascinates me. I am seriously considering studying psychology in college, as a minor to literature. Joyce is a master at layering symbolism, while his language is a pure delight to the ear.

Everything that I love about Joyce bewilders Jake. I am determined to make him realize that there is more to life than being a jock. The mathematical and technical portions of his brain need to be nurtured with some appreciation of art, literature and music.

"There is no practical reason why I need to be reading this story, Gabby. It doesn't even make sense, and the language is archaic. ...how am I supposed to even understand the epiphany, when the character doesn't even know?" Jake says in frustration.

"That is exactly why I am here. And the reason why the humanities are essential, smart ass.... it teaches you to have empathy, and respect ideas that you may never even knew existed. Fundamentally it makes you human," I respond, passionately.

Jake leans across the table that separates us and gives me a quick kiss, before the Liberian can see him.

"I suppose that is why you showed me the poem by Kean.... Or Kern .... whatever his goofy name is?" Jake is shuffling through his notes to find the poem.

"That is John Keats. Don't bother looking in your notes... I have it here. The title is "Ode Upon a Grecian Urn" and as I remember, you liked the part where the guy is chasing the maiden". I finally find the exact lines.

"Here it is...'Bold Lover, never, never canst thou kiss... She cannot fade, though thou hast not thy bliss... Beauty is truth, truth beauty, - that is all You know on earth, and all yea need to know '... Very wise words. Brilliant," I say, eagerly.

Jake shakes his head negatively, pointing out,

"What I didn't like was that he never caught the girl. And I still don't get that truth and beauty stuff, Gabby."

I was learning to be very patient with Jake. But, no matter how much I loved him I just knew that most of these objections were only a facade.

"I know that you understand all of this a lot better than you pretend to."

He winks at me acknowledging that I am right.

Today I am determined that Jake will understand epiphany. Together we read the passage from "Portrait of an Artist." It is when Stephen Daedalus, the main character, is mesmerized by a young girl frolicking in the waves.

For the very first time there is a moment of clarity. From this vision, he realizes why he must be an artist.

Watching this girl from afar, lifting her skirt to avoid the wet waves, playing with a flock of sandpipers, Stephen feels an "outburst of profane joy".

I explain to Jake that it is profane because there is conflicting emotions. The church is convincing Stephen that the aesthetic beauty that he witnessed is evil and perverted.

"Jake,are you listening to what I am saying to you?" He is in a daze until I call his name.

"Yeah, yeah.. When Stephen realizes that 'her eyes had called him' and his destiny is to 'live, to err, to fail, to triumph, to create, life out of life' he is a changed man. It is the bird girl, in those few, brief, moments that release the tension pent up his entire life," he finally answers.

I looked up from the passages that Jake had just referred to. I am in shock.

"That is exactly right. And you said it profoundly.... how? I mean, what made this so obvious to you?" I ask.

For the very first time, Jake looks like a scholar, not an athlete.

"Gabby, you're my 'bird girl, my destiny and my reason to live," he says, looking up from the text.

As I listen to his personal epiphany, I sense that we are moving beyond the literature lesson. It was both thrilling and frightening.

At the Tybee carnival, I always avoid the roller coasters. Jake can never convince me to ride on them. But, at this moment I just might enjoy a thrill ride.

When Jake asks me the following weekend to arrange a sleepover, I immediately go to Molly's house. We have been friends since first grade, when I got caught trying to take the class goldfish home and she took the blame.

Molly and I are as opposite as any close friends can be. Physically, she has short strawberry blonde hair, brown eyes and is built like an athlete. Which is why, she is on the girls' softball team. The only reason why she even joined drill team was because I begged her.

"Molly, my favorite person in the whole world, my beautiful friend," I say, as I walk into her room.

I can barely find her, buried beneath mounds of clothes, art canvases, and Rolling Stones albums.

"You must want to spend the night with Jake on Saturday? I think you are the only couple in the universe that sleep together without having sex," she says, without looking up.

Molly is working on her latest art project, which is, really impressive for a sixteen-year-old.

The oil painting is a collage symbolizing her motivations in life. Although it is a work in progress, I notice that most of the objects Molly chooses is French.

"Looks like you plan on spending some time in Paris, Miss Molly?"

It always impresses me how the colors she uses are both vibrant and subdued; very much like Molly herself.

"Well, that is the plan. Maybe when I become famous you will come and visit me. That, is if Jake will let you." She keeps painting, focusing on her immediate object.

"I don't ever have to get approval from Jake to do what I want Molly." I know that I sounded agitated, but it disturbs me when people think that Jake rules my life.

"Okay, Gabby....chill. I just would like it if sometimes we could spend an evening together. I miss those pre- Jake days."

Molly is serious now and I begin to realize that she may be right.

"I'm sorry Molly. I promise that we will make some time to spend together." It is a promise that I intend to keep, but I am not sure when.

Saturday night Molly's mom is working at the local all-night diner. It is a shift that she prefers, now that Molly is old enough to leave alone at night. The diners are better tippers at two in the morning, after the bars close.

When Jake comes by to pick me up, he rings the door bell, instead of honking his horn. That should have been my first red flag that something different is in the works. It is Molly that answers the door.

"Oh, Jake....how sweet of you. You shouldn't have?" Molly grabs a bouquet of red roses and dances around the room.

"Cute, Molly....where's my girl?" Jake has managed to grab the flowers back just as I walk into the living room.

"Why Jake Chevalier, so nice of you to stop by and visit us old spinsters. Are these red roses for moi?" I curtsy in front of him, waiting for a response.

But he doesn't even bite. I smell the roses. Jake has NEVER given me flowers. Even if he had wanted to give me flowers before, I would never be able to hide them from my parents. They still had no clue that we were a couple.

"Now this really must be serious. You have never even given me a dandelion before. I should be very worried."

Ignoring my question, Jake waves goodbye to Molly, and pulls me out of the door, with my free hand. I hold the roses in the other hand.

"Seriously Jake, what is all of this about?" I kept asking.

Being romantic was... well let's just say, not one of Jake's shining qualities. He showered me with affection, but things like flowers and poetry were not on his repertoire.

"Have I ever told you Gabby that you just ask way too many questions? Just relax and enjoy tonight." He refuses to divulge any more..

He opens my door for me, another first, and I take my designated place right next to him.

"Will you at least just give me a small clue about where we are going. I mean, come on Jake....I'm wearing shorts and a T-shirt." He turns away from the road to take a quick look at me.

"Looks good to me sweetheart."

And he continues driving, silently.

It did not take me long to realize that we were not going to the barn. And then Jake turns, on to Tybee Road highway. But it is not the normal road, where the fire pits are. Instead, we are on a dirt road heading toward the Lighthouse. As we pull up to the door, I am now really confused.

"You do know that we can get arrested for trespassing, don't you Jake?"

29

He turns off the car engine. Ignoring me, he begins taking things out of the trunk and proceeds toward the front door of the Lighthouse.

"Well? You coming? Or are you going to just sit there all night with your roses?" Jake asks, smiling.

I am not sure if I want to take a chance being busted. Then I notice that Jake has a key to the door.

"How did you get a key?" I ask.

"Just follow me in and it will all be clear in a few minutes. I promise you babe."

I nod my head yes, although my inner self is very confused.

Jake's body is holding the door open. His hands, are holding a cardboard box containing some unknown treasures.

As I continue to follow behind him, I notice an all glass window circling around the room. The moon beams are iridescent, making the waves look like sparkling diamonds dancing in the water.

It is mesmerizing. And I am speechless.

"Do you like this, Gabby? It's as we are floating on water, just the two of us, our own private island." He waits for me to respond. It is breathtaking.

When I don't say a word, Jake approaches me and wraps me in his arms. Finally, after a few moments I say,

"How, did you ever get the keys to this place? It is special, but can we be here?"

My voice expresses the momentary anxiety I am feeling.

"It is all ours for one night. And I intend to make it MAGICAL for the entire time we are here, Gabby."

He then walks over to the cardboard box ,that is now on the small round table, and removes a lovely gift wrapped in gold foil.

I sit down on the bed, that is covered with a sunflower patchwork quilt.

"This is for you, Gabby." Jake hands me the box.

It is the first real present that I ever receive from him. I have his class ring and Saint Christopher medal, oh, and of course his Letterman Jacket, but never a real, wrapped gift. I stare at it. It is almost too beautiful to unwrap.

"Gabby, you have to open it," I hear Jake insisting, encouraging me to continue.

As I carefully removed the foil wrapping, it reveals a beveled crystal bottle with a blue sapphire ornate orb on top.

The label says, SHALIMAR. I have, of course heard about this expensive fragrance. Molly and I probably even sampled some at Dillard's department store once.

"Oh my goodness Jake... this is so... so... outrageous! You can't afford to spend your money on extravagant ..."

Jake stops me from continuing as he starts to kiss me. And, it is kissing like we have never done before.

His hands are in my hair. His mouth feels like I am being inhaled into his, passionately without a need to even breathe. Then it all just stops.

"Gabby, before we go any further, I have to tell you why I bought Shalimar for you.... will you listen, please?" My heart is beating so fast that I can only barely respond.

"Yes... Jake, but, only if you will kiss me like that again when you are finished with your little story."

By this time, he is also trying to control his emotions and I see him grinning, obviously pleased by what he has accomplished so far.

"Okay, then this is the story: Four centuries ago, Emperor Shah Jahan fell hopelessly in love with Princess Mumtaz Mahal. He built for her the Taj Mahal in India, and the enchanting gardens of Shalimar. It is known as the forbidden fragrance."

He takes the bottle from my hand, opens it and places several drops behind my ears and on my cleavage. It smells like vanilla, ambrosia and nectar from some enchanted Island.

Then Jake's mouth once again is on mine. His hand rubbing my inner thighs. We are lying on the bed, still clothed, when he looks into my eyes and says softly, "Tell me what you want Gabby?"

My entire body is quivering. His hands pull down my jeans, and then his fingers are stroking my vagina, but I can't say a word.

"Baby, you have to tell me if this is what you want " he whispers.

Just then I feel him plunging deeper than he has ever gone before.

I yell out, in ecstasy, "YOU, JAKE. I want to feel you inside of me. All the way inside of me."

I am nearly delirious as my hands clutch his massive arms. My bra has somehow been removed.

I feel him sucking on my nipples. Then he mounts me again gently. My legs wrap around him. I start to arch my back.

"Gabby, baby, let me do all the work. I love you so much. Just remember this forever...." He is whispering in my ear and his cock is going deeper and deeper until.... I feel the ripping sensation.

It is like sweet and sour flowing inside. I want to scream and cry but I just hold on to this moment forever.

I hear Jake moan with such intensity that I know that he has come inside of me. It is warm and natural.

I see a kaleidoscope of colors flashing. There is no time for a condom, but I don't care.

It takes a few moments for Jake to move off me, and when he does, I already feel empty

He holds me close to him. He finally asks me," Are you okay, Gabby? I am so sorry for hurting you."

"I am more than okay. You have given me something unbelievable. I can barely express the joy I feel."

"You are the only virgin that I have ever had sex with and the only one that I will ever love." My eyes fill with tears.

I replay in my head the conception and creation, between the motion and the act.

For this is life as I always want to remember it, now and forever. Unknowing at this moment, that the world will end, not with a bang but a whimper.

32

CHAPTER 4

The beating of my heart, the passing of blood and air
through my lungs,
The scent of green leaves, and the shores
dark colored sea rocks,
And the hay in the barn.
Houses and rooms are full of perfumes.
The shelves are crowded with perfumes.
I breathe the fragrance myself, and know it
And like it.
This atmosphere is not a perfume.
It has no taste of distillation- it is odorless
It is in my mouth forever.
I am mad for it to be in contact with me.
A few light kisses, a few embraces,
A reaching around of arms.
Battles of horrors, of Fratricidal war,
The favor of doubtful news, the fitful events.
There was never any more inception than
There is now,
Nor any more heaven or hell as there is now.

-Walt Whitman
Leaves of Grass
(recast)

Gabby, Spring 1965

Tybee Island Lighthouse, was erected in 1736. It was the first one on the Georgia coast. Standing only ninety feet high, it's original purpose was to alert ships into the Savannah port.

After my first sexual experience with Jake, in that tower, it became my beacon of light. Until 1967, it represented my safety net. When I was disillusioned, frightened or confused, my mind would soar to Tybee Lighthouse for consolation.

This sanctuary, became our private oasis, from that first October night until Jake graduated that following summer. It was so much more than a sex haven. Whenever I had doubts, or regrets the Lighthouse drew me to its outstretched arms soothing my inhibitions.

If it had not been for this radiance which was once so bright, soon to be taken from me forever, I could never revel in the comfort, knowing that nothing would replace my splendor in the grass.

Later, in life, this recollection encouraged me to move along faithfully, with soothing thoughts of intellect, imagination and creative prowess into a new journey.

That moment when Jake anointed me, with the mesmerizing scent of Shalimar, it gave me a confidence to confront most obstacles. It also provided me with an "edge" that leveled the playing field on campus. Not even the popular, "mean girls", in their exclusive cliques could make me feel inadequate.

Losing my virginity was a rite of passage, but Jake was very adamant that sex was not going to be a reoccurring event.

"Gabby, you must trust me on this issue. Even using a condom is not one hundred percent safe. This is risky for both of us and we are so close to being out of school that we must be careful." He was absolutely committed to be in control of our future.

I only agreed with him because I knew he was right. But it was now March and we had only been intimate three other times. In a few months, Jake would be leaving Savannah on a football scholarship to Alabama. I, would be by myself, with the exception of, Molly.

Ironically, being exclusive with Jake allowed me to spend all my free time studying. My counselor was so impressed with my grades that she began showing me college options.

"Gabriella, you have impressed most of your teachers. Especially the English department. I realize that you are only a sophomore, but, Mr. Johnson, your honor's English teacher, is so amazed at your literary analysis that he is advising me to enroll you in a college literature class next year." Mrs. Thompson, waited patiently for my response.

"I am very flattered that Mr. Johnson has such confidence in my ability, but really, I do not think that I am ready for that," I said, softly.

My response was unexpected.

Mrs. Thompson removed her black rimmed glasses and looked directly into my eyes, "Gabby, may I call you that?"

I nodded affirmatively,

"This is a lifetime opportunity for you. My generation did not recognize talented young ladies like you. This position, as a guidance counselor is as far as I can go. But, you Gabby....your talent is noticed. One day, you may be able to break through that glass ceiling. Do you understand what I am saying to you?"

I was paying attention to every word she was saying, but I still had difficulty believing she was talking to me.

"I really don't think that I have that ability, Mrs. Thompson, but I will try taking that class. Maybe, I will even surprise myself".

When I told Jake about my visit to the counselor, he wasn't even surprised.

" I told you Gabby, that first night we went out, nearly two years ago that you were brilliant. Together babe, we will make some beautiful and amazing children one day."

That left the opening that I needed to plead my case for us to get married sooner than later. My plan was to move to Alabama with Jake, married of course, and while he was in school I would enroll in Community College. I knew that passing the GED would be a breeze. But every time I would suggest this, we ended up fighting.

Because of graduation, there were many senior parties this time of year. We attended most of them. It was after one of those parties that the reality of Jake really leaving. became too much for me.

Once we were in the car, I started to cry almost hysterically. As Jake tried to calm me down, I just stopped suddenly and without even realizing it, demanded that we get married or split up.

Once it got quiet, and I waited for his reaction, I regretted how hostile I sounded.

Jake simply turned to me and calmly said,

"Okay, Gabby. You win. I will give up the Bama scholarship and stay here in Savannah. I will get a job, and when you graduate in two years, try to go back to some community college."

I was stunned. Speechless. He continued.

"You do realize, however, that we cannot run away and get married in Kentucky, like you want to do, because there will be no money for a long time."

As Jake was talking in a very subdued tone, I began to come to my senses.

"Alright. You have made your point eloquently. I would never deprive you of the opportunity to play football at Alabama."

I was still sniffling and hardly audible, when he began to draw me close to his chest, I could hear him whispering in my ear ever so softly.

"This is for us, baby. What I always do is for us. You have to trust me Gabby."

And, of course I did trust him. He was my life and when he held me in his arms like this, the world could end and I knew we would survive.

Then it happened. In 1965, the United States drastically increased the number of soldiers deployed to Vietnam. Soon news reports, in color now, would depict the images of young men on their way to this "conflict". The word "war" was being avoided, as if that would make the situation less horrific.

Dr. Martin Luther King, began to speak against this engagement, pointing out how many black men were being recruited to the front line.

When the National Guard shot four white students at Kent State, there was a national outrage. Ordinary people were questioning the validity of escalating a conflict that was not even being recognized as a war.

The third and final phase of troops made up the first cavalry. It departed from Fort Benning, Georgia with 13,500 men. At that time, it was just another statistic. And then, it became real.

ROTC (The Reserved Officers Training Corps) had infiltrated Savannah High School, seducing young men to volunteer for combat. Bonus pay was a main feature that tempted many boys to sign on the dotted line. Then there was, of course, the appeal to "serve your country honorably, like generations before you."

Every Friday, in April *the cruelest month, breeding lilacs out of the dead land,* there was a patriotic assembly. In June, we were told that all the new recruits would be honored with a special tribute demonstrating the branch of the service that they had chosen.

The recruiting officers, always dressed in official military attire. The Marines, proudly wore their Dress Blues; the most traditional and formal of all the other armed branches.

It was a basic blue jacket with red trim. Equivalent to a "black tie" affair. This was what all the officers wore in the advertisements plastered on walls throughout our campus.

"Don't you just love a man in uniform?"

I would hear girls, saying in the hallways on the way to class.

For me, it resembled how the citizens of Oceania, in George Orwell's prophetic novel, **1984**, were forced to publicly support the government, or risk being banished from society. What I was witnessing, had overtones of similar propaganda techniques.

During these months of recruiting, there was never any mention of how many of these young men returned home

37

in body bags. And, it would be decades later when the deadly effects of Agent Orange would surface. At this moment there was only fanfare.

When ROTC finally left Savannah High School, they had met their quota for recruits. It was soon obvious which boys had made the commitment to join the forces.

They were the ones driving to school in their shiny new mustangs, or buying their girlfriends diamond engagement rings.

In my opinion, it was still a throw of the dice if any of them would come home alive.

One afternoon, shortly after the recruiters were gone, our history teacher let us out early to do some research at the library. Once I was finished there, I decided to wait for Jake in his car in the senior parking lot.

I opened the passenger front door and slid over to my designated place next to the driver's seat. The dashboard was piled with military pamphlets. I reached for one as I heard Jake open the car door.

"Hey, babe," I said. Then I noticed the dark circles under his eyes.

"Have you been getting enough sleep lately?" I asked, genuinely concerned.

He started the car, and drove out of the parking lot without looking or answering me. By now, I could tell if he was being moody or just absorbed in deep thought.

Past experiences taught me, to let him make the first move. But, after about fifteen minutes of silence, I couldn't take it any longer.

" Do you want to talk about this, or are we going to drive around in circles all day."

Never turning his head from the road, he finally said, " Yes, we definitely need to talk."

There was never a time that Jake was this serious with me. I could not even begin to imagine what had happened.

What are those roots that clutch? What are those branches that grow out of the stony rubbish? And that dead tree gives no shelter; the cricket no relief...But, I will soon see the fear in a handful of dust.

The familiar dirt road leading to the Lighthouse provided me some assurance, recalling that only good things ever happened there. Jake stopped the car, removed the key from the ignition and took my hand.

"Today, Gabby, we are going to the top of the Lighthouse to see the beach and the sunset from a different perspective," the tone of his voice continued to be serious.

"Okay. You know that I like to see things from all kinds of angles," I tried to sound playful.

"I am counting on that Gabby," he leads me to the front door. While turning the key, he added, "This will take a little more patience on your part."

I was becoming more confused as we entered the Lighthouse and began climbing the wrought iron circular stairs to the top floor. The window seats around the glass had inviting gingham cushions.

The only other piece of furniture was a roll top desk with a pair of binoculars on the upper shelf. *This is where the Phoenician soldier drowned, here is Belladonna, the lady of the rocks, the lady of situations.*

Looking out to the sea, using the binoculars, I felt Jake's arms around my waist from behind. He then turned me, so that I was facing him. I put the binoculars back. He firmly held my arms with his hands, like he was restraining me.

"Gabby, I have to tell you something, and I want you to listen to everything before you speak, or do anything."

I looked up at him, trying to stay calm. Whatever was about to unravel, he wanted me as high up as possible, preventing me from running away. I must have looked like a deer who sees headlights for the first time before it is going to die, because Jake was talking very slowly.

I watched his mouth move in slow motion, barely comprehending what he was saying.

"I have secured a future for us that will make it possible to get married sooner than I thought. I have joined the Marines and will be in boot camp for sixty days right after graduation.

Then, I will be overseas for six months, home on leave for three months, with the last leg at Fort Benning. "Jake waited for my reaction. But, all I heard was "Marines".

My body was stiff, like rigor mortis had taken over. When I did not react, he continued to add that,

"We will see each other every weekend and when you graduate, with all the money that I will save ...oh, and the GI bill, we can get married and go to college together."

The words would not come out of my mouth. I imagined myself as the "screamer" in Edvard Munch's famous painting. Unable to compose myself, I Just started crying and using my fists to punch Jake, pushing him back as far as possible, in this room the shape of a coffin.

Finally, my voice was making a screeching sound, "Do you have ANY idea what you have done? " was all I could say.

"Yes, Gabby. I have made an ADULT decision for both of us because you are incapable of looking at life realistically. You depend on Eliot, Keats, Joyce, and Whitman to guide you and they are all **DEAD.**"

Jake looked at me exhausted. Then he added,

"This war is real. The opportunity to prosper from this war is REAL. And it is real that I love you and I need to take care of you. "

Again, he paused, looking at my eyes that were flooded with tears.

At this point it was not clear if he was trying to convince me or himself. *So, intelligence, what do I do now? What shall I do? I shall rush out as I am, with my hair done like Ophelia before her death by water scene.*

"Do you even know how many soldiers lose their lives a day over there? Jake, if that happens to you.... I will no longer want to live."

By this time, I was nearly collapsed on the floor. Jake sat me down carefully. He then held me in his arms like I was a wounded bird.

"Oh Gabby... My Gabby! I will never leave you. You will be the reason I will not die. Have I ever lied to you, Gabby?"

I wept sweet Thames, run softly till I end my song... For I speak not loud or long.

August 10, 1965, the night before Jake left for Vietnam, I insisted that we spend the night together at the Lighthouse. Until five AM he would be all mine.

When he arrived, he brought me stacks of travel folders from all the places we had decided we were going to visit after college. He explained each one to me.

"Here is Ireland, Gabby. We will follow in the steps of Joyce. Then to Paris, France where we will see the Louvre, and of course the Eiffel Tower, where I will propose to you formally, and then on to Scotland and England to visit the Romantic poets. Finally, we will conclude our trip in Venice, at a gallant masquerade ball. Then home to make babies."

At last he was back to being himself, controlling but always charming. For the following twelve hours, we would share Chinese food, drink champagne, lay on the bed staring at the stars reflecting into the massive ocean, feeling safe for the moment in our private world.

"It is almost impossible to believe, that in the morning you will be on a plane that will take you on the other side of the world," I said.

Up until this moment I really did not want to accept that reality. I knew that Jake did not want to talk about it either.

" Let's just live for the moment Gabby. You know, Carpe Diem! Isn't that what all those dead romantic poets tell you to do?"

I wasn't even going to take his bait tonight. I nuzzled as close as possible and soon we were making love for what would seem like eternity.

Quietly, when the dawn was breaking, Jake prepared to leave, for the bus depot. Dressed in his Marine fatigues, he bent down and gently kissed me on my mouth. There was only moonlight shining through the windows, when I awoke realizing that this would be goodbye, at last.

"Gabby, I promise, this will go by fast, sweetheart," he said, his voice nearly inaudible. I looked up into the eyes that always saw through my soul, and was determined not to cry. With the blanket wrapped around me, wearing his plaid flannel shirt, I kissed him and said,

"Go now Jake, and come back to me, as you promised. God Bless you, my love."

CHAPTER 5

There is an unspoken grief
When empty chairs, at empty tables,
Remind us of those who are now,
Dead and gone.

When did the dawning of Aquarius
Become the Death's Angel?
And where are all the young girls now?
With their wilted flowers and songs,
Of peace, long times passing,
Long ago.
                    -Gabriella Girard

October 1966
Gabby

Jake never did come home from Boot Camp. Unexpectedly, his unit was immediately sent to Vietnam. That was when I became engrossed in the details of this war.

I tried to rationalize, that the more I knew, the easier it would be, to accept Jake's decision.

As much as I tried, I could not understand how he could walk away from a college football scholarship, and of course me. Instead, I discovered some horrifying details, that were being hidden from the general public.

Berkeley, California in 1965 initiated an underground student newspaper called, The Tribe. A group of students, and even some liberal arts teachers, at Savannah High school, began to meet in the evenings, at local coffee houses.

The objective was to read the latest news, often documented by legitimate reporters, on the "true" progress of the Vietnam War. It was heinous.

In Laos, where Jake was stationed, the United States bombing was part of a secret war. From 1964-1974 more than two million tons of ordnance, (weapons) in this case bombs, were dropped. That is equal to a plane load of bombs every eight minutes, twenty-four hours a day.

The more research that I did, the more frightening the situation became. The first objective was to destroy the enemy's material and control the traffic along the Ho Chi Minh Trail. Jake was currently assigned to the Intelligence Force, responsible for that specific ground mission.

Not only was it the duty of these soldiers to gather intelligence, depicting where the enemy was, they also planted bombs on tracks, minefields and main artillery paths. Since there were no reliable records kept, or films made of the area, American troops would also be blown up by their own bombs.

Laos was complicated. The Royal Lao Government (RLA) consisted of tin soldiers being led by straw generals. And, once again, there were no statistics kept on how many troops lost their lives in Laos or Cambodia.

That overwhelming fear, that starts in the pit of my stomach, and turns my blood ice cold, left me feeling helpless. At sixteen, my pathetic life, now centered on only one objective; receiving a letter from Jake.

Since he was on the front line, mostly doing secret missions, those letters were few and less frequent.

May 16, 1966

Hi, Babe,

I never imagined how much I would miss you, Gabby. All of us are just waiting for our orders. To keep our minds from going stir crazy, we decided to build a lawn mower from extra scraps. When we finished the job, we proudly told the Sarge that now he could mow down the jungle. He didn't find our humor very amusing. He made us tear it down, claiming that it wasn't an "authorized" piece of equipment. That cracked us all up, since nothing we have here is "authorized" equipment.

Can't wait until I see you. Keep writing please. I know that it is hard waiting for me to write, but the mail here is real slow.

Love, Jake

By the fall of 1966, I was lucky to even get one letter a month. I found it nearly impossible to stay focused, on anything but the Vietnam war. I was torn between my loyalty to Jake and my commitment to protest a war that made no sense.

Soon, I was actively, yet secretly opposing the war. Even my physical appearance was changing.

Whenever I could leave the house without being interrogated, I would stop at Molly's and change my clothes into what became my new image.

" When I suggested that you should get a life Gabby, I didn't mean that you should be sneaking around protesting the war. I mean.... what happens if your Dad finds out? Can you just imagine...., Gabby?" Molly lectured me often on this subject.

I looked at myself in the full length mirror. My long dark hair was held back by a bandana with peace symbols. I always wore black tights and a mini skirt, with Jake's flannel shirt over a white blouse, tied in a knot. The shirt was a reminder of why I was protesting. This was more than a statement against the establishment.

"I just can't be quiet anymore, Molly. Jake is risking his life for a war with no purpose, " I responded emphatically.

I knew that I could never convince my Dad, or Jake that they were wrong, but I also needed to express my own feelings in my own way, among people that believed that our voices would be heard.

If the conservative adults, refused to take the necessary action, needed to bring our soldiers home safely, then it was our generation that must continue to demand the truth. During our coffee house meetings, the college students would distribute copies of Henry David Thoreau's "Civil Disobedience" doctrine.

"That government that governs least, governs best" became a motto that we would adopt as our philosophy.

"I just know Gabby, that one day I am going to get that call from you, asking me to find a way to bail you out of jail. Can't you find another way. Perhaps, less dramatic, to protest?" Molly said, looking directly at me.

"Good Golly Miss Molly, " I was hugging her, on my way out the door, "you don't ever need to worry about me. I am just a small pebble in a river full of boulders. Nobody is going to hardly notice me," I tried to sound reassuring.

What Molly, didn't realize, was that most of the protest marches were well organized by both college students and liberal adults. Prior to any marches or sit in demonstrations, we were all being taught the fundamental rights and obligations of citizens to peacefully change the course of history.

Finally, the stability that resonated in the 1950's, was now replaced with an obligation to fulfill President Kennedy's challenge to, 'not ask what your country can do for you-ask what you can do for your country.'

During those one thousand days of optimism, in 1961, more than eighteen thousand people applied to join the Peace Corp. That number of dedicated people made the protest that I was involved in, appear minor.

Whenever I began to feel that my voice was not being heard loud enough by the "warmongers", I would reflect on Robert Frost's poem, "The Gift Outright".

It was meant to be read at President Kennedy's inauguration. However, the original poem, the eighty-seven-year-old poet, wrote, titled "Dedication", needed to be replaced when the glare from the sun on that freezing January, morning, prevented him from seeing the words. That is when he recited the "Gift" spontaneously.

Frost's message resonated the price our nation pays for battles. *We were withholding from our land of living/ And forthwith found salvation in surrender the deed of gift was many deeds of war.*

My obligation was to remind the generation before us, that each life lost in war, is a tragedy. We must strive for a more civilized way to solve disputes.

By October, as dedicated as I was to the Peace Movement, realistically, it was time to seriously review my college options. Jake would soon be home from Vietnam and we needed to discuss what college would be best for both our needs.

Thanks to Mrs. Thompson, my guidance counselor, I was taking several English classes at Savannah Community College. My parents, decided to reward me for such good grades and commitment to my future, with a car for my Birthday.

It wasn't just ANY car.... It was my dream car; a 1957 Ford Thunderbird sports edition. This model was white with silver chrome, and reshaped grille and tail fins.

When I got in the driver's seat my dad, proudly showed me the Dial-O Matic feature that turns the seat automatically when the ignition is turned off.

The feature that I loved the most, was the porthole windows and the thunderbird hood ornament. Years later, George Lucas, in the movie "American Graffiti" would attempt to recreate this moment that I was now experiencing.

"American Graffiti," symbolized the end of an era; the end of youth. Included in that nostalgic film, is a replica of my Thunderbird.

As soon as Molly found out that I had "wheels", she began to plan ways to wean me from my political agendas and back into the social circuit. At lunch, one afternoon she brought up the idea of "crashing" a party.

"You may be my best friend, Molly McGee...no, I should say, my only friend, but I am not going to escape reality by being a party animal. " I said.

Molly kept on insisting that this party was not like those private parties that all the sosh attend.

"Caden Cassidy and a few other jocks will be there so it should be fairly civilized. Anyway, my mom knows his family. They are Irish, and own the local deli," she said.

"I remember hearing that name before, somewhere?" I replied.

Then it became clear who Caden was. He was at that awful party that Jake dragged me to right before he left last year to Boot Camp.

What I mostly remembered was how he almost knocked me down when we were on a collision course in the school hallway. Some girl, known mostly for being "easy" Allison, came out of nowhere and attached herself to him, like an octopus.

"No, Molly. A hundred and fifty times no. I remember now who Caden is. He may be Irish but, he is bad luck. I would rather stay home and wash my hair, than be caught dead at any party he is at," I replied.

Molly was trying to convince me that I must be mistaken. She knew Caden, and he was a really good guy. She added that I was just jumping to conclusions that had no factual supporting evidence.

Rather than go into detail on my experience with this Caden "nobody", I merely avoided any more discussions that included him. I may have been over sensitive about Caden, but the only thing lately on my mind was praying that Jake would be home soon, and not in a body bag.

Chapter 6

By the water, I sat down and wept,
And ran softly, for I speak not loud or long
I hear the rattles of my bones.

After the red torchlight,
After the Agony
The shouting and the crying
He who is living is now dead
With little patience.
(Wasteland, TS Eliot)

An ocean could never laugh
If clouds weren't there
To kiss her tears.
A river would stop its flow
If only a stream were there
To receive it.
The world is not a pleasant place to be
Without someone.

-Niki Giovani

December,1966 Vietnam
Jake

Gabby brought colors and texture into my life, with so
much exuberant passion that the Italians called this phe-
nomena, "Colpo di fulmine". A thunderbolt, like lightning
so powerful and intense that it cracks the chest wide open,
spilling the soul out, for the world to see.

That was how I felt about Gabriella Girard, the very first moment I laid eyes on her. That long chestnut hair flowing like a cascade down the middle of her back, she reminded me of an exotic gazelle, moving in slow motion. She turned me inside out. No going back; my life irrevocably was changed forever.

Then came the moment that I had to tell Gabby that I had enlisted in the Marine Corp. Her emerald green eyes looked as if she had just seen the earth collide with Mars. I had never imagined that she would react so emotionally. It was a decision that I made to secure our future.

Once more I needed to convince Gabby, to be patient for just a little longer. I really did not know what to expect this time, but, whatever happened was already in motion.

Finally, I was boarding the "Ghost" plane headed home for one week of R&R (rest and recuperation). A ghost plane is one that doesn't exist. The soldiers are told to report to the airstrip and wait for their name to be called. In my case, it took two days before I boarded my flight from Cam Ranh Bay on December 16, 1966 on flight N267A.

Some might call it a coincidence; Gabby, would say it was irony. I was leaving from the same station that I arrived at. My life had come full circle. Once I was on the flight, I realized that I was by myself. My good buddy, John, who was also scheduled to fly to Atlanta, was now flying home in a special army provided casket.

I had plenty of hours on this plane to reflect on what and how I was going to break this news to Gabby. When I originally enlisted, the decision seemed not only logical, but practical. Gabby had two more years of school, and by the time she graduated, my stint would be over.

There would be no further obstacles to prevent us from being together. What I had not anticipated was being sent to Special Forces and transferred to the middle of the jungle five miles from Cambodia.

When we arrived to Vietnam, at first it was just a waiting game. We were known as Grunts (low ranking, disposable soldiers). When the monsoon season came, we were coated with thirty to forty layers of insect repellant.

I was soaked from head to toe, for nine straight days. My buddies, who had been here for a while, warned me that this hell hole would consume so much of my life, that I would never want to return stateside. This world, they assured me, would make me "a dead man walking."

After several months, when the opportunity came to advance to Special Forces, my Lieutenant made sure that I was going to go with him.

"Jake, this transfer comes with a promotion. You are a smart guy. Take advantage of the opportunities that come your way... Hell, who knows, you might even end up a lifer, like me," said Lieutenant Chandler.

I knew that the Marines would never be my life choice. That epiphany came shortly after I witnessed how the Viet Cong blew up runways, limiting our ability to receive resources.

One night, when we were overrun by the enemy, all we had was our gun barrels to fight them off. Then, after witnessing bodies thrown out of helicopters, and human remains landing everywhere, I was past the initiation stage. All I wanted to do was go home.

Nothing ever got easier. It was not uncommon to be talking with your buddies during patrol duty and seconds later see their head blown off right next to you.

Or, a mine might engage while you were scouting the area. The soldier in front of you just detonated a mine. Arms, legs, and torso thrown in different directions in the swamp, like a rag.

This was our Apocalypse. Yet, something inside kept reassuring me that I was making a difference. *Something happening here, what it is ain't exactly clear. There's a man with a gun over there--there's battle lines being drawn. Nobody's right if everybody's wrong.* Those lyrics by Buffalo Springfield were branded on my mind.

And, despite all the red flags flying in my face, I still signed up for a second tour of duty.

I checked my watch. Two hours before landing. Once again, my reasoning was sound. It was not because I thought that I could endure any more of this nightmare; it was because the military was offering me more money, a promotion, and all this for only six more months of duty.

The caveat was, I had to return to the front line in one week. What made the offer acceptable, was that I already knew my destiny was to be with Gabby. Now all I needed, was to somehow convince her that in six months we would never be separated again.

Nobody knew that I was coming home. Soon I was on the Greyhound Bus in Atlanta, headed to Savannah. It was Christmas break and Grant Gibbs, my closest friend in high school was home from the University of Atlanta. He would pick me up at the bus depot.

"Hey man, you are looking good Jake,"

Grant said, as I grabbed my duffle bag and threw it in the back seat.

" So, is it as ugly over there as everyone says it is? " Grant asked, trying to be politically correct.

"Let's just say, I am here now and I don't want to think or talk about any war stories. How is college life in Atlanta?" I sincerely wanted to know.

"Football isn't the same without you. But, I have to admit that the college babes are really hot. And most of them are ready to give it up," Grant answered.

Surviving the horrors of war, made Grant's sexual conquests seem irrelevant. But, listening to him, made me aware of how much I had changed.

After Grant dropped me off at my house, the strategy was to go directly to Molly's place. She would be my liaison to Gabby. After, a hot shower and clean clothes, I was on my way.

"Oh, my Lord! Jake Chevalier." Molly was poking me all over. "You feel real...what the hell are you doing here? Are you wounded?" Molly was talking so fast I couldn't stop her.

"It's me Molly. Alive and well, just like I promised Gabby. I need to surprise her. Will you help me do that Molly?" I said seriously.

"Oh Jake, she is going to be so excited. But, I don't want her to breakdown...I mean, she isn't expecting you until June. Hell, she is just getting used to you being gone." Molly's arms were moving at the same pace as her voice.

"If you aren't wounded, why are you here?" Molly asked me directly.

"I got lucky and they sent me home for Christmas," I tried to make it sound true. I knew better than to confide the real reason to Molly. She would be as bad as Gabby if she knew I had reenlisted.

My plan was for Molly to take Gabby to a favorite restaurant, **Tony's**, on the pier at Tybee Beach. Hopefully, from there, after the initial shock, we would go to the loft in the old barn, where I could explain to her reasonably, my decision.

Gabby was putting the finishing touches on the Christmas gifts she was sending to Jake. All the PO's (post offices) were staying open late to guarantee shipping to the troops overseas.

Gabby had included her homemade fudge, chocolate chip cookies, Leaves of Grass, a collection of poems by Walt Whitman, and a few of her own original poems, that she had written for Jake. The last item was a Saint Christopher medal, that she hoped would keep him safe.

Not a religious person, in the past, she began attending church with Molly every Sunday. Gabby found the Lutheran Church, with its casual service, to be more comfortable than the Catholic Mass that her parents attended. Besides, she didn't feel comfortable confessing her sins to some priest every week.

"Gabby?" Her mom was calling her from downstairs. "Molly is on the phone."

"Hey Molly. What's up?"

"How did you know it was me, Gabby?"

"Who else would call me? Do you want to go with me to drop off Jake's gifts at the post office?" Gabby said. "I could use some company."

"Sure, but, let's go have some Christmas cheer at Tony's on the pier first. I will pick you up in twenty minutes." And the phone went dead.

There is something strange going on with Molly, but I will just wait until she gets here to figure it out, I was thinking out loud.

When I saw Molly's Volkswagen Beetle pull up and honk, I ran out with my hands full of packages to mail.

"I still don't get why you insisted on driving?" I said, really confused.

"Gabby...really? Sometimes you just need to go with the plan someone else has. We are going to **Tony's** and celebrate the season. Please, let's have fun...okay?"

Molly, was really trying to lift my spirits, so I decided to do my best to seem excited.

As we entered the restaurant, I couldn't see any empty tables. "Molly? Did you call ahead for reservations? We won't get out of here for hours," I said looking around. That was when Molly took my hand and started to drag me to the back of the restaurant.

"Where are you taking me?" She was just about to break lose when Jake stood up from the last booth.

All Jake could see was Gabby, running into his arms, with her legs off the floor as he lifted her up.

When our lips met, her eyes were sparkling with happiness and for one brief moment we were on an unknown stratosphere. Then I heard the people cheering and clapping.

As I gently released her, all I heard her say was, "I can't believe you are here! But why?" The only thing I could do to postpone the inevitable, was kiss her.

CHAPTER 7

Once upon a time, where nothing is real,
We both heard a lonely saxophone,
A solo sound,
That told me to hold you tight,
Until the memories subside,
Before the silver rain, washes away
All hope.
It is a make belief life,
Where nothing is real.
We share a sound
 Never heard before,
Never heard again.
We dance
Alone, on a sheet of glass,
With misty, forlorn shadows.
The last dance
In this, our world.

1966-1967
Gabby and Jake

"Is this awful nightmare finally over?" I ask Jake. The noise in the background, makes it impossible to talk. People are cheering the return of their native son, a war hero. I am, of course, proud of Jake, but at this moment all I can do is thank God for his safe return.

When Jake finally puts me down. My hands are already sweating when I clutch his hand. If I release it, I will fall into a state of amnesia, forgetting how good this feels. We are surrounded by people crying with joy. My mind, however, is recalling just how last week, the ominous, black, military sedan was parked across the street.

The Madison family had two sons that enlisted in the army. On this day, two enlisted officers had the grim obligation to deliver the news that Harold, their youngest son, was an MIA (Missing in Action). My heart stopped momentarily. Now, whenever I see that sedan nearby, I...

But, now...now, it is over. Jake is really here. His hand is in mine. He...We, have survived this ordeal, just as he promised.

"Gabby, baby...tonight let's just spend our time together, alone," he was whispering in my ear, as he wiped away my tears,

"I guess that means no lobster, for me?" Molly said laughing.

"Well, at least I know now why you insisted on driving," I said to Molly.

Then looking at Jake, I said,

"This saved me a lot of postage. Now I can give you the Christmas gifts, in person. They are in Molly's car."

"You are the only gift I want Gabby."

Jake said, while ushering me through the kitchen, to the back door.

"Whoa, soldier! Why are you in such a rush Jake? I have things in Molly's car..."

I was almost out of breath, as my short legs were racing behind this six foot four man with his long strides. My feet were barely touching the ground.

"Did you miss me that much, crazy man?" I could barely talk at this point, outside the restaurant. My hair was flying wild in the wind and I was trying not to stumble in the dark. At last Jake stopped in front of his car.

"You will **NEVER** know how much I missed you Gabby." Jake was looking directly into my eyes. There was something frightening in his penetrating stare. I had never seen that look of hungry desperation before. If it had not been Jake, I probably would have run away as fast as possible.

Without even blinking, I said, "I do think that I might have some idea Jake. I was the one who went nearly hysterical when you told me that you enlisted," I then, reached up to him, standing on my toes, and added,

"But, you were right. You came home to me. And, I will never doubt you again. But that is now the past. And, we will never need to go through this again," The relief in my voice was obvious; as obvious as Jake's silence.

In the car, we were on the road to the deserted barn. I wondered why we weren't going to the Lighthouse. But, then he may not have had time to prearrange it with, Joe, the groundskeeper. It was not important where we went, as long as we were together.

The loft held many wonderful memories, including the last night we spent together, before Jake went to boot camp. Tonight, there is, a quick stop at the Piggly Wiggly convenient store, for fried chicken, fries and coleslaw, and a bottle of chilled champagne.

Once inside the barn, we carry everything to the loft. Bundled in warm blankets, with hurricane lamps lit, there are shadows dancing on the walls. The orange smelting pots provided that familiar aroma, that always reminds me of my first time here with Jake. It feels that same way now; Comfortable, but a little uneasy.

Sipping champagne, I begin to tell Jake what has been going on at home all these months. He asks the typical questions, about the football team, his friends, Molly, all the common chit chat that eight months away from home will generate. Then, I make the error of bringing up the war. Almost immediately I know that it is a mistake; it is like a Gorilla in the room. I decide to face it head on, before it starts throwing banana peels at me.

"I don't want to talk about it Gabby." He isn't yelling at me, but the tone is ominous, almost reprimanding me for bringing up that subject.

"Vietnam is another dimension. A chaotic, Nietzcheistic world, as close to the Apocalypse that I have ever imagined.

This right here, the hay on the ground, the sounds of crickets, the smell of burnt oranges, THIS, is reality."

I was silent for some time. How and when did Jake ever learn anything about Nietzsche and his chaos theory?

I was fascinated by the Butterfly concept myself. It was something I studied, when Mrs. Thompson enrolled me in a Philosophy class at the local Community College. Molly had taken an Art Appreciation class on the same evening to keep me company.

"Come on Gabby. This will be just like college in a few months. Everyone will think we are coeds," Molly said.

After hearing Molly whining and Mrs. Thompson pushing me, I finally acquiesced. Once in class, the instructor was inspiring and the philosophies amazing. If it had not been for the fact that Philosophy is such an unrealistic major, I might have considered it.

"Can I at least ask you Jake, how did you ever meet Mr. Nietzsche in Vietnam?"

I was trying to lighten up the conversation, but Jake's reaction was unexpected.

"You are not the only intellect that I know Gabby. Our captain was a Philosophy Professor, before being drafted. While we were waiting for our orders he would read Nietzsche. One day, he asked me if I would be interested in reading it. I thought, why not? And that's how we started to discuss it," Jake replied, once again his tone was solemn.

This was a totally different person that I was trying to communicate with. Before he went to Nam, Jake was always mellow. Now, he is intense, determined, mature. I was trying to adjust to the change.

I wanted to ask him if their discussions included the Butterfly effect, but if they had not, I was afraid he would consider me mocking him. There was no need to make clean waters muddy, at this time. Tonight, was a celebration, not a competition.

Perhaps later I would share with Jake the short story by Ray Bradbury, "A Sound of Thunder". The "old", familiar Jake would have appreciated knowing that when Bradbury published this story in 1956 it focused on the same Butter-fly thesis.

A hunter pays a scientist to take him back in time to kill a Tyrannosaurus Rex, using the time machine that he has created. During the safari, the group discusses a recent Presidential election, whereas a Fascist dictator has been defeated. The travelers have been warned to minimize the events they change before returning to the present.

Any alterations to the distant past could cause a cata-strophic effect on history. When one of the travelers, inad-vertently steps on a butterfly that dies, a paradox occurs that could change the course of the world.

Wisely, I decided to change topics and enjoy my evening with Jake. Crawling under his blanket, with my head on his chest, I asked, " How long is your leave, baby? And, do you know if they will station you at Fort Hunter?" Gabby asked calmly.

The time had finally come when he would have to tell Gabby the truth. He had hoped that he could wait until the end of the week, but, he knew she would keep asking ques-tions.

Jake sat up and turned his body toward Gabby. She, in-stinctively felt his body grow tense, like a panther that is preparing for the kill. He was still holding her close to him.

"I am only here for a week. I need to leave the twenty third of December," he said quietly, waiting for her reaction.

"What happened?" Gabby was still calm, waiting for an explanation.

A million things were going through his mind. Finally, what seemed like eternity, Jake decided he had no choice but to tell her the whole truth.

"Gabby...." He helped me to sit up. With my legs crossed Indian style on the floor, I was staring into his captivating blue eyes. His dimples, barely noticeable, he gave an un-comfortable half smile.

59

"Without going into all the Hellish details, I decided that after six brutal months of combat, that I had made a terrible mistake. You were so right Gabby..."

It was getting more difficult each moment. She looked so young ...so innocent. Then, he knew the time was NOW.

"Will you promise to hear me out completely before you say anything?" Jake asked. I shook my head, yes. Things were getting very complicated and serious very quickly.

"Okay. I should have taken that scholarship to Bama. Hell, we should have run away and got married, like you wanted to. "Jake was watching my every reaction.

"Are you trying to tell me that you are AWOL (away without leave)? Because that is ok. We can go to Canada until this stupid war is over. I know people that can help us..."

"Stop. STOP. Gabby, I have reenlisted."

Jake had finally said it.

I stopped in mid-sentence. Then I stood up.

"You did what?" I wanted to hear him say it once again before the atomic bomb went off in my brain.

There was nothing left to tell her. I knew as soon as I saw her stand up that there was no way that she could wrap her head around this idea. I would never be able to convince her that this was the best decision for us.

How could I convince her that, by extending my time on the frontline would mean I could come home permanently, and sooner. When I returned to duty I already knew that I would be stationed South of Saigon at Cat Lo. My job would be to protect ships traveling up the river to Saigon.

We were all being offered huge bonuses and an early ticket home. The additional six months seemed tolerable. None of us who took this deal believed it could get any worse than what we had already experienced. Once again, fate would prove me wrong.

"How do you expect me to react to this news?" I said, totally outraged. This time, I refused to break down and cry.

"I really don't want to argue with you Gabby. Please do not make these next few days miserable for us," he said, in a very controlled tone.

Was he really blaming me for this catastrophe? By this time, I was on my feet, staring directly at him.

"Jake, I cannot go through this insanity again. Every day, when I wake up I wonder if you are still alive, or is today the day you will die. And, once again you make this arbitrary decision without even talking to me." Now I was in tears and losing focus on how I was going to continue with this new development. Then I just started running to the stairs. That is when Jake stood in front of me blocking my exit.

"Fuck, Gabby. How can I talk to you when I am fighting a war halfway around the world, and by the way, trying to stay alive," he refused to let me past him.

I began to push him, until I realized that it was impossible. He refused to move.

"Will you just listen, baby. I came home with no injuries. I am well trained, and I know what I am doing. "He couldn't stay angry with her. Gabby was standing there like an injured bird. She looked like any moment she would collapse.

"There is nothing that we can do to change this." He was pleading with me, desperate for me to accept the inevitable. Before I could answer him, Jake was kissing me with such intensity and passion that I was sure that I was melding into his embrace. *That was the moment I knew I had surrendered my life to him.*

"Let's get married before you leave, Jake. We can drive to Kentucky. We don't need to tell anyone. Please, Jake at least let me have that." I didn't know what else to say.

I watched the color fade from his face. He almost turned an ashen shade of grey.

"I couldn't do that to you Gabby... if I lose a leg, or worse..." I put my hand over his mouth to stop him from saying anymore.

"That's not in our contract, Lieutenant."

I said, regaining my composure.

He tried to smile, and kissed my hand.

He already knew too many guys that came home with missing body parts. There would be no way in hell that he would ever put Gabby through that torture.

"Darling. Do you remember when I was tutoring you in math? " Jake asked.

"Yes, Jake, but what does..," Gabby replied, confused.

"Do you remember what PI is used for?" Jake asked.

"I think it has something to do with a circles circumference ...why does any of this even matter?" I said, obviously annoyed.

"Well, let me refresh you on that mathematical lesson, and then maybe all of this will make sense to you. PI is the ratio circumference to its diameter. "He illustrated this by drawing a circle on the floor with my marker.

"Now, Gabby, consider this circle you and I united," he waited for a moment making certain that I understood the analogy.

"Regardless the size of the circle, PI is always the same number. There is no final digit of Pi. Therefore, Pi is infinite. No matter how far the circle takes us from each other, we will never really be apart. You, and I Gabby will be infinite, as in forever." He said this with the most emphatic conviction.

For the moment, Jake had won again. Making love all night in the loft, nearly convinced me, that there was no need to worry about the future. We would beat all the odds. I had no way of knowing then, that this would be our last night together.

Jake told me, that someone once asked him , what was worse than dying? " Black rain is worse than dying," he answered. "When it is falling, contaminating the ground; war killing sons and daughters, blood running down like water. You'll think you got away, but your deader than the scattered bodies."

That image of a flag draped over a coffin, Angel of Death standing by, spraying black rain on the survivors, with twisted psyches watching the madness rising like hollow straw, like souls, empty and polluted, is etched in my mind forever. That is worse than death.

CHAPTER 8

Silent storms, cause wild dreams.
A love that returns from the grave,
Only to put another bullet in my head.
Then, reruns flicker in my mind.
Our hands let go,
So that I can search for us.

Needles, and knives, and beautiful lies.
I say, listen carefully to the echo,
It is your loneliness,
It's your heartbeat,
In the stillness of remembering
What you lost--and, what you had.
It will drive you mad.
You can tell when it's over,
If the high was worth the pain.

Jake's montage recast
, 1967 Vietnam

We stayed in the bush, without food. Sometimes, if we were lucky, C-rations were shared among us. Sleeping on the ground, carrying seventy-five pound packs, with no vehicles available was now normal. To stay alive, meant constantly moving. New fox holes were dug daily. I had malaria twice.

One evening, during night patrol, the Viet Cong did a surprise raid. Those of us on duty attempted to kill as many as possible, before they invaded our camp. After rescuing two of my buddies that were wounded, I felt the explosion under my left foot. And then, nothing. Only darkness.

It was several days later that I finally woke up in the hospital. I thought that I was dead. I was so heavily sedated that it was a week later that I learned that my foot had been amputated. Immediately, my mind fast forwarded to Gabby. It was then that I realized that the nightmares I was having was real.

I was in Special Forces, in the middle of the jungle, five miles from Cambodia, when everything ended, in one loud explosion. *Nowhere safe to hide. A surprise, and, the last thing that I saw were your eyes. A camera's flash. I vanish from the picture of you and me. Ride the snake, ride the snake to the lake. The snake is seven miles long. He's old with skin that's cold.*

That killer wakes at dawn, just like me. Puts on his boots, killing machine in his hand, while kissing his wife and the children that he loves. *The ones we will never have. Stolen from us. Kill! Kill! Kill! The end of a beautiful friend, laughter, soft lies; the end of nights I tried to live, resulting in being only half a man.*

Memories of graceful arms, supple lips and flowing hair. My shield, my armor, my invincible tomorrow. *It hurts to set you free, but you no longer are allowed to follow me. I am lost in a journey of wilderness pain, surrounded by children that are insane. I patiently wait for the summer rain, to wash away the black rain, but never MY PAIN.*

"Lieutenant, Jake Chevalier. I am Dr. Nelson," The white ghost was saying.

"Do you know where you are, soldier?" The ghost was still speaking.

I tried to speak but my voice was silent. I reached for the ghost's hand. He then pulled a chair up next to the bed.

"A week ago you were brought here, to Landstuhl, Germany, when you were wounded in Cambodia. It was necessary for us to amputate your left foot to prevent the gangrene from spreading. Unfortunately, the latest tests indicate that the gangrene is still in your blood," The Doctor paused to allow me to understand the severity of the situation.

As I attempted to speak, once again my voice was not audible. A tall, blonde nurse walked on the other side of the bed and handed me a pen and notepad.

"It is not unusual, with the trauma that you have experienced, lieutenant Chevalier, to have your voice temporarily gone. It is not a permanent situation," The Nurse interjected in a soft, pleasant tone.

On the pad I wrote, "What do you do next? And will I be sent home soon?"

Dr. Nelson took the note and smiled.

"It is a very good sign that you are coherent. And, yes, you absolutely will be sent home as soon as you are able to travel after the surgery," Dr. Nelson said, but returned the pad of paper to the nurse, not me.

"Isabella, I am going to finish my rounds now. You may explain to our patient what will happen next," Dr. Nelson said as he left the room.

Once we were alone, Isabella, sat in the chair vacated by the doctor. She wiped my forehead with a cool wash cloth and then took my hand. Her hand felt much more comforting than the Doc's.

"Jake? May I use your first name?"

I shook my head yes.

"The Doctor has made the decision that part of your left leg will need to be surgically removed. I know that this is not what you expected, or wanted to hear. But, I can personally tell you, that Doctor Nelson is the best surgeon here and once this is completed you will be on your way home."

Isabella's voice was as soft as her touch.

I reached for the pad in her hand.

"Is there any other way to save the leg? And when is the surgery?"

Isabella read my note. She placed the pad and pen on the bed stand. And then stood up.

"I wish that there was another way, Jake. But, it is crucial that the gangrene be completely removed. If not, you will die. The surgery will be tomorrow morning."

She was now waiting for my reaction.

I felt nothing. I was nothing. I did not care any longer if I lived or died. Isabella must have had to deliver this news to other soldiers many times. She moved closer to my hospital bed. Then, without any warning, she reached across me and kissed my forehead.

It was such a loving gesture that I grabbed her arm and whispered, "Thank you for caring about me."

"I know how devastating, this news sounds, but you will walk again. And you will get your life back. I promise you this," Isabella said, with conviction. And then she left me.

Promise is an interesting word. We use it frequently, without really knowing if we can fulfill the situation that we pledge to. *What happens now with my promise to Gabby? How do I explain to her that we may no longer be together? And, does Isabella's promise even matter now?*

The surgery was successful. However, it was necessary for the entire leg to be removed, and a bullet in my spine was still there. It was decided that attempting to remove it could possibly leave me paralyzed.

There was a numbness that lingered for days during my recovery. I drifted in and out of sleep. I was in a state of limbo. Not dead, but certainly not alive. The only image that I could not rid of was Gabby. Visions of Tybee lighthouse would not fade away. *I am an inmate in an asylum.*

I was so sharp back then. I had all the answers. In this jungle, we came in spastic, like wild horses, and came home in plastic; some in numbered caskets. Soon, we learned to travel light, when our arms grew heavy, and our bellies tight. There was no camera to shoot the horrid landscape, that is etched in my brain, but I always shot my weapon on sight like I was taught to do.

Every night, I thanked Jesus Christ, played my Doors tape and passed the hash pipe. It was my brothers that got me through the night. *Who was wrong and who was right? Does it even matter anymore?*

Back at home, those singing and marching to save our souls from mortars and countless rotors were the only ones who realized that men named Charlie and Smitty, left their childhood in paddy fields, in the thick of this endless war.

It seemed like weeks before anyone told me that my parents had finally been informed of my injuries. I concluded that it was because they wanted to be certain that I would survive the trip home. No reason to let anyone know that their only son was shot until they knew if they were going to send a telegram or a Casualty Notification Officer.

I hoped that my letter to them proceeded any other formal announcement was made. It was imperative that Gabby not hear anything until she could hear my voice and know that I was alive.

Isabella was my angel of mercy. She would write my letters, read to me and personally sit for hours while I was recovering. Her hands were therapeutic and her voice mesmerizing. I learned that she lived near the hospital. Her mother was a German attorney and her father, a retired General from the US Army. She had dual citizenship, but had never been to the United States. When her father retired, they made the decision to stay in Germany with Isabella.

What I needed the most right now was someone to listen, to all my complaints without making any judgement. Isabella was that person. She encouraged me to continue my physical therapy, when I saw no need to ever be mobile again.

As boys, they sent us to fight, and we did just as we were told. But, now, I had lost hope, and never wanted to speak about what I had seen or done. *The world that I had left behind had ceased to exist, replaced by a private hell, in the shape of an inner shell that I crawled inside, leaving reality behind.*

That would not last long. Once I was told that my parents had been informed of my condition I asked Isabella to write them a letter. The medication that I had been pre-scribed, made it difficult for me to focus.

She had agreed to be my scribe. As I began to dictate the letter, I noticed how Isabella's blonde hair was pulled back, in a French braid, just like Gabby would sometimes wear her hair. I tried to ignore the similarities.

Dear Mom and Dad,   Feb. 21, 1967

I am now in Landstuhl Hospital in Rhineland-Pfalz, five kil-ometers south of Kaiserslautern. I know that none of this will make sense to you, but the reason I am here, is be-cause during an evening raid by the enemy I stumbled on an active mine and got a little banged up. Nothing too seri-ous and the good news is I will be home permanently in a few days.

I was able, to get the Sgt. out of danger and was return-ing to help another buddy when the bomb exploded caus-ing a fracture to my left thigh bone. And, then a shot to my right chest-- none of it that serious.

Put the beer in the ice chest, this kid is coming home, all in one piece, just not all pieces moving normal yet.

Just don't worry about me, I'll let you know the details when I know them myself.

All my love,
Your son, Jake

"Could you read it back to me, Isabella, so I can hear how it sounds?"

I wanted to make certain that it wasn't too dramatic. Knowing my folks, they would be on the next flight out if they suspected I was in danger, here. I listened to Isabella read the letter exactly as I had dictated it.

"Do you want me to send a letter to Gabby, also Jake?" Isabella asked, casually.

69

I nearly fell off the bed when I heard Gabby's name. "How do you know anything about Gabby?" I asked her, obviously irritated.

"Calm down Jake," Isabella was pushing me back on the bed, afraid that I might dislodge the tubes attached to my body.

"You talk about her all the time in your sleep, and your mail just arrived from the front line with about ten unopened letters from Gabriella Girard. She must be going out of her mind, waiting for a letter from you."

Isabella answered.

"That is none of your business," I snapped back, regretting how I sounded.

Isabella just walked to the door, and replied very sweetly, "I will make sure personally that your letter goes out today. I will be back later for your bath, after you have rested." Isabella was gone almost immediately.

I decided to comply with Isabella and rest my mind from all the chaos that has changed my life. *Destiny waits in the hands of the gods now, shaping the now unshaven. I have seen things lately that mold in shapes that mortal men should never see.* When at last I heard the door open and saw Isabella with the bathing tub and sponges, I was ready to begin accepting my fate.

For several weeks, when Isabella would wash my body, I would feel nothing. Today would be different. As she lathered the sponges, I allowed my mind to imagine how she would feel next to me. Her long blonde hair caressing my chest. *A fool may believe that he may turn the wheel of his own destiny, that the impossible may change its course..*

In the past, Isabella's touch, would make me flinch; my muscles tightened no matter how good it felt. Another woman's hands touching my body, was so foreign, as if I was cheating on Gabby....*but that temptation to return to voices, that have taken residence in my mind, have no chance of waking a dead world.*

However, this time, things were different. My eyes were wide open as I watched Isabella stroking my inner thighs

70

and groin. ....*I am like the eagle that lets the doves roam free, but now I have taken the shape of a wolf, hungry for recognition.*

It took a lot of control this time to ignore my sexual desire, that was making me naturally hard. Isabella, recognizing my embarrassment, turned her back to work on my right leg.

"It's alright Jake, I promise you. It is just a normal impulse. It means that you are alive and recovering. We would be concerned if you did not have an ejaculation for this long of a time. " Isabella was trying to comfort me, but I knew that what I was feeling for her was not just a stage of recovery.

The following days, Isabella would come and visit me even on her days off. If the weather was warm enough, she would take me in the wheelchair to the rose gardens outside and we would talk for hours. Reluctantly, she admitted that she was twenty-four years old. And, I reassured her that the minor age difference in this world is inconsequential.

I shared with her my dream of being a football legend, and how now I would be lucky if I could even learn how to walk again. Isabella insisted that once I was fitted for my prosthetic leg, there were only few limitations preventing me from accomplishing my goals.

It was very obvious that Isabella would never be Gabby. She could never take her place in my heart. But, there was another door beginning to open inside of me that was willing to let her enter. There were these strange puzzle pieces that appeared from nowhere, beginning to fit somewhere, somehow.

"Why haven't you ever married Isabella? If that's too personal, just ignore my rude behavior," I asked one afternoon in the garden.

Without even a hesitation, she answered me. "I have never found the right guy at the right time. Really quite simple, don't you think?" She then added, that "I am a nurse. It is a profession, not a hobby. The men that I have met do not want to accept my commitment to my career."

Trying to lighten up the conversation a little, I said, "Well, I can definitely attest to the fact that you are an amazing caregiver,"

I then took her hand, and added, "And, these hands are wonderful. The softest and yet strongest hands that I have ever felt in my life." I then kissed them, which startled Isabella.

Our eyes met in a moment of admirable affection, when she suddenly pulled away, and said, "Gabby is a very lucky girl, to have a man who loves her like you do," she said quickly, and without another word, she asked the nurse approaching us, to take me back to the hospital ward.

It was such a sudden departure, that it left me confused at what I might have said to initiate that response. What I was left with, was a definite feeling that I had discovered a new emotion, what it was I was not yet certain.

Isabella was now working the night shift and visiting with me frequently in the afternoon. It had now been several weeks since I had planned to be going home. There were so many excuses and delays that I stopped asking and decided to let this dilemma take its course.

Then one night, I finally had my first night terror, that would later be more frequent. I began screaming so loudly that the entire night shift ran to my bed. I dreamt that I was in the jungle, but this time it wasn't Cambodia, it was a jungle with a lovely beach, wild animals roaming peacefully on the grass.

Two white tigers approached where I was lying. I stretched forward my hand to allow them to smell my scent. It was a universal sign of peace. One of the female Tigers began to lick my hand with her rough tongue; while the other one said very clearly,

" *Come with me Jake. I will set you free. I am the best, worst thing that hasn't happened to you yet. You take the full truth, then you pour some out, and you can kill me or let God sort this out. As you drift off to sleep with those dirty thoughts in the shape of your mouth. I am pity sex and nothing more, and nothing less. Stay with me until the lights go out. Let the other go free, and stay with me."*

As I looked at the other white tiger, I heard the gunshot. I saw the pieces of her shatter, like a kaleidoscope, into millions of tinted glass. Then, the outrageous scream of pain was unbearable.

I was drenched in sweat. Isabella was the first one by my side. She waved the others to go back to their stations. In her arms she was cradling me, like a child, rocking back and forth, until I was calm enough to stop trembling.

In my ear, I could hear her softly saying," It's going to be okay Jake. I will be here with you. I will help you fight the night terrors. So many of you soldiers from the front have them. You will never be alone."

I looked into her dark brown eyes, that held secrets I wanted to discover.

"Will you help me overcome these nightmares? Can you make them go away Isabella?" I was begging her.

She bent closer to my face, her mouth inches from mine, and said, "I will be here as long as you want me to."

I could no longer hold back, what I had been feeling for weeks. I sat up and kissed her mouth and tasted her foreign lips, pressed next to mine. I could see the ocean when I closed my eyes, but it was Isabella holding me close. No rockets were shooting through the sky. No centrifugal motion, perpetual bliss, that I felt when Gabby and I made love. But, it was an unstoppable, unthinkable kiss, that I would learn to enjoy and appreciate throughout the years.

"Isabella, could you... ever learn to love me?" I could see the tears in her eyes and the smile on her face.

"Jake, I fell in love with you, when I first saw you lying on that gurney. I knew you had someone back home, so I didn't want to get too close to you and get hurt," she said.

It was absolutely imperative, that I be as honest as possible with Isabella about my relationship with Gabby, and just hope that she would still want me.

"Gabby and I have been together for nearly four years. She is graduating from Savannah High School in June. I have always loved her. We were planning on getting married after my tour of duty. But, now, everything has changed," Jake said, with remorse.

Isabella, looked away, from me and took a deep breath. "Does Gabby even know about your injury Jake?" Isabella asked quietly.

"No, Gabby knows nothing, " I said, watching Isabella's reaction. She was so composed and patient. Nothing like Gabby. Then, she asked the one question I did not want to answer.

" And now? Do you still love her? Do you want to be with me because I can care for you?" Isabella was now looking directly into my eyes. I knew that she deserved an honest answer.

"Yes, I will always love Gabby. But, I also know that I love you. It may sound crazy, but it is the truth. For weeks, I have been contemplating this. I let Gabby down, I never want to do the same thing with you, Isabella," I said as straight forward as possible. Then I added what I knew was true at this moment.

"I am not the man that I used to be, but what I feel for you is real. If you let me I will love you forever. Isabella, you are all I need and want.... Please, let me be that man you have been waiting for. The man that will complete you. Will you marry me?" I said, very naturally.

Isabella had waited a very long time to hear those words, but now she was reluctant. She knew that she loved Jake, but was she enough for him. Could she ever take Gabby's place? Should she even try?

"Jake, this is a very serious commitment, for us both. We need time to be certain that these feelings are not just a re- action to the recent trauma you have experienced."

Isabella had to be carefully optimistic. Although, I could understand her hesitation, I already knew that my feelings were real. What Gabby and I experienced was a perfect storm, doomed from the beginning. It was my responsibility to set her free. Not an easy decision, made nearly impossible from a hospital bed across the world. But, I did owe Isabella the time she needed to trust me.

A few days, had now turned into three months. Dr. Nelson, the surgeon who removed my leg, stopped by to let me know that I was finally being released to go home. It had seemed like another lifetime, since the military air ambulance brought me here from Cambodia.

"I wanted to stop by Jake, and talk to your one last time before you leave here," said, Dr. Nelson. The Doc was a twenty-five-year military man that confided in me the most horrible injuries imaginable. All those years, and he treated each case he was assigned to with empathy.

"It is time now to honestly prepare you for your return home. The rehabilitation for this extensive injury, is a minimum of five years. The round that hit your chest, is so close to the spine, that if you have any further, even minor injuries, you could be completely paralyzed," The Doc waited for me to ingest this news before continuing.

"How will this affect my intimacy with women... I mean, will I be impotent? I need the honest truth Doc," I asked, not really wanting to hear the diagnosis.

"No Jake, your sex life will return to normal as soon as it is safe to stop the medication. The gangrene is no longer an issue, so we will stop all intravenous medication today. And, once you are stateside, you will be fitted for a prosthetic leg. At your age, the chances are good that you will have a very normal life," said the Doc on his way out to do his normal rounds.

Once alone, I began to write a letter to Gabby.

Dear Gabby, was as far as I got. Isabella interrupted my thoughts, as she entered the room.

"I heard the good news! Aren't you excited? Finally, you are going home, Jake."

She was acting very distant. But, I refused to let her continue acting indifferent.

"Have you thought about what we discussed? I have been as patient as possible, but, I am not leaving Germany without you, Isabella. I don't know how else to tell you that I want to marry you.

I love you now and always," I said.

I began to crumble the letter to Gabby, that would never be sent. In the other hand,I reached in my pocket and pulled out a solitaire diamond ring.

"Will you, Isabella, do me the honor of being my wife?" I had her hand in mine, waiting for her to say yes.

"How did you ever manage to get this ring?" Tears were in her eyes.

"Will you please just say yes, and stop with the questions." My hand was quivering now.

Finally, I could hear her voice full of excitement, "Yes, Jake, a thousand times yes!"

This time when she bent down to kiss me, I knew that we would be perfect for one another. I slipped the ring, that I had sized for Gabby, months ago, on Isabella's right finger. Then I put the ring box back in my pocket. I was thankful that Gabby and Isabella had the same ring size. The only common denominator in this equation.

CHAPTER 9

Desire, in itself is a movement,
Not in itself desirable.
Love, in itself is unmoving.
Then what causes,
The end of a movement?
Time is an undesirable form
Caught in between being
And not being.
TS Eliot

Gabby Jan-June 1967
Savannah, Georgia

When an atomic bomb hits a target, everything is immediately destroyed. Fireballs, shockwave, and radioactivity are the three main effects that such a catastrophe yields.

The Hiroshima and Nagasaki explosions resulted in two hundred different kinds of isotopes; nuclear fusion particles of uranium and plutonium, that escaped fission.

The mixture of enormous amounts of airborne, irradiated materials, combined with heat and thermal currents from the firestorm, caused rainfall in both cities within thirty or forty minutes of the bombing.

When the fallout particles were mixed with carbon residue, from citywide fires, the result was the amazing, and deadly BLACK RAIN.

Weeks had passed since my last letter from Jake. Our final night together was both passionate and desperate. Both of us knew that this might be our last night together, but neither of us wanted to admit that.

The days and nights that followed, were haunting. My mind would wander off, without warning. My wings spread open to hide me from the sunlight and the nightmares, raining bloody, brilliant lies exploding from the sky.

Nowhere to run. Tears are piercing through my heart. Hands over my ears. Pounding, pounding, relentlessly contaminating the ground. I feel the Angel of Death, crossing many borders, collecting half dead corpses infested with maggots.

Mouth wide open, I am unable to say the words pounding in my brain, "STOP this FUCKING madness. Does anybody care?"

When, finally I feel that I have been eaten alive, left here with nothing, unable to hide the damage any longer, I ask pleading,

"Does this whole thing seem just as damn ugly to you?" *I try to erase all the scars that you have left on me. But, the taste of betrayal will never be washed away. It will be with me 'till I'm not alive, 'till the day I die.*

The months of torturing, has lead me to playing possum. Molly is my only visitor from the outside world. My psyche walks a very thin, tight rope between mourning and unleashed rage at unidentifiable objects.

I am not prepared to accept that the man who pledged his undying love to me, is now providing food to the hungry beast; last year's words belong to last year's language. Next year's voice awaits a new response.

My spirit has left my body on a distant shore. *That constant impotence of rage at human folly, of laughter that ceases now to amuse me with trite promises lacerating my wrists.* My foolishness stings the open wounds with flames and ice.

"GABBY! GABBY!"I hear him screaming. So far away. Closer to the Dead Sea than Moon River.

"Listen to me Gabriella! This is enough tragedy for a life-time." Molly was frantically attempting to shake me out of my self-inflicted limbo.

"I refuse to let you continue to move between these two worlds that you are hiding in. Jake is alive ...yes, he lost his leg. And, what he is doing to you now is ridiculously painful... but, baby... there is nothing you can do about it," Molly said, softly.

Then, like the climax in a tragedy, February 14, 1967, the Postman delivers fifteen bundled letters that I had sent to Jake, marked "Undeliverable ".

At this time, I had no idea what this meant. I could not ask Jake's parents since we had never formally met. I had heard from other people that they, ironically, were blaming me for his decision to join the Marines. Did that even matter anymore? All I knew was that I could not go to them for any answers now.

It was Molly that finally broke the news to me, that she had heard Jake had been injured, and possibly lost a leg, but it was all finally confirmed, with the aid of The Savannah Herald.

"Now, Gabby....I have some news about Jake," she briefly hesitated, like she was almost going to change her mind.

"But, before I decide to share this with you, I need to know that you won't go all crazy on me," Molly was holding something in her hand. I wasn't certain what it had to do with what she was going to tell me but, I agreed to be reasonable.

"I don't understand why all of you are treating me like a mental case. I do have a legitimate reason for being upset. My boyfriend is in a war and suddenly..." I stopped to gain my composure before continuing.

"...If there is anything that you can tell me...well, I would hope you would tell me, knowing how...upset... worried..."

I couldn't finish my thought. Molly just handed me the front page of the newspaper.

I took the paper, unfolded it and read the headlines aloud.

"Jake Chevalier, native son, 1965 Savannah High School graduate, and all-star football player, sacrificed his leg in battle, while heroically saving three of his fellow officers." I read the words, but the reality was not totally penetrating. *I began to feel as if I was being quartered, torn apart in pieces.*

"That must explain why I haven't received a letter. Oh my God, Molly...Jake must be in such terrible pain ....and confused," I said, feeling guilty for not understanding. And, then, before Molly could reach for the same paper, I saw the photograph.

It was a picture of Jake with his arm around a tall, blonde lady. The caption read, " Isabella Remington, is the nurse credited for bringing Jake back to life. The two are planning a wedding next January, 1968."

The newspaper article was dated April 15, 1967. That was nearly a month ago! *Was this really the way Jake wanted me to know that he was no longer in love with me?*

All I could do was start sobbing. Molly held me close to her. I was speechless.

"Gabby, I am so sorry you had to find out about Jake in this way. I was hoping... no praying that he would send you a letter. But, when no letter arrived ...Well, I thought that it would be best if you heard it from me. Gabby, I know that you are hurting now, but believe me, in time even this will fade away."

Molly said, crying along with me.

I put my head on the pillow, to stop it from spinning. How could years together be dissolved like grains of sand washed away into an ocean with a lost horizon.

I bored a train that is going nowhere, an angel with a grotesque smile hands me empty promises. They are on petals that scream, "he loves you, he loves you not".At that very moment, when we both feel passion through our veins, you disappear.

These streets are so much colder;

Jake I am finally older. You left me shy and humble, with eyes that made you stumble. And, now I am a woman, who refuses to accept the world we knew, is gone. Know this, forever more, that my name is carved inside your beating heart, until the day it stops.

Somehow, I pulled myself together barely, long enough to complete the last few finals I needed to graduate. If it had not been for Mrs. Thompson encouraging me to take those college classes, I may not have graduated. Then, totally unexpectedly, I was called out of my Civics class. The small pink slip of paper said to report to Principal Saxon's office.

As I walked down the empty hallway, my first instinct was to continue walking out the door. I already knew that I had met all the graduating requirements. Graduation meant nothing to me. Leave the Pomp and Circumstance to those seniors who appreciate it.

Before I could walk out the doors, Mrs. Thompson met me.

"Gabby, I do believe that you and I are headed for the same meeting," she said, in a jovial tone.

"Mr. Saxon, pinked me out. Do you have any idea what could be the problem, Mrs. Thompson?" I said in return.

"Well, I might Gabby but I think Mr. Saxon would like to be the one to tell you."

She replied, opening the office door to let me enter first.

"Please, Gabby.... Mrs. Thompson, take a seat. "Mr. Saxon had walked over toward the door and pulled out two leather chairs for us. This was my first time, in four years in his office. If I had been that same Gabby that started here at thirteen, I would have been petrified. But, there was very little that I now cared about or was intimidated by.

" I am quite certain that you must be taken back by why you are here right now Gabriella? Let me assure you, that it is not anything negative. As a matter of fact, it is quite wonderful," he said while taking a seat back at the massive oak desk. He then handed me a letter.

As I removed the letter from the envelope, I noticed the Georgetown embossed gold seal on the front.

"Go ahead, Gabriella...You may open it," Mr. Saxon said eager to hear my response.

Dear Mr. Saxon,

It is with great pleasure that we notify you that one of your senior students, Gabriella Girard has been accepted on full scholarship to Georgetown University, as a declared English major.

Please provide her with all of the necessary forms enclosed, which will instruct her when to arrive on campus, how to select her residence hall, and many other pertinent factors highlighting our campus.

I would personally like to congratulate you and your academic faculty for preparing three of your students for our outstanding University.

Sincerely,

Chancellor Omar Ferrara

I placed the letter neatly back in the envelope. And said nothing. What was there to say? At seventeen years of age, I had lost my desire for everything. The future was in my past. Going to college would not change that. Jake may have lost a leg, but I lost my soul.

"Gabby...I am very aware of the changes recently in your life," Mrs. Thompson was speaking to me in nearly a whisper.

"But, you MUST not let anything prevent you from taking advantage of this lifetime opportunity," Again, she paused to let me think about what she was saying. Again, I was silent.

"Gabriella, I am going to have my secretary arrange all of this data for you. And, let me congratulate you for being accepted to one of the most prestigious schools in the country," Dr. Saxon said, standing up, signaling to us that our meeting was now over.

I am thankful that it is the end of the day and next week there are no more classes. Seniors are celebrating. Parents are preparing for their lives to change, and I wait for Molly, who has volunteered to be the one in charge of the "suicide" watch.

Without Molly and her optimistic approach on everything I would never be leaving Savannah High School. It was Molly that continued to remind me that life is a risk that we take, and when it is dark inside our self-made stage, we must listen to the curtain call, before the lights fade out and there really is no final call.

"What do you need time to consider Gabby? It isn't like Jake is coming back, and even if he was, I wouldn't let you go back to him," Molly was relentless about this.

The inside voices keep reminding me that it is fate that weaves the threads that hold the soul.... Now, let him go. Do not allow those demons to override a new beginning.

Nothing is ever final, except death.

Molly, loved to remind me, that in the play Romeo and Juliet, the real tragedy is that neither one of them trusted the other enough to believe that it was possible to overcome a rather simple dilemma. Their death, according to Molly, was, "A spontaneous reaction that solved nothing."

There was no known sedative that worked better than my Molly. Her over simplified logic, finally resonated a sense of reason that I lacked. The synthetic, psychoactive, "Molly" that was both a stimulant amphetamine and hallucinogenic mescaline, would later produce feelings, of increased energy and euphoria.

Maybe it was a combination of both Mollies that made me finally realize that the distortions would finally become normal once again in another background. Georgetown would be the place where I could disappear; no one would know who I was. It would be a new start at life. Once I boarded that plane, I vowed to myself that I would never return to Savannah again, and I almost kept that promise.

CHAPTER 10
Part II

Among the graffiti
In some deserted alley
Life scribbles my epitaph.
It is the beginning of my end.
I am the keeper of the torch,
The singer of the Blues.
Like a thief in the night,
Syncopation warns me,
To walk away, and let
The flame die out

Caden Cassidy :2004

In everyone's life there comes an intermission. In some cases, we are also given an opportunity to insert a semi-colon between moments that need clarity; an audible pause between closely linked subjects. That would be me, Caden Cassidy. Without a choice, I became Gabby's semi colon.

Even before I formally metGabby at Georgetown University, I knew of Gabriella Girard, from Savannah High School. We were in the same graduating class, 1967, but in reality we were light years apart.

You see, just as the community was in constant turmoil in 1965, our school, a mini metropolis with varying circles of hell, was also tumultuous.

Students formed "castes" within these circles, that in-cluded all groups, ranked by popularity. The social minded movers and shakers, affectionately referred to as the "sosh" ruled the turf. These were the cheerleaders, student government officers, and jocks.

One level down from the "sosh" would be the intellectuals, speech competitors, honor students, debate team members, and service club students.

In an outer circle, suspended in space, there you would find the drama students, band, choir, and journalism. Yearbook was known as panderer's, since they paid homage to the "sash", but were never allowed in that circle.

Finally, at the bottom of the circle were the outcasts, loners, "rough/tough " boys, "easy" girls and everyone else too poor to own a car, or shop at Dillard's, Sacks, or Macy's. There were even songs that paid tribute to those "on the poor side of town" or that were like "Gloria" or "Sloopy".

I was basically an intellectual. Too busy for the social scene, yet for some strange reason, still accepted by the elite. Gabby, from my observations, was on her own Island, with that football quarterback, Jake Chavalier, two years her senior. They basically isolated themselves from everyone else, which was really quite astute of them.

Literally, on the same day that I earned my Varsity letter for track, my sophomore year, it was like the world stood still; the Saran Wrap that made me invisible was finally removed. That Letterman Jacket was a chick magnet.

It was such a sudden transformation, that I felt awkward and clumsy. I began to take my clues from other jocks. Being a quick study, in no time I was now moving around with the pros. Finally, I felt that I was ready to attend my first "sosh" private party.

The other jocks that I was now hanging with picked me up on a Saturday evening, at about nine pm. When we got to our destination, there were no lights on, and I was sure that these guys had the wrong house.

"Chill, Caden. Lights are out because parents are out. Nobody wants to draw attention to what's happening inside," Roy, my "cool" mentor said, poking me in the ribs.

I wasn't sure what he meant by that, but it didn't take long to discover, that private parties were definitely the "A" list on the party scale. They were very exclusive, and since the jocks were always invited, they also acted like bouncers when needed.

Once in the main "great room" of this classic, traditional, colonial, mini mansion, it became a challenge to find our way to the bar, where everyone started the evening. It was so dark inside, that all I could do was follow Roy and Chad, who I knew had a bloodhound nose for anything with alcohol.

From nowhere, somebody handed me a cold beer. My eyes were beginning to focus again and I recognized most of the girls from the cheerleading squad and homecoming court. Most guys were either sitting on couches with some girl on their laps, or in the corner passing around some weed.

Once Roy and Chad found their "prey", they disappeared into some room, leaving me standing alone with my beer. That is until a very busty, strawberry blonde, chick, with the most provocative smile, took my hand and coyly, said, "Hey, Caden, let's get you loose with some tequila shots."

Before I could protest, she had taken the beer and was pouring tequila down my throat. It didn't take long after that for any inhibitions that I might have had, to literally go down my throat. After a very short time, I was definitely loose.

Soon I discovered this mystery girl's name was Allison and the "looking glass" that we were about to enter came with its own psychedelic lights. Allison took hold of my hand and led me down a narrow hallway. When she opened the door all I could see was a bed.

Without saying a word, Allison closed the door. She then put her arms around my neck and while, blowing in my ear, she whispered, "Caden, baby. Unsnap my bra, please," Like a trained puppy, I did exactly what she told me to do.

With her bra now on the ground, we began to kiss. I had kissed girls before, well a few...Okay two girls, but none of them were rubbing their naked breasts on me. It was FAN-TASTIC.

Then she sat me down on the edge of the bed, her tongue went directly into my mouth, and her long legs wrapped around my waist. Sitting on my lap, face to face, she began gyrating to the music in the other room.

Her hands were guiding the hard nipples of her breast into my open mouth. Instinctively, I began sucking while my dick was throbbing between her legs.

"I am gonna rock your world, jock boy," she was breathing in my ear.

Alternating between breasts, my own hands were now holding those supple tits, squeezing first, then my mouth began sucking.

I barely heard Allison say, "Now, you just relax, Caden and let me do you first."

I wasn't really paying attention to what Allison was saying, but I could feel my cock getting harder than it ever did when I masturbated. Then she unzipped my jeans. On her knees in front of me, once released, my cock was in full throttle; her wet mouth, with paradise pink lipstick, all around it, she first started licking and stroking.

Finally, her whole mouth began to inhale my cock. .I put my hands on her head guiding the pace, groaning uncontrollably, I felt the final squeeze as I came in her mouth. She didn't seem to mind.

"Now" she said face to face with me,

"It's your turn Caden."

My turn? I had no idea what she expected. I wasn't going to fuck her, that was made clear when the guys told me we were coming here.

"These girls... well, let me just tell you Caden, they will satisfy you...they will make sure you cum, but none of them will let you have intercourse with them. They are all virgins.... well, most of them," Chad, said.

So, what did Allison expect ME to do?

She pulled down her black lace panties, and rubbed them on my nose.

"Keep smelling me Caden," Alice said while dancing in front of me, fingering her pussy, and making me lick her fingers. By now, I was hard again.

Without a warning, she pushed me down on the bed, and with her knee on my chest she made me lie face up. Then, with her hips straddling my head, her pussy was on my mouth. She was telling me to eat her, lick her clit, use my tongue to make her cum. I followed all her directions. *It was my first feast.*

When I finally heard her scream, and tasted her for the first time, I knew what true ecstasy really was. My cock was ready to explode. Allison handed me a condom and like everything else, I did what she said. The lubricated condom was easy to put on. With my dick getting harder each moment I was definitely ready to fuck her now.

"I'm probably safe, but why take any chances," She said, winking, making sure I had it on right. Once again, she straddled me, but this time she was putting my cock in her vagina. Once she felt it was steady, she began to ride me, each hump penetrated deeper inside.

Her long hair was shaking above me as I began to suck again her firm breasts keeping the same beat as my cock. I could sense Allison contracting her vagina, pulsating as I went deeper inside of her, never ending pussy. And then, we both felt it at the same time. She comes and I feel the warm juices flowing into my inner thighs. As I remove the condom my penis drips, whatever is left on her stomach. She lets it remain on her as she rolls of next to me.

When it is over, we both lay still. No touching. No kissing. Allison is the first one up and dressed,

"Not bad for your first time Caden. It won't be long until you are poking all the girls with that fine pecker of yours."

I really didn't even want to look her in the face. She knew that I was a virgin when she brought me in this room. Sensing my discomfort, she stroked-my hair, kissed my mouth one last time, and said, "Caden, there has to be a first somewhere, with someone. Each time you will get better. When you do, call me. We can have some fun together."

The thought crossed my mind that this might have been a set up by the guys. It really didn't matter. Allison was right. There had to be a first time.

When I exited the bedroom minutes, later, I headed to the john, to clean up. A couple of the guys were pissing away the beer they had juggled down. As I joined in, someone noticed the paradise pink lipstick still on my cock.

"Hey, man...see you met Allison," he grinned at me. "Yeah, that Alice knows how to give you a good time," He said before leaving.

I zipped up my jeans, threw on my T-shirt, and walked into the living room. But, Allison was gone. Turning toward the kitchen, in the dark, I almost knocked down this girl, with her long chestnut hair, flowing to the middle of her waist.

When she turned her head, our eyes met. Those eyes were the color of polished jade, shimmering. Stunning.

"Excuse me, I almost knocked you over."

I said, grabbing one arm for balance. She giggled softly. Her other hand was attached to another male. It was Jake Chevalier, the football quarterback.

But, I had never seen this girl before on campus. Almost reading my mind, she said, "I'm, Gabriella Girard, but everybody calls me Gabby."

I was still overcome by how exotic and beautiful she was. "And, I am..." Before I could finish, Jake was leading her out the front door, "Caden! My name is Caden!" But, she was gone.

The following week at school, I couldn't get that Gabby out of my head. I tried to focus on academics, which was what I needed to do, if I was going to be accepted to Georgetown University, my first choice in colleges.

But, then it happened. Right outside of my Civics class, I had one final opportunity to connect with Gabby. As she was walking past my class, the hallways overcrowded as usual, once again I physically ran right into her.

"Oh, my God! I am so sorry. It seems like it is our destiny to meet," I said. *That was so lame... did I really say that?*

As I bent down to pick up her books, for a brief second, I thought that I heard her call my name. But, when I stood up, Allison was hanging on me. Where she came from, I have no idea. By the time, I processed what had just occurred, Gabby was history.

The community surrounding me was in a different kind of turmoil, then my own personal life. I was living in Georgia during a time when the youth was setting the pace for changes. The Freedom Movement fascinated me. It challenged those of us in the very heart of the south to take a "less traveled" road, when making choices.

On March 9,1960 a group of Atlanta University students, published in the local

newspaper, "An Appeal for Human Rights".

I am including an expert from that text, primarily because it was the foundation for much of my liberal views in life.

"We (AUC students*) have joined our hearts, minds, bodies in the cause of gaining those rights which are inherently ours as a member of the human race and citizens of these United States... We do not intend to wait placidly for those rights which are already legally ours, to be meted out to us one at a time. Today's youth will not sit by submissively, while being denied all the rights and privileges and joys of life... We must say in all candor that we plan to use every legal and nonviolent means at our disposal to secure full citizenship rights as members of this great Democracy of ours."

Perhaps, in 1965, I associated with these demands more passionately than my fellow "white" students because I knew what it felt like to be different. Both my parents immigrated from Ireland to the United States when I was only three years old.

And, although our color was never an issue, we were made to feel inferior.

That was why, in part, my family saved enough money to open their own convenience store and deli. It gave us a sense of pride as well as a way to be respected by the community.

Today, Savannah is a thriving tourist attraction. Visitors stroll down Bonaventure Cemetery, where the "Bird Girl" statue was immortalized by the now famous author John Berendt's who wrote, **Midnight in the Garden of Good and Evil.**

When I was in high school, before the cemetery became famous, we would search the grave stones for eccentric names, and then brass rub them for souvenirs. Now, Johnnie Brown, a tour guide, points out the gashes in a tree trunk that once was used as a whipping post for black slaves.

The Savannah that I returned to, after leaving Georgetown unexpectedly, was like many other cities in Georgia. It seemed to thrive, almost intentionally on the ability to remain in its own Antebellum bubble wrap; far from reality. In fact, it is possible to roam around the cities haunting boulevards, without a clue, how my hometown, the oldest African American community in Georgia, influenced this country.

Today, as an owner of two well established businesses, the original Cassidy Deli and The Molly Pub, I am able to recognize, the pioneering black designers, artists, musicians, and philanthropists. That evolution is still in motion.

Now that you know a little more about my background, and even some of my intimate details in high school, I can move on to discuss the real purpose of my life.

Without revealing too much at once, I will begin by vaguely stating that Gabriella Girard entered my life with more destruction than a Tsunami. Similar to how the gravitational pull of the moon and sun creates havoc, this is what I am experiencing, thirty-seven years later.

When it started to torment me, I first imagined it was only because we never had closure. But, as it became increasingly more painful, I had to finally resolve that this

91

was more than merely a curiosity of what her life had become without me.

It was in the autumn of 1967 at Georgetown University that I finally caught up with the elusive Gabby that I first laid eyes on at Savannah High School. There is a cliché that says, "the best always comes from the worst" nights. Well, I am here to declare that thirty-seven years later is like a forever hangover, that I cannot wrap my mind around.

The snapshots are filed in my brain. My fingers playing with her long chestnut hair. The taste of cinnamon on her tongue. The way those jade green eyes sparkled when she looked at me. All of this is triggered by the scent of Shalimar that comes from nowhere.

Over the years, I have had my share of girls to drink a bottle of gin and lemon *with under the sheets, the heart is so cold when you fuck without love, take aim and reload, no pain, just pleasure, until the movie reel starts over again, in my fucked up head.*

I began to find other ways to rid myself of this girl that wouldn't stop haunting me. Then, one time when I decided that the gin wasn't working; it was time to graduate to snorting coke. Calhoun and Murray were brothers, who used to hang out at my folk's deli before going to their own "parties"

It was on one of these occasions that the brothers offered to help me overcome the funk I was in.

"Listen to us man...snorting this pure Coke up your nose is guaranteed to get you past these blues.... well, at least it will be a temporary fix for a while," Murray said with conviction.

I figured, what the hell, nothing else was working. Once we got to the flat, everyone started first with some weed. After a short time, the Coke was brought out. Murray was an expert, and showed me how to get the most from my high. After a while,

I was spilling my guts to them about Gabby.

One of the bros, I don't remember which one now, showed me proudly the Anaconda tattoo on his left arm.

Then, I think it was Murray who said, "This broad, Gabby, isn't she the one that was Jake's bitch... you know in high school?"

If I was feeling normal, I would have punched that asshole in the mouth, but the Coke made me feel nothing. And, then Calhoun added that he heard Gabby was married to some prick doctor who lived in Kentucky. I thought that would be enough to drop this Gabby insanity.

That was until I told them that Gabby and I had dated for a few months when I was at Georgetown. That was when Murray started to ask me how sweet her pussy tasted and to tell him how it felt to fuck her.

Maybe the Coke was wearing off, or maybe I had just had enough of these low life losers, but I no longer could hold back.

"You ever even as much as say her name again, and I will pull out your tongue with pliers, you mother fucker ape. Do you understand me?" Calhoun was pulling me off of his brother, who by this time he was dripping with blood from every cavity in his face.

Everyone stopped talking and stared at me as if I was crazy. I was. That was about thirty years ago. After that night, I decided to stay away from the drugs, before It did any permanent damage.

Nothing was working. I HAD to find out what it was about this girl that kept me hanging on. Don't get me wrong, I wasn't consumed 24/7. Life does go on, but as it does, the small hole in my chest keeps getting wider. I was beginning to believe that I was missing some chromosome that would eventually kill me, if I could not stop this insanity.

Then, I finally found the answer. In the waiting room, at my annual Doctor's appointment. I picked up the Relationship Enquirer from the lobby, to pass time. That is when I come across an article about the effect of intense emotion. It concluded that, single or married, everyone aches for a deep, satisfying, intimate connection that doesn't fade by time.

As humans, we are "hard wired" with this need, although rarely, are we able to recognize it when it happens. This phenomenon is referred to as Lost-and- Found love affairs. Those who have experienced this will testify they are not fantasy.

These are relationships that never ended. The most cataclysmic, powerful, rekindled love is heightened by ephemeral chemicals of new love, combined with the profound, satisfying, deeply relaxing chemicals of long term love.

The brain is actually exposed to heightened levels of testosterone and progesterone, the steroid sex hormones involved in sexual intensity, according to Thomas Lewis, the author of **A General Theory of Love.**

Even after learning all of this, and slightly reassured that I was not insane, for years, I still live in a fog so dense that eventually I recorded my feelings on a cassette tape. Occasionally, it would rewind, interfering with my current thoughts, lingering in my mind, playing along with the overpowering feeling of love. That is when I would revisit my last night with Gabby.

Or from time to time, when the winter breeze makes some young girls ponytail dance like a loose kite, or every New Year's Eve, when it is time to ring in the hope for a new beginning, my heart stops beating for a mere second; I pay homage to a memory that refuses to die.

Thirty seven years pass, as fast as a flirtatious wink, or a "hello", to a perfect stranger. The satin sheets that we first made love on, are granted the immunity from the wrinkles of time.

Out of nowhere, while driving on the highway, my thoughts of Gabby reoccur, lately more often than ever. I try to make the necessary adjustments, and cruise control once again takes over. I am soon back to moving with the ebb and flow in a complex world.

Most of my relationships have a short shelf life. For me, it always had to be me in control. When the warning lights started flashing, it was time for me to walk....no RUN as fast and as far away as possible from Gabby. Now, I am counting on the same forces, with the same impetus to bring us back together, thirty-seven years later.

Jake Chevalier, may have experienced where I am now. I will never really know. But what has become very clear, is that time is finally working in my favor. Once, I have the opportunity to talk to Gabby, I am confident she will share the same desire to reunite.

CHAPTER 11

Stars screaming in an unknown
World, with no tomorrow
Worth another sorrow.
Breathless moments
Are now, too close for comfort,
Yet, they cure the pain;
Keep me sane, until everlasting,
Becomes, a never ending light,
That watches me slowly dying,
Too late to seize the crying.

Gabby October, 1967

Freshman housing at any university can be an ordeal, but never more so than when I decided to accept the scholarship weeks past the deadline. That must have been the reason that I was placed in Darrell Hall. It was the newest housing available, and named after the mother of Georgetown University founder, John Carrol.

The other three girls had already moved in a week ago. I was the last one. I dreaded walking in on this group that had already settled. But, at this point all I really wanted was a desk, a bed, and a closet. I soon learned that bathrooms were communal. That would definitely take some time getting used to.

Once I arrived on campus, I realized that Molly was absolutely right. This was my opportunity to get an education as quickly as possible, find a rewarding profession, and most of all kick the Jake habit. The University was far enough away from Savannah, that I could easily blend in with all of the other coeds. If I keep to the program maybe this won't be that bad.

My three roommates were all different. The first one that I met was, Ophelia. Immediately I knew we would be friends. After all anyone named after a Shakespearean tragic heroine had to be amazing.

I knew she would be my favorite before I even met her. The only time I ever heard that name, was in the play Hamlet, and the name my English teacher gave to her cat. When I learned that Ophelia and I were both English Literature majors, it sealed the deal.

"Welcome, Gabriella. It isn't the Waldorf penthouse, but I think you will find it cozy. How rude of me... I am Ophelia McIntyre. "Ophelia said, extending her hand.

"Oh, please call me Gabby. Are you an English major like me?" I said, excited.

"Well, yes and no. I am an English major because it is the best route to take on my way to law school. I want to be an entertainment attorney, eventually, that is."

Ophelia added.

I soon discovered that Ophelia's family owned a luxury spa/bed and breakfast establishment in Sedona, Arizona. It catered to the rich and famous exclusively because they knew that their anonymity, would be kept private.

Ophelia reminded me of the legendary Hollywood actresses like, Lana Turner or Greta Garbo. She had naturally silver blonde hair that framed a face that was like porcelain and eyes that were brighter blue than sapphires. Everything from her perfectly shaped breasts to her model legs, were only the exterior. It was her memory that was faster than a steel trap that mesmerized everyone who met her.

What was equally amazing about Ophelia was her confidence, that never appeared pretentious. She worked hard and partied just as diligently.

"We came here to change the world, ladies, and we can certainly do that with a flute of champagne in one hand and a diploma in the other," she reminded us whenever there was an invite to a party. There were definitely times when her stamina was spellbinding.

My other roommate, Veronica Taylor, was the polar opposite of Ophelia. Whereas, Ophelia was dedicated to becoming an attorney and eventually a Supreme Court Justice, Veronica made it emphatically clear that her major was art/ music with a minor in SEX. The first two years she would dedicate herself to discovering the evolution of the sexual revolution by personally "fucking" enough men to determine if they were more satisfying than women.

The last two years, which she surmised were the most crucial ones, she would commit herself to finding a doctor, dentist or millionaire playboy to settle down with. Gender did not matter.

Veronica was only five feet tall, but never underestimate her ability to play a room like an experienced Diva. She had the charm of a southern belle, the wit of Mark Twain, and the beauty of Liz Taylor.

That Raven black hair, blue eyes, with a hint of amethyst, lured anyone, brave enough or just unsuspecting enough, into her web. The innocent subject, of her temporary affection, would always return with parched mouth, pleading for her nectar, unknowing that all their promises and begging would only result in their demise. Once Veronica tired of her male conquest, she would quickly move on to another with no remorse.

Veronica's hometown was New Orleans, Louisiana. Most of her weekends, since arriving to Georgetown, resembled Mardi Gras. She could party with the best Fraternity Brothers on campus, and still make it to mass the next morning.

My final roommate, Sydney Alleyne, was probably the most fascinating member of our dorm group. She was from Barbados. A glamorous and mysterious foreign exchange student, whose mother was from Australia, thus the origin of her first name. Her father was a member of an elite family, whom did not approve of the interracial union. That was one of the reason she chose to attend Georgetown.

The engineering major was, at this time, primarily dominated by men. This did not discourage Sydney, who spoke English fluently, when she wanted to, and was familiar with people objecting to her defiance of tradition.

Before she even stepped foot on campus, she had declared that she would be first in her class. Not an easy accomplishment, since no black woman had ever attempted this before.

Sydney's second objective was to return to Barbados with the necessary skills to make significant changes to the quality of life for the middle class and those in poverty.

Everyone around me seemed to have a drive to succeed; a direction that they were moving toward, except me. All that I knew about Georgetown that inspired me, was, that in the 1950's, when John Kennedy was a mere Senator, he moved to 33rd and N Street in Georgetown.

The social and political elite had finally returned, after a long hiatus. This was attributed to, mostly the very glorious Jackie Kennedy who began to entertain famous and influential guests at their home.

What I soon learned, was that Georgetown University, unlike the city, has a unique mixture of beer guzzling college students and a more resolved, intellectually aristocratic, success driven crowd.

Although most tourists would prefer to take pictures of the chapel at the south end, where the Exorcist was filmed, the enormous National Historic landmark of Healy Hall, where the first African American earned a PHD is difficult to ignore.

On a personal level, I was battling with my own demons, *where I could never find a warm day, among saints layered with false gold; the beast inside of me screaming hysterically through the same eye sockets that now weep tears of blood.*

I even sarcastically played with the idea of printing Victorian calling or visiting cards, that were widely used during a more genteel era, and left by prestigious ladies at the homes they would frequent. Mine would say, in an elaborate vintage font, of course:

"Lady Gabriella Girard. Toxic, approach at your own risk."

It remains very dark inside the stage of my inner world. When I hear, the curtain call, loud and clear, and the sinners crawl as the lights fade away, I see my freshly dug grave.

Yet, far off in another chamber, the unknown voices remind me, that "It's what you make of this; not what it makes of you. It's up to fate that wove the threads in your soul; now let him go, release those demons. Do not let them hide, or override a new beginning.

There were days when everything fascinated me. Then among those moments I was determined to explain the complexity of love. Music, art, poetry, drama, not only capture but suspend time. I needed to solve this mystery. Why do we fail to recognize, that we are our own architect, not only of our future, but the past and present; all united by a common bond, much like a Mobius strip.

Like a Möbius strip, the human psyche has no inner or outer limits; no beginning, no end, no single port of entry or exit. No hierarchical ladder to climb up and down. I would continue to reexamine this metaphor at different stages of my life.

At this stage, I was going to experience my first real college party. Georgetown University has some conflicting views about sororities and fraternities. The general rule is, that they do not exist.

But, take a campus stroll in the main courtyard during freshman orientation, and there are advertisements for various club events, sanctioned or not. There may not be any formal Greek system, but the pledges are everywhere.

Personally, my focus was only academics. My minor was, kicking the Jake habit. At seventeen, life was inviting me to experience the illumination of harmonies, that are constantly modifying different rhythms with a variety of accompaniments.

One of my first lessons was when I realized that a sun reflecting on an empty fountain, is a ridiculous waste, that prolongs misery beyond its premeditated boundaries.

Early in October, I had my first opportunity to test my inner and outer limits.

The Order of the Crown and Dragon, sometimes referred to as "Seven", was hosting an invitation only, private party at their Frat House.

They had been on probation many times for violating, the code of conduct, even though they were not recognized on campus.

This, of course, only made "Seven" more appealing, especially to sorority pledges, who were not allowed to attend any parties. The frat brothers, knowing this rule, were determined to entice as many unsuspecting coeds to their, " den of Iniquity."

The limited invitations must be presented at the door to enter, but everybody on campus knew that this was an annual party that "celebrated" the ascending virgins on campus. It was unlikely that any of them would be shunned away, invitation or not.

It was said, that next to the Seven's Coat of Arms, in the foyer, were ornate flags and banners, with names of all their conquests. Naturally only the first names were displayed, as to not totally ruin the girl's reputation. Some girls even donated their panties, after a night of debauchery. They were proud to claim that their names were displayed, even if they weren't.

If the plan was to have a hook up, I wanted no part of it. My plan was actually to go to this masquerade party, to test the waters, not to swim in them. I saw this, as an opportunity to go from step A to step B without any emotional repercussions. In a few weeks, I would turn eighteen. Perhaps, I would celebrate with a "quickie" in the bed, or the bathroom, like in and out, just enough to remind me what all the hype was about. This might even be momentarily pleasurable.

So far, I had accomplished disengaging myself from dwelling on sex. But, I had to admit when Veronica would come home from her orgies, sharing graphically what she had done, the hormones began to rage. I was no virgin, but I may as well be one. I had limited experience with only one man, that knew what he was doing.

"Gabby girl, there is nothing to it. When that one eye monster shows his head, you will instinctively know what to do," Veronica assured me.

When any man would notice me I always found it quite peculiar. Even those men, who were merely friends would say, " You are one of those exotic, rare creatures that one finds in the art galleries of Brussels, or the Louvre. Men are fascinated by you from afar, but do not want to experience the rejection they are certain you will give them," I, would hear this often.

I believed that those people were simply being kind. My legs are too short, boobs too large, and what some refer to as exotic, to me is grotesque. I would truthfully be quite happy with cookie cutter features, fading into the masses, without calling attention to any of my oddities.

Jake always made me feel ethereal, fragile, breakable; his very own captured goddess. But, I never felt that admiration from any other men. Once I agreed to attend Georgetown, Molly was the one who enlightened me, that in high school I might as well have been walking around with a giant "J" on my chest.

No matter how discreet Jake and I thought we were, everyone knew that I belonged to him, and no male would dare approach me. At least, now miles away from Savannah, I would not have that stigma to plague me.

The afternoon that Veronica proudly shared with us, the invitation that was personally delivered to her, by a "Seven" frat member, seemed like forever ago. But, now, only a few hours away, it began to feel real. Ophelia, had decided she would not attend, but Sydney, Veronica and I all agreed to dress as classical literary characters.

Veronica chose a very revealing Tinker Bell costume. I argued that Tinker Bell was not an authentic classical character. But, I soon gave up, attempting to convince her rationally. It was a moot point. In the end her only objective was to be laid, and unless her wings would interfere, it was a sure bet that she would get her wish.

We all agreed to arrive together

" Come on Gabby, seriously? You aren't going to this party as Juliet, are you?" Veronica was complaining.

It was clear that she thought that I was totally crazy. "But, of course I am. Juliet is a legitimate classical heroine, unlike Tinker Bell," I retorted defiantly.

" You're missing the point, Gabby. That costume covers too much of your body," Veronica, continued emphatically.

I walked passed her to the full-length mirror, and added, "Excuse me, but my boobs are my best asset, and this corset is so tight I feel like I am falling out of the bodice, " I replied.

Sydney started laughing, adding that, " She has a point Veronica."

Then looking at me she added, "But, then again it will limit your choices to only boob men. They will be lining up, hoping to get at least a quick feel on the dance floor. We both should be thankful that you are not showing off the rest of that terrific, wicked body or Veronica and I would never be noticed," she said.

Sydney was being more than kind.

"Like you and Veronica have any flaws? When you walk in a room, all eyes are on you, and only you," I responded.

Veronica, Sydney and even Ophelia knew how to act instinctively in every situation, with such prowess, that I might just as well be wallpaper. I accepted this, because I was new to the game, and preferred being an observer.

It was time to add the final touches to my costume. I put on the ornate mask that Jake gave me as a gift on his first visit home from Vietnam. It went perfectly with the empire style gown, laced cinched bodice, with long train flowing when I walked. The royal burgundy, with gold trim was a replica of the newly released movie, "Romeo and Juliet" starring Olivia Hussey. With my long dark hair loosely hanging down my back, I, actually felt like Juliet, on the night she met Romeo. Would my fate be similar, to hers tonight? Star crossed lovers, doomed at first sight.

The massive historical building, that currently houses the "Seven" Fraternity, was lit up like a Roman Candle. As we began to approach the massive oak door, I noticed the gold carved crown surrounding a dragon. Standing outside, there were two robust bouncers resembling giant cyclops.

"Ladies,

Ladies, Ladies...Please, come right to the front," said a fine-looking gladiator, wearing a helmet, but no mask.

Veronica handed the prestigious invitation to the Roman soldier, who was eager to show us inside. His wide mouth grin, looked like he was about to devour Veronica immediately, wings and all.

"Follow me, you fine maidens," he said jovially.

"And good evening to you, Ben- Hur. Can I pollinate you with some of my pixie dust?"

Veronica said, rubbing close to him.

I thought that I might regurgitate. I grabbed Veronica by the arm and dragged her into the hallway.

"First of all, bees pollinate, not fairies,"

I said, in an emphatic whisper.

Sydney added, "And, please, for me... try not to come across like a whore," She said, as Ben -Hur came closer.

"That's okay, Miss Juliet. I really knew what she meant," he said seriously.

It must be true that there is someone for each of us. And, then he winked at her adding, "I'll be here all night, baby... and when I'm ready to be "pollinated" I will find you," he said, and then grabbed her ass.

Now it was Sydney who looked directly at Veronica.

"If you want everyone here to think that you are a slut, fine...but, I do not want them to think that I am like you!" Sydney said.

"This is the end of the 60's and women are liberated. We are open about sex....and if I am horney, I am going out and getting some ass and I am not ashamed." That was the last that we heard of Veronica. We never saw her again that night.

In some strange way, you have to love the Veronica's of the world. They are uninhibited and honest. Suddenly, I realized that I was standing alone. Feeling out of place and awkward, I began to move slowly to the bar. When I turned around, I literally, nearly fell over this fine specimen of a man. His eyes were staring into mine. Through my mask it felt like he had hypnotized me. I turned away, feeling uncomfortable.

That was when he took my hand, and bent down on one knee.

"Is this the fair maiden, Juliet? come out to play with thee?" He said.

I gained my balance and stepped back slightly. I recognized that voice, but not the well chiseled body, that was barely covered by a red toga.

"Let me introduce myself. I am Caden, faithful and loyal follower of Mark Antony himself," he said with confidence.

Caden? Where did I hear that name before? Oh no, not tonight. It can't be the same Caden from Savannah High School. The same one that almost knocked me over in the hall. The one that I barely met, at the only party Jake ever took me to .Please, if there truly is a God, make this not be the same man.

Not now, when all I want to do is be my new self. I do remember now that Mrs. Thompson said there were three of us accepted at Georgetown University. My first instinct is just bolt, as fast as I can. But he is still holding my hand. Maybe he won't even remember me. He only saw me once... maybe twice.

According to Molly, he was very smart and popular. All the girls thought he was hot; and maybe he was, in a preppy way, but not my kind of hot. What I didn't know then, was that he was more of a "bad boy", like Warren Beatty or

105

James Dean. Even at this moment he looked very cool. Sizzling cool!

I removed the mask, and took a chance, that he would not recognize me. But, Caden was stunned.

"Good evening, kind, Sir" I said, with a curtsy. His hand still holding mine.

I know this chick. I've seen her before. Yes...we went to high school together... and that party.... where I was shooting tequila and Allison gave me my first sex lesson.

"Are you from Savannah, Georgia?" He asks directly.

"Yes. But, Savannah is a large community," I tried not to look at him directly in his eyes, still hoping that I could escape from what might be a terrible scene.

"Okay. We can catch up later. That song the band is playing, by Fleetwood Mac, is great," he is still talking when I realize we are suddenly on the dance floor.

Somehow, I am in his arms. I hear him whispering and singing in my ear, "*Like a stillness of remembering what you had, and what you lost. Thunder only happens when it's raining...,*" I didn't want to; I couldn't listen to those words.

His breath on my neck and the intensity of the music, made my head start spinning. I broke loose, and left him on the dance floor. His eyes searching the room for where I might have gone.

Trying to get passed the crowds, all I wanted to do was find the door I came in and exit as quickly and discreetly as possible. And, then I heard Caden directly behind me.

"Abby? Stop... Please...," he was saying.

"It's Gabby! .My name is GABBY!" I answered him, not really knowing why.

His arms have now caught up to me. They are around my waist. By this time, I am furious.

"Before you attempt to seduce a girl on the dance floor, moron, you should get her name right," I say.

But he is moving me to a dark corner, away from all the loud noise.

"Hold on for just one second, Miss Abby with a 'G' " Caden said, now looking directly in my eyes.

"I was maybe serenading you, but I was not being pushy," He said, waiting for me to respond.

Clearly, I was not ready for this high stake poker game. He was way out of my league.

"Do you even remember me from high school?" he was asking.

"Because, I could never forget you, Gabby?" Caden added as I started to walk away.

It was then, that I just couldn't let it go. I had to be a smart ass and say,

"Oh, yes, I do remember you Caden Cassidy. You were at a party I went to a few years ago. As I recall, you were Allison's latest project and conquest. "My face flushed as I said that, and it wasn't from the heat in the room.

Caden just wouldn't let it go. His reply was on the money.

"And, you Gabby were Jake's girl, back then. But, that never meant I wasn't interested, or even stopped being interested," he waited to see if I would come back.

"Can we start over? A new beginning?"

Those words caught my attention. That was why I was here. Caden was right. If I left him now, Jake would have won again.

"I am Gabby Girard...," I put my hand out to him. "And, I would be glad to meet you, Caden Cassidy," I said, as he took my hand again. It was warm, safe and almost too comfortable.

"Well, at least you got my name right,"

We both laughed. He then asked me for my dorm phone number and wrote it on the back of a laundry receipt. I was fairly certain, he was just being courteous when he asked me for it.

"It's still early, Abby with a 'G'. Can you stay for one more dance? "Light my Fire" is next," he says, smiling. "I promise not to seduce you.... please?"

"One more only," I agree, but added that " I have a lot of studying this weekend for mid-terms."

"Okay, school girl, just one more dance. I will take what I can," he says, leading me to the dance floor.

At first, there is plenty of space between us. Then he approaches me, suggestively, moving closer, and closer. We are looking directly into each other's eyes, as if we are alone.

His mouth is moving to the words of the song, but he never loses eye contact.

"You know that I would be a liar, if I was to say to you.. Girl, we couldn't get much higher... Gabby, let me light your fire..." Then, he is holding me so close that our bodies, are nearly one, and the crowds have vanished. The band is loud, but I only hear him now,

"Let me be your fire... Your only desire... baby, trust me, I can be your fire,"

And, the music stops. His mouth has found mine. His tongue is learning how to gently, but strongly, pursue mine. Then, he sucks my lip, and it is nearly orgasmic. Caden Cassidy will be a force to reckon with.

CHAPTER 12

If doors of perception were cleansed everything would appear to man as it is, Infinite. For man has closed himself up, till he sees all things through narrow chinks of his cavern. -William Blake

Caden October, 1965

Five hundred seventy nine miles from Savannah. What are the odds of running into Gabby Girard here at Georgetown at a Frat party? How the Hell did that happen? In my shirt pocket is her phone number. Maybe, what I should do is throw it away right now, before I am tempted to call her. No... better yet, I should burn it.

Caden takes out some random matches that he always carries in his pocket, just in case there is some weed that becomes available. He lights the match and then almost instinctively, blows it out.

I can't deny that holding her in my arms earlier felt amazing. Almost like she belonged right there. It was so natural to talk to her that I was almost believing that we were together, like a real couple... but, wait.

Where is Jake? And why is she even here?

Do I really want to take the chance that she will want to go out? I mean, let's be real. From what I remember and heard about her and Jake, was that they were in a serious relationship; I mean as in potential marriage relationship.

But, I would be lying if I didn't admit that she got to me tonight. Those green eyes, like the color of emeralds, sparkling when she looked directly at me.

And, that dark chestnut hair reaching nearly to her waist, made me lose all my senses. When we danced her body fit into mine like a lost puzzle piece, at last completing the riddle.

When she left, my next stop was the Tequila Bar, set up at all Frat Parties. My goal was to get rip roaring drunk, grab a quickie from any sorority babe, leftovers, and forget about any chick with baggage.

Then I ran right into Dylan. Dylan Thomas. Yeah, he's named after the famous poet and all the girls dig him. He quotes lines from romantic poems and it works every time.

"Hey, buddy. Caden? Hand over that bottle. Where is that cute brunette that was all over you earlier?"

My head was playing like a roulette wheel, spinning so fast, that suddenly I lost my balance, landing on the nearest sofa. Sitting next to me was an attractive, petite blonde with fairy wings that nearly blinded me each time she turned. Here was what I needed to get that Gabby taste out of my mouth.

"Hello. Tinker Bell, any chance that you can remove those wings?" I was already getting my groove back. Until... the fairy girl gave me the most piercing glare.

"My wings are part of my costume, moron. The only way they come off is if everything does," Veronica replied.

I must have moved toward her at that point, just a little too aggressively, because the next thing I remember is her pulling my arm nearly out of its socket.

"What's your problem playboy? Gabby not good enough for you? You were all over her earlier."

How could she possibly know Gabby?

"I know your type, but Gabby is my roomie. She is trying to get over a really bad break up. She doesn't need someone like you making it worse. Scram before I turn your ass into a frog, Prince Charming."

That was just perfect timing. Over two hundred eligible girls more than willing to hit the sack with any of us, and I try to score with Gabby's roommate.

It was time to make a midnight run to my Aunt Selena's pad in nearby Alexandria. If I left now I would just make the last train, there. She was probably out partying with one of her senator boyfriends.

I could sneak in quietly without too much attention. In the morning, I could look forward to a homemade Sunday breakfast. Selena's home was my favorite sanctuary.

Finally, I have no idea how, but I see the Metro station in front of me. I stagger around for a few moments, as a light breeze blows through my hair. There is a vacant bench that I claim, seriously considering lying down for just a few seconds. The fresh air is, thankfully bringing me back to normal.

A Metro security guard walks toward me, with a condescending grin, and with his wood night stick, starts to poke my stomach.

"Hey Caden, you ever going to get on this train sober?" Stanley asks.

My many midnight excursions have made us on a first name basis. I don't dare throw up, although I still feel slightly nauseous.

"Don't you worry about me Stanley... good buddy," I give him a polite salute.

"I am going to turn my life around, starting tomorrow morning," I said, trying not to slur my words.

"Well, Caden, I sincerely hope you do. Someday, if you don't change your wicked partying, that window of opportunity will pass you by like a New York minute."

Stanley was always trying to get through to him, but nothing seemed to be working.

"Do you have anyone special in your life, Caden?" Stanley was still talking.

"Man, you only get one opportunity, when it comes to the right girl. She will flash across your world, like a shooting star across the Milky Way." Stanley was finally getting my attention.

Once on the train, I begin to realize that in all the four years I was at Savannah High, I might have seen Gabriella...Gabby, ten times, and never close enough to even say "hello". Jake Chevalier, the football quarterback, that led

111

us to the state championship, and won, was always close to Gabby.

She was only a sophomore, like me. Being with a guy that much older, surely means she is no virgin. More like a freshly picked gardenia. Lucky Jake, he popped her cherry early. So why was she acting like she didn't understand the hook up game?

Ever since Allison, my high school sex mentor, I found scoring with girls easy. I knew what they wanted, and more important, I knew how to satisfy them. As long as they wanted to cum, I could fill their empty vessels. I had the fortunate ability to reset myself quickly and sustain my erection long enough to have multiple orgasms.

That kind of talent gets around to the ladies like wildfire, and I have just the hose to cool them down. That was why, Joe Madison, President of the Seven Fraternity and I became friends so quickly.

My new world was filled with exploding fireworks, that released a cascade of colorful streamers in blues, greens, reds, purples, yellows and oranges. I was a live wire, with indefinite ever ready batteries, lasting all night; until tonight.

Looking out the train window, all I can see now is, GABBY surrounded by stars and driving me NUTS. I am hoping that Aunt Selena will have some solid advice.

Aunt Selena, has always been considered the "black sheep" of our ultra conservative family. She is my Dad's half-sister. When Selena's husband passed away, five years ago, she never even hesitated to leave Savannah, and come directly to our capital, Washington DC.

"The men in Savanna, are just too inhibited, serious, and boring. I need more excitement in my life than an evening playing dominoes, or joining a bowling league, " Selena proclaimed.

With the substantial inheritance that Uncle Ralph left her, Selena was able to buy a three bedroom, Brownstone, in a very posh but quaint suburb of Alexandria, Virginia.

Close enough to the excitement of the political hub and just far enough away to privately entertain some of the most powerful senators and congressmen in office.

Soon after Selena arrived, she began volunteering at the most notable local charities. Her support for, Young Athletes of America, The Animal Welfare League, and Abandoned Children, allowed her access to the most elite, eligible or not, bachelors in DC.

When she wasn't organizing a charity event or an auction extravaganza, Selena would assist with various lobbies, many that promoted women rights. It was not surprising to hear her name linked with many powerful politicians. It was because of Selena, at least in part, that I chose Georgetown University to attend.

It was difficult to accurately put an age on Selena .I estimated between fifty and sixty-five, but it was a moot point since she captivated the attention of men and women of all ages. It was more than beauty that attracted everyone to her.

Although she was small in stature, a petit five feet tall, her stunning Raven black hair and equally captivating grey blue eyes,that resembled a polished silver, metallic glow. This was only the frame that accentuated her free spirit.

Everyone in DC knew when Selena had arrived. She would make her grand entrance in a candy apple red Mustang, with the convertible top down, weather permitting. When it was too cold to drive from Alexandria, a town car or limousine would be available to her, most of the time.

Aunt Selena was always being invited to White House Charity Balls, Embassy dinners, and International lunches. It was on one of those occasions that she was seated next to the Irish Ambassador.

The planning coordinator knew that Selena was Irish and lived in Dublin. Thoughtfully she decided it would be a nice gesture to seat her next to the Ambassador. What followed, from that innocent decision was a typical Selena moment.

After a short time of idle talk at the table, Selena leaned close to the Ambassador and whispered to him that on this occasion she had gone commando. She then discreetly placed his hand on her very wet pussy. Minutes later, she handed him a cocktail napkin that said, " follow me to the restroom, nearest the kitchen for some Irish cream."

Selena gracefully excused herself from the table. Five minutes later the Ambassador followed. When they returned again, respectfully at different times, the rather flushed Ambassador announced that he had not ever had such delicious Irish Cream before, even in his hometown of Dublin. It was of little importance that he was drinking a martini at that moment.

I could always count on my Aunt Selena, to offer me a story that would lift my spirits or share her stash of weed. If it was possible to have cloned her, she would be my perfect life partner.

Searching for a woman who was willing to swim by moonlight, hike the Himalayas, marvel at Macho Picchu and take midnight drives to watch a meteor shower was rare to find in any generation.

"Caden. You look like shit," Selena greeted him at the front door.

I was used to this response. Lately I was in this condition most of the time when I "visited".

"Love you too, Selena" I replied on cue, as I walked past her to my guest room, banging and bumping my way up the stairs and down the hallway.

"Can we talk in the morning? I've got a bummer headache," I was yelling, as I kept walking, anxiously looking forward to my own bed.

"That's called a hangover, smart ass. The best cure, is to stop partying every weekend," she said, as I closed the door.

Thankfully, the next morning, the aroma of freshly brewed coffee, sizzling bacon, and Selena's homemade blueberry Belgian waffles, with an old family recipe syrup was calling me downstairs. If I forgot to mention earlier, in addition to all of Selena's other attributes, she is a gourmet cook.

"Girl problem, Caden?" She carefully approached the subject.

"This one is totally different, Selena.

I can't be accused of a hit and run this time. I barely made it to first base with a kiss."

"Sounds to me like you ran into an air-conditioned gypsy. The hardest kind to tame. Extremely difficult, but not impossible," Selena said while serving me her remedy for a hangover.

"Now you got my attention. What the hell is an air-conditioned gypsy, Selena?"

"Okay, Caden. The best way to describe this girl would be to say that she is an outcast, hippie, beatnik, yet very cool. Unlike the standard "make love not war" hippies, this one is going to be selective. She is not an easy catch; from what you are saying." She warmed my coffee and added,

"Why is this girl important to you Caden?" Selena waited for me to respond.

That was a very good question. My game plan was always to score and move on before any serious relationship develops.

"Gabby is very different from anyone else that I have met. I like to call her Abby with a G. It is hard to put a rational explanation to this. I do not want to blow the chance to know her better," I could not say what this mystic about her was, but it was definitely still here.

"If you are admitting Caden, that this Gabby is worth respecting, then my advice is to move very slowly. Do not play any games with her. If her name is Gabby, call her that. Respect everything about her. She is looking into your soul, not your sack," she said

I was listening, but still thinking about how I would make my next move.

"Caden. You must be very careful, because this Gabby might be the one to steal your heart forever. "Selena was serious by this point.

I was most definitely going to be careful. Still, I could not let the opportunity to get close to Gabby pass by.

"Caden, you will know soon. She will give you clues. It is up to you to listen. Talk with her, not at her. Eventually she will reveal to you her most intimate desires. The question will be; how will you respond to them?" She continued to make him realize that this was a serious decision, not to be taken lightly.

"Women like the chase as much as men do. But, in the end we want only one man, to care for all of our needs. You need to give up the notion that it takes many women to satisfy that voracious appetite. " Selena seemed as curious as I was.

"Invite her for a visit. I am fascinated that there really is a young woman out there that is making my favorite nephew spin in circles," Selena said.

Now was the time to reflect on all that had been discussed.

Two days later, while I was sorting my laundry, the receipt with Gabby's phone number fell down on the ground. Dylan was the one to find it and pick it up.

"Hey... Caden, were you ever going to call this Gabby chick? Because, if not.... can I have it?" Dylan already had the number memorized.

"Back off Don Juan. Hand over the number. You have your harem quota already."

I looked at the number. It is now or never, I thought as I walked toward the Frat phone, that miraculously was not being used.

"Hello....I would like to speak to Gabriella Girard, please. This is Caden Cassidy."

CHAPTER 13

Performance, perseverance, and persistence in spite of all obstacles, discouragements, and impossibilities; it is this in all things that distinguishes the strong soul from the weak. - Thomas Carlyle

Caden and Gabby October-November Georgetown 1967

Forty-eight hours later, Caden Cassidy called me. It was much more awkward on the phone than on the dance floor, but at the end I did agree to meet him for coffee at the nearby Hamilton Arms.

According to the Washington Post, the collection of Swiss style village houses and apartments was a "deteriorating" community. Those of us at Georgetown University thought it was the perfect place to congregate.

On the outer walls of many buildings, Dickens characters were permanently sculptured. Delicate flowers, painted on window shutters, and ceramic tile glued on park benches, invited those free- spirited beatnik and artists a welcome place to gather.

It was where we shared poetry, smoked pot openly, and enjoyed the latest protest song playing from a nearby window.

Adjacent to the coffee shop that Caden and I had agreed to meet at, were open apartments, where the residents were notorious for throwing wine parties that would last for weeks.

No one seemed to work, but there were many Vietnam veterans that lived here. They were some of the most vocal protesting the war.

This was my favorite place to come and mingle with a different group of people from a different world. Here there was no social hierarchy and no one made judgements of anybody. This lifestyle, promoting and encouraging a peaceful coexistence appealed to me.

It was a place to experience the creative power of a bohemian culture, that fueled the movement of visionary literary heroes, passionate poets and unrestrained sexual desires. Bebop jazz, playing with Mary Jane, among esoteric philosophers challenged all the established morals.

Coffee and Confusion, was the most popular hangout. It also takes credit for Jim Morrison sharing his early poetry, on a makeshift stage, when he was a teenager.

Our coffee date went well, but I had the distinct feeling that Caden was not comfortable with this free spirit atmosphere. The weed didn't seem to bother him and he was polite, attentive and a real gentleman. Maybe, just a little too reserved.

Since that night at the Frat House, there was only that one passionate kiss, when his mouth took total control, and my pelvis was trembling, enough to make Jake a far off memory.

Caden was the antithesis of Jake. Where Jake was tall, blonde, athletic, and confidant in any group, Caden's dark hair, and crystal blue eyes, could turn a room of ice into a sauna.

He knew what to do and say with any woman. Inside that "good boy" exterior, was a very appealing, bad boy persona. Even after a very short time with Caden, I knew he was spontaneous, edgy, and maybe even a little dangerous.

It was Sydney that I trusted the most with advice on men. She was the wise one. Her motions were in check. There was no doubt what her priorities were.

When the two of us were in the dorm alone, during a study session, I would glance up from my notes to see her long legs and slender hips moving to the captivating calypso or reggae sounds from her headphones.

None of us had headphones that resembled those worn by pilots. In this decade, any earphones we had, were attached to a transistor radio with limited listening choices.

But Sydney's friends were brilliant. Many of them experimented with electronic devices as a hobby. One male friend, that was obviously hoping to impress Sydney, invented a prototype tape recorder that included all her favorite music and artists. Bob Marley, Mighty Sparrow, and Sir Lancelot, were just a few examples of the music genre that Sydney thrived on.

On the few occasions that I was deemed worthy of sharing this experience with her, I was fascinated by the alluring melodies from an exotic Island that tempted me to escape from my shabby existence. Most of the music arrived in contraband packages from Barbados and Jamaica. None of these artists had been discovered yet by the mainstream disc jockeys.

I was lucky to get a leftover song when Sydney felt unusually generous.

"How is it going Gabby with that new boyfriend?" She asked, never removing the headphones.

It was easy talking to Sydney. We knew our boundaries. There was a controlled friendship that neither of us pushed.

"I don't know if I would start referring to Caden as my boyfriend, Sydney," I said, firmly.

"We are not exclusive, and I have only had coffee with him once, at Hamilton Arms. He seemed a little uncomfortable. That was a few days ago. You could hardly even call that a date," I added, as a support for my conclusion.

Sydney removed the headphones, took a deep breath and sat comfortably on my bed, resembling a cat ready to play with its mouse.

"Men here in the US are not really that different from back home. They all just want to get into our pants," she gave me a moment to respond before elaborating.

"I guess that's the reason I might be avoiding all his calls lately," I said honestly.

Sydney began adjusting her headphones once again, and then made one last comment before she went back to her dancing.

"Gabby girl... it's time to send those demons back to hell. They've been casting shadows on your happiness for far too long. Give this Caden fellow at least a chance to help you get your groove back." And off she went, bumping and grinding, refusing to hear any of my excuses.

There was a slight flashback, and I was back home with Molly in her bedroom just a few months ago. God how I missed her now.

Aunt Selena had no idea how difficult this Gabby Gypsy was going to be to tame. Now, I was back on the warm up bench, with not even an opportunity to get on base again .My semi date with this Ice Princess at the off campus coffee house restricted me.

The banjo playing, pot smoking atmosphere had possibilities, if it weren't for all her "friends" interrupting us whenever I started to get close. It was useless to talk, let alone "listen" like Selena suggested.

When we finally left, and I walked her back to the dorm, I was sure that at last she would invite me upstairs to her room for a little recreational "play" time. But, what I left with was a "brotherly" kiss on the cheek and a polite "call me" as she walked up the stairs and disappeared.

Now, do not get me wrong. I never really expect to score on the first night. Although, when it does happen, I am ever so grateful. It avoids all this messy game playing. Why can't we both be honest.

"I like you. You like me. Now let's go fuck each other." Then we can both just move on and stop wasting precious time.

Alice taught me the basics, and the rest came naturally. And, I will add, that most women appreciate this honesty.

But, now it has already been two weeks since Gabby and I have kissed at the Frat party, and nearly a month since I had sex. Something needed to shake down soon or I am moving on to more open arms; and believe me, on this campus they are everywhere.

The thought of walking away from Gabby has crossed my mind many times. But, something is evolving that I do not recognize. Gabby is playing the "Master Player". *There is no escaping..., there is a spell on me.... I cannot explain how or why I feel this way...I'm not sure if I can take it...if I'm the last romantic, star crossed lover alive, then I'm surely dying.*

And, right then I knew what I had to do. I have to get her in the sack, where I am in control again.

That is the challenge I cannot walk away from the chase. Once I win her, she will be like all the rest. Yet, at this moment, I have invested more time on Gabby than any other chick, ever.

Finally, Gabby returned my call, and this time she sounded much more relaxed, even anxious to see me again. With Aunt Selena's help, I planned the perfect date.

Andy Warhol, Paul Morrissey, Niko, and Eric Emerson were speaking on campus, promoting their latest film.

The Chelsea Girls, had recently been banned from the Cannes Festival, because the organizers feared a scandal over the ten seconds of male nudity.

Everyone on campus was eager to hear Warhol discuss the many controversial projects he was tackling, including, the most ambitious film, "Imitation of Christ." The title is a reference to **Imitation Christi**, a spiritual guide written in the fifteenth century, by Dutch mystic author Thomas a Kempis.

Warhol's film is a dramatic interpretation, a dark comedy of a handsome young man, whose name is "Son".

The character is a moody introvert, who enjoys most of his time with the family maid. She feeds him, pampers him, and reads to him the **Imitatione Christi**.

It is a complex study of how, "Son" deals with his analytical parents, abrasive girlfriend, and his journey with a hobo in San Francisco. I knew that once I told Gabby that I

121

had tickets to this one night only event she would not only be impressed; she would go NUTS.

Personally, I could care less about hearing this bull shit, but if it gets me closer to fucking Gabby, it is worth the money and two-hour investment. The Andy Warhol lecture was a sellout, and the entire campus was raving about it.

When I broke the news to Gabby that we were going to hear Warhol talk, she was speechless. Score one for team Cassidy.

"Hey, you think I can just stop by for a quick visit? I am close by, and I can tell you about the plans for the rest of that night."

There was a long pause, and I thought we might have been disconnected.

"Sure, Caden. Can you give me about thirty minutes to get ready? " I heard her finally respond.

I was beyond ecstatic. My old charm was finally coming back.

I could hardly believe that Caden , actually took the time to arrange this perfect date. I was not sure why my first instincts were so critical. This was technically only our second date, and it was so thoughtful of him to consider the Andy Warhol event. Somehow, he was able to not only get the tickets, but they were orchestra center seats. This event was not only sought after on campus, but everywhere in the Capital, as well.

After the lecture, Caden had arranged a late- night reservation at the very posh and famous 1789. This restaurant is located in the Federal period house, off of 36th street, which meant we needed a cab to get there and back. Not a cheap fare, especially on a college student's budget.

Inside, there are six different dining rooms. Each decorated with antiques, famous prints and equestrian art. The restaurant's name is derived from the year the constitution was signed. Caden had reserved the highly-coveted, Middleburg Room, located upstairs.

As we entered, the ceiling was adorned with tree branches, covered with tiny twinkling lights. Our table was located next to the window, as well as a romantic view of the very inviting fireplace.

The maître de pulled out my chair and Caden sat directly in front of me. He reached over to hold my hand lightly.

"Are you having a good time, Gabby?"

He asked. His eyes were sparkling as blue as the feathers on a timid starling.

"I have no idea, Caden, how you managed all this, but it is breathtaking. It is the best date that I have ever gone on," I said. And, that was not an exaggeration.

Caden tilted his head, rather confused.

"Certainly, Jake wined and dined you some of those years you were together."

He said quietly.

Startled to hear Jake's name coming from Caden's mouth, I retreated my hand and stared at the fire, flames dancing freely on the crackling wood.

"Can we please not go there tonight?"

I finally said with definite hostility. I could tell already that Caden knew that he had made the wrong move. But, before he could respond, the waiter was at the table with a bottle of Cabernet and two glasses.

Without any hesitation or checking ID's, he poured a small amount for Caden to taste. Once he received the affirmative nod, the waiter continued to pour both of us glasses of wine. Then there was that awkward silence, once he had left.

"There is nothing on this menu that will disappoint you Gabby," he said.

I continued to read the five-page menu, ignoring any eye contact. This would end up being a very long evening. Then spontaneously, out of nowhere, Caden dropped to his knee, and began singing, in a very Irish accent,

"Oh my love my darli'n, I've hungered for your touch, a long lonely time , and time goes by so slowly, and time can do so much, are you still mine?"

Everyone sitting anywhere near us, broke out clapping, and whistling as he took my hand again. This time I looked directly at him.

In 1986, the movie "Top Gun" with Tom Cruise reenacted this very moment. When I saw the film I thought that some screenwriter must have been at the restaurant when Caden spontaneously performed his act for me.

" Forgive me Gabby for being an insensitive jerk?" He then kissed my hand gently.

"Sometimes, words just come out of my mouth without even thinking. Seriously, whatever you have heard about me, tonight I am a different man. I promise you," Caden said, waiting for me to respond.

This time when I reached across toward him, I kissed him. The sparks ignited once again, and I knew that we had crossed an important threshold tonight.

I could never thank Selena enough for the fantastic lecture tickets, impressive restaurant, and even arranging the wine. It was all, in spite of my faux pas, a terrific evening.

Back at the Frat house, I had arranged for Dylan to find another room for the evening. A bottle of champagne was chilling. Another one of Selena's generous gifts, waiting for our return. Outside the restaurant, while Gabby was getting her coat, a lady was handing out roses. I slipped the lady a five-dollar bill and hid the roses behind my back.

The doorman hailed us a cab, and soon we were headed back to campus.

"Gabby, it is still rather early. Would you come up to the Frat house for awhile? Just so we can talk and get to know each other a little better?" I handed her the roses hoping that would clinch the deal.

As I put my arm around her, I could smell the sweet scent of vanilla nectar that always reminded me of Selena.

"I really do want to know you better, Caden. And this was such a memorable evening. Thank you so much for everything. But, if I go with you to the Frat house, how will

I get home?" I asked, wanting to make it clear that I was not planning on staying the night.

"Curfew is at two, and I must be back by then," I added just so that there was no confusion.

Not wanting to blow this, and still hoping that I would convince her differently, I assured her that I would make certain that she would arrive home safely. It was all falling into place perfectly.

"Is that Shalimar you are wearing, Gabby?" I asked.

She looked astonished that I recognized the scent. She was so close now, that I could feel her breathing.

"How did you ever guess the perfume I was wearing? Not many people know what it is," she said.

I just smiled thinking how much Aunt Selena would approve of this girl. Then it occurred to me, that this could really happen.

"My Aunt Selena, who lives in Alexandria, wears that same scent. I will take you one day soon to visit her, I mean if you would like that?" I added.

The cab pulled up as close to the Frat House as he could. I paid him the fare. Holding on to Gabby's hand tightly, I was anxious to get her to my room. I was saying a little prayer that Dylan was good on his word, and not back until after two.

Leading her upstairs, past the banner of iniquity, made me even more anxious to have sex with Gabby. But, I knew that this would take patience. Once inside, I immediately opened the refrigerator, mostly packed with beer, and took out the chilled bottle of champagne. POP...it was uncorked. I poured Gabby a generous amount in a red plastic glass, leftover from a recent party.

This was going to be an epic celebration. Touchdown! Blow the whistles and ring the bells. I was almost laughing at the images playing in my crazy head. I turned Gabby so she was facing me, so we could make a toast.

"To the beginning of forever," I said, looking directly into her eyes.

"To the beginning." That was as far as she would commit to. She then, gently pushed a piece of my hair away from my eyes.

It was now that I drew her close to me. Our tongues playing hide and seek, until at last they come together, neither of us needing air to breathe; neither wanting to release the other.

Without warning, my hand slips into her panties. She does not object I begin to stroke her pussy with two fingers, gently entering her vagina. My tongue is mimicking the fingers.

"Oh, baby...you are so wet... is that all for me?" I am breathing heavy and I can tell when I move her hips closer to me that she too, is moaning. Then my finger feels her contracting, squeezing tightly, and I ask,

"You don't want me to stop do you Gabby?" I am nearly in a state of euphoria, when I hear her call out my name,

"Caden! Oh, Caden! Make it last baby. Don't stop, please don't stop."

She is almost begging. Hearing her, almost desperate, I move my fingers from her pussy and in one motion her dress is on the floor, and she is on the bed with only a bra. That quickly is unsnapped, releasing her full breasts with hard nipples. As I am sucking them, her fingers are in my hair.

She cries out, "I need your hard cock...now, Caden...Fuck me, NOW...Caden," she says, her back arched ready for me to enter her.

"Not yet, Gabby. Trust me. I want to make you cum baby, and climax over, and over. Your cum in my mouth will be like honey. I will lick your clitoris and you will then cum with me when I fuck you," I said, preparing to eat her pussy, when, suddenly, it all stopped.

Gabby was up and had her clothes on faster than I had removed them.

"Hey, what's the matter? What did I do?" I said, while holding her in my arms. I could feel her tears on my chest. She was sobbing uncontrollably.

"I am ... I am...so...sorry, Caden." She was trembling.

I held her head between my hands and wiped the tears away, kissing her until she stopped crying.

"Just tell me what I did wrong. I have been crazy about you since the first time I saw you, two years ago at that party."

I was clueless at what went wrong.

"It isn't you Caden. It is me. I thought that I was ready for this, but when you started to talk about licking my vagina, I had no idea what to do. I never have felt that before." She was looking into space, while trying to explain all of this.

The reality was just now hitting me.

Gabby may not technically be a virgin, but whatever she experienced with Jake was limited.

"It is alright, sweetheart. It is all my fault." I moved way too fast. As I looked into those deep green eyes, I knew that sex from this time on was going to take a whole new meaning.

This Gabby, my "Gabby", needed to be handled with extreme care. The next time we would have sex, we would make love, and it would be an unforgettable experience for us both.

CHAPTER 14

How many loved your moments of glad grace,
And loved your beauty, with love false or true,
But one man loved the pilgrim soul in you,
And loved the sorrow of your changing face.

And bending down below the glowing bars,
Murmur, a little sadly, how love fled
And paced upon the mountain overhead
And hid his face among a crowd of stars.
                                        -William Butler Yeats

Gabby and Caden November 1967

Something had changed since that awkward evening in Caden's dorm. It resembled some other natural phenomenal stages, like sunrise, tidal waves, auroras; rare fire rainbows. Occasionally, the shift was like extreme snow donuts, or even Hessadalan lights. Fascinating, yet terrifying to experience without warning.

When a comet crosses the atmosphere, an eclipse casts shadows, on the sun or moon. A meteor shower lights up the sky, and the force of nature makes a powerful statement that can lead to an unsolvable mystery.

Without even knowing, Caden and I were experiencing something resembling a solar eclipse. For some odd reason, we were destined to travel on the same path, at least temporarily. We became inseparable, with the exception of classes.

In the mornings we would plan to meet for a quick breakfast, part with a kiss, and always reunite at the end of the day. I began leaving Caden love notes, in various languages, inside his backpack. Tam I'ngra leaf, meaning I love you, in Irish, later lead to the Italian; amo.

Then eventually African; Ek het jou lief; Cantonese, Ngo oiy ney a; French, Je Taime adore; Hawaiian, Aloha; Russian, Ya tebya liubliu; Spanish, Te quiero, Te amo.

Caden was always affectionate, but never said the words, 'I love you' in any language. There was no doubt, however, that we were growing closer each day. Almost overnight he had changed completely. Now, he was protective, not possessive. Declaring that we were exclusive, was not necessary. Our actions were obvious to everyone.

This was an entirely different experience than the long term relationship that Jake and I had. Caden never tried to control me. We both felt comfortable in each other's circle of friends. It was a mutual decision when we planned our activities. The only thing that we did not do together was intercourse.

There had been several near misses. The more that it happened, the worse I felt. I knew that Caden had been sexually active regularly before we were a couple. As frustrated as he must be, he would always reassure me that we would have time to get it right. Even with only heavy petting, our relationship was moving very quickly.

Sydney suggested that we join her at the underground dance club that she frequented often. These clubs featured "mento" bands. They were a fusion of European and African folk dance music with just enough rock to make it a popular, exotic, dirty dancing, and sexually appetizing for the college crowd.

Alcohol was served without restriction, which encouraged the libido to the maximum. Sweaty bodies gyrated, uninhibited, as close as possible; genitals rubbing next to each other. Dancing couples lost in each other's eyes, sometimes stopping for long embraces and prolong kisses.

"This is just what you need Gabby to loosen those shackles that are keeping you from a healthy sex life." Sydney was always trying to help me put into perspective why I was so frigid. I wish I could say she was wrong, but it was something I just could not shake.

Watching the various provocative moves on the dance floor, stimulated many of us. It was almost like open voyeurism or a simulated sex orgy. Having clothes on and mentally fantasizing, was a great foreplay that lasted well into the morning hours with Caden.

Hamilton Arms became our comfortable refuge. Similar to a hippie compound, there was a remarkable group of Georgetown artists, writers, poets and musicians who embraced the Bohemian lifestyle, while encouraging a life of sexual freedom.

This counter culture movement, challenged those restrictions that inhibited a women's desire for sexual pleasure. It defied the purpose that women could only enjoy marital sex, specifically with the objective to bear children. My literature classes were also aligned with these new values.

DH Lawrence, a British writer, published Lady Chatterley's Lover in Italy, 1928. It was considered so sexual and graphic that the United States banned it until 1959 and in England until 1960. Previously in 1918 The Rainbow and in 1920 Women in Love, addressed specifically a women's desire for sexual independence.

As the Women's Movement got stronger, it became clear that Capitalism demanded self-restrain, and sexual regression to control the masses. It was not surprising that our parents' generation, believed that all revolutionary movements, including civil right , decolonization, gay and lesbian liberation, and even the peace movement included Communist hidden agendas.

In retrospect, it is clear why it was difficult for many of us, primarily me, to accept sexual desire as a natural reaction, and not an evil obsession. Once I understood this, it

130

became easier to allow Caden into my private, secluded world.

"Gabby, have you ever considered that maybe we should just move in together. I mean off campus?" Caden, asked one afternoon.

"I have no objection to that. I mean, we are almost living together now. But, convincing our parents.... that is another issue," I said.

It would be impossible to explain to either of our parents why we wanted to do this. More so, I knew that my parents would insist on a marriage certificate. Rarely anyone older than twenty-five, or outside the academia environment, would accept our relationship as normal.

At the moment, what we could agree on, was to stay at Georgetown, during the winter break. Neither of us wanted to go home and be separated during the holidays. Most of our friends were leaving soon for snow vacations or family reunions.

Caden suggested that we spend some time with his Aunt Selena in Alexandria. Never meeting her before made me reluctant.

"I am sure that your aunt is fantastic, Caden. But, how does it look, if I just show up during the holidays, when we have never even been introduced."

"But, Gabby, Selena is family. She expects me to spend time with her, and she has already asked me to bring you over on the Wednesday before Thanksgiving. We will have our own room and celebrate on Thursday with her."

Caden, seemed very determined to finalize this arrangement.

"Well, we will be out for winter break and I do not think I will be working in the bookstore that week. So, it might be a nice change for us," I said, pleased that we had made a decision.

Another option was to pool the money we had been saving from our campus jobs, and take a long weekend off campus.

The one point that we both agreed on, was that before moving in together we needed a test run.

"This time, alone, away from the stress of classes should allow us to work on all the issues in this relationship," Caden said, while we shared a plate of sushi.

"Do you really think that this will be enough time to decide if we can live together? I mean, we do have to face that our sex life is not what you expected," I said, knowing that we could not continue to ignore this issue any longer.

"Gabby, the sex will change once we are really committed. Once you trust me."

Caden, lifted a salmon roll with his chop stick and placed it on my mouth.

"Now, not another negative word from you, Miss Abby with a 'G'," he said.

A few days later, Caden called the dorm asking me to meet him on the walking trail near the Potomac River. I was bundled up in my warmest wool coat, snow boots and skull cap. Why, Caden wanted to meet out here in nearly freezing conditions was beyond my understanding.

On the park bench, I patiently waited, admiring the college sculling team, practicing during these chilly afternoons. I was fascinated at their stamina, not even noticing when Caden came up behind me. When he leaned over to kiss me, I was slightly taken by surprise.

"Hey, beautiful. How's my Alpha Girl?"
He said.

"Really, Caden?" I looked at him with my eyelashes nearly freezing together.

"If this relationship is ever going to move forward, I better be more than the Alpha girl. I better be the ONLY girl in your life."

I said, half joking. But Caden could tell that his smart comment had hit a nerve with me.

With Jake, there was never a doubt that we were exclusive. As Molly had pointed out, I may as well be wearing a letter J on my forehead. But, with Caden, we never really discussed this. Realistically, it would have been impossible for either one of us to see anyone else, since we were always together. Nevertheless, I never really felt confident.

Before I could even finish my thought, and without saying another word, Caden just took off, like a kite being lifted into a sudden tunnel of wind. Then, just as quickly, he was back, right in front of me.

"Okay, Gabby, promise to keep your eyes tightly closed, until I tell you to open them. Promise?" he insisted.

"Yes, okay, I will play your little game," I answered, not sure what to do next.

"Now open your mouth."

I could feel something light, ethereal and sweet, resembling cotton candy. Then, his tongue touched mine. It was wet, juicy and salty all at the same time. The combination of something you know is lethal but irresistible.

"Okay. You can open your eyes," he said.

When I did, I was staring into his cobalt blue eyes, drawing me into his soul.

"That incredible taste that we just shared? That is what stays with me whenever we are apart. You are always on my mind Gabby. Practical, logical, thoughts do not make sense to me anymore. " He was still talking, but his arms were holding me firmly, as if he thought I might not be understanding this revelation.

"My life will never be the same again, and it scares the shit out of me, how much I love you Gabby." He was finally done.

I was stunned. It was the first time that he had ever said he loved me.

"You brought me out to the Potomac River in mid freezing weather to declare your love to me?" I was shaking with happiness and from the cold.

With my arms now around his neck, and standing on my toes, I kissed him with a passion I did not even know that I had.

"That was the very first time that you ever said you loved me, turtle," I said smiling.

"Really, your nickname for me is turtle?" he said, and then kissed the tip of my nose.

"Well, it did take you a long time to tell me that you loved me. And, you still haven't hit a 'home run', so, yeah, I think turtle is a great name for you," I said.

"Tomorrow, when we get to Selena's, you will be so glad that this turtle belongs to you," Caden said as we started walking back to the dorm.

"Oh, and Gabby, pack enough clothes for an extended long weekend. Aunt Selena's Christmas present to me is a trip to the Big Apple, all expenses paid, and baby, my Aunt Selena travels in style." Caden was half way up the block before I could get any more details about this trip.

Just the thought of visiting New York City during the Christmas Holiday, was unbelievable. By the time I was finished packing, it was nearly two AM. I was alone, since all the girls had gone their separate ways days ago. When the alarm went off, I felt that I had just closed my eyes.

I was on my way to a totally new experience with a man that I could definitely be falling in love with.

Caden had arranged the perfect amount of time for the taxi to get us to the Metro Station. It was unusually busy, with many people leaving early to beat the holiday rush to Alexandria.

At the station, Caden carried my one suitcase, with his duffle bag toward the entrance, when a kind porter stopped us.

"Nice to see you Mr. Cassidy. And under such better cir-cumstances than your last visit with us," Stanley said, with a smirk.

"Good to see you, too Stan. This is my girlfriend, " Caden looked briefly at me for my reaction.

"Glad to meet you, Stan. My name is Gabby," I said, hoping that now we could be seated.

"Well, well, Caden, looks like you are finally moving TO-WARD something and not AWAY from something." Stanley grabbed the luggage and let us board the train.

Before, Stan went to assist other passengers, he stepped back, and in a whisper he added, looking directly at me, he said, "Man, she's a keeper. You play nicely, now, understand?"

And, before, I could respond, Stanley was out of hearing range. I then turned my attention to Gabby.

"We can move to the back and make out all the way there," he winked at me. I jabbed him in the ribs.

"You behave yourself Turtle. We will be together for five days. " I said, noticing him sulking.

Once settled, I move close to him, and lay my head on his chest. I can feel his fingers running through my hair, and he squeezes my hand tight. Neither of us need to say a word. It is a silent understanding that feels like a security blanket.

Aunt Selena's bungalow, is located in the center of Old Alexandria's historic district; walking distance from the center of town. Caden takes out his personal key and opens the door.

"Shouldn't we knock first?" I try

to hold him back from entering.

"It's okay Gabby. Aunt Selena won't be home until late tonight or even early tomorrow morning," Caden assured me.

"We have the house to ourselves, Princess," he adds as I reluctantly follow behind him.

Caden then leads her to the upstairs bedroom. *I hope that Selena knows what she is doing. She is my last hope.* The door opens and it has been prepared like a honeymoon suite. The queen size, four poster bed has rose colored, silk sheets, with a black cashmere comforter. It sits in front of an inviting, crackling fire with two winged chairs arranged next to each other.

There are mood lights turned down to a comfortable warm glow, but also several candles are lit throughout the room. In the corner, next to the bed is an ice bucket, chilling with what appears to be champagne.

The magnolias, immediately remind me of Savannah. They are arranged, with red and white roses. The scent is intoxicating. Even the sound of a classical harp has been included to make this the most inviting room I have ever witnessed.

Caden is even slightly taken back. Silently, he

thinks *this is definitely the E ticket that will take us to the moon tonight.*

On the wall Gabby recognizes a painting of the Moulin Rouge and another larger one of the Eiffel Tower. She smile silently, thinking of Molly. Caden drops the luggage in the corner, closes the bedroom door and almost in one continuous motion they are on the bed.

"Let me just taste that tongue, baby.

You smell so inviting Gabby," he says, pulling my pony-tail out of the clip.

With his fingers running through my hair, I can feel his hard cock through his jeans and my pussy is moist already.

"Oh, Gabby....your hair smells like forever. I want to get lost inside you, baby." Caden is moving his hand now to my nipples. Without removing my blouse, he traces my breasts with his fingers.

"Oh, Caden. You have made me feel alive again. I really do want you," I am saying these words and really trying to mean them, when I feel his hands removing my bra and then my blouse.

"Gabby, baby, tell me what you want. I am here to please you." His hand is now on my wet pussy, and his tongue strokes my mouth in a perfect rhythm with his fingers that are fondling my clit.

I cannot hold back the desire to feel him plunge into my vagina with his full total force.

"I want you Caden. Let it be NOW," I am nearly scream-ing losing control.

"Gabby, baby. I need you to release complete control to me tonight. Will you do that, please, Gabby? Do just what I say sweetheart. Trust me?" I can no longer restrain myself.

"Yes. Whatever you say. Just please, dear God...Fu..." His mouth stopped my words. And then I could tell how truly hungry he was for me.

I feel his wet mouth now moving down, between my legs, and his tongue is licking my soaking pussy. He carefully separates my pubic hairs allowing full access to my vagina. His firm tongue is sweeping up and down in full length motion, as my pussy lips part allowing maximum pleasure.

Caden does not stop licking my clit, and then I feel his teeth with just the right pressure nibble me to the point that I release part of my cum into his mouth.

Somehow, he manages to stop it from all flowing. "Baby, I'm going to fuck you now. Can you hold on? That's it Gabby," he then takes out a condom. I push it away.

"No, Caden. I want to feel all of you," I say, determined.

"Are you sure?" He asks one last time.

"Yes, I am damn sure. I want us to cum together inside of me."

I am on top of him now. His hard dick is in my hand, and I guide it to my aching pussy. He takes it from there, slowly inserting it fully in.

"The slower the better," he whispers in my ear.

It gives me incredible pleasure.

"The entry is the best, baby, right before the final orgasm."

My pelvis is now moving sometimes slowly, sometimes fast, but always continuous with the seductive music. I want to climax so badly. But, Caden moves his cock inside of me at just the right rhythm.

And then, just when I cannot hold back any longer, I feel his buttocks contract, and there is an explosion, like an erupting star. Suddenly we come together, with such a magnitude and unison that we become one, for a split second, eternally.

"That was the most incredible feeling I have ever experienced Gabby," Caden says.

"How did you ever manage to make that happen, Caden?" I asked, still breathing heavy.

"I know that you won't believe this Gabby, but what we just experienced was an ultimate connecting bond. Somehow, I think that we managed to join physically. I mean, even now, I feel like we are still together. "

Caden was genuinely moved.

"I never knew that sex could feel like this. At one point it felt like nothing would separate us. I am going to just allow myself to feel this and not even try to understand it," I replied.

Caden opened the bottle of Dom Perignon Champagne and poured us each a glass.

"Let this be our first night of forever."

And for the first time in my life I knew that I was in control of my own destiny.

CHAPTER 15

Krishna means, among other things, or one way of putting the same thing, that the future is a faded song, a royal rose, or a lavender spray of wistful regret, for those who are not? yet here to regret..."

TS Eliot, Four Quarters

Gabby and Caden 1967

Waking up the next morning with Gabby's body next to mine, made last night real. I watched her breathing peacefully, her chest rising up and down, just like last night. Yet, this morning there was something distinctly different about her.

She was deep in sleep, yet glowing with just a slight trace of a smile on her lips. I gently pushed away a cascade of dark curls from her supple breasts, making them slightly visible.

I had never noticed before how perfect she was. After that first truly intimate moment last night, we managed to make love two more times, until exhaustion overtook us both. We fell asleep entwined in each other's arms most of the night. It was the first time I had ever spent the night with any woman.

There was never a time, in the past, that I stayed longer than a few hours; a one night stand . Most of the time I was gone minutes later. This was new territory.

Gabby was incredibly fragile emotionally, but once I convinced her to trust me, sex would become my ultimate desire. This changed my entire concept of sex. . I was now, only satisfied when she was. My penis became hard while still inside her vagina. The more that I came inside of her, the deeper I needed to become one with her.

Satisfaction would never be the same with any other woman. I was both thrilled and scared out of my fucking mind.

"Whatever, and however you did THAT last night, well I want more of it," Gabby said.

Her hand felt my dick already stiff. As she began to move beneath the sheets, I felt her tongue licking my shaft at precisely the same moment I heard the knocking on the bedroom door.

Gabby lifted her head up. I grabbed the cotton Terry bathrobe at the end of the bed, and opened the door for Sarah, who was carrying in a tray of coffee, tea, cream and sugar.

"Good Morning, Mr. Caden. Aunt Selena sends this to you hoping that you will meet her downstairs to watch the Macy Parade." Sarah, politely left the beverages on the Queen Anne's table near the window. Arranging the drapes to reveal the morning sun, while waiting for my response.

"Please tell Selena that we will be down stairs in ten minutes, Sarah. Oh, and thank you for the starters," I responded.

Sarah was satisfied and out the door before Gabby had a chance to say a word.

"Does your Aunt have domestic help, Caden? That is very impressive, I must say," Gabby said, scooting to the end of the bed, ready to resume what she had previously started.

"Oh my Gabby....I could spend the whole day in bed with you," I said, lifting her up to my eye level. "But, unfortunately, we both need to go downstairs. Aunt Selena doesn't ask much of me, but she does expect me to be polite," I kissed Gabby on the nose, threw her a matching bathrobe and went into the bathroom to brush my teeth.

"Alright. I will forgive you this one time, but only if you promise that we can play later," Gabby said, now using the sink next to me.

"Baby, I intend to make you my permanent playmate," I replied with a sensual pat on her rump.

Downstairs, Selena and Sarah were sipping tea and watching the pre parade commentary. At first I felt rather awkward coming downstairs in a bathrobe, but once we were in the family room, it felt very inviting.

"Aunt Selena, let me introduce to you my girlfriend, Gabriella Girard."

Caden rarely used my full name so at first I was a little taken back. Selena stood up to greet me. Caden did not do justice when describing his aunt. She could have stepped out of a Renoir painting. There was no doubt that she evolved from a more gentile era. That stunning raven black hair, without any trace of grey, fell well past the middle of her back. Loose curls were held with a mermaid rhinestone hair clip, original, as she was.

"Please, call me Gabby. Thank you so much for graciously inviting me to join you for the holidays. Your home is magnificent," I said, trying not to stare at how perfect her alabaster, smooth skin was.

As I stretched my hand out to meet hers, I noticed that she had the same deep blue eyes that Caden had. As a matter of fact, there was a great resemblance between the two of them. There was no doubt why she was the 'darling ' of the DC social circuit.

"I am so happy to finally meet you Gabby. I have been anxious to see the young lady that has finally tamed my wild nephew," Selena said.

"Later this afternoon you will meet a few of my Washington DC friends who will be joining us for dinner. But, now it is time for family," Selena said.

"It has been a tradition in the Cassidy family, since we arrived here to watch the Macy's parade on Thanksgiving and go to Midnight church services on Christmas Eve, regardless of the weather," Selena added.

I was beginning to feel a part of this family. It also made me realize how committed Caden was to our relationship.

Sitting next to each other on the leather couch, it was hard to imagine being anywhere else today.

Sarah had just brought out a platter of scones, and homemade blueberry muffins. That was followed by individual servings of eggs Benedict, with hash brown casserole and a pitcher of Bloody Mary's. I was beyond impressed.

"Sarah and I have been friends for many years. She enjoys cooking and serving and I appreciate being taken care of. So, it is almost like a perfect marriage," Selena laughed.

After the parade was over, it was time for Selena to prepare for the next stage of what was becoming an elaborate event.

Once we were finally back upstairs, I decided to shower and change into a suitable outfit. Caden explained to me that for dinner Selena had invited a few Senators, political aids, Lobbyists and Doctors.

Some would be with their wives, but mostly they we're bringing their girlfriends.

"Selena has a wide range of friends Gabby. I never know what to expect. But, one thing will be certain, it will be entertaining and formal. That is until the first two rounds of drinks," Caden said.

Soon I was back downstairs offering my help to Selena. I thought that would be the least I could do. However, by this time, the dining room was already set for twenty guests.

The peach colored linen tablecloth, was set with gold flatware. Next was the gold plated chargers and Waterford crystal goblets, and champagne flutes. Candelabras on both ends of the table were anchoring several chrysanthemum floral arrangements.

Gold leaf name cards were strategically placed at each seat. Selena explained that with such a diverse group tonight, she was careful not to place the wrong people next to each other.

"It is sometimes a great challenge to entertain politicians that rarely shake hands across the aisle," Selena informed me.

Tonight there would be a professional serving staff and bartender. The dinner was being catered from Gadsby's, a landmark restaurant established in 1785. John Gadsby, the entrepreneur, owned a popular tavern that the founders of the American Revolution, such as George Washington, Thomas Jefferson, John Adams and James Monroe regularly frequented.

Selena was pleased that on such a traditional day, she, an immigrant from Ireland could serve such an authentic meal to a group of elite Washington socialites. And, the menu was outstanding.

There would be succulent turkey, stuffed goose, prime rib, leg of lamb, oysters Rockefeller, shrimp cocktail, sweet potato purée, cranberry compote, crab beignets,fresh baked bread, mashed potatoes, gravy, asparagus with hollandaise sauce, Brussels sprouts and black caviar.

The grand finale, was two dessert trays with pumpkin pie, Apple pie, pecan pie, English Truffle and New York cheese cake flown in from Carnegie's Deli.

Caden and I sat next to Selena at the head of the table. That was when Selena first recognized the Shalimar I was wearing.

"My dear, we apparently both share a common perfume. It is rare that I ever meet anyone who can wear it properly. You must have just the right chemical balance," she said.

It was actually the only time that I thought of Jake. Caden had done a good job at making me forget about him for a while. I knew that I could never tell either Caden or Selena how I came to wear Shalimar.

"It was given to me by a close friend a few years ago. It has always made me feel special," I responded, actually quite accurately.

"And, that you are my dear." Selena patted my hand, and I felt that the two of us shared a secret bond.

Most of the guests who attended were so far removed from not only my generation, but the real world, that I got the impression that they resided in a self-imposed bubble.

Ironically, they were all being paid to thoroughly understand and support those of us on the outside. It wasn't so much that I felt out of place, but more like an exotic bird in a gilded cage.

Prior to dinner, the only thing Selina requested was no talk of politics for one evening. I was actually relieved, since I had some very strong opposing opinions about the Vietnam War. I did not want to embarrass Selena with my antiwar sentiments, but my wounds were still open from the trauma that Jake had experienced.

Thankfully, most of the guests were more interested about my college major and Savannah, my hometown. Hedging politics, a few people asked my opinion on Gloria Steinem.

They were curious on how I perceived her "radical" stand on women's rights. I avoided the obvious traps by sharing with them that I was impressed that in 1960 she was hired as the first employee for the magazine HELP.

That of course lead to her support of pro-choice. I was well prepared, and quite capable of debating all night those principles. Nevertheless, Caden gently reminded me that it was after eleven and we had an early morning tomorrow.

Although most of the guests had left by this time, the President's physician, who was clearly Selena's date for the evening and a few other couples had moved to the formal living room to finish their after dinner cordials.

Both Caden and I gave Selena kisses goodnight as we began to ascend our way to the bedroom. Once in bed, we were both so spent that all we had left was enough energy to barely remove our clothes. Once my head was on the pillow, I fell into a deep slumber.

Memories of s lovely evening became tangled with yellow leaved pressed between a book that has never been opened..

My subconscious mind was creating images of Caden and Jake playing tug-a-war, with me in the center, desperately trying to find my balance.

Once I became free, I ran into a maze, where the way up is the way down, the way forward is the way back. And as I kept running there would be neon signs flashing with messages:" Time is no healer" and "the patient is no longer here."

While I restlessly moved around in the bed, I tried not to wake Caden, who had no problem sleeping.

Finally, I resolved that I had to get up and take a sleeping pill. My doctor gave me a prescription a few months ago after I learned that Jake and Isabella were engaged. Now, I only took them on the rare occasions, like tonight, when nothing else would work.

I was thankful that I had avoided alcohol tonight, when I swallowed two Xanax, and slipped back into bed.

After a few minutes I was on a train watching grieved faces turn to relaxed expressions. Listening to the sleepy rhythm of the rolling train, I begin to escape from the past and enter the future.

That is when a small child, with flaxen curls, hands me a sunflower with a note.

The note says, " *You are not the same person who left the station. You will never know when the past has finished or when the future begins.."*

When I ask the child who has given her this note, she turns around laughing.

"You. You. of course gave it to me."

When I turn around I notice that the train has left the station without me. Panicked, I then ask when the next train will arrive. , but that is when I hear the alarm clock ringing.

Caden has no problem waking. I have decided not to say a word about my dream, or nightmare. I haven't determined yet which it is.

"Are you excited about our trip to the City Gabby?" Caden asks.

He is dressed in jeans and a long sleeved knit shirt with a Georgetown logo on the pocket.

His dark hair naturally falls into place and he walks toward me with an air of confidence.

"Hey...babe, are you okay? Gabby, is there something wrong?" His voice has changed now. He sounds legitimately concerned.

"No, of course not...I am fine. Maybe a little tired from last night, but I will be good," I answer, trying to sound jovial.

Once the taxi has arrived to take us to the train station, I thank Selena once again and promise to be back on Christmas Eve with Caden.

We walk to the cab, Caden opens my door and I settle in. But, Selena calls him back. I can see her talking to him and him shaking his head, but I cannot hear a word.

"Caden, do not ruin this opportunity for real happiness." She was walking him slowly back to the curb.

"Remember what we talked about a few months ago? Gabby is a keeper. You may not even realize it yet with all of the intense sex and all..." She keeps talking.

This is beginning to make me uncomfortable. She is bringing up my sex life and at the same time talking to me like I am twelve.

"Don't be so obsessed with the physical Gabby that you don't recognize and appreciate the real woman she is," Selena adds.

I wanted to remind her that this is why we are going to New York.

"Don't worry Selena," I was about to open the door, then I added, "I do not plan on letting her go. Believe it or not, I do listen to everything you tell me."

I kissed her forehead and she handed me the envelope with all our travel documents and credit cards.

That was when I knew that my life was starting to change. On the train sitting next to Gabby it felt like we were newlyweds, on our way to our honeymoon.

Caden held me close as I watched snowflakes smiling at me from the outside, as to say, "Gabby, remember every moment. Everything will pass so quickly. Treasure this joy, and recall it when it becomes a memory."

On the way, we talked about the must see landmarks. It will be a short time but, The Empire State Building was first on our list.

"You're not scared of heights are you Gabby? I want to go to the very top. You know like King Kong?" Caden said enthusiastically.

He sounded like an anxious child. Caden was talking so fast that I thought he was on an adrenaline high.

"Because, you know if you're scared of heights, I will be right there to protect you," he stopped finally.

"And, Mister. If I was scared, would you make me go anyway? Or even worse, would you leave me all alone and go by yourself?" I tried to sound authentically worried.

"Of course I would never leave you there alone. What kind of boyfriend would do that? But, I would convince you that I would always take care of you. You do trust me, don't you, Gabby?" He said.

When I started laughing he knew I was kidding.

"Caden Cassidy, you are definitely one of the last living romantics. And that is just one of the many things I love about you," I said.

"Okay. My first pick is MOMA...you do know what that is, don't you? "I added.

Caden didn't have a clue what MOMA was, But, then he answered, out of nowhere,

"Of course, I know what it is. Museum of Modern Art," he said, quite satisfied.

I was impressed until I turned around and saw the advertisement on the overhead.

"You cheated, Caden!" I said emphatically.

"I didn't know that we were playing games. But now that I do know, I will give you harder landmarks," he said.

"You know that I never play games that I can lose at. I am a terrible loser. If I don't play, I can't lose," I said.

We both started laughing and after a few moments the rocking of the train put us both to sleep. Before we knew it, we had arrived at Grand Central Station. I knew exactly how Holden Caulfield felt, when he arrived at this magnificent historical train depot. While Holden was trying to escape the phonies that were suffocating him, I was hoping to find the real answers to some very complicated questions.

From the time I first read, **Catcher in the Rye,** I was captivated by Salinger's ability to portray such vivid settings and characters that challenged our own interpretation of reality.

In some strange way Holden and I were both trying to escape the demons that keep us hostages to the past.

Everyone should experience, at least once in their lifetime, arriving to The City via Grand Central Station. Not only is this where all NYC subways originate and terminate, but, based on the forty-four platforms, it is the largest depot in the world.

Before I even stepped off the train, I was overwhelmed and quite comfortable at the same time. Holden's coming of age and Caden and I coming to terms that our relationship was about to move to another level seemed to have much in common.

Our view of the world was so very limited, but entering this" Emerald City," did not, for some reason feel threatening or foreign. Neither of us, had been here before, yet we both felt we belonged here together. Silently, I marveled at how much chaos and confusion surrounded us nevertheless, Caden knew exactly how to take the lead. He got us out of the station and into the taxi line, like he did it every day. Hand in hand, with luggage in tow, we were the next in line.

"Well, Gabby, Welcome to New York," I said to myself, feeling giddy.

"It is amazing that it is everything I expected it to be," I now said aloud.

I looked up, seeing the tall skyscrapers, the urban morning lit up with glitzy marquees, and the smells and sounds that later become poems or song lyrics. Using an umbrella handle, Caden places his imaginary microphone in front of me, and asks,

"Welcome to The Big Apple Miss Girard. Would you share with our viewer's what you are thinking right at this moment?"

"Honestly?" I answer.

"Of course honestly, Gabby," Caden responds.

"Okay. Well, honestly I was thinking, why do the ducks stay in the pond at Central Park during the winter?" I asked.

Then Caden put down the umbrella, lifts me off the ground and says to the people walking by, "I am definitely, in love with this lady. And I wouldn't have her any other way."

He said as the Taxi pulled up, "Where you crazy kids headed to?" the driver asked when we opened the door.

"The Waldorf Astoria, Sir," Caden replied.

"Nice digs for you two love birds. Honeymoon?" he asked, winking in the mirror.

"Not this trip," Caden answered. He squeezed my hand.

"But, soon.... maybe, very soon," Caden hinted, giving me a long kiss.

Jesse, our driver, was a Yankee fan. He had a shirt and hat that proclaimed his loyalty. But, this morning he was going to give us a little history lesson on The Waldorf Astoria.

"This Grand Dame, opened on October 1, 1931 on Park Avenue. At the time, it was acclaimed the tallest and largest hotel in the world. The first film that was shot there was titled 'Weekend at the Waldorf.' There are so many famous people haunting stories and great events that take place there that it is legendary. You two will make some of your own memories, I am sure of that," Jesse said, as we pulled up to the VIP entrance Caden paid the fee and added a generous tip. Aunt Selena had assured him that she was covering enough for tips, since so many of the "little" people, as she called them, are the ones behind the scenes making everything perfect.

"Never be afraid to tip well', Selena, told me. 'You never know how many mouths need to be fed with that tip'", Caden shared with me.

As we entered the lobby, I was recalling what Jesse had told us. "This is the hotel where Arthur Miller and Marilyn Monroe, once checked in together. I don't believe that they were married either," he winked at Caden.

I held Caden's hand tightly, to make sure that this was truly happening.

"I don't think we're in Kansas anymore, Toto," I said quietly.

This place was dripping with grand tradition. Art Deco lamps, and Peacock Alley, where Oscar Tschirky invented the Waldorf Salad, eggs Benedict, and Thousand Island dressing. Beyond the lobby, was the main corridor, leading to the Empire Room and Grand Staircases.

In the Marie Antoinette parlor, eighteenth century antiques were displayed, including a bust of the eccentric queen and a clock she once owned. I was reading this from a flier in the lobby.

"Why don't you sit here and soak up all the history while I get us checked in," Caden asked, but had already decided, since he walked directly to the line waiting for check in. For just that split second, it reminded me of how Jake would always take over.

It must be a male thing. Women's Lib movement was just in the early stages, and men still felt it was the gentleman's duty to take care of their ladies. In one way chivalrous and in another way antiquated.

As I was beginning to people watch, I noticed an elegant, older woman, wrapped in a chinchilla fur coat. She was wearing oversized dark sunglasses, and carrying a white toy poodle.

The lavish rhinestone collar that the dog displayed, reflected the lights onto the glass doors in a kaleidoscope effect. I imagined that this is how Gloria Swanson would have looked arriving.

At the opposite end from 'Gloria Swanson," was a rather "fluffy" small man, wearing a brown derby. He apparently was complaining that his room was not facing Central Park.

The clerk was apologizing, but tried to explain that due to the Thanksgiving Holiday weekend there were no other rooms available.

I could tell that, since there were three other guests in front of Caden, that I had time to do some exploring. I wandered over to the stairs leading to a Grand Ballroom. One door was ajar, so I decided to slip inside to see what was going on. People in white shirts, black slacks, black vests and black bow ties were scurrying around with lavish flower arrangements that looked like orchids, roses, and gardenias.

There were gold lame streamers being positioned around the head table, while others we're placing the famous blue Tiffany boxes with white ribbons on each gold rimmed plate that had the Waldorf Astoria initials stamped in sapphire.

"Excuse me, Miss? Are you with the wedding party?" A man in a black tuxedo was asking me.

"No... Oh, I am so sorry...I was...I mean, I was just admiring how lovely everything was."

I sounded like a scared child that was caught doing something mischievous.

The elderly gentleman, dressed in a tuxedo, I could now tell, worked for the hotel. He bowed his head to me, and said, "By all means, my lady. Admire all you want," he motioned his hand with pride.

Then, just as I was about to compliment him on how wonderful the room looked, Caden was at my side.

"There you are, Gabby. We are all checked in, sweetheart. Are you finished here?"

Caden sounded anxious.

I once again thanked the gentleman and followed Caden to the last set of elevators.

The porter pushed the eighteenth floor. When the door opened, I immediately noticed that our room directly faced Central Park. "Thank you, Aunt Selena," I said, admiring the outside view.

CHAPTER 16

I'm standing on the edge of some crazy cliff. What I have to
do, I have to catch everybody if they start to go over the cliff.
I'd just be The Catcher in the Rye is all.
Catcher in the Rye by JD Salinger

Gabby and Caden Thanksgiving Weekend 1967

New York, New York. The epitome of world class. From the
eccentric "bag people" to the exquisite architecture, it is a
natural high that fills my lungs with enough oxygen that I
feel like I can soar above Manhattan, like a loose balloon.

The smell of Coney dogs from the street vendors, is the
only thing that would tempt me down from above the skyscrapers.

People from all walks of life, around the world, gather
near the street vendors to buy a plump frankfurter, smoth-
ered with your choice of: sauerkraut, cheese, onions, mus-
tard, and ketchup.

In the early morning, at Liberty Park, once the morning
mist lifts, I can hear the oohs, and ahhh, as the Lady with
the torch beacons everyone to her island. Caden, was only
three years old when he arrived at Ellis Island in 1952 with
his parents, Selena and two other cousins.

"I do not remember much of that day. But, if you do not
mind I would prefer just admiring the Statue of Liberty
from here," he almost pleaded.

"No... of course, that was not even on my list. Actually, I
believe that she looks much more grand at a distance," I
said.

Perhaps someday, Caden will feel like he can share that experience with me, but today was not the day to visit skeletons in the closet. There was enough baggage of my own to deal with.

Later today, after visiting the Empire State Building, we were headed to Rockefeller Plaza for an hour of ice skating. We stopped at the corner for a moment, and I began to search through Caden's pockets for anything edible.

"What are you doing to me, out here in public, crazy lady. Control yourself," Caden said, just loud enough for a few people in front of us to turn and stare.

"I just know that you have some sweet morsel hidden from me. You always have, mints, or gum, or hard candy in some pockets," I say to him as I continue to frisk through any possible places I may have missed.

"Gabby, the only hard candy I can share with you, requires us to go back to the hotel, baby," he says, giving me a seductive kiss with his tongue in my mouth.

Then, as we cross the street, he runs off, yelling at me to stay under the tree and wait for him. Given that I have no other option, I take a seat on the bench, and wait for his return. We had planned on skipping breakfast in order to leave early and be the first ones at the Empire State Building. Then go to Rockefeller Plaza, where we were now headed, and then to MOMA, and finally a late lunch at Tavern on the Green. Definitely a full day.

I could see Caden running back to where he had left me. In high school he ran track for varsity, and it was clear that he was in excellent physical condition.

"Okay. Now where were we?" Caden sat down on the bench next to me and started kissing me again. That was when I tasted how salty his mouth was.

"Did you run off and get something to eat without me? " I was only half joking.

Before I could really get angry, Caden pulled out of his pocket a warm bag of chestnuts.

"I was keeping them right here, next to my heart so that they would stay warm, just for you," he said. Pleased that he caught me off guard.

"You know that I will always take care of you, Gabby." He started feeding me the chestnuts, lovingly.

Before moving on to the ice rink, we noticed that men in overalls were gathering around the giant Norway Spruce. Some of them were even on a scaffold. The tree must have been at least ninety feet tall. We would be back home when the official lighting would take place. There would be over eighteen thousand lights. But, just seeing this magnificent tree in its natural beauty, was a delightful and unexpected surprise.

"Can you just imagine Caden, how many people will be here for the lighting ceremony? "I said.

We both got up and moved as close as possible to get the full effect of the gigantic tree.

"People from all over the country and even the world come here for this event. But, I bet that no one will be as close as we are right now," I said.

Caden's hands were on the back of my neck, as I was tiptoeing to see the top, when suddenly a bright flash made me almost lose my balance.

"What the HELL was that?" I heard Caden yell; but I still could not see anything. My eyes were out of focus.

"Sorry Guy and Doll!" A well-dressed lady, wearing a London Fog trench coat, was talking to us. She was probably in her forties, with a camera hanging around her neck.

"I hope you don't mind, but I wanted to get a fresh, natural shot. Pre-lighting and all that garbage. The two of you added just the right personal interest that I was looking for," she said.

"Are you going to print that in the paper?"

I didn't want anyone back home, in Savannah to see that I was in New York alone with Caden. If my parents, or Caden's parents, or even Jake saw this there would be a lot of gossip.

"How rude of me. Let me introduce myself. I am Diane Arbus,a free-lance photographer. Usually my subjects are deviants, marginal people, nudists, circus performers, gypsies, you know, the misfits in our society. But, you two, well you actually look quite normal," she said, smiling at the observation. Adding, "Go figure,"under her breath.

Then I heard Caden respond, "Looks can be deceiving."

She must have heard him because she then said, "That's exactly what I was thinking, when I saw the two of you. A lovely looking couple, but just something a little odd. Like a mystery unfolding and maybe my camera lens can capture it."

As I heard this, I felt chills run through my veins. What did she possibly see that made her say that?

"Well, this is my girlfriend, Gabby. She is definitely mysterious. She would make a great subject for your collection," Caden said.

"And what does that mean exactly, Caden?"

I asked, looking as annoyed as I felt.

"Chill Gabby. It's just a joke Princess." He walked over and put his arms around my waist.

"If you two will just give me your address, I will send you a copy of the print. If nothing else comes of it, this will at least be a nice keepsake of your trip," Diane said.

She then took out her journal and handed it to me to write the address.

"And, who knows, this might be hanging someday in my first photo exhibition," she said.

I gave her my dorm address, which was safer than my home. I was still curious to know what she saw that might fit her "deviant" profile. *Thirty eight years later it would become very clear.*

Finally, with rented skates on our feet, and holding hands, more so for balance than affection, our goal was to make it around the rink without falling. For some odd reason, my mind kept on flashing back to Holden Caulfield, *caught between two polar extremes, child and adult, not knowing how to fit in either world, creating his own dimension, finally.*

"Gabby... Oh Gabby? Come back to earth. Come back to me," I heard Caden's voice.

I snapped out of my vision, almost startled to see Caden next to me.

"Sorry Caden. I really am paying attention."

I tried to convince him and myself.

He led me off the rink to sit at the warm up bench. "Okay, Gabby. I agreed not to bring up the past, but you need to tell me what is wrong? Out of nowhere, you begin to drift, and I don't know how to bring you back. " His voice sounded as troubled as he looked.

"I don't know how to explain it to you Caden. It's not you, and it is all of you. It is everything I experience. I mean, maybe I am just more sensitive than other people," I said.

Caden held both of my hands in his, stroking them gently while I spoke.

"It is just all the music that I hear and the poetry that I read. The novels, the paintings that I see, I absorb them and connect it at a different level. Sometimes those images, or sounds, interrupt what I am doing, and meld together. Does this sound like I am insane?"

I began to move around nervously.

"Of course not baby. You just need to sometimes let your inner child come out to play with me. Enjoy this show called life. Don't analyze why, or how. Sometimes NOW is all that matters," Caden said.

I knew that he was right. I just wasn't sure how to accomplish it. "How about with hang up the skates and head over to MOMA. That should get your mental juices flowing. Then we have reservations for a late romantic lunch at Tavern on the Green, followed by a carriage ride in the park. Sound good to you?" He said, relieved to move on.

I smiled with all my heart, hoping that my mind would start letting him into the secret chambers that only Jake knew how to release.

"It is after one. Do you think that we can get to Central Park from MOMA before it gets too late?" I asked.

All that I wanted to do was to move on without further discussion on the topic of dazing. Caden grimaced.

"Of course we can make it. Did you forget that I ran track in high school?"

"No, I did not forget. But, first I didn't run track, and next, walking is different than jogging," I said, continuing to un-lace my skates.

"I think that we are having our first fight, Caden," I add-ed.

"No, we are not fighting Gabby. If we were, you would win. So this is merely a discussion," Caden replied.

I reached over to tie his scarf and we both started to laugh at how ridiculous this was sounding to any bystand-ers.

I quickly changed the topic to a little background to what we were soon going to see.

" In 1929, the wife of John D Rockefeller Jr, and two of her closest friends developed an outstanding art collection, and built a home for it. That home is now referred to simp-ly as MOMA".

I recall Molly raving about the Japanese American pho-tographer, Soichi Sunami, who according to what she told me, was the museums official documentary photographer.

"What I found most amazing, Caden, was how Abby's husband was so opposed to modern art that he refused to release any funds to her."

Without elaborating, Abby became very resourceful and determined to make her gallery successful, in spite of her wealthy husband. In 1930, in addition to obtaining loans and gifts that included, Van Gogh, Gauguin, Cezanne, and Monet, she acquired Picasso's retrospect of 1939-40, which presented a significant reinterpretation for scholars and his-torians to study. As I was reading this aloud to Caden, he gently pushed the booklet down.

"Are you certain that the ladies name was not originally Gabby, and she decided to drop the G?" He interrupted.

"Very cute, Caden. But, no, she was always Abby, and I am always Gabby. Can you keep that straight?" I said.

He shook his head no. "I like my version better." I tried to ignore any more nonsense.

It was hard for me to believe that now I was here, about to see Picasso's earliest works, Le Demoiselles d' Avignon, Paris 1907; Girl Before a Mirror, 1932. This was of his young mistress Marie-Therese Walter. In addition to these, there were some newly found sculptures.

"I know that you could spend the next forty-eight hours here Gabby, but we need to start walking over to the Tavern pretty soon." Caden reminded me.

It was obvious that Caden was getting bored and anxious to move on, but he was definitely right about me spending days here. On the destinations that Jake and I had on our agenda to Europe, The Louvre, in Paris, was definitely one of them.

"The Eiffel Tower is where I will officially propose to you," I could still hear Jake's voice.

"But, I won't believe that you will say yes, until I hear it again in The Louvre. "Jake insisted.

This was our private joke. Since The Louvre is the home of so many priceless masterpieces, when I agreed to marry him, he would be walking out with his own irreplaceable masterpiece, that he promised to cherish for life.

That myth ended now. This was not The Louvre and Jake no longer cared about me. My eyes were beginning to tear.

"Gabby, are you melding again?" I heard Caden ask softly.

"No, Caden. I absolutely am not. Let's go have a fabulous lunch," I said.

There had to be some way that I could learn to control these distractions. And why can't I shake these feelings?

"Good. I am starving. Do you see, over there? Just past that open grass field. About, I guess ten miles, maybe." Caden was pointing to where we were going. The ten miles got my attention.

"You are kidding, right?" I said, my voice in panic mode.

"Yes, I am kidding. Just checking if you were paying attention." He tilted his head to one side for effect.

"Of course I am paying attention. Have I told you today how much I love you?" I retorted.

"Well, now you have MY attention. You never say that to me unless we are having sex," he said, leading me to the taxi that had stopped in front for us.

"Yes, I have said it. But, you must have been fading in and out at the time" I smiled, and kissed him before getting into the cab.

I was anxious to know why so many people were impressed with this iconic restaurant, Tavern on the Green. As soon as I saw The Elm tree room, which was built around this massive tree, I knew this was going to be more than just an eating experience. We were led down a narrow hallway. On one side there was a Tiffany peacock window with opalescent glass, and multi colored floral patterns.

Once seated in the Crystal room, named for all the ornate windows, we could see the outside patio. Trees wrapped in twinkling lights from the tips of their branches to the base of their trunks. A carved stone lion statue in repose, was guarding the green shrubs, shaped as elephants, sheep, rabbits, kissing swans and one quite giant APE.

In the center of the room was an amazing 19th century green Osler chandelier of Baccarat crystals, originally made in Austria, for India's Maharaja of Udaipur. Even more spectacular was the Tiffany glass ceiling the chandelier was hanging from. The rainbow of colors was only outdone by the cascading floral arrangements in huge baskets in every corner of the glass room.

"Oh my gosh, Caden. I am speechless," I said.

"I think that must be a first for you, Gabby. Not too shabby for something that started out as a sheepfold for the sheep that grazed right outside the meadow," Caden said.

"How do you know all of this?" I asked surprised.

"You are not the only one that reads you know?" He responded, pointing to the back of the menu.

Funny. Jake had said that exact same thing to me when I asked him about Nietzsche. Maybe I did come across like I knew more than anyone else.

The waiter was dressed elegantly with a white shirt and green velvet vest. The cufflinks and brass buttons on the vest were stamped with a leaping deer.

"I don't think that I ever want to leave this place. I feel like Alice must have, when she stepped through the looking glass," I said.

Caden was loving how impressed I was with the entire ambience. I was beginning to understand what he meant about "enjoying the moment."

The wine steward brought him a bottle of Cabernet and two wine glasses. Nobody questioned our ages. It was all very natural. I watched as Caden was handed the wine cork to smell. After just the right amount of time, Caden nodded that all was well. First, a slight amount for him to taste, and then both glasses were filled.

"How did you ever learn to do that? And how do you know if the wine is acceptable," I asked, genuinely curious.

"I have all kinds of hidden talents that I have yet to reveal to you," he said, his eyes sparkling.

Outside of the restaurant, the horse and carriage that our hotel concierge had arranged, was waiting for us. It would be the perfect ending to our first day in New York. This enigmatic Irishman, with many hidden talents, made me realize that there was still hope for happiness.

CHAPTER 17

It is not the stars to hold our destiny, but in ourselves."
  William Shakespeare

Gabby and Caden

.289 square miles; population 22,785, in the borough of
Manhattan, is the birthplace of both "Beat" and the 60's
counterculture movements in the East Coast. Fondly referred to as the "Village", Greenwich was definitely a place
we both agreed we must visit.

The Avant-garde lifestyle was as established as early as
the nineteenth century, when independent presses, quaint
art galleries, and experimental theaters found its home.
Caden was particularly interested in the Tenth Street Studio Building, commissioned by James Bormann Johnston,
designed by Richard Morris Hunt and housed the first architectural school in the United States.

"Can you just imagine, Gabby? This is where it all started. Hunt designed this national architectural prototype
with a featured dome central gallery. The rooms intercon-
nect , radiating into parlors, where artists eventually displayed their masterpieces," his voice was full of energy.

Whenever he spoke about blueprints or building designs,
there was an eagerness that was distinct from any other
topic.

"And, right across the street, Caden, at the Hotel Albert
famous people like Mark Twain, Harte Crane, Walt Whitman, Anais Nin, Andy Warhol, Jackson Pollock, all resided
for years," I was eager to pint out.

"How is it Gabby that you always know so much about everywhere we go? We just arrived, and there are no flyers or anything else posted telling us such details," he asked, confused. On the landing I began prancing around him like a forest Nymph, goading him on. This was so much more fun than divulging my secret.

"I told you Caden. Strange stuff just pops up in my mind from nowhere," I said playfully. Although this was true most of the time, these details were readily available to me courtesy of the hotel magazine, which just happened to feature Greenwich on the cover.

I read the articles while Caden was showering that morning. "Hey....you.... Caden?" I had temporarily lost him. "Uh, huh. What is it Gabby?" I could tell he was totally engrossed in whatever he was doing. "When we leave here, can we check out the Cherry Lane Theater?"

"Anything you want to do, babe." I heard him from some staircase close by. And that was when I finally saw him captivated by a handbill with an eerie looking woman staring directly at us. "'Angel Eye Astrology. Esmeralda, expert at Tarot Reading. Best Psychic in the Village.' Let's go visit Esmeralda, Gabby. It sounds like so much fun," he said.

My first immediate reaction was to rip the sheet to pieces. But, instead I tried to react rationally. "I really do not think that this is a good idea, Caden. All these people are fakes. Why waste our money and time on it?" I tried to be calm.

"It is only for fun, Gabby. Lighten up. Relax. People do this all the time. You even check your astrology sometimes. I have seen you," Caden was insisting.

He was right about the astrology, but I think that going to a fortune teller is like playing with lightening and we did not need any more complications in our lives. "Her place is really close to that theatre. The Blooming Cherry, or whatever it's called. We can jump in for a quickie and then visit Esmeralda. I meant a quick reading."

He was being impossible. "Cute, Caden. On one condition. That you do not take any of this serious, and later

163

bring it up when we don't agree on something," I said, still skeptical.

"We agree with almost everything. But, okay, just for fun," he said.

Now, the witch hunt, begins. Well, she may not really be a witch but close enough. Trying to find the address on this flyer wasn't easy. She needs a new publicity manager and advertising guru.

"This has got to be it," Caden was confirming. The old exterior was not very appealing, and the fake geraniums in the window box seemed an omen on her reliability.

"How can you trust a fortune teller who has plastic flowers outside," I made one last argument.

As it turned out Angel Eyes and Esmeralda were the same person. After a short bartering session, about how much we were willing to "donate" since it was illegal to charge a fee, Esmeralda gave her disclaimer.

An accurate reading depended on how well the planets were lined up. Nevertheless, she claimed her readings were always dependable. Her objective was to let us see just enough of the future. This allows, people to make wiser choices. There would be no serious readings that involved catastrophic results.

Her method was Tarot Card reading. "In most people's minds, Tarot Cards are frightening because the purpose is to foretell impending doom." She looked at both of us, waiting for a reaction. "But," she continued, "The Hermetic Order of the Golden Dawn asserts that the real purpose of Tarot is awareness of the higher self."

Again Esmeralda paused, before continuing. "What exactly does the higher self-do?" I had to ask.

"Without getting into complicated details, let me first clarify that Tarot is not intended to ask simple yes and no questions, without carefully reviewing all the facts. Nor should the cards lead you to make rash decisions," Esmeralda added.

The more she elaborated, the more it sounded like a legal contract. But, now that we were here, I was anxious to get it over with.

"I have chosen to give you both an Open Reading. This will address the larger aspects of your lives, rather any specific problems. I believe that the two of you may be entering a new phase of life?"

This time she waited for us both to respond. Caden answered her directly. "Well, yes. We are both hoping to learn some new ways our relationship will develop. Is that general enough?" Caden asked.

I, quite honestly did not want her to delve into that subject at all. I kept reminding myself that this was only for entertainment.

"Good. Now that we all agree on our expectations, it is time to begin," she said, as the lights dimmed on their own.

My grandmother, who had an Arabic heritage, knew a great deal about Tarot. According to her, the name Tarot came from the conjunction of two Egyptian words, "Royal road", which implied that the tarot was the path to wisdom. I was certainly hoping that I would benefit from that wisdom, so that my brain would stop spinning like a roulette wheel.

Esmeralda was proud to show us her French Tarot de Marseilles Taro cards. During a psychology class I took last semester, I recall Carl Jung connecting the symbology of the trumps to archetypes, concluding that Taro might play a significant role in psychoanalysis.

Joseph Campbell, an American mythologist, best known for his work in comparative mythology and religion, prepared the groundwork for *The Journey of the Fool*, who jumps heedlessly off a cliff, only to come full circle into the position of magician.

I had to wonder if that is what happens to Holden Caulfield, in Catcher in the Rye? Oh, my God. I have to control this mindless moving from one idea to the next, grasping pieces from everywhere, and connecting without control.

FOCUS Gabby, or Caden will leave you just like Jake did. You must LIVE, without analyzing.

Esmeralda started to shuffle the cards asking Caden to first cut them, and later me to do the same. She then proceeded to place the cards face down in a circle of eight. Then three cards in the middle, representing, past present and future.

As she was explaining this, she added that the top card in the center would represent Caden and the bottom one would be mine. The crackling fire was comforting, but my hands were ice cold. The closer that we came to the actual reading of the cards, the more nervous I became.

As Esmeralda turned over the outside card she identified each one. And for the remaining hour it was Esmeralda's show.

"The Knight's Cup will encourage you to remember that victory is more than strength, and can also be achieved with intellect. Seven of cups is speaking to your inner self, trying to tell you that hopes, dreams are all fair game. Look carefully at your own motivations and re-examine your goals.

In the past you have lost time. I have seen those conflicts in your life. Presently you will be rewarded for your mental and creative activities. However, the future will slow your progress, but a constant effort keeps you moving forward if you are honest with yourself.

Page of Cups: In the past the obstacles you are aware of, will lead you to a better understanding of the ways around those obstacles. Presently good news will remind you of a fresh outlook on life, and the future will urge you to seize the day, by taking emotional struggles you pass through and learn how to love deeply and intimately.

Three of swords: in the past there is a great emotional pain that you cannot let go. Presently there will be an intense emotional upheaval. This leads you to a future path that is being cleared, but it is your decision how to benefit from those opportunities.

166

King of swords: A person who has the professional authority to aid you, but may seem to dominate. He only intends to help. In the past you have relied on the strength of your intellect. In the present, a person with authority may help set plans in motion, but, the future shows opposition to those goals. Your ultimate superior intellect will lead you passed these distracting barriers.

Queen of Wands: You are an extrovert, outgoing and friendly, but self-contained. In this position, the card indicates that someone close to you can be trusted. In the past, patience has been your virtue. You or someone near to you, has made wise decisions for you. Presently, a loving friend will provide you with important advice. It is a woman and you will never forget her identity. The future will lead you to seek positive self-development.

The queen of Wands is a lively, passionate and independent woman.

Eight of Wands: Be prepared for an abrupt increase in the pace of your life. Good news for relationships, although there is a possibility that travel will be necessary. The struggle that has been occupying you will pass, followed by a brief peace. There will be a discomfort that is necessary to remove you from a sedentary present. A new venture will bring you future success, but you must be ready to make the right choice.

The Lovers: There will be difficult choices ahead. The paths are mutually exclusive into different futures, but each will provide a temporary peace. Choices are likely painful, but the correct decision and positive outcome are within your grasp. The emotional burden of a recent conflict will soon be lifted. Presently you will need to make a decision between love and career. Neither will disappear forever, but the choice will be your priority.

For the future it would be wise to remember that opposites are two sides of the same coin. You will find that without your other side, there will be chaos."

And then it was over or at least almost over. Caden had been holding my hand; one hand cupped over the other, fixated at every word that Esmeralda spoke.

"I thought at some point you were going to give us separate readings," Caden said, disappointed.

All I wanted was to leave here before any more warnings were included. Honestly, I just wanted to breathe normal again.

"Oh, young man. You and your young lady are a wonderful couple, who are discovering the mysteries of love. Do not ignore the pull that is bringing you permanently together. There are few who experience such a powerful connection. What I found, while I was reading the cards, is that it was impossible for me to know where you stop and Gabby begins."

My hands were shaking again. "Can we please, just leave now Caden." My voice was pleading by now.

"There is just one more thing that I saw," Esmeralda added, reluctantly. "I am not certain that this is the right time to share it with you. But, it is so strong that I feel that I must tell you," she said, determined to give us her last message.

I already had my coat on and was pulling Caden toward the door. "Hold on Gabby. We have come this far. Let's listen to the end." He broke loose of my hold.

Esmeralda, with her very large and probing grey eyes, looked directly at Caden and said, "No true happiness will ever occur between any other partners. Without each other, you will both be searching for the missing link. What is worse is that this bond will increase, over time, and during separation. Together there is balance, apart there is chaos, and at the worst extreme, death. This love is so intense that it can only be compared to conjoined twins, who when separated, can still experience the physical and emotional needs of the other. Please take what I have shared with you seriously." Esmeralda, blew out the last remaining candle.

Caden handed her the fee, but she brushed it off. " No payment for this reading. God be with you both."

Outside the modest apartment, Caden and I were both speechless. We decided to walk back to the hotel and let this very strange afternoon just find a place somewhere safe.

Once in the room I felt exhausted. "Gabby. I am sorry. I hope that Esmeralda didn't ruin your weekend?" Caden said. He removed, from his jacket, a small bag from Sacks Fifth Avenue, and handed it to me.

"When did you have time to go anywhere without me?" I asked him, truly surprised.

"I have my ways. I just hope you like it. The name of it is everything that you have given me. I love you, my Abby with a 'G'," he said.

I opened the bag. Inside was a small, simple bottle of perfume. JOY.

"The bottle was created by a French architect, Louise Sue and it is a blend of 10,000 jasmine flowers and 20 roses to create 30 mg of this perfume. I never smelled anything so beautiful and I knew it had to be yours. How do you like it babe?" Caden said, hoping this would make me forget the earlier fiasco.

Only, Caden could have discovered a bottle created by an Architect. And, it was exquisite. *This was the moment I knew that I had to leave Shalimar and Jake forever.*

"Thank you, my darling. I will never forget this wonderful trip. Each time I use this JOY, I will know you are with me," I said, truly content for the first time in my life. It was the perfect ending to an afternoon that I no longer wanted to remember.

CHAPTER 18

Love knows no barriers, it just hurdles, leaps fences, penetrates walls, to arrive at its destination.
Maya Angelou

Gabby and Caden December 31, 1967

For one afternoon only, December 31, 1967, Fay Jones, a protégé of Frank Lloyd Wright was lecturing to an elite group of student architects at Georgetown University. When Sydney told me that she had two tickets to this event, I knew that somehow I needed to convince her to take Caden with her.

Almost immediately, after our short trip to New York, we had decided that living apart was just impossible. During our winter break, was the ideal time to find just the right apartment that we could afford, and still be walking distance to the campus.

This would be our Christmas present. Our entire paycheck was going toward our living expenses. We both agreed there would be no gift exchange this year. However, Mom and Dad sent me a generous Christmas check, that I was saving for emergencies.

When Sydney asked me to have coffee with her at the Bean and Brew, I finally had the nerve to ask her about the extra ticket for today's lecture.

"So, my beautiful, genius Sydney, have you decided who you are going to take with you this afternoon to hear Fay Jones," I carefully asked, sipping my tea.

Caden's dream was to be an architect, and Frank Lloyd Wright was who he admired the most. When he told me about The Fallingwater home, that Wright, in 1933, was commissioned to build, in rural southwest Pennsylvania, I was spellbound.

The Kaufman family, had told Wright that they wanted a view of the water falls, however, what Wright decided on, was to build the home into the waterfall. He named it Falling water, because it appears to stand on solid ground while stretching over a thirty-foot waterfall.

This design became an historic landmark Wright told the owners that he wanted them to live with the waterfalls, to hear them and make them a part of their everyday life.

"Actually, I have been thinking that I can scalp this ticket, and make about $500. Can you imagine? Some people are just crazy. Jayden gave these to me, hoping that I would feel obligated to have sex with him. Poor, foolish boy. He has no idea who he is dealing with." Her smile was intoxicating. That is what drove these boys crazy.

"The most that I could offer you is $300." I decided to just throw it out there. "Girlfriend, I know why you want this ticket. That man of yours, he better appreciate how much you love him," Sydney said. "Does that mean you will sell it to me?" I started to look for my checkbook before she changed her mind.

"Put away your money. What kind of a Sista friend would I be if I took your money, child!" Sydney said reaching into her purse and handing me the "golden" ticket.

I was nearly in tears; I was so happy. Making the decision to live with Caden was so spontaneous. But, now that we were actually doing it, made me a little nervous. *I sometimes questioned if I really loved him. If so, did I ever love Jake? Do I even know what love means?*

One thing I was certain about, was giving Caden this gift would make us both happy.

"I will never forget this Sydney. I owe you so much," I said, safely putting away the ticket.

"You owe me nothing. Tell Caden to meet me at the front entrance. I want to make certain these tickets aren't bogus," Sydney said, as she ran off to meet another admirer.

With that "golden" ticket in my hand, I couldn't wait to get back to the apartment to show Caden. When I walked in, the room was still empty.

There were boxes in the hallway, a new bed, Aunt Selena's house warming gift to us, a rented refrigerator, and two giant pillow chairs that came with the apartment.

Caden had found a broken table in the alley. A few days later he managed to make a bookcase by adding crates from the bookstore where he worker. But, the most amazing transformation was an old antique door that we found in the alley at our favorite Italian restaurant.

Soon, Caden had converted the door into a functional desk. It reminded me of a Renaissance replica seen in the background of a famous painting.

"Hi, babe," Caden walked in with his arms full, " I bought a few snacks for later, and some sparkling wine, to toast the New Year," he said, heading right for the small kitchen. "And I have a surprise for you," I said snuggling up next to him.

"Now, Gabby....you better not have spent any money on me, remember our agreement?"

"Can you just please just live by your own philosophy. What happened to 'enjoy the moment' attitude that you always tell me?" I said, coyly.

I held up the ticket and gave it to Caden to read. It took him about thirty seconds to realize what it was.

"Oh my God, Gabby! Where? I mean how? Where did this come from? Oh, but this is for today. I'm not leaving you home on New Year's Eve," he said, realizing the date. "No you are not going to leave me alone. Now, go get ready. Sydney had an extra ticket and she is going to meet you at the main door at seven 0' clock. She says you will be home by nine. Plenty of time to initiate our new bed, and ring in the New Year," I said.

"Well, I have a surprise for you too tonight, baby," he whispered in my ear, nibbling a little before he started to look through some boxes for a clean sweater.

"Here you are," I handed him a navy colored crew neck that I had hung up earlier. "Enjoy tonight, I know how much you admire Fay Jones. I will be waiting here when you get back." I gave him a long kiss and watched him walk out the door.

We were close enough to the lecture hall that Caden could ride his bike and be back home before the cold evening winds started to blow. Once Caden was gone I began to reflect on how far we had come. It was hard for me to believe that so much happened in less than a year.

Only a few months ago I learned that Jake had his leg amputated, and was marrying another woman. *1965 was also the year that I graduated from Savannah High School, came to Georgetown, met Caden, spent a long weekend in New York City, and decided to move in with a man that I knew I was falling in love with. And, I am only eighteen years old.*

There was an optimistic feeling in the air that I just could not identify. Although my mind and heart were still playing tug-of-war, it bothered me less. My spirit was leading me to an unchartered territory and although sometimes I was vulnerable, it was okay.

What I now realized, was that Jake was always in control. Which was always okay because, there was never a doubt in my mind that he loved me, until, of course I saw that engagement picture of him and Isabella.

Caden, from day one, encouraged me to always, be his partner and "dance" equally with him. While Jake would always talk tender to me after we made love, Caden, speaks to me throughout our lovemaking. That sensation is with me for hours, or even days later.

Caden and I truly do fit together, like Esmeralda predicted.

1968 is going to be a stellar year. Life has finally become a worthwhile adventure that has direction, purpose, and an optimistic vision.

I am focused on achieving my architectural dreams, but more so, I am committed for the first time to be a participant, not an observer.

Tomorrow, New Year's Eve, I am going to make Gabby officially all mine. Thanks to my Aunt Selena, I am ready to ask Gabby to be my wife. Just as the fireworks are going off, in the background, and the New York mirror ball is ready to proclaim a new year, I will be placing a diamond ring on Gabby's finger.

It was Aunt Selena that made me think very long and seriously about my decision. Rightly so, she was concerned that I was moving too fast.

"Not that I want to spoil your elaborate plans, Caden, but the entire idea of cohabiting is so you know if you are ready for marriage," Selena reminded me.

"I know that this seems sudden, but being engaged does not mean that we are going to rush to get married. It just means that we are committed. And that is what you always want me to be, isn't it?"

"Alright Caden, you do seem serious. And because I want you to know how much I trust you, I have something for you," Selena said, she then walked directly to the hidden wall safe behind a painting of an Irish landscape.

She handed me a small velvet jewelry box. When I opened it, there was a magnificent two carat diamond ring, surrounded by emeralds. Immediately I thought of Gabby's eyes. "I want you to take this ring, Caden, and when you are certain that Gabby is the ONLY woman you cannot live without, you put this ring on her finger," Selena said.

"But, where did this come from? I never saw you wear it," I asked, totally confused. "I never married the man I loved. This ring was given to me by his brother shortly after he died. We shared an eternal bond that not even time could break. That magic, is also what you have with Gabby. I recognized it that first morning you introduced me to her. When the time is right, you will know," Selena handed me the ring.

Aunt Selena knew nothing about Esmeralda, and yet she told me nearly the same thing. That is what convinced me to propose to Gabby.

Gabby, Caden and Jake December 31, 1967 OH MY!

We had declined, several party invitations from friends. Instead, we had both decided that the best celebration would be in the privacy of our very own, first apartment.

Theoretically, we were not to move in until the first of January. But Sam Jonas, an elderly widower, took one look at how anxious we were, and let us start moving in on December 30th.

It was a one bedroom, loft apartment located at Hamilton Arms. Caden and I had made friends with several older couples, in their twenties. When a vacancy became available, we took it immediately.

Living without a marriage contract, seemed less intimidating. There was no need to follow our parent's rules, when we could make our own. For me, it was perfect. After spending years with Jake, I needed to be certain that Caden was just not too good to be real. As much as I wanted to believe in the fairytale ending, I was not ready to run away with the first knight permanently.

There were those moments, when I would be singing a song to myself, and Caden would start singing the same song out loud. That is how close we had become. if only the montage of dreams with no beginning and no end would stop weaving through my mind with no control, I would feel almost perfect.

I admire the masters who create moments, using mediums that not only withstand time, but add a new dimension to time. The love I was experiencing now, was like an art form. It has developed into suspended anticipation. The

British Romantic poets Wordsworth, Coleridge, Byron, Shelley and Keats all discovered the secret ability to capture the essence of time, in an ode, a ballad or a sonnet. The layers of poetry, music and art, intertwine together creating my physical and emotional state. It is an experience felt only by few; a rare evolution that is not easily recognized, nor controlled.

Esmeralda identified this phenomenon. We were both warned about this powerful attraction. Like a tornado, sporadically devastates its surroundings, Caden and I were unprepared for the aftershocks that would never cease.

On the way back to the apartment, after leaving Sydney, I stopped at the dorm to pick up a cardboard box that held Jake and my remains. I wanted to dispose of it properly. In hindsight, I should have left it in the dumpster on my way out. Instead, I brought it with me. Now that Caden was gone for a few hours, I would have time to set that box on fire in the alley.

As I was about to grab my sweatshirt to go outside I noticed on the kitchen counter that Caden had left the lecture ticket. Just as I was contemplating how I could get this to him, there was a knock at the door. "You don't need to knock at your own..." I said, when, suddenly I noticed, standing in front of me was Jake, dressed in his formal Marine uniform.

"Jake? ...My God...I mean how did you... No...why are you?" I thought that I would pass out. Jake must have sensed this because he was holding my arms. All I could do was stare at him for at least one full moment.

He looked perfect, with the exception of his right leg missing. *Bring me all of your dreams. You dreamers. Bring me all of your heart melodies, that I may wrap them in a blue cloud cloth away from the too rough fingers of the world*

"What the hell are you doing here?" Once I could talk, I was damn angry, and happy, and scared, all at one moment. Instinctively, he stepped back. I think he thought I would slap him. Which I came very close to doing.

"I HAD to see your one last time Gabby."

"Why, Jake? And, why tonight?" My voice was beginning to crack. "I am here right now because I needed to explain to you in person what happened," Jake said, as he walked past me into the living room.

"I already know about Isabella. I know that you and her are getting married. What else Jake...what else do I need to know!" Tears were running down my face. I could not stop crying. And then he was holding me in his arms. The same arms that I always ran to for three years. We were back at Tybee Lighthouse, just the two of us, alone.

"Just listen to me, please, Gabby." He was still holding me tight, whispering in my ear. He would not let me go, and I didn't want him to. " I will never stop loving you Gabby. I couldn't stop, even if I wanted to. You are only eighteen. I love you more than I desire to live. When I stepped on that mine, and my body was shattered, it was your face that I saw flashing in my eyes. And, when I did wake up it was your name that I called out. But, Gabby it is BECAUSE I love you that I have to leave you." And then he kissed me.

I heard nothing. All I felt was his familiar lips on mine. In his arms, the beat of his heart next to mine was all I needed. *How could Caden ever replace this love I had for Jake?*

"You know that I have someone else Jake." I was nearly hysterical. I wanted to hurt him. "And, we love each other. So you go off with your little nurse..."

"I know Gabby. It's okay."

"It's OKAY. How can you say that after you just kissed me? Are you insane?" I didn't know what else to say.

"Yes, baby I am. But I could never be able to watch the pain you would go through to take care of me," Jake said, never raising his voice

"I don't care about your leg. You need to believe in ME Jake. I am stronger than you think I am. And I CAN'T live without you." *There I said it. I thought that I could live without him, but now I knew I was wrong. I had to convince him if this.*

177

"Gabby, listen to me. It is more than just my leg. I should be dead. I am a walking corpse. Nobody knows how long I have to live," he said.

"Then spend whatever time you have left with me Jake," I was now begging.

"I can't put you through that torture," he lifted me off my knees. I looked right into his eyes and said, "It isn't your choice Jake. It is mine." And as always, he took final control.

"Oh, but it is my choice. And you my love will continue your life. I wouldn't have it any other way," he said with conviction. Then he turned to leave. I grabbed his arm, pleading one last time.

"Please....Please don't do this." Before he was out the door, I reached down and lifted the cardboard box that held the remains of our life.

"This is what is left of our dreams, Jake. I was planning on burning it tonight. But, it is more appropriate that you be the keeper now." In his arms, he held three years of our life. His letters from Nam. Pictures from Tybee Island. My Yearbook, his letterman jacket, class ring, dried flowers, commemorating my rite of passage and an almost empty bottle of Shalimar.

As he walked out, the last thing I heard him say was, "That new perfume you're wearing is a nice scent on you. I approve entirely."

Outside on the way back to the official military jeep, he and Caden nearly collided. Caden was just there long enough to see Gabby and Jake embracing. There was no need for Caden to go back for his ticket now. The only ticket he needed tonight was a one-way ticket back to Savannah.

I ran upstairs to the loft and threw myself on the bed that Caden and I were going to initiate.

How could I do that now. What the hell was wrong with me? How was I going to ever explain all of this to Caden? Well I wasn't. He must never know how I feel about Jake. Loving Jake must never interfere with Caden, I will make certain of that. And in time, Jake will just be a memory. Was I even listening to the words in my own head? This must be the very last time I think of Jake. I went to the mirror to see my face blotched with red spots and mascara running from my eyes like a voodoo doll.

Esmeralda! Suddenly, I remembered what she had told me. This had to be all a very bad nightmare. When Caden gets home everything will be better.

Then the phone began ringing.

"Caden, where are you? You left the..."

"No, Gabby it's me, Sydney. Caden never made it to the Lecture Hall. I was wondering what was going on?" She sounded worried. I couldn't answer her.

"Gabby. Honey, are you there?"

"Yes, Sydney. Caden left his ticket by accident. But now, I have no idea where he is?" *Or maybe, I do.*

"Don't panic. I am on my way over there. There has to be a logical explanation for all of this."

And the phone went dead. *Maybe, I really did not want to know the truth. I just needed to talk to Caden, and soon.*

CHAPTER 19

"'Twas, brill if and the slithy toves, did gyre and gimble in the wabe: All mimsey were the borogroves, And the momes raths outgrabe " Jabber wok Lewis Carroll
Gabby December 31, 1967

What was taking Sydney so long to get here?
Meanwhile, I keep coming back to the same conclusion. When Jake showed up a few hours ago, I was hoping that he came to his senses and left Isabella.
[*And then what would you have done, Gabby? There is no doubt that you still love Jake and that he still loves you. But, you also claim to be in love with Caden. Ask yourself this, when does one love end and another begin?*
If Jake claimed to love me so much, that he had to let me go, and I could never live with his handicap, was I just settling for Caden? You know, like a consolation prize?
The doorbell, thank God, jolted me out of this mind warp.
"Gabby! Oh, Gabby," Sydney had her arms wrapped around me as soon as she saw how I looked.
"Oh, poor baby. You look horrid. Let me get you a cold wash cloth for those swollen eyes." Sydney was always the mother. Must be because at home, in Jamaica, she had seven siblings.
When she returned from the bathroom, I was sitting on the floor in the corner of the room. "Okay. Tell me what you think happened to Caden, and we will piece this whole thing together," she said, stroking my head gently.
I explained to her my theory that Caden must have seen Jake and I through the front window and became angry and hurt. Apparently, Caden came home for the ticket he

forgot and saw Jake and I together from the front window, embracing in the apartment.

He deserves an explanation and I should be able to give him one. But, at this moment, I was angrier than hurt. During times of crisis, I always have delayed reactions. Once my mind begins to function in "normal mode" "rather than "safe mode" the reality that two men that I love, and who claim to love me, both rejected me on the very same day, which happens to be New Year's Eve.

Ironically, everyone knows that Auld Lang Syne, means farewell to the old year and welcome in the new. I was once told by a young Scotsman, that it is also sung at funerals, which for obvious reasons, seems very appropriate to me at this moment.

"So, what you are telling me, is that Jake, your old lover, just pops in from nowhere, and comes to your apartment, for exactly what reason?" Sydney sounded rightfully confused.

"I know, Sydney. I was so shocked; I didn't know what to do. I should have just told him to leave. I know that now. But, at the moment, I just lost it. All those old feelings just took over," I said, almost ashamed.

"I tried to warn you Gabby, that rebound relationships never work out. Jake just left your apartment an hour ago. And you admitted to me that you still love him. I know that this hurts, but you need to let Caden go. He was your rebound. Next time take it slower. Go out and date, but without sex, and let time heal this mess," she said, wiping my tears that wouldn't stop.

I was not ready to accept any of this logic. I know how Caden I are when we are together. I just couldn't explain how Jake factored into the equation. Maybe that was the answer. I don't really love Jake anymore.

The feelings I have are just residue ashes from a flame that seemed eternal. Once I could fall asleep, I would be able to rationalize these emotions.

Tomorrow. Yes, tomorrow there will be plenty of time for understanding why I feel so empty. Real love is when nothing is expected. I never felt that I was settling for Caden.

Sydney sat with me until I finally fell into a deep sleep, and when I awoke, by myself the next morning I knew that I needed to take that short, but very difficult ride to Alexandria to face my destiny head on. I decided to wait until after New Year's day to approach Selena. Nothing could be gained by hysterically showing up, demanding answers like a lunatic.

Once on the train, Stan, the friendly train Porter, approached me as I was settling in my seat.

"Good morning, Miss Gabby. Sorry to hear about you and Caden breaking up," he said politely.

I turned around suddenly, and nearly snapped his head off. "What did you say? Have you seen Caden?" I asked.

"Well, yes, I most certainly did. Let me see. Yes, that would have been New Year's Eve. That boy was so wasted, that when I asked him where you were, all he said was that 'Abby lost her G ', and something about wearing the letter J. Can you figure that out, Miss Gabby? It's been bugging me for days," he said, shaking his head.

"Oh, Stan.. I really don't know what he's talking about. I am going to see his Aunt Selena, and hopefully she has some answers," I said.

"Well, you take care of yourself, Miss Gabby. If that fool walked away from you, he must be on some nasty dope," Stan said.

Now I at least I knew that Caden had been to Salina's on New Year's Eve and he was quite drunk. And, he definitely saw Jake and I together.

As I settled into my seat, I remembered that first time on this train, when Caden cradled me in his own arms, his breath caressing my neck, whispering, "Baby, you and I will one day look back at our trip to Alexandria, as the place our love came to life, like magic."

Was all that just a lie? Did I just want to believe that somehow the universe tossed us chaotically on this path, only to make us combust into microscopic particles, lost forever? I need Caden to slam me gently against a wall, kiss my mouth passionately and turn my world inside out.

Together we created a new us, a melodic opus; a self-portrait that took on new forms of life each time our bodies became one. Like a perfect tango appears effortless. My body was aching at this moment to have Caden fill me with his juices.

Sex was never crass or vulgar; it was always bold and vibrant, and real. *Desire itself is a movement, not in itself desirable. Love is itself unmoving, only the cause and end of the movement/ Timeless and undesirable, except in the aspect of time, between unbeing and being. TS Eliot*

The trains motion was thankfully lulling me into a deep sleep. Then I heard Alice asking "when do we arrive at Oz?"

At first I thought it rather odd that it was Alice asking, instead of Dorothy, who actually traveled to Oz. Then I concluded, that it only made sense that the rabbit hole would eventually lead Alice to Oz.

Nevertheless, the Cheshire Cat did seem out of place.

"The flying monkeys found it quite disturbing when the Cheshire cat disappeared, leaving only his silly grin behind." Alice was talking directly to me this time.

"Cheshire cat was not very helpful to me in Wonderland either, but you may feel free to ask him any questions that you would like," Alice continued.

I looked around, perplexed, still trying to determine why and how I ended up in Oz. Alice politely offered to show me how to address the contrite cat.

"Cheshire please tell my friend Gabby where her Caden is?" Alice asked for me.

As Cheshire's often ponder questions prior to answering, we watched his tail curl around, several times before responding.

"It really is a matter of whether she really wants to know, or if she just likes asking silly questions," The Cheshire was done speaking.

I thought about this for a moment and soon realized that, I really didn't care to know, as long as I get out of here.

Hearing this reply, the Cheshire gave a long grin once again and said, "Brilliant. Then I will send you to the Jabberwocky and into the maddening crowd. "

"Oh no! I definitely do not want to go among mad people. "I quickly answered.

"Too late, "the Cheshire cat replied emphatically, "we are all mad here. I'm mad you're mad"

"But, I'm not mad," I insisted almost in tears.

"Oh my dear you must be mad, or you wouldn't have come here." Then, finally I heard the loud speaker announce, that Alexandria was the next stop.

I looked around reluctantly, hoping that no one had heard my moaning or wild conversation with Alice and the Cheshire cat. At this moment my world was definitely feeling like a fractured fairytale.

As the taxi approached Selena's house, I regretted that I had not phoned first, but it was too late now. As soon as Selena came to the door, I broke down in tears.

"Gabby, oh my child. It will be alright. Just let it all out." She was holding me in her arms trying to console my trembling.

"I am so sorry that I never called first. But, I haven't been thinking straight for several days." I was trying to explain between the whimpering and the sobbing.

"Come inside with me now, and I will make some hot tea. You can tell me everything and then I will tell you what I know." She led me to the couch and soon came back with a lovely pot of tea, matching Bone China cups, sugar bowl and creamer.

Immediately it reminded me of the play **Tea and Sympathy** when Deborah Carr invites poor Al, the dejected college boy for tea and begins having an affair with him. Naturally, that would not happen with Selena, but I was bracing myself for what she was going to reveal to me about Caden

This Sympathy, I believed was going to come in the size of the sugar cubes in my tea.

"OK, darling, before you begin with all this madness, I want to let you know that Caden was here, also extremely upset. I listened to him, gave him my advice, as I will give you, and be as impartial and fair as I know how to be." She took my hand emphasizing her honesty.

That word "madness " keeps following me. After I shared with her what I thought had happened, Selena began to flesh out Caden's reasoning for leaving.

"My dear, Caden was in a total state of confusion that night. Do you know that Jake and he nearly knocked each other down when they passed each other outside the apartment? Caden was overwhelmed with pain and anger. By the time he reached my house, he had consumed at least one bottle of Jack Daniels and maybe more. And we were up together most of the night smoking weed, trying to determine what and why all this happened. " She said.

I was not surprised that Selena smoked weed, but I was curious about the advice she gave him.

"I told Caden that he needed to sleep all of this off and the next morning, or even a day later, I told him to call you. He was a real mess. But, I have to tell you Gabby, men do not take rejection well, and Caden, just shuts down completely." Selena was obviously worried.

"I know that this seems like I do not understand how he feels, but, Selena, I just need to tell him that Jake came over on his own, unannounced and unsolicited. It was his way to have closure. What Caden saw was a goodbye not hello".

Selena took a long sip of her tea and gently put her cup down. "But, Gabby, was this closure for you too? You must honestly and deeply look into your heart and ask yourself, if there ever was a choice between Jake and Caden, would you still choose Caden? He does not believe so," Selena made her point clear.

That response stunned me. I was not ready to confront that issue. Selena was absolutely correct. I needed to be certain that I love Caden and Caden alone before I confront him.

"You are a very wise woman Selena. And everything that we talked about is definitely more clear now. I need to allow it to settle in before I make any more impulsive decisions. Thank you so much for sharing with me.

" We both rose at the same time, maybe instinctively knowing that it was time to conclude our tea and sympathy session.

"One more thing Gabby. Caden has returned to Savannah, for at least the time being. His parents could use some help at the deli, and he could also use some time alone. It may be wise to give him his space," she was pleasant but firm.

At that news I felt a bit melancholy, recalling how passionate Caden was about being an architect. I hoped, that meeting me, and our break up, would not stop that dream from becoming reality. I kept that thought to myself. Sharing those thoughts with Selena would only make this more difficult.

"This is not goodbye Gabby. You are always welcome here. I will call you in a few weeks for lunch. Always remember, my sweet, the heart knows what it wants, and it will tell you if you listen. "

As I walked out of Selena's house, I realized that eternity is where true love lives, and timing is everything in love and loss.

CHAPTER 20

Beware the Jabberwock my son! The jaws that bite, the claws that Catch! Beware the Jubjub bird, and shun,
                    -The frumious Bandersnatch.

Caden Cassidy

December 31, 1967 -January 1 1968

Ever wonder how long it takes for the male ego to go from ecstasy to anxiety; from jealousy to detachment; from abandonment to revenge?

"What the fuck did I just see? Was that really Jake holding Gabby in his arms, and kissing her. In OUR APARTMENT!". Is this reality, or some sick New Year's Eve prank? I feel like the dumb pawn in someone else's chess game. How could I be this STUPID.

I feel like the dumb pawn in someone else's chess game. It makes perfect sense now. All those times when Gabby's mind would wander, she was thinking of Jake...that Bitch.

"Oh, Caden, I can't live without you. I love you so much." Her voice is pounding in my brain, like a steel drum.

I find myself screaming the words out loud. I turn on a dime so fast that Peter Rabbit could not keep up with me.

"Fucking Bitch. I'm outta here. Sleep with your ex, or sleep by yourself, but never again with me." I look around and have no idea of where I am.

Some people are starting their New Year celebration off early. Wherever I am, some idiot with a blond wig and 1968 rhinestone glasses is blowing a party favor in my face. I reach back and my fist is ready to smack him in his Fucking mouth, when I suddenly feel an arm from nowhere, pull me back.

"Caden? What the hell, man, what's up with you? "

I look up and notice, it is Dylan, my old roommate from the frat house.

"Where is Gabby, and what are you doing out here by yourself, man?"

Like a bucket of ice water has just hit my face, I stop and look up. I pull his hand off my arm.

"I'm OK. I will take care of this my way."

"Well, you look like shit. Why aren't you wearing your sweater?"

I look down and realize that when I ran from the apartment screaming, crying, and mumbling incoherent nonsense, I must've pulled my sweater off.

"Right. Well, Dylan thanks for that observation."

I immediately put the sweater back on realizing that it must not be any warmer than 20° out here. No wonder people were freaking out around me.

"OK, Caden, I hear you loud and clear, Man. But if you need a place to crash, stop by the frat house, we're having a big bash there later.

Tonight is not the time to be alone, out here, on the streets."

I shook his hand. Before I continued in the store, I asked him to call Aunt Selena, and let her know I had to talk to her. It was imperative that I see her tonight. I handed him her number and hoped that she was not having a party at her house. If she was out, there was always a spare key in the flowerpot, so I could wait for her until morning.

What are you doing Abby without a G? You tell me one thing, and then I see you kissing Jake. And fuck you, Jake. You asshole. Fucking with my woman, well now, my ex woman. You can't just accuse me of hit and run Abby. I saw those tire tracks all across your back. I can see clearly that you have had your fun two timing this tortoise. I got your fucking turtle shit. I shake my head just in time for the light to change as I head across the street. I am screaming deliriously inside.

"Hey man, "I say to the clerk. "Where are my good pals Jack Daniel and his partner Jimmy Bean?" I am attempting to be as normal as possible.

"On the back wall right behind you," he says. I walk over to where he has pointed, and do not realize that I am talking out loud to myself.

Reaching for two bottles, I say, " Thanks. Ring these two pints up for me. Tonight I drink alone. Yeah, with nobody. Good riddance to 1967 the worst year in history. Time to get shitfaced."

"Cool," the clerk says. After a quick look at Caden, the clerk asks to see his ID. Caden pulls the driver's license from his wallet and shows it to the clerk. The clerk holds it in his hand. First, he looks at the license picture and then glances up at Caden. Perfect match, the clerk thinks.

Next, he checks the date and says, "Okay, your good to go. All I ask is you don't drink and drive."

"I won't man. I already got stabbed in the heart and back, no need to bring anybody else innocent around for this hearse ride to hell."

My fake ID works all the time, and it is the only thing working for me right now. Once out the door and in the alley, I uncap the Jack and proceed to empty the pint. I toss the glass bottle in the trashcan. Within minutes I am on my way to Aunt Selena's place.

My favorite metro policeman, Stanley says, "What kind of hurricane hit you boy?"

"Never you mind Stan, I got my problems and you got yours. "I could tell my voice was beginning to slur, and I could not control it.

"Where is Gabby tonight? It is New Year's Eve, you know. First kiss with your main squeeze, and all that."

"Oh, you mean that Gabby? She lost her G and decided to wear that J again. "Stan looked totally confused, but thought it best to leave it at this point.

"Just try to stay out of trouble. No throwing punches; and no puking. And No drinking on this train!" It was obvious that tonight, Stan was serious.

I waited for Stan to retreat to a small cubicle and settle in for the rest of the train ride. I tap into the 'Jimmy' and take one long pull. I notice a suit sitting near me. Another redneck going somewhere. His eyes are moving but there's no life showing.

"Man, you got any weed?" I finally ask.

"No, dude," he snaps back. "I'm Wall Street. I snort coke, you fuck."

"Fuck? Who you calling' Fuck? I outta take your fucking head off, you prick."

Then I remember Stanley's warning. It is one thing to show up to Selena's drunk and another entirely different story if she has to bail me from jail on New Year's Eve. With tension in the air, the situation goes no further than a Mexican standoff.

I take another jug of J Bean and decide to focus on how I'm going to walk off this train and to Selena's without barfing. When the train finally does pull up to the depot, I see Selena wrapped in a silver full length mink coat. Her sable black hair, pinned up in a perfect French coiffure.

Dylan, you are the man of the hour. You came through for me at my darkest moment. Then I notice Selena's feet. She is wearing a pair of glass slippers and I suddenly realize that Dylan must've called her just prior to her leaving the house.

Well, now both of our New Year's Eve will be ringing in with a silent chime. Once Selena sees me, exiting the platform, her driver, Maurice came over to me, and she walks back to the Town Car. Just as we were approaching the car, Maurice stops as I began to heave the first part of my Jack in all directions of the street.

I look like a broken fire hydrant. Before I was allowed in the car, we went to the restroom, where, wisely, Selena had brought a change of clothes for me. Once cleaned up, I slid into the backseat where my Aunt was waiting.

"I don't know what any of this is all about Caden, but it better be good. I am missing the event of the year, tonight." Her voice was not very sympathetic.

I made the decision to let her cool off, and let me sober up before I told her what had happened. It was a very long, and silent ride home.

"Are you feeling a little better now, Caden?" I could tell that Selena was back to her normal self.

"Well, I can at least see straight again. That driver must really be experienced with drunk people. He knew just what to do," I said.

"I am not surprised. He has been a driver for many politicians here in DC, so I am sure by now he has seen it all," Selena answered.

Once in the house the first thing Selena removes is her glass slippers. She then takes a seat in her overstuffed chair and waits for me to start.

"The floor is all yours Caden. Tell me everything, do not leave out any sordid details, do you hear me?"

"Well, to be as straightforward as possible, I saw Gabby and Jake kissing through the front window of our apartment." I waited for her reaction.

"Can I get you something to eat Caden?" Selena had already risen from the chair.

"Did you hear me Selena ? Gabby was kissing another man. No, not just any other man, the man she was desperately in love with before me, and all you can say is 'am I hungry'?" Selena sat back down.

"Caden, did you approach her and ask her why? Or did you just come directly here to complain to me? There has to be a reason for this, and a good one. Did you propose to her yet? What happened prior to this, Jake character, showing up?" She waited for me to respond.

I thought silently for a few seconds. I wish... damn it Abby without a G, you fucking drive me crazy. Why?

"All I know is that I saw her kissing Jake. That is all I need to know. Sometimes when we are together she goes in these weird trances and I think she's wishing she was with

191

HIM. Hell, she may be thinking of him when she is fucking me, how do I know. Thankfully I still have the ring you gave me."

I pulled out the diamond ring surrounded by emeralds and handed it to Selena.

"No Caden. I want you to keep this ring and when you find the woman that you cannot live without, you put this ring on her. Promise me this Caden."

The tone in Selena's voice was now very serious.

"I am going back, back to Savannah tomorrow. I won't stay here any longer than I have to. Will you loan me the money for a train ticket? And, I will keep the ring like you have asked me to, but I doubt that it will ever go on any-one's finger." He placed the ring back in his pocket.

"I do not think that you're making a wise decision, but of course I will give you money to go home and it will be a plane ticket not a train. Just, please make sure you know what you want this time. No regrets." Selena was looking directly at me, or more like through me.

"It has been one hell of a night. You got any weed? A couple of tokens and I will be over the line. I don't think I will fall asleep any other way."

"Yes, I do have some pretty good quality weed from Columbia, fresh from the FBI raid last week. Don't ask me how I got this confiscated contraband, just enjoy it. But this time you're not going to bogart that joint. "

Caden does as she tells him and passes the joint to her. They both soon begin to feel the effect and crash before the munchies get to them. And, then the following words come into his mind; " hast thou slain the Jabberwock? Come to my arms, my beamish boy! Oh frabjous day! Calloh! Callay! Chortled in his joy. When he wakes up this will finally all make sense.

192

CHAPTER 21

Hello darkness, my old friend
I've come to talk with you again
Because a vision softly creeping
Left its seed while I was sleeping
And the vision that was planted
In my brain still remains
Within the sound of silence.
                    -Simon and Garfunkle

Gabby 1969

For nearly eighteen months, after I saw Jake and Caden , both for the very last time, I refused to date anyone steady. The advice that Sydney had given me about rebound relationships was now my roadmap. Sex is restricted to some serious petting, but intercourse was definitely out altogether.

Sydney, tried to convince me that I was taking extreme measures, when I decided to literally take her advice. But in my mind, if I never let anyone close to me again, I would avoid the pain that still ached when I began to think too deeply about either Jake or Caden.

According to Molly, my inside" mole "to all Savannah's gossip, Caden had basically taking over the deli from his mom and dad who were almost totally unable to handle the daily operations. According to the latest report, Caden worked in the deli all day, and in the evenings he was taking classes at Georgia Tech. Reluctantly, she also added that he was dating some Irish girl named Kaitlyn, but she did not know how serious that was.

There had been a time, that she thought he was also doing drugs. That apparently ended once Kaitlyn entered the scene. It made me sad to hear that he was not pursuing his architectural dream, but that may have happened regardless of our relationship.

Jake and Isabella had moved to Boston, but it was not known why or what he was doing. And of course Molly was still in Paris, living her dream. She leased a loft, no larger than the top floor of Tybee Island lighthouse. It cost her a small fortune, but it was on the couture, Avenue Montaigne. That area, Molly said, was surrounded by iconic historical landmarks, and without a doubt the most fashionable, trendy bars in all of Paris.

Originally, in the early 18th century, it was called the alee des Veuves (widows' alley) because women who were in morning, would gather there to support one another. The current name comes from a very well-known French author, Michael de Montaigne, who during the French Renaissance was credited for inventing the essay genre. Now, most people are attracted to the sparkling Mabille balls.

On Saturday nights it becomes the most popular place to attend, with its illuminated fountains and some 30,000 gas jet lamps, along with Chinese billiards, and bands inviting couples together in the streets to dance and drink. It was definitely a place that I could envision Molly thriving in.

Molly loved the idea that she could buy fresh food daily, paint on the weekends near the Seine river, and still work during the day as a tour guide at the Louvre. I missed her terribly.

It was amusing to me that somehow she knew more about everyone from Savannah, living thousands of miles away than I did, living only five hundred twenty two miles away.

"That's because you have turned yourself into one of those hermit crabs, Gabby. If someone begins to show the least bit of interest, you scuttle under the nearest rock," she would remind me often.

Molly knew me better than anyone else on this earth, with the exception of perhaps Jake, and I was hoping that with time, Jake would no longer be a part of my new life.

"I would rather be hiding under that rock Miss Molly, than be smashed by some stranger's boot, "I retorted back, quite content with my new found philosophy on life.

"There will come a time Gabby, when even you will need to put down those guards and let someone in. Not every man is out to ruin your life and unless you plan to become a nun, this abstinence will eventually come to an end, even for you my lovely ice princess," she often said.

Molly and I made a pact to speak at least once a month. We would have been on the phone more, but neither of us could afford the overseas phone charges so, we made the most out of our monthly chats.

The life that I had been living in Georgetown was now on the fringe of reality. The closest I ever came to the "real world" was when Caden and I lived together for two days. Now, since I returned back to the dorm, the electric bills are paid by some mystery person, food prepared by kitchen staff, and mornings don't start at 8 AM like most jobs; for me, 10 AM is the earliest class I ever take.

Academia life is quite appealing. So much so, that I was seriously considering going directly to graduate school and applying for a fellowship to study at Oxford. I would be close to Molly and far enough from the past. One thing for certain, I never wanted to return to Savannah. Too many wounds that I did not need any salt poured on.

If I was ever going to move forward I could never see Jake or Caden ever again. My parents could not entirely understand my reasoning, but so far they were pleased with my current studies, and enjoyed visiting me in DC.

Literature and writing had always been my passion. Now that I was close to my final year of undergraduate courses, several professors recognized me for a number of insightful thesis' and outstanding contributions during Socratic discussions.

Named after Socrates it is a form of inquiry between individuals, based on asking and answering questions to stimulate critical thinking to illuminate ideas. It felt very natural and easy for me to do this.

The buzz around campus was that I would undoubtedly receive the English scholar award at graduation; but as far as I was concerned It was just a pleasant rumor and nothing more.

Whenever I begin to feel that I have some control over my own destiny, IT happens. Call IT perhaps fate, but to me it is just another unexpected whirlwind, or better yet tornado, that seems to follow me.

The past several years, Selena and I have grown quite close to one another. She cares for me like a surrogate mother, never referring to Caden or Jake, which I am forever grateful. So, when I received a call, one afternoon in January, while there was still snow on the ground and most people were hibernating to a warm fireplace, Selena was inviting me to the Willard Continental Hotel, often referred to as the crown jewel of Pennsylvania Avenue.

"Gabriella thank you so much for being prompt on returning my call." I knew that it must be something important or serious because rarely does Selena ever refer to me by my formal name.

"Of course, Selena . Is there anything wrong?" I could not imagine what would be so urgent that she was glad I called immediately.

"I know that this is short notice, but I am sending my driver over 11:30 to pick you up and deliver you to the Willard, where we will be having high tea with Dr. Jacoby, Randall Blair, the owner of one of Kentucky's most prestigious horse ranches, and his delightful son, a premed student at Johns Hopkins, Alexander Blair," she said, sounding rushed.

I was not certain how I was supposed to react to this news. There was a moment of uncomfortable silence.

"Gabby, dear, are you still on the line?" I could hear Selena inquiring.

196

"Yes, Selena I was just curious why I am being included in this group," I asked reluctantly.

"I have decided my darling that the time has come for you to be introduced to the elite. Consider it your coming out party. These gentlemen, all of them, can change your life. And God knows you deserve a change."

I could not argue with her logic. I did need a change. The only good news was, that since all the drama was centered on my love life, my scholastic grades had soared. Currently I was fifth in my class academically. If I continued on this path, I would graduate with honors. At least my education was moving in the right direction.

"I do appreciate all that you have done for me Selena. I am anxious to meet your friends. I won't ever embarrass you."

"Oh my Gabby, I am never worried about that. I just want you to be among a group that could lead you to whatever you want to accomplish. These gentlemen have keys to doors that can open your future. " She said.

Selena was referring to my latest aspiration, about Law school. It was be something I was considering after Oxford. There was no definite decision, yet, however.

The thought of being a lawyer in Washington DC did appeal to me. What I was not ready for was Alex Blair. Native Son, of Louisville, Kentucky. Heir to the Blair Equestrian fortune, with a bloodline that dates back to Prime Ministers of England. Closer to home, this family breeds horses that not only compete in the Kentucky Derby, but have won Triple Crowns.

I never expected that not only would this southern gentleman melt the Ice Princess, but he would lift me into a world that I only fantasized about in classic novels.

Chapter 22

Consciousness is an end in itself. We torture ourselves getting somewhere and when we get there it is nowhere, for there is nowhere to get to. - DH Lawrence

Caden Cassidy 1969

Returning to Savannah, I had hoped would help me forget Gabby, and move on with my life in a new direction. What I never did expect or foresee, was that Savannah ran through Gabby's veins.

Those months we spent together in Georgetown, could have been right here as well. It wasn't long after I arrived here, that I regretted my decision. Oh, there was no doubt that I was in love with Gabby, but I never realized how strong that love was until years later.

Like Savannah, Gabby is a quintessential Southern Belle, with the genuine charm of a smooth glass of fine Sherry, the strength of an ancient magnolia tree, and the radiance of a painter's palette, that softens and glows without overpowering.

How could I ever escape her beguiling presence in a city that dares you to explore wisteria draped gardens, in secret passages along golden marshes and bustling waterfronts. Even little six-year-old Gracie, who died of pneumonia and is buried in Bonaventure cemetery, has a spirit that is said to linger around the old Polaski hotel. I walk past that statue and something draws me to it. I fantasize that Gabby, perhaps resembles her as a child, with the long hair and slender fingers. Or maybe even, it is the daughter that we will never conceive together.

There is no peaceful place in the city, or even in my solitude; and so the years continue to move on with no reprieve for this dead soul. A pawn in someone else's chess game is indeed a humbling experience. What I did discover, was that relationships can be extremely complicated.

The unwritten rules are not always practical or black-and-white. And by the time that I figured out all the turns and twists, I no longer cared about when or what might happen.

Living together as an unmarried couple was still considered radical by many people, but it was beginning to be a normal transition before marriage. To me, it seemed like a safe haven. I never really had a chance to experience living with Gabby, but for some unknown reason I still believe that eventually we would have gotten married after college.

Now that Kaitlyn and I have been dating for six months, it seems that everyone just expects that the next step will be a proposal. Everyone, that is but me.

My parents, insisted that I meet this" very nice Irish Catholic girl," that had recently moved to the neighborhood. The word "nice" usually is a red flag that the girl is not a keeper most of the time. However, to keep mom and dad quiet, I always agreed on one date. I was pleasantly surprised when I met Kaitlyn. She was very attractive, intelligent, and quite witty.

At first, our dates were just a fun diversion from my melancholy attitude about life. Once I realized that my plans to attend the University of Georgia would have to be postponed, because my mom and dad were getting too old to run the deli by themselves, my goals started to change.

With that new reality check and recognizing that Kaitlyn and I shared many of the same interests, it became much easier to suggest that Kailtlyn and I move in together. *Sometimes everything has to be chiseled across the heavens in one long flowing line before you can realize the truth written inside of you.*

The very first time Kailtlyn and I had sex, I was pleasantly surprised how much this "good Catholic girl " knew about pleasing me. There was even a good chance that in time, Gabby would be just a memory of my reckless youth.

It was 1969 and the Beatles had just released their eleventh album called, "Abbey Road". I remember, distinctly, walking past the local music store, downtown, on the way to deposit a check in the bank next door. That was when I stopped suddenly and stared at the giant poster that read, Abbey Road, and immediately I thought that someone had forgotten the **G**.

Abby with a **G** was still playing havoc with my gray matter, although most the time I was able to control it from embarrassing me. Like some kind of mystical vibe, I was being drawn into the store to hear this album.

[*Because the world is round it turns me on. The wind keeps me high; your love is new but it makes me blue; the sky alone makes me cry, just because it blows my mind.*

And then I heard "Something "and I almost lost it right there. It was all that I had been fighting to hold back for the last two years, captured in the lyrics by George Harrison on this new track, called of course, "Abby Road".

I of course, saw it as missing a **G**. I must've spent three hours in that listing booth just mesmerized by the words. Then I did something insanely stupid. I bought the album, took it to my house, and used a sledgehammer to break it into as many minute pieces as possible. That next evening, I went to Kaitlyn's house and asked her to marry me.

Six months later, while I was waiting for my beautiful bride to reach the altar, I felt in my pocket the ring that Selena had given me several years ago in Alexandria. When I proposed to Kaitlyn, I knew I could not give her Selena's ring. And even at this very moment, as stunning as Kaitlyn was walking down the aisle, I knew that I could never love her like I still love Gabby.

Somehow I just knew that one day that ring, still in my pocket, would eventually be on the right finger of the right woman.

Only Selena recognized and admired the other "ring " that Kaitlyn was proudly showing off at the reception.

Selena caught my attention while holding Kaitlyn's left hand and nodded discreetly at me, but I understood clearly the message that she was sending me.

Shortly after our marriage Ma and Pa decided to retire in Florida and leave the business to me. Kaitlyn was a great asset and business manager. After some wise investments I decided to buy the lot next-door to the deli and open a local Irish pub called the Molly McGee.

It became my preoccupation. I was determined to make it the most popular bar in the city. For the first time in many years I was having fun creating and personalizing The Molly, named after Gabby's best friend of course, began to be a memory house of Gabby.

First I asked a friend I knew, that was working on animated characters, to stencil several Irish turtle with a shelalee, wearing a fisherman's hat, and carrying four leaf clovers. Of course, no one but I knew the significance of this. Turtle, was an endearing name Gabby used to call me, when we made love, because I moved slow and allowed her to enjoy every moment. Now, these charming Irish turtles were conversational pieces that everyone noticed.

Next, there was a special champagne cocktail that I asked my bartender to create called the Gabriella Enigma. It became a favorite of the local ladies, but the bartender wouldn't even tell me what the recipe was.

Finally, in memory of all the times Gabby would leave me notes that said "I love you" in various languages, I had those same words posted throughout the bar. Sometimes, they would appear on the menus, some were written on the bar and others on the wooden tables.

And, of course, I cannot forget the Abby Road Album cover that I placed next to the Jim Bean. I had commissioned a local artist who frequented the Molly, to take the famous cover and create a framed picture. She included the letter **G** crossed out, and embellished the remaining letters with rhinestones.

Over the years I had really hoped that maybe on a visit home to her parents, or a class reunion, Gabby would recognize the name of the bar and just wander in. But, as time went by, I resolved myself that this would never happen. Even, my attempt to locate Molly was futile. At least my financial situation was stable. Both the deli and the pub assured Kaitlyn and I that we would be solvent for the rest of our lives.

It is really difficult to say that Kaitlyn and I ever drifted apart after 35 years of marriage, because there really wasn't ever anything to drift apart from.

After three years of marriage we had twin boys. Our lives from that point on revolved around their sports, academic achievements, camping trips and family vacations. Finally, the boys were grown with their own lives to pursue. On the outside we were the model for the modern family. Indiscreetly, we continued to live our lives somewhere between unbeing and being, caught in a form of limitation, without a desire to really admit that whatever was once, if ever, at all, was now dormant.

There was always an uncomfortable sense that something was lacking; incomplete, not enough. And then, it happened. At the breakfast table, Kaitlyn started to read out loud to me an article on the third page. It was about a local lady, from right here in Savannah, who was showcasing her art in a prestigious Paris gallery.

"Listen to this Caden. 'Molly McGee' native of Savannah, Georgia is displaying her latest local paintings in a Paris gallery. Most of her objects depict her hometown and portraits that capture the quaint American spirit.'

I almost spit out my morning coffee, when I hear Molly's name.

"Let me see that article, Kaitlyn." I practically rip the paper out of her hands.

"Isn't that a curious coincidence that her name is the same as our pub, Caden?" I could tell by the tone of her voice that Kaitlyn was suspicious.

"Was she your old flame, Caden?" she asked me directly.

I ignore her question, and smile like I haven't in years. In the paper is a picture of Molly. Her strawberry blonde hair, cut short, she still looks the same. In her right hand is a portrait of a young woman with her long dark hair, slightly tinted with blonde streaks being blown by the wind as she frolics in the sandy beach in front of a lighthouse in the background. There is no doubt that this is Gabby. My Gabby! I finally answer Kaitlyn's question, without taking my eyes off of Gabby.

"No Kaitlyn, my darling, she was just a dear friend of the family and I thought the name was catchy and very Irish."

Kaitlyn seemed to be satisfied with that explanation, which was by most accounts the truth. What she would never know, was the joy I was feeling came from now knowing how to find Gabby. I knew that Molly would have that answer. If I needed to fly to Paris to find out where Gabby is, I would do that too. This would be my mission, and yes maybe my obsession. All I knew was that I had to talk to Gabby one last time. What would happen after that would be up to the fates.

CHAPTER 23

Dreams pass into the realm of action. Action stems the dream again; and the independence produces the highest form of living. - Anais Nin

Gabby 1969

The first time that Alex and I made love, it was raw, tender, and zesty, but far too fast. At the ripe age of nineteen, with only two other sexual experiences, I obviously was not a valid critic.

What I was able to realize is that Jake took me past this hemisphere. He produced inside of me a light so transparent, so powerful that the Aurora borealis would look pale in comparison. He was my holy grail; the cause for my pain, and the only cure for that pain was him.

When Jake left me on the precipice, it was Caden that caught me. Those very short three months with him, I learned how to give and take without guilt, or fear. Our relationship was like a Chinese Lantern festival. It celebrated the future, acknowledged the past and released the lighted lamps into the heavens, carrying away past demons. Without knowing it, that release from Caden and Jake led me to my formal meeting with Alex Blair.

He was, without a doubt, a gorgeous specimen of a man, who unfortunately, lacked the intimacy gene. This definitely was not due to the size of his manly shaft, nor was it because he wasn't skilled at using it. Alex was a polished master at finishing, with an impressive amount of ammo. I never felt physically unsatisfied, and on those rare occasions that I desired more, he always delivered. It was more of the afterglow that never happened, like both Jake and Caden were able to leave me with.

Those mental images that Jake permanently branded in my mind would never be erased by any other man. And Caden, well he made our love making seem effortless, spontaneous, natural, pure, and intense, every time.

What Alex did contribute, was a new beginning at. A time when I had really thought that there would never be one. Similar to Jake, he would take control, even in the beginning.

As Selena and I approached the Round Robin Bar, at the Willard Hotel, all three gentlemen rose from their seats. The youngest of them, I presumed, was Alex Blair. Immediately I was impressed with his black ebony hair, and steel grey eyes the color of polished silver. He reminded me of a combination George Hamilton and Warren Beatty.

"Miss Gabriella Girard. Pleased to make your acquaintance." His arm outstretched, he takes my hand firmly and draws me closer to him.

"I am Alex Blair, at your service," he said while pulling out my chair next to his. His eyes have never left mine. Trying to maintain my composure, without looking overly anxious at this southern gentleman, I merely nod my head in appreciation.

Selina was already engaged in full conversation across the table. I recognized Dr. Jacoby from last year's Thanksgiving dinner, and presumed that the remaining elderly man must be Alex's famous father, Randall Blair. Just as I was beginning to acclimate myself with group, waiting for an appropriate time to join the conversation, Selina announced that I was an English major at Georgetown University with aspirations to continue my fellowship at Oxford.

"My dear, have you ever been across the pond?" Mr., Blair inquired, while he was sipping his dry martini. Never hearing the term 'pond' used to describe the Atlantic Ocean, I hesitated before I answered. It must have been enough for Alex to recognize that I was uncomfortable. He gallantly came to my rescue.

"Dad, really....is it necessary to drill Gabriella at this moment about her previous traveling experiences. After all, she doesn't need to have visited Great Britain to attend Oxford," he said, reaching under the table for my hand that was slightly trembling.

The smile, that accompanied his strong hold on my hand suggested that he would not allow this conversation to. Get out of control. It was the first time in two years that I felt safe.

Three months later, I was invited to Blair's Hampton Estate for an intimate cocktail party with their closest one hundred friends. It was going to be a weekend soire, that began on Friday evening with cocktails and ending with a Sunday champagne brunch on the veranda, surrounded by lush gardens and the Atlantic Ocean.

Naturally, Aunt Selena was there, escorted by Dr. Jacoby, but most of the other guests were part of the elite horse breeders from Kentucky Intermingling with this group were several powerful Washington DC politicians, and of course a fair amount of young attractive socialites and DC interns.

It was an interesting group that masses me feel extremely self-conscious and uncomfortable. It reminded me very much of the high school cliques that I despised at Savannah; pretentious, bogus , and calculating. The food, however, was undeniably the most impressive spread that I had ever seen.

It started with finger sandwiches to red and black bowls of caviar. On the beach, directly in the back yard, a clam bake with corn on the cob was being prepared. For those who preferred the cool marble floors inside, there was rack of lamb and lobster thermadore. And if that was not enough, hot dogs and hamburgers served with SKYLINE chili, flown in from Cincinnati was always a popular addition.

Cristal Champagne and Dom Perignon were paired with barrels of every imaginable beer, malt and ales from around the world.

For those guests who preferred a cocktail, three bars were arranged throughout the compound. I would be remiss to say that this entire Gala Event was beyond my imagination. It was my first, but not last encounter with what the Blair fortune and power meant.

I had found a few moments to escape from the crowds. Standing outside on the balcony watching the dolphins frolicking in the afternoon, was almost surreal. That was when I saw Alex run up the stairs. His strong, golden brown, tan arms were embracing my bare shoulders lovingly. He had left early that morning on a sailing excursion with a group from the local Yacht Club. Our first kiss of the day made my body tingle, just slightly. I was careful not to show too much public affection among the surrounding guests.

Although we were practically living together by now, it was made clear to Alex, that while at the Estate we would have our own separate rooms. What happened after we retired for the evening was inconsequential, but appearances must be kept civil.

"How is my baby this morning?" Alex whispered in my ear. "Did you fall back to sleep when I left before sunrise?" I could feel his warm breath on my neck, and when he started to nibble on my ear I began to rub my body as close to his cock as I could.

He was wearing a pair of cream colored linen pants and looked like he had just stepped out of a GQ billboard. His erection was obvious by now.

"You know how I hate it when you leave me before I wake up, babe," I said, reaching down to stroke him, out of sight.

"Want to find an empty closet where we can play hide and seek for a while. Just the two of us." This time, he didn't seem to care who saw us. His mouth was own mine and our tongues were ready to explore. Just as I was about to whisk him away to the pool cabana, an entourage of bikini clad starlets interrupted us.

"Come on Alex. You promised to play sand volleyball." The obvious leader of the group said, as she pulled him away from me.

"Gabby. Meet us down by the beach. Where the tide pools are. It will be fun...I promise, only one game," he was yelling as he left. And then he was gone.

It was something that I was learning to deal with. Even in the sand playing volleyball, not one hair was out of place. His long, strong muscular legs, naturally tanned, decades before any of us worried about skin cancer from the sun. Shirtless, his upper torso begged to be stroked, and fondled with wet kisses. He had lived in this limelight his entire life.

"That is why I am so in love with you Gabby. You are real. These other Barbie dolls have never attracted me. I have been waiting forever for someone that I can share ideas with, not just the bed with," he said.

Alex was always trying to reassure me that I never had to worry about competing with any of his many admirers. "Believe me Gabby they are all plastic. In time, you will understand that all of this hype is just a facade. At the end of the show, I only want you."

It was no secret that I felt uncomfortable in this setting. When I started considering that people really live this way, it made me reconsider my feelings for Alex. These parties just may be the red flag I need before I get too deeply committed.

Ophelia was the one, this time that I relied on. Ophelia had grown up with Alex in Kentucky and ran in the same circle of friends. Later, her parents moved to Sedona, Arizona because of the climate and to open their famous spa and wellness center.

Many people assumed that Alex and Ophelia would eventually marry and produce the most remarkably, beautiful offspring's and then rule the world. Unfortunately, no one bothered to check with Ophelia and Alex, who were more like siblings than every potential lover.

When Ophelia realized it was the Alex she knew, that I was dating, she is assured me that, "there were more sparks between a deer and a tiger than between Alex and me. And by the way I would be the tiger. " We both laughed at the dominating image that she flaunted so well.

"Don't misunderstand me, Gabby. Alex is a great guy, with a pedigree of positive attributes that any woman, including you should appreciate," she added. "He is just not that wild and crazy guy, or girl, that makes the hair on my neck stand up when he comes close, or makes my nipples hard when I am next to him."

She waited for my reaction. That was fine with me. Alex Blair didn't have to blow any of my whistles, or start any sparks. I have had enough of that kind of excitement forever. And if anyone is keeping score in the romance game, I am losing 0 to 2.

Someone steady, wealthy, loyal and permanent, fits very nicely on my agenda for a lifetime partner. Marriage would be just another fringe benefit. After my three-month tumultuous romantic interlude with Caden, I was ready to admit that he had been my sensual soul mate. He was more than a passionate lover. He and I shared some emotional tempo that I regret will never be the same. I still do not know why, but we fit together like a precise jigsaw puzzle.

Since I was now in a place that I could reflect on my past relationships, I was determined not to make the same mistake with Alex. The metaphysical poet, John Donne in his poem, 'A Valediction Forbidding Mourning' eloquently compares a compass to that of two lovers; if they be two, they are as two, stiff, twin compasses are two; thy soul the fixed foot, makes no show to move; it leans and hardens after it, and grows erect as it comes home.

I knew that however desperate I was to leave the past behind Jake's shadow would somehow always be with me. The real question was; would I allow Alexander Blair to challenge that apparition?

CHAPTER 24

"And so, with the sunshine and the great bursts of leaves growing on the trees, just as things grow in fast movies, just as things grow in fast movies, I had that familiar conviction that life was beginning over again with the summer." - The Great Gatsby

Gabby and Alex July 4, 1969

Bartholomeu Gosnold, a British fisherman, in 1602, discovered an island, as t as the legend goes. He chose to name that new island after his first born daughter, Martha. There were no vineyards at that time, but there were wild grapes, we providing the necessary inspiration for what would later be known as Martha's Vineyard.

I wanted to learn as much as possible of this whimsical island. It had captured my attention, ever since President Kennedy and his family had been featured in Life Magazine, before the tragic assassination. What I recognized immediately, was that it was less sophisticated than the Hamptons. And yet, stunning, in a delicate, cozy way that I preferred.

The one hundred and twenty-four pristine miles of tidal shoreline, attracted a vibrant group of artists, writers and musicians. It was also, a cultural magnet for the rich and famous. One of the unique features and charm in the village, was that there were no chain stores, restaurants, or hotels to distract from the natural beauty.

Even prior to the Kennedy Compound, there were high profile people, like Elizabeth and Ryan Reynolds, who owned oils rigs not only in Beaumont Texas, but currently investing in a crazy business opportunity known only as

TAPS (Trans Alaska Pipeline System). According to Alex, the man was a genius. But, I personally thought the idea of pumping oil underground from Alaska to Texas was impossible.

Nevertheless, the Reynolds we're hosting an anniversary celebration at their estate on July 4, 1969, for Alex' parents. It was apparently going to b the seasons highlight event.

Another historical moment that caught my interest, that I read in The Vineyard Gazette occurred on August 3, 1941. FDR decided to get some R&R (Rest and Relaxation) on board the USS Potomac docked at New London, Connecticut.

After engaging in a few hours of fishing, with the Prince and Princess of Norway, who just happened to be cruising on the high seas at the time, he received a White House wire.

"Going around the south end of Cuddfhunk, Island, we anchored in the midst of seven US Warships at about 11pm, at Menemsha Blight, on the western end of Martha's Vineyard." End of telegram.

On August 5, The Vineyard Gazette ran an article, speculating that the Warships were there doing military maneuvers.

No one ever discovered until years later, that the President was transferred from The Potomac, to a flagship, headed to the coast of Newfoundland in absolute secrecy,

FDR had his first meeting with Winston Churchill to draft the Atlantic Charter, that later became the basis for the United Nations.

"I bring you to one of thc most idyllic places that I know on earth. We stay at a villa, just steps from the beach, and you have your nose in the historical archives even before daylight," Alex said.

I was curled up on the overstuffed coach, wrapped in a terry cloth bathrobe, with my hair in a towel turban, still engrossed in my reading.

Alex moved closer to me, now, and removed the article from my hand, to get my attention.

"Do I have to hide all printed words from you to notice me?" He said towering over me. I could tell that he was teasing, but I also knew by now that he did not like being ignored.

Before I had an opportunity to respond, he had lifted me off the couch and was twirling me around.

"Alex...put me down, you Brut," I was demanding, but laughing at the same time.

"No, not until you put down those papers and promise to go with me to watch the sunrise, NOW!"

"Okay....Okay. Alright. Maybe I was a little over grossed in the reading. A walk on the beach is a very good compromise. " I conceded.

Alex looked impeccable, as usual. His white cargo shorts, aqua marine Ralph Lauren polo shirt were perfectly matched. The cologne he wore was a blend of sandalwood, oak, lavender and jasmine. Not every man could pull off wearing that scent. But, then again Alex was not just any other man. He was nearly perfect. Almost too perfect.

People admired us as a couple, yet I always felt that Alex was the star attraction, and that I should be grateful that he chose me. Like my role in his life, was an accessory.

None of this was caused by Alex. He never had an ego problem. It was always me. My insecurities, I had determined was just a part of my DNA.

"Remember Gabby that the whole point of us staying here at the Sandpiper Villa was to seclude ourselves from those annoying crowds, and unreasonable sleeping arrangements, my parents insist on. Not to seclude ourselves from each other." He was stroking my hair with his long, perfectly shaped fingers that were meant for a surgeon or pianist.

"You are absolutely correct, my love" I replied. My hands together like I was praying,

"Can you ever forgive me?" I leaned my head on his chest, like a cat begging to be pet. "I will only forgive you if we make it to the giant rock that we found the other afternoon...you remember.... the one near Lambert's Cove? We

MUST be there by sunrise or the Pirates will capture us," he said.

This was the Alex that I was falling in love with. The laid back version that could make me spontaneously smile at any time. The man who swept me off my feet, but was willing to listen to my opinions, even if he disagreed.

"And don't forget your sea shell bucket. I left it right here on the porch, behind the chair swing."

He was talking to me from the front door, as I rushed to put my swimsuit on, under my shorts and tee shirt. On the porch, Alex was holding a wicker lunch basket, that no doubt, had warm croissants, quiche,
and fresh fruit, prepared early this morning by Maggie, our domestic cook, who was sent over by the Reynolds, because I am sure they thought that I was
incompetent at such chores. And, they were correct.
As I reached down for the tin bucket, I noticed for the first time, a turtle painted on the front. Like a lightning bolt, immediately Caden's image shot through my mind. Up to this point, Alex was able to preoccupy me with so many new experiences, glamour and glitter, that I was no longer the naive girl that Caden had swept away.

I was now Bathsheba, Thomas Hardy's young heroine, in his novel, **Far from the Maddening Crowd**. I wasn't inheriting any money from a wealthy uncle, but I was certainly surrounded by an abundance of wealth. Alex had
lavished me with so many extravagant trips, meals, and social events that remembering my humble background was nearly impossible.

I was thankful that the Jakc's flashbacks had ended and with the exception of just now, Caden's memory was finally in the past.

"Gabby? Are you still following behind, me? We need to make it there before sunrise."

Alex was insisting, again. Why was this so important? I had no idea.

"I am on my way, babe. Right behind you." I slipped the bucket handle with the turtle image behind me, and forced the Caden memory back to the past where he belonged.

The grains of sand this early in the morning felt cool on my bare feet. In just a few hours, the heat would penetrate through this beach. Then you could see barefoot people hopping from one shadow spot to another trying to escape the inferno.

At this early break of day, only the sea gulls soaring around searching for an early breakfast were easily visible. Further down, the sandpipers, with their tiny, yellow -green legs. and high pitched creep call, are hunched over like little elderly people, probing for crustaceans, insects and other invertebrates.

Thus far, we are the only human specimen for miles around. Further down, we continue to walk, with just a mellow moon in the sky; it resembles more twilight than sunrise.

I stop for a moment when I notice that above us on the cliff, is a nearly completed multi-level home. Using the binoculars that Alex gave me, specifically, for bird watching, I can see Chinese lanterns slightly glowing, perhaps left over from an evening party.

"That house you are spying on..it is Carly Simons new abode, Gabby. I heard some locals say that it looks like a fairytale cottage, with four bedrooms, five bathrooms, and five thousand square feet of living space," Alex said without stopping to observe with me.

"I like her idea of what a cottage should look like," I added, still staring through the binoculars.

"Maybe we can have Martha bake some Alice B Tokias cannabis brownies, and stop by with a welcome gift from us", Alex sounded perfectly serious.

But, I refused to put the binoculars down.

"Really, honey.... you can put the binoculars down. My parents and I both know Carley, or at least we have met her socially. Her father and my Dad had some business deal together. Did you know that her Dad was the first half of Simon and Shuster? He died a few years ago, in 1960 I believe. Anyway, I am sure if we were to bring her a housewarming gift she would remember me," he said.

It was remarks like this that made me question when Alex was serious. In 1972, a few years later, Carly Simon recorded, "You're so Vain" became a mega hit. Everyone was trying to determine whom she was referring to. That was when Alex claimed it was him, that she wrote about.

I naturally thought he was joking, but Carly and he were the same age, and it could be possible.

Finally, Alex had reached our destination and was arranging the patchwork blanket neatly on the sand. He then sat back and watched me gather my shells.

The closer I moved to the ocean I could feel the waves kissing my feet It was so comforting that I could have stayed here forever.

When I turned toward the seashore to see how far I had wandered, I realized that Alex was signaling me to return. The sunrise was about to begin its grand entrance.

"Hey, Princess...come share with me the treasures that Neptune sent you." I skipped over to Alex, careful not to get sand on the quilt, and sat down Indian style, legs crossed, facing him.

Nearby, Alex grabbed the Frisbee that he always brought with him to play with the local chocolate Labrador Retriever, that lived nearby.

"Okay, now let's see what you found," he said emptying the bucket into the inside of the Frisbee.

This brought back fond memories of when I was six years' old and my Baba would take me to Tybee beach during the summer. Those wonderful memories seemed so very long ago.

As I began to shift through the sand, buried between a chipped periwinkle, underneath a spindle and harp shell, I could see a sparkling object. Most of the times, these would be shards of glass that retained its. glitter even after the salt water has made the surface smooth. Just as the sun was rising, I could now see that the sparkle was not glass, but a massive diamond ring. When I finally was able to separate it from the other shells, I realized it was an exquisite emerald cut diamond ring, at least five carats. Surrounding the diamond were opulent sapphires, the color of the Mediterranean Ocean.

"Oh, my God, Alex!" I jumped up and started to look around the beach.

"Someone must have lost this ring while recently walking on the beach! We need to find the owner as soon as possible ...She must be going crazy out of her mind, Alex," I was talking so fast that Alex finally grabbed my arms gently, and made me sit down on the quilt.

"Let me see the ring, Gabby," he said. I followed his instructions, trusting he would know how to find the owner. That was when he stood up.

With one knee now bent down on the sand, he looked directly into my eyes, and said, "Gabby, this is YOUR RING. And, if you accept it and promise to always be mine, we will never have to watch a sunrise or sunset by ourselves again. Please Gabby....will you marry me." Before I could even register what was happening, the ring was on my finger and it fit perfectly. For the very first time in my life, I was speechless.

After what must have been a fairly long time, Alex asked again, "Well, Gabby? Will you be my wife?"

My world had just stopped. Jake must have by this time married Isabella Caden was with someone named Kailtlyn, living in Savannah. And, the most eligible bachelor on this island, perhaps even the country was asking me to marry him. What was I waiting for? Why was I suddenly crying?

Alex finally broke the uncomfortable silence, "I can only hope that those tears of joy, Gabby." I was trembling, while he was holding me in his arms.

"Just tell me yes, sweetheart, and I will always be here for you." He may not have even understood at the time, but those were the only words I needed to hear from him.

"YES! YES! Of course I will marry you." I was taking deep breaths between my yeses, but there was no doubt in my voice.

"You had me scared there for a few moments. But, I promise you, you will never regret this."

Two weeks later, Ted Kennedy drove his Oldsmobile off of a wooden bridge in Chappaquiddick Island, with Mary Joe Kopechne, and left her to drown in the river, while he escaped unharmed.

July 8, 1969 the first US troops withdrew from Vietnam.

July 20, 1969 Neil Armstrong takes his first step on the moon.

August 8, 1969 The Beatles, Abbey Road has a photo shoot on a zebra crossing as their cover album.

July 4, 1969 Gabriella Gerard accepts engagement proposal from Alexander Blair, son of multi-millionaire Kentucky Equestrian breeders, William and Eleanor Blair.

CHAPTER 25

The loneliest moment in someone's life, is when their whole world falls apart, and all they can do is stare blankly. - F. Scott Fitzgerald

Gabby and Alex. July 4, 1969

Part Two of this very long and monumental day came while I was preparing for the Blair's Anniversary Bash. Sitting in front of my vanity, staring at myself in the mirror, I suddenly became very aware what I had just committed to. Soon I was to realize that it was not only a marriage proposal, as much as a binding contract. Like acquiring a new acre of prime land, or a prize breeding mare .

At this time I never considered myself an asset, but it would soon become clear that my obligation was not only to Alex, but to the entire Blake Estate. Like Spanish moss absorbs life from other sources, the Blairs were ruthless negotiators that were known to suck the life from anyone who opposed them.

There was still time to change my mind. Alex was not Jake; nor was he Caden. As early as fourteen, I knew that I was madly in love with Jake. To be perfectly honest, I still loved Jake.

With Caden, the attraction at first was entirely sexual. That, however, grew into an intense body and mind experience. Not even Jake was able to make me feel as complete and yet independent at the same time. We were, without a doubt, connected.

But, was that love, or lust? What Alex offered me, that neither Jake not Caden could, was security. Alex promised to never leave me, and that I believed one hundred. percent .

He was also, generous, easy going, cautious , and sexually satisfying. If I had met Alex before Caden, there would be no doubts. But, was I in love with Alex? And, did it even matter?

Maybe I should have been more like Ophelia , and slept with more men. Perhaps there still was someone out there who had the best attributes of Jake, Caden , and Alex but, I did not have the patience or energy to continue that Quixotic pursuit.

When in doubt, turn to Molly. Her advice was always practical, except when it involved her own choices. A few years ago, she withdrew from Savannah Art Institute, packed a small duffel bag, and purchased a one way ticket to Paris with a small amount of money that she had earned as a waitress the previous summer. Nobody even knew that she had a passport.

When I enquirer as to how she intended to live in one of the most expensive places on earth, her response was classic Molly,

"Marie Antoinette said 'let them eat cake' and I have enough for that, at least for a short time. Sometimes, Gabby, you just have to live Carpe Diem."

As it turned out, after only a few weeks, she met John Paul, at a local bistro. His sister, Gigi was conveniently in need of a roommates.

Consequently, she introduced her to an affluent art gallery, where she worked Monday through Friday and part time as a travel guide for the Louvre on the weekends. During her down time, Molly took art lessons and painted chalk portraits of tourists on the Seine River. While Molly's dream was in full production, mine was still a work in progressed.

During a surgeon symposium while Alex was in his last year of medical school, he met Molly in Paris. It was only six months after we had started dating . Since I was in the middle of midterms, I could not accompany him. Molly was very impressed with Alex, like anyone who ever met him.

But, then when he took her to dinner at Maxims, one of the most internationally well known restaurants in the world, he won her heart. It was not only a symbolic place for Art Nouveau but an artists haven as well. The fact that Alex selected Maxims, a place known for showcasing such French artists as Galli, Guimard, Mayoroule, and Tiffany endeared him to Molly instantly.

Dragonflies , butterflies and exotic birds, surrounded by red poppies, lilies , irises and even chestnut leaves are ornately represented on the walls, windows, and lamps.

Molly would never been able to afford such an extravagant place for dinner, and Alex was fully aware of this. After that visit, Molly could not stop talking about Alex. It was like she had become his own personal advocate.

""Gabby, it is about time that you came to your senses and are appreciating the finer things in life....and Alex Blair is REAL FINE."

That was Molly's reaction when I called her at 3:00am her time. Receiving Molly's blessing was more important than even the Pope's. It meant that my life's script was now moving in the right direction. The only reservations that I still had was if the leading man would be the right one.

"Gabby....sweetheart? You do remember that we will need to at least make an appearance at the Reynolds Fourth of July picnic. How long will it take you to get ready?" Alex was persistent but never demanding.

"Not long Alex. But, I have to let my Mom and Dad know about out engagement, before they read it in some paper, or magazine." I was trying not to yell, but I was upstairs and Alex, was of course ready and waiting for me downstairs.

I was always trying to be as punctual as him, but, for whatever the circumstance he would always be waiting for me. There were times that my punctuality became a contentious subject.

Unfortunately, my folks must have been celebrating, with the rest of Savannah, at the local All State Parade, neighborhood BBQ's , and swimming parties, because there was no answer. As much as I wanted to be the first one to personally deliver this message, my first priority now was finding a suitable outfit to wear for this party. After staring at what I brought with me for longer than I needed to,

I settled on the only suitable, floral, spaghetti strap summer dress that I owned. I had been searching a year for a comfort zone around the Blairs and their friends. No matter how much I tried, it was useless to believe that I was anything more than simply, Gabby from Savannah.

For some very strange reason, that I was not privy to, Alex thought I was marriage material. It was only a few weeks ago., when I was told about this anniversary celebration, that I even contemplated how marriage "forever " actually lasted. That was when I asked Alex,

"Do you think your parents are really happy?"

"That is an interesting question, Gabby. I suppose they are. I mean, they are celebrating forty years of marriage," he replied.

I should have realized then, that Alex and the Blairs measure value on either money or years. Anything else is worthless or time consuming. Eleanor Blair was the only one that sometimes seemed uncomfortable with those standards.

There was no doubt that she had a commanding presence; her voice resonated money when she spoke. It sounded like an arrangement of musical notes, carefully orchestrated to produce a symphony of anticipation.

Looking directly at Eleanor's face, there was a definite melancholy glamour that resonated a different past . Her glistening eyes, still revealed the traces of a mischievous girl, perhaps full of life and wonder, not that far removed from myself. What was very obvious, was that Alex was a replica of his mother.

A strange and mysterious bond that was so strong that no woman, and certainly not I, could ever change that.

Perhaps, the woman Eleanor was, is partly what attracted Alex to me in the beginning . It also may have given him the patience to overlook many of my idiosyncrasies, and for Eleanor to graciously accept me into her family.

As I got to know Eleanor better, it became obvious to me that she was more like a "poor little rich girl" caught in a conundrum, with no escape. Later, I learned from Alex that, "Both Mom and Dad come from inherited wealth, but Dad brought the blood line and aristocratic pedigree."

"Do you think that they were in love Alex, or was it a union based on convenience?" I asked, honestly curious.

Alex was in the bathroom shaving, during this conversation, when he stopped what he was doing and looked at me confused

"I never have really thought about it. But, I do know that I love you, and that is really what is important. " He said this and patted my ass at the same time.

"Gabby? Oh, Gabby." It was Alex again from downstairs.

"We need to arrive at the Randolph's BEFORE the firecrackers go off." He reminded me again.

On the drive over I expressed once again how self conscious I was around this crowd.I knew by now that this "picnic" was not going to be like the normal, potato salad, hamburger, hot dog event I was used to.

No matter how much Alex attempted to ease my mind, it always sounded patronizing.

"You need to get over these panic attacks every time there is a social gathering. There are many people that you have already met at The Hamptons and Louisville . They all love you, because they know you are my girl."

If Jake or Caden had ever suggested that people accepted me only because of them, I would have been inconsolable .At this point, it seemed petty to even point that out to Alex. Maybe , Molly was right. It was time to be realistic.

When we finally arrived at the Randolph's, everyone was outside sitting at round tables with white canopies. The tables, naturally, were themed in red, white , and blue table cloths . Flickering lights , that looked like sparklers at each table were accentuated with mini American flags . The stars on the flags were glittering with small rhinestones.

All the guests had apparently completed their meal and were patiently waiting for the fireworks to begin shortly over the Atlantic Ocean. The grand finale, was a gigantic wedding tiered cake , also decorated with red, white and blue frosting and stars scattered randomly.

What caught my attention, for just a brief second, was that there were two brides and groom statues on the cake. But before I could examine the cake in more detail,

Alex was leading me to the bandstand where his father, Winston was standing holding a microphone.

Although I thought this was rather awkward I followed suit, obediently. Then from the corner of my eye, I caught Eleanor gliding over to stand next to me. Everything was happening so fast, that I felt like this was a staged performance, but I did not know what my lines would be.

Suddenly, I heard Winston speaking through the microphone to the entire audience. "Ladies and Gentleman. Please forgive me for interrupting this evenings festivities, for a very special announcement. At this time, I was nudging Alex, trying to indicate that we needed to find a table. Ignoring me, he finally said,

"It's fine Gabby. Just stand next to me and smile."

The next thing that I briefly remember, is Winston, leading us to the front of the stage and the band behind us playing, "Get me to the Church on time."

As that melody was playing confetti from somewhere began to fly all around us. Then the band stopped and Winston continued.

"I am pleased to announce, that our only son, Dr. Alex Blair, has proposed marriage to the magnificent Gabriella Girard, southern belle from Savannah, Georgia."

As the band began to play again, there were waiters at all the tables with champagne flutes and bottles of Dom Perignon being poured to everyone.

Then they all stood up, for the toast , while the sky lit up with fire crackers in n the shape of ariel shells, aqua shells, barrage blossoms, and comets so bright that I thought it would last forever. I was not sure how I felt about all of this attention or that The Blairs already knew that we were engaged.

Alex looked at me innocently, and shrugged his shoulders, like he was as surprised as I was. As soon as the fireworks ended, the flash bulbs started. The local newspaper as well as, several magazine photographers, were conveniently present to get their story. Standing next to the Blairs, my future in-laws, and Alex, hand in hand we lifted our arms in unison, above our heads. It reminded me of a political convention.

That was the moment that I knew my life would change permanently, I just never could imagine how drastically.

CHAPTER 26

*When power corrupts, poetry cleanses, for art establishes
the basic human truths which must serve as the touchstone
of our judgment.* - John F Kennedy

Gabby and Alex 1970

On February 8, 1967 Dust Commander was foaled. Dust
Storm was the dam and Bold Commander the sire. It was
noted that this new colt had a bloodline connected to
Nearco, one of greatest racehorses of the twentieth century.

Before Nearco became the patriarch of the most dominant sire line in Thoroughbred history, he retired unbeaten
in fourteen races. Nearly every Kentucky Derby winner is
linked to Nearco.

When Robert E. Lehmann, was searching for a race-
horse, he approached his close friend Winston Blair for advice. Blair introduced him to the Pullen Brothers, who
shared the Blair Equestrian Estate. Three years later Dust
Commander, who remained on the estate was ready to be
entered in The Kentucky Derby.

The only reason that any of this concerned me, is that
Eleanor Blair had insisted that our wedding date needed to
be compatible with the Derby schedule . Her rational, was
based on making it convenient for the invited guests, who
were also planning to attend the Derby. They could remain
in town, after the wedding and attend the remaining pre-
race social events.

"Alex, I know that your mother is planning the perfect
wedding, but why must she also pick the wedding date?
Why can't we just have a simple summer wedding," I asked,
for probably the tenth time.

"We have been over this many times before, Gabby. For me, the earlier the better. If there was any possible way we could elope I would do it. But you, and I both know that it would cause an avalanche of trouble in the Blair kingdom."

Alex had decided to begin his residency in Maryland and then transfer to Louisville soon after the wedding. I usually took the train after my last class on Thursday and would stay with Alex in his penthouse until late Monday afternoon.

It was a two and a half hour train ride, but lately Alex arranged a Town Car to pick me up and take me home. That made the commute fifty-five minutes or less, depending on the driver. This Friday, I was relaxing on a supple leather chaise, reading the latest New Yorker, and trying not to allow this wedding to make me miserable.

Alex could sense my frustration. He was buttoning his shirt when he just stopped. Then he was bent down, next to me snuggling and lifting my chin near his. Those steel grey eyes, were making me hot.

"Let me worry about my Mother. You are the Princess. Let everyone else take care of the details . All you ever need to do is be beautiful and smile. Really, Gabby....it is that easy." He ended this advise with a long kiss. The minty flavor of his tongue made my throat tingle. Instinctively, I began to unzip his slacks, and release his penis, hoping to prolong a few more minutes of playful sex.

He was panting, but managed to say, "Be a good girl Gabby, I have an important meeting with the Chief of Staff this morning."

But, by this time, I was on my knees, with only a tank top on and no panties. He could tell that I was disappointed, when I hissed at him, trying to lure him back. Then, when I thought that he was turning away, suddenly, his mouth managed to find my breasts. Within seconds my nipples were hard and my pussy was wet. My legs began to wrap themselves around his waist, and I was so ready for him, until he leaped up, zipped his slacks and raced to the door, without even looking back.

"Sorry, babe. I love you, but I HAVE to go, NOW." And, it was all over, just like that. Even moments like this it was difficult to stay angry at Alex. His simple logic was almost always right. He was not only an Adonis, but, he was also a brilliant surgeon.

Renowned specialists already were inviting him to join their practice. That confidence reminded me of Jake. Maybe, if I had been more confident I could have convinced him to change his mind about enlisting in the Marines. It was too late now to keep thinking of my insecurities. What I did know, was that these last six months had been the most serene and peaceful times of my life.

Then why was it now beginning to be stressful? Maybe it started when I realized that Dust Commander was predicted to win the Kentucky Derby. I couldn't ignore that he was born in the most devastating year of my life. Jake had nearly died in Vietnam. He became engaged to another woman. Then returned on New Year's Eve, only to assure me that we could never be together again. On the very same night, Caden Cassidy irrationally, or maybe rightly so , determined that our relationship should also end.

Perhaps I should chose to look at Dust Commander as a good omen. With his speed and agility he would overcome all the other contenders and win the Kentucky Derby. A love everlasting finale for us both.

Another required condition for our wedding to be spectacular, meant it must take place at Louisville, Kentucky, rather than Savannah, Georgia. Which ironically was the only thing that Eleanor and I agreed on. I had vowed never to return to Savannah, and I was committed to that pledge.

It was my Mother that became outraged.

"It makes no sense, Gabriella, that you get married in Louisville." It was the first time in eighteen years that I heard my mother call me by my formal name. "You grew up in Savannah."

This is your hometown. You are our only child; Our ONLY DAUGHTER." My mother was screaming into the phone, and I could sense her crying. Although I sympathized with her emotionally, Louisville was where Alex grew up, and he too was the Blairs only child.

"Mom, please, just try to be reasonable. I have told you many times that I will never return to Savannah . So, get that out of your mind . Once you meet Eleanor and hear what her plans for this wedding are, then you will understand that there is no other reasonable way," I said

It was not easy to convince my mom that the Blairs were like royalty in the state of Kentucky. Neither my parents nor I had ever been exposed to such opulence. There was a dead silence on the other end of the phone.

"Mom? You didn't hang up on me did you?"

"No Gabby, but I will not hide my disappointment. No boy should be that important that you allow him to dictate your life. This just isn't like you."

I wanted to respond by first pointing out that Alex is a man, not a boy. And, unfortunately, I allowed the only two other men to dictate my life.

Mom was right about one observation. I refused to remain the "Loser Gabby". Alex would be the one to change all of that.

"Mom, I have matured. I now know what I want. I am asking you to be happy for me, enjoy being the mother of the bride and celebrate my marriage to Alex. Can you just do that?" I said, pleading.

She at last, resolved it was a losing battle and accepted Winston and Eleanor's invitation to visit the ranch for the weekend. I realized that this was not easy for my mother to relinquish her wedding duties. But, by the end of her visit she had accepted all the terms that Eleanor would share with her, with the exception of the invitations. Mom and I would pick them out together, address the envelopes and have them postmarked from Savannah.

It was not until we sat down to complete this task that she realized how huge this wedding was going to be.

" There are over four hundred and fifty invitations, Gabby. That means at least four hundred guest, if you estimate fifty percent Surely, most will not show, I imagine?" She said.

"Oh, quite the contrary, Mom. I would not be surprised that some of these tickets will be scalped, to get into the reception. From what I hear, our wedding is being talked about as the event of the year. Only the Derby, might be bigger," I shared.

My mother and father, even after their weekend being catered by the Blairs, had no idea of the true significance of this families power, or their elite status.

Since graduation from Georgetown was only one week before my wedding, it was a great excuse to stay in DC while the plans were being finalized.

Thankfully, Eleanor had not hired a Father of the Bride to walk me down the aisle and she did "allow" me to select my brides maids. When I insisted that Molly had to be my Maid of Honor, she graciously took care of the airline expense. But, unfortunately, we had to use the measurements that she sent, and had little time for alterations. At that point I didn't care if she had to wear a gunny sac. All I cared about was that MY MOLLY was coming back.

Everything else was progressing like a Broadway play. There was no doubt that on Saturday, April 18, 1970, "opening night" all the players would be well rehearsed. The Seelbach Hotel, recognized as one of the first and finest American hotels was booked for our venue.

Not only did it capture the French Renaissance design of an old world grandeur of European hotels, but it also became immortalized by F.Scott Fitzgerald in his novel, **The Great Gatsby.** I, of course was familiar with that novel, and immediately began to consider any significant similarities between the characters and my personal life. In the novel,

Jay Gatsby, is obsessed with finding the love of his life, Daisy Fay. Unfortunately, he only spent a very brief time with her while he was on leave , from the Army., before, being sent to war.

Some critics noted that Fitzgerald chose Daisy's last name, Fay as an allusion for fairy, suggesting that she put a spell on Jay.

While Gatsby is at war,the extremely wealthy Tom Buchanan becomes enamored by Daisy. It is implied that he buys her love when he presents her with a strand of pearls valued at $100,000

I briefly look down at my enormous diamond engagement ring. Is it possible that I may be making the same mistake? Absolutely not.

Alex is nothing like Tom Buchanan, and there will never be a Jay Gatsby, determined to win my love at any cost. Neither, will there be a Benjamine Braddock, from the movie **The Graduate,** , running into the church at the last moment to prevent me from some life tragedy.

I refused to allow my mind to even suggest that my life is a sequel to **The Great Gatsby** or **The Graduate.**.

The Seelbach Hotel was selected first and foremost, because it is the most regal, and romantic Ballroom in Louisville.

There were, however , some details about my wedding that I found disturbing. For example, how many brides never see their wedding gown until the final fitting? I had just graduated from Georgetown, third in my class with a Bachelor of Arts degree in Literature. I was also invited to study at Oxford during the fall semester. Obviously, the wedding , and my marriage took precedent over that dream.

Eleanor had arranged for a limo to pick me up at the dorm, where I was packing up my few personal belongings. Most items were already in Louisville. The Limo took me to a private air pad where the Blair's jet was ready to take me directly to the Dior studio in Manhattan.

I had never been on the private Jet before. There was a flight attendant, on board to serve me drinks and a fruit salad for the short flight. Jacob, the pilot, reassured me that this flight was safer than driving the turnpike. He suggested that , I relax and enjoy the sights.

The flight only took thirty minutes. I never knew that I could hold my breath for that long without breathing and still be conscious.

Once at the Dior studio, Maria greeted me at the front desk and escorted me to a private dressing salon. Inside the gigantic chamber, there was an army of seamstresses.

Finally, I had the gown on and the "army" began their mission, the scene looked like something from **Cinderella**, when all the mice begin sewing her ball gown.

Each of my "mice "had a specific task and there were ten of them all diligently working.

"Did anyone tell you, Miss Gabriella, that your dress pattern is a replicas of that worn by Grace Kelly at her wedding to Prince Ranier III of Monaco, April 19, 1956," Maria announced.

I looked at the full length mirror, imagining the famous actress seeing her reflection and anticipating her future. Maria was explaining what minor changes were made and how they were able to retain the same regal effect.

"We designed a bodice with a plunging neckline, to compliment your assets. Then there are the puffed lace sleeves, with a full ivory peau de sole skirt, imported from Scotland. "Maria seemed as excited as I was to see my reaction.

"The embroidered Irish lace is created by the carrickmarioss technique, allowing us to hand stitch these roses and star appliqués with Svoroski crystal throughout the skirt, as well as the train, and on the tiara headpiece. When the light reflects on the crystal, it transforms the room into a multitude of rainbows." Maria was anxious to demonstrate the effect. Using a hand held flood light, and darkening the room, the crystals projected a brilliant rainbow image. I was spellbound.

"That is amazing Maria. But what exactly is this carrickmarioss technique, anyway?"

I was curious now, how all of this came together, and exactly how many people were working on it. I would never ask the cost, although I could only imagine it was phenomenal.

"Without getting too technical, basically it is a traditional form of fine embroidery, net tulle and cotton organdy, sewn together with a couching stitch. The organdy is then cut away to expose the net. The technique is visually appealing because of the dimensions and fabric thickness and pattern created on the net," Maria said proudly.

I later learned that those individual patterns were then hand sewn into the gown with the crystals. It took twenty people stitching for several weeks here, and nobody knew how many people were employed in Ireland to create the flowers and stars.

"Is it too late to add just two more small patterns?" When I heard that the lace was from Ireland, Caden found his way back into my mind.

"No, my darli'n. Not at all too late. As long as they are small and something Maggie can copy. "

" Maggie was currently working on the veil, but looked up when she heard her name.

"What did you have in mind Missy?" Maria asked, hoping it was simple.

"Just a few shamrocks and perhaps a Claddagh ring. Nothing too pretentious."

"Why yes, I think that would be lovely. Of course I can add that for you, m'lady," Maggie said with a smile.

I was not sure why I wanted those two symbols. Perhaps, because they represented both Caden, who was from Ireland and Jake whom had insisted that our honeymoon would begin in Ireland. Either way, it would be my interpretation of something old and something new. In less than one week I would finally be able to purge my soul from all my past inhibitions.

Jane Austin's quote from **Sense and Sensibility**, surfaced unintentionally, "To wish was to hope, and to hope was to expect. " This kept me grounded , while I anxiously waited for the day my life would finally begin anew.

CHAPTER 27

'Tis better to have loved and lost, than to have never loved at all." '.
Alfred Lord Tennyson

Gabby, Alex and Sterling 1970-90

The only moment that I recall during the actual wedding ceremony was walking down the never ending aisle, clinging to my father's arm, not wanting him to let me go. I was later told that St. Martin's Tower had a capacity of eight hundred and fifty people, and nearly every pew was filled.

Once at the altar, everything began moving now in slow motion. After pledging my spiritual everlasting soul to Alex and God, the priest blessed us with holy water. Once the unity candle was lit, Alex and I sat together to the right of the alter.

The Blair's were not really devout Catholics yet,, nevertheless,,insisted that The Nuptial Mass and Blessing follow the Order of the Rite for Celebrating Marriage. During the entire time, I heard none of the Gospel, nor the Sermon.

Silently, I retreated to my literary world. *April is the cruelest month, breeding lilacs out of the dead land,mixing, memory and desire, stirring dull roots with spring rain. .* "You gave me hyacinth first a year ago. Your arms full and your hair wet, I could not Speak, and my eyes failed, I was neither Living nor dead, and I knew nothing. She turns a moment in the glass Hardly aware of her departed lover "Well, now that's done: and I'm glad it's Over." I breathe not his name, let it sleep in the Shade

Where cold and unhonor'd his relics are Laid.. Sad, silent and dark are the tears that I shed And the tear that I shed, in secret it rolls Shall long keep his memory green in My soul.

If anyone knew how my mind was wandering today, this wedding would quickly become an Inquisition.. Thankfully, it was nearly over.

Sandra, our official "wedding consultant immediately ushered us out of the church for a lengthy photo session. When it concluded and the photographers were all satisfied that every pose was captured for posterity, we proceeded to the horse drawn wedding carriage, that delivered us to The Seelbach Hotel for our reception.

"You haven't said one word since our vows, Gabby?....I hope you are not already regretting marrying me?" Alex asked

"No, of course not Alex. This has just been so overwhelming that I am trying my best to remember it all," I said, honestly.

"This is really your day, darling. I hope it is everything you always dreamed it would be," Alex said, really not expecting a response.

Which was wise. I never could really share with him that I had never dreamt of this wedding and he was never the one I dreamt of marrying.

Thankfully, we had arrived at our destination. The moment we entered the spectacular Grand Ballroom, on the tenth floor, every round table was occupied. The table cloths were the exact mauve shade that my bridesmaids wore.

Silver runners with our initials A and G were scrolled also in silver calligraphy. Replicas of my wedding bouquet were in the center of mini candelabras, with flickering candles. Each guest also received a wicker basket with a sterling silver frame in the shape of a castle, a wine glass embossed with The Blair crest, our name, and date. Finally, a bottle of Dom Perignon, Godiva chocolates, and a small box, to take a piece of wedding cake home, with A &G stamped in silver.

On each basket, there were mauve silk ribbons and a mini bridal bouquet. A scroll explained the significance of each flower selected. Since, I knew nothing about any of this, including why Eleanor selected the arrangement for my bouquet, I became fascinated at what each flower represented.

Was it ironic that Hyacinth was selected, I wondered? Hyacinth: The constancy of love. Ivy: Fidelity, friendship, and affection. Lily of the Valley: The return of happiness. Tulip: The Perfect lover.

I truly tried not to think of the past, but, my mind flashed back to that first lavish wedding reception at The Waldorf Astoria, years ago. This spectacular vision before me was beyond anything that I was capable of imagining."

Are you ready to rock n' roll Princess?" Alex was whispering in my ear. I could not stop my hand from trembling, even with Alex' comforting grip. "Not really," I managed to barely say to him.

"Just take deep breaths, and smile." Alex reminded me.

The orchestra began playing, "You are the Sunshine of My Life" as all eyes were on us when we entered the room. Someone on the loudspeaker signaled the band to pause as he said,

"Ladies and Gentlemen, let us all welcome Dr. and Mrs. Alexander Blair." The crowd was now standing. Everyone clapping as the band began to play once more.

Alex led me to the head table, where I almost collapsed in relief. Molly, my Maid of Honor had her arm around my back reassuring me that all was well. This was a well earned rites of passage, not unlike an underground tunnel, that leads to a road with no bends, forks or turns.

Up to this moment, my life was a circus ring. I had followed the lead Elephant, seeing only his tail. Now at last, I had my Bachelor of Arts degree in Literature and my Mrs. title from Alex. That feeling of accomplishment did not last long.

Our first few years together we're predictable. Learning to compromise, accepting a new living condition, and negotiate whenever possible, sometimes was emotionally exhausting.

I, nevertheless, was determined to complete graduate school, although, no one in the Blair family either supported that idea or encouraged me.

Alex and I were expected to be a "team". That translated to, my duties as his wife, included charity functions, promotional benefits, volunteer duties at the local hospital, and weekly lunches at the Country Club.

The Blair's, including us, were members of both the Louisville Country Club and The Idle Country Club in Lexington. It did not take too many visits to determine that there were only very wealthy "white" members at all events.

The Idle Club, *founded in 1924, established an astronomical in*itiation fee of $50,000. It was later discovered that current members were somehow able to use that fee as a charitable tax donation. It also prevented most people of "color" from being interested. When I discovered this travesty and brought it to Alex' attention, you might have thought that I was challenging that the earth was round.

"How can any intelligent, well educated man like you Alex, who has taken the Hippocratic Oath, be racist," I asked, disgusted.

"Hold on just one minute Gabby...I would never refuse to treat any person who needed medical assistance," Alex immediately retaliated.

"No, of course not Alex, you just refuse to 'break bread' with THEM, or play golf with THEM," I added, getting more annoyed as we continued.

"And., why do you believe that I have to be forced to be with anyone that I have nothing in common with? Have you ever considered how uncomfortable they may feel also?". Alex insisted.

That was the beginning of the end of our relationship. I knew at that moment that I could never love a man who discriminated against other races.

We continued to go on vacations together, usually with the Blairs. I continued my wifely "duties", and my charity obligations, but the gap in our marriage was widening.

Perhaps it may have also been due to the fact that I was unable to conceive a child after seven years of marriage. All the tests indicated that I should have no problem. But, the real reason ran deeper than medical results. I refused to bring an innocent life into this shallow existence.

There were times when I recalled how Jake was so concerned that I might get pregnant when I was only sixteen years old. Or when I prayed that I would have his child, and he would return from Vietnam permanently.

And, by the time I decided to take the new available "birth control" pill , Caden was history. Before that, he never used a condom. Once I accepted this fate, Alex and I rarely were intimate. We lived our lives separately during most of the day. In the evening, we sometimes shared dinner, and talked politely, but we both were emotionally distant.

Thirteen years later, in 1983, Sterling Powers, mysteriously, from nowhere, appeared one afternoon , at all places, a charity committee meeting. Not only was this man wildly handsome, he redefined the meaning of wealth.

"Gabby, did you notice that tall, dark, handsome gentleman who slipped in the back door a few moments ago?" Kennedy whispered so only I could hear her. Kennedy Burton was the chairman of the Hermitage Gala this year.

"I am not blind Kennedy. He is gorgeous. Who is he? And where did he come from?" I could not resist asking.

"That my dear, is Mr. Sterling Powers, lifelong bachelor, retired Cleveland pro basketball player, billionaire, part owner of a little known company called Google."

There were many times that I later was grateful that I had not met Sterling when I was single. He was without a doubt, the most alluring man I had ever met. It was so much more than his physical presence, which in itself, left any woman he was introduced to, wet and hot.

Sterling resonated an aura of empathy that was visible in his blue.violet eyes, his gentle touch, the serene tone of his voice and the seductive movement of his body. The man was definitely not feminine, but his masculinity was god-like.

When Sterling spoke, it was with such sincerity, that regardless the size of his audience, everyone felt they were in his spotlight. I recall horse breeders telling me that when a foal stood up and walked within hours of birth, they could tell if it would be a contender for the triple crown. Sterling had that same charisma. My charity committee was sponsoring an event to raise funds for local underprivileged children.

Some of the funds raised, would also allow autistic children to attend horse camp during the summer. I had learned, by talking to the grooms and trainers, that daily interaction with the horses and eventually horseback riding, greatly improved autistic patients quality of life.

One of the most popular fund raisers, weeks prior to The Kentucky Derby was the Hermitage Grand Silent Auction. As far back as, 1789, when the first race course was laid out in Lexington, and the Kentucky Derby was inaugurated on May 17, 1875 this auction was established.

The names of all the horse contenders were arranged in alphabetical order. By invitation only, the wealthiest patrons on our list would arrive and bid for an opportunity to share 1% ownership of the horse they selected. All the money earned at this auction was handed to the Heritage Farm Charities. If that horse was a Derby winner, the owner and Churchill Downs would match the amount raised.

This year, Sterling Powers was one of the entrepreneurs bidding at the silent auction. As I was about to circulate the room, Kennedy grabbed my arm, and I was standing in front of this seven foot gentle giant."

"Gabriella," I was no longer Gabby.

"I would like to introduce you to Mr. Sterling Powers, who has graciously agreed to serve on our board of trustees.

You will be working directly with him next year on the Heritage Gala," she said.

At that moment, all that I heard was that I was responsible for this gigantic event. Sterling had his hand stretched out waiting for me to acknowledge him,

"Please forgive me Mr. Sterling." He was now holding my hand with both of his. Kennedy began to walk away, leaving us alone. She could tell that I was annoyed at the news.

"Do not blame me Gabriella. Eleanor submitted your name and the vote was unanimous," she said. Before I could respond negatively, she was gone.

Sterling took control, and led me to the cocktail bar that was adjacent to the dining room, but far enough away for privacy. He chose a secluded red leather booth, made sure I was seated and proceeded to the bar. This maneuver was so fast and smooth that I never had an opportunity to protest.

Returning to the booth, he slid extremely close to me. "I hope that you do not consider me too bold for ushering you away, but I prefer to discuss certain arrangements in more civilized settings," he said, looking directly in my eyes.

"Do you consider a cocktail lounge a more appropriate place for business?" I was attempting to remain serious, when he reached into his lapel pocket, removed a silk handkerchief with the initials SP embroidered.

He, then just slightly touched my cheek.

"No, Gabby....may I call you Gabby?"

That is when I noticed his violet blue eyes staring at me so deeply that I could sense him swallowing me. That was when he showed me the tiny eyelash on his handkerchief.

"Those long eyelashes can be so annoying when they decide they want to free themselves.." He never took his eyes off of me. I had a feeling his comment went deeper than my eyelashes.

While I was trying to decide just how to respond to all of this, the cocktail waitress brought us our drinks. "Does this drink look familiar Gabby?" Alex said, continuing to call me Gabby.

It had been years since anybody, other than Molly or Alex had called me that name. .

"Is this part of my initiation, Mr. Powers?" I was beginning to relax a little.

"Now how can we have any fun if you insist on calling me Mr. Powers while I call you Gabby. The games cannot even start until we agree on the rules," Sterling said.

This felt like a blood transfusion, given to an anemic patient. My life had been in life support for so long I was not sure that I still had a pulse.

Once again Sterling asked me if I recalled the drink he had ordered for me. "I honestly have no clue. Should I know for some reason?" I asked. It was wonderful, but very potent.

"Nearly twenty years ago, over seven hundred people were toasting you with The Seelbach cocktail at The Grand Ballroom. Does that now sound familiar?"

"Oh my God....You were at my wedding?" I nearly spat out my drink.

I had never tasted this drink before, because Alex and I had champagne only.

"Yes, I most definitely was. A true jealous admirer from a distance. That was the most elaborate, wedding I had ever attended. And, by the way, the bride was drop dead gorgeous.

Sterling only took one sip, and then switched to his normal, dry martini with two olives. "

Too potent for you, Mr. Powers...I mean Sterling?" I was now in a relaxed, playful mood.

I later discovered that this drink was made with aged bourbon, dashes of Angostura and Peychatfd's bitters, champagne, and a lemon twist. I want from 0 to 80 in record speed.

"This is the only drink in my life, I am ashamed to admit, knocked me on my ass. After your wedding, I was hung over for two days," Sterling shared.

It was hard for me to accept that anything would cause this man to lose control. "So, Sterling....am I to believe that although this drink is too lethal for you, I should be able to deal with it. How safe am I really with you, here alone?" I asked.

Sterling responded by moving even closer to me in the booth. With his hand on my knee, and looking directly into my eyes, he said in a serious tone,

"Whenever you are with me Gabby, there is absolutely NOTHING that I will allow to harm you. That is my promise to you."

Without hesitating, but a little more lightly he added, "Besides Miss 'Daisy' you are so much stronger than I will ever be. Just look around you. This is your domain, and you have survived it quite nicely."

I really was not certain how to respond to that observation . What I wanted to tell this stranger, who appeared to know me better than the man I married thirteen years earlier, was that I was definitely not Daisy Buchanan, but I certainly could relate to her superficial life.

"You don't really think that I resemble Daisy, from **The Great Gatsby,** do you Sterling?" I asked rather serendipitously.

The longer I was here the more I was dreading leaving. Thankfully, Alex was out of town this week at a conference in Chicago. I could bask in the attention that Sterling was pouring on me.

"Only time will tell. There is definitely some hidden secrets buried in that beautiful heart of yours," he said, putting his gigantic hand on my breast. When I didn't object, I was convinced that he would kiss me. And, I would not have stopped him. This was the beginning of

a twenty year relationship.

CHAPTER 28

There's not one cosmic meaning for all; there is only the meaning we each give to our life; an individual meaning, an individual plot, like an individual novel, a book for each person. - Anais Nin.

Gabby and Sterling 2001

Alex never did leave me, although for all intense and purposes there was no longer a real marriage. By this time, we were sleeping in separate rooms, and had entirely different interests

Only on rare occasions did we even share dinner. There were days, especially lately, that I wished that he would discover my affair with Sterling and never return home. Then a few days prior to Eleanor's passing, she shared with me , what I had already suspected on my own, about the Blair men.

"I probably should have told you these things many years ago Gabriella , even before you married my son. Forgive me. I was being selfish. I knew how perfect you were for him. It reminded me of how I was, when I met Winston," she said faintly.

Looking at this frail being nearing the end of her life, I realized what a commanding presence she once had on me. And, now as she was dying, I felt no fear, only pity.

"Winston, Alex, and I assume all of the other men before them, lacked the faithful gene in their DNA. However, we can be thankful that at least they were all discreet about their extramarital affairs. And, that my dear, is all we can expect from them."

Those were the last words that she spoke. Her feeble hand reached for mine, as I could feel her grip loosening. The spirit to live does not relinquish easily. Although, she never spoke again, those final hours she faded in and out of life.

"Will this be the way I die?" I thought silently. No. It will be worse than this. Eleanor at least had her son and me. "Would there be anyone, who would even mourn my passing when I die?"

Eleanor's admission about the Blair men now confirmed all I needed to know. It may be all that I could expect from Alex, but it was not how I intended to live the remainder years of my life.

With Eleanor's passing, most of my obligations to the various charities ceased. Winston had secluded himself to the ranch, allowing his management team to take over all the daily responsibilities. The only obligation that I was assumed to have now was to maintain the Blair's honorable name.

" I believe, Gabby that without getting deep into the dirty details, you understand, as I do, that divorce is not an option," Alex said one day. Although, I was never asked to sign a prenuptial contract, Alex and both his parents made it very clear that divorce would never be an option. Under the Kentucky Marital Property Laws, anything owned by either spouse, prior to marriage was nonnegotiable during a divorce.

Since respecting their honorable name was really the only thing that they ever expected from us, I decided long ago that I would respect those wishes. I owed that to Alex, but nothing more.

Sterling accepted that I was married. He never suggested that I leave Alex. There were even times that I believed he preferred that I was married.

"Single women are mostly neurotic, sometimes psychotic, and at the very best frightening," Sterling would say.

We were at the Meta Bar, our favorite rendezvous meeting place, sharing with each other anything and everything. Comments like this were not unusual, and never prompted by me. I never in eleven years, expected, or even cared if we were exclusive partners. And, I never pried into his personal affairs.

"Surely, you remember Alexandra Forrest, don't you Gabby? Fatal Attraction? Remember how Dan Gallagher? I think that was his name, played by Michael Douglas. He has this weekend affair with Glen Close....and then she goes mental on him, killing his daughter's pet rabbit and left it cooking on a pot on their stove," he said, still serious.

I started laughing, almost hysterically, which made Sterling even more emphatic.

"Gabby. I am not kidding. There are single women everywhere just like that."

"That is a very astute observation, coming from such a sophisticated, confirmed bachelor. Why don't you just tell 'Mama' who it was that bruised that delicate ego of yours. And I will kiss it and make it go away," I chided.

This verbal foreplay usually resulted in a few hours of afternoon delight at his penthouse. In contrast to Alex, sex with Sterling was always stimulating and spontaneous. Guaranteed never to be mundane.

We might be attending an early afternoon art auction , and he would lean over and whisper in my ear that he needed to lick my wet pussy. Then, in the same breath, purchase a $600,000 Monet for the hospital atrium.

Later, then we would meet in his Limo. It always provided the privacy Sterling demanded.

There I would discover a chilled plate of sushi and always a silver bucket of ice. With the sleek movement of a determined panther, with one hand , he would pull down my panties, and then begin to lick my clitoris, with his powerful tongue.

Using the sushi to add spice to his own personal "honey pot" it would add the desired flavor he was craving.. I never disappointed him. Then with ice in his mouth he would once again proceed into the wet canal. The long strokes on the clitoris and his tongue tasting my labia, would continue until I could no longer come.

We would then kiss. His mouth , still with traces of sushi and cum was the best aphrodisiac possible. Only then would he mount me. His mouth still frothing from my pussy juices, his powerful cock began to work its magic. I was certain that there was no one on this earth that could please me more.

In those early years, after Alex and I had basically stopped having sex , I was concerned that Sterling would soon grow tired of me. Instead , he became excited about my tight vagina. Making certain that I climaxed was his priority. Sometimes, it would take hours for him to lubricate me. When the clitoris would start swelling, he would use first his tongue, with his pierced stud. Other times a peacock feather might work, until he could feel a contraction around his tongue .

Once the clitoris became less visible, and the contraction tighter, he would stimulate the anus, preparing for the orgasm to begin. Once his mouth was filled with cum juice, he was satisfied that he could mount me, and begin to pulsate his erected penis, this time filling me with his semen, ejaculating inside of me. That sensation was like no other; a natural high that always made me came back for more.

" I don't know why you want to have sex with ME Sterling. It takes so much effort before we can actually have intercourse. There are so many other women you could be with, that could please you better than me," I would say, sometimes frustrated.

"My poor, wonderful, abused darling. It is never up to you to please a real MAN. What pleases me is when YOU are sexually satisfied. Whoever has made you feel otherwise, needs to be taught a lesson," he said earnestly.

Sterling may not have been able to reload like Caden, or make me feel that emotional high that only Jake could provide, but he was my gentle giant, and the safety net he provided for me was more than I ever expected.

The possibilities that Sterling offered were endless. Anything from a few hours of random talks , to weekend ballet and cocktail parties in Istanbul, Turkey, to sharing useless information for hours on the telephone, when we were right across town. There were times that we would sometimes randomly, find a broom closet at a restaurant and minutes later we were fucking like crazy.

On elevators, Sterling would hold the close button and I would be on my knees with his huge penis in my mouth sucking to make him cum. We started a game that would time how long it took me. I then would try to break my own record.

The rare evenings that we actually spent the night together, I became accustomed to sleeping in the buff. Sterling claimed it relaxed him, and soon it did the same for me. It was how he shed all the days complications, returning him to his natural form. Often times, I would awake with his mouth sucking my nipples. Then his hand gently found my vagina, and like a maestro, setting the pace for a magnificent opus, all my inhibitions were set free.

When he taught me how we could both have oral sex at the same time , it was not only my physical world that turned upside down, it introduced a newly found arousal method.

It was pure genius, how Sterling was able to satisfy me without an ounce of emotional stimulation. I loved how he could make me feel complete without either of us needing, or wanting a commitment. We were together for that moment and nothing else mattered.

I was convinced that this arrangement could last a lifetime, if I wanted it to. Our invisible bond was stronger than most marriages.

Once Sterling was comfortable about our relationship we moved on to a new way to assure that sex would continue to be rewarding. This was always the main mission.

When I was finally introduced to the private orgy clubs, I was more than skeptical, Honestly, I was afraid. It never repulsed me, but, personally, it threatened my comfort zone.

"The private orgy clubs that I am a member of, and the ones we will attend together will introduce you to a totally new and exciting world of sexual pleasure. I have been attending these for years, and I am always better when I come back," he said, enthusiastic.

"But, Sterling....seriously, I have a limited knowledge of sex. I would feel completely inadequate among experts," I said knowing that my insecurities were once again surfacing.

"There are so many varieties of sexual options that it is like going to a spa and selecting what service you chose for that visit. And, by the way, nobody is going to assess how well you performed. Everyone there is normal, just like me." Sterling had concluded his persuasive speech.

I was not sure why he thought that adding that everyone was as "normal" as he might convince me to go with him, but what I did know after all this time is that, our relationship lasted because it was based on a cat and mouse game. If he ever caught the mouse, in this case it would be me, he would devour it and the Game Ends. What we did share, was a live on the edge mentality. A double life, that made reality exciting and sometimes mysterious for both of us.

I may not be that sixteen year old hippie that rallied for peace, or marched for women's rights but I was intelligent enough to discover a mental exit from this life sentence with Alex. And if it sometimes meant taking unconventional risks I would do so.

One thing that I was certain of, I was determined not to die like Eleanor or live with the attitude that this was the best I could do.

A few weeks after Sterling had introduced the idea of the private orgy clubs, we were having dinner at Bourbon N' Toulouse, a well known Cajun and Creole restaurant, located in a wooded area in Lexington.

"This is for you Gabby, that is, if you will join me?" Sterling handed me an elegant envelope, totally black, with a fascinating hologram of an old colonial manor.It was addressed to: Sterling Powers and Guest.

"Go ahead and open it Gabby. I already know what it is," he said, grinning.

I carefully, ripped away the sealed closure, and began reading it silently, using the candlelight to see better.

Mr. Sterling's presence is requested at this years annual Erotica Halloween Haunt, located at The Belvedere Mansion, on October 31, 2001, at New Orleans. Please use the exclusive key provided. Directions will be sent Special Delivery , along with instructions for your guest once you confirm. We look forward to your attendance, as usual. This years committee has provide an exceptional package of special effects for our VIP guests. RSVP is required.

It was definitely tempting. I was curious to see first hand what not many get to experience . I just knew it would be a life changing event. Ever since Jake's funeral in February, I needed desperately something to get my mind off of him. Sterling was teaching me that sex and beauty are inseparable, like life and consciousness. And, that intelligence which goes with sex and beauty, is intuition.

"Yes, Sterling. I would love to join you. But only if you allow me to pick our costumes. " I said with no hesitation.

I knew that would be a condition that Sterling would never object to. It was a wild and wicked idea that I had wanted to try during our role playing. This was even more perfect.

"Great, Gabby. What did you have in mind? I trust whatever you decide will be fun," he said. Obviously relieved that I was not only willing to attend, but anxious to participate.

"We will be, Lestat and Claudia from the bestselling novel, **Interview With A Vampire**. What do you think? Isn't it just brilliant," I said, enthusiastically

. Sterling was delighted. We would be the perfect couple. Since this novel, by Ann Rice, was now dated, I was certain that no one else would think of it. It was just frightening enough to make it fun.

The juxtaposition between Lestat and Claudia and Sterling and I, was more ironic than I wanted to delve into at this time. What I would admit is that Sterling had a hold on me that I could not pull away from. It was beginning to feel more like an addiction than pure pleasure.

"I love this idea Gabby. I remember how Lestat transforms Louis into a Vampire in New Orleans. Then later he recounts how he discovered the innocent, exquisite, Claudia!" Sterling was definitely excited about this transformation. Thankfully, he had not made the same connection that I did with the characters. Or, perhaps, he did not recall, how Louis can no longer resist making Claudia a vampire, trapping her forever in a child's body.

When Louis and Claudia form an alliance they must travel half around the world in search of others like them. Similar, in many ways to how the two of us are exploring new people in erotica clubs that share similar desires. In Paris, Louis and Claudia discover a theater of Vampires, but no real solution to their dilemma.

Will Sterling and I be like that one day? Untouchables, lost in our own world of fantasy. An irresistible, burning desire toward the abstract; Like flirting with Death when he asks you to kiss him.

Finally, Halloween had arrived. Traveling to our destination was indeed part of the entertainment. Once the private jet landed, a limousine would be our transportation through a deserted swamp area, on the outside the city limits of New Orleans.

The driver had been arranged by the Erotica Halloween Party Host, who would never be revealed. The Mansion that we were headed to, apparently, is rented out only once a year for this exclusive event. We were also informed, that the micro chip key that Sterling received by a private courier was time sensitive. It was only good for twenty four hours after it was received.

Along with the key, was an attractive rhinestone tracking device that all guests were required to wear. Once on, it could only be removed by the person they accompanied. It was for my own protection, I was assured.

"Protection from what?" I asked. There was no reply from the driver, nor from Sterling.

Once in the very dark forest, on a dirt and occasionally gravel road, flashes of lights outside would reveal hanging bodies, or I was hoping mannequins, from weeping willow trees. As we continued through the dense fog, there were large signs posted, warning us about The Labyrinth of Terror ahead.

It was the location where a decapitated spirit known as Lady Cassandra, would guide us to the Trail of Torment. Here the tortured images of wandering ghosts would lead us to the front entrance of the Mansion.

The exterior of the dark house, with its inviting wraparound porch, was less intimidating than the journey to get here. A few broken windows, with some gigantic spider webs was not really spectacularly spooky. Then we went inside. A very tall man, or woman, it was not evident which, had a mask that covered the face, only revealing a white distorted mouth.

Immediately, they placed the ankle bracelet on me, and handed the key to Sterling. He was my designated master for the evening. As I looked around, I realized that this practice was not gender related. Women would also be given keys to male or female guests.

"This event is much more guarded. I assume it is because everyone is in costume. Are you okay with this, Gabby? If not we can leave now," Sterling said, determined to make the decision entirely mine.

"It will be fine. I am good with all of this. As long as I know what all the rules are, there should be no problems," I said. Most of what we were being told was just common sense, until the "safe word" was introduced.

Due to the anonymity of the guests, each person was provided with a word they could use to stop the sexual advances if they became threatening or unbearable. After listening attentively, to all the conditions, Sterling and I were ready to enter the main theater lobby.

Within a few moments the room became totally dark. Then, we were being lead by someone, on a marked path. At the crossing, Sterling and I parted, going opposite directions with a guide dressed in black robes with white screaming masks.

I am being seated in a theatre chair, a few rows from a stage. There are strobe lights everywhere. The stage curtains open, revealing a huge movie screen. On it appears, Satyrs, goats, horses from the waist down, all taking turns fornicating a blonde female strapped to a gurney.

The various beasts take turns fucking her. Then she is flipped over, allowing only her anus to be visible. The beasts now take her from the rear. At the same time, on stage a live show is beginning with another, woman that had so many tattoos it was difficult to see much of her flesh.

This time. Before the live half man, half beast begins to pay attention to the female, he splatters what looks like blood over her naked body.

The remaining beasts now begin to lick her savagely . This is when the Gladiators enter from the stage right, with spears threatening the beasts, who wisely flee from the left stage. As the female begins to moan loudly, the Gladiators take over, licking the insides of her thighs, taking turns at the pussy.

The screen and live event are celebrating simultaneously. Finally, in both arenas, a Satyr appears with a gigantic cock exposed moving close enough for the maiden to suck, while the Gladiator is fucking the Satyr from the rear. There is pandemonium in the theatre as people begin to openly master-bate, while other couples seek private salons to continue role playing in private.

I have never partaken in any of these rituals, but Sterling has shared private Videos in his home theatre and we later improvised. My guide, gathering that this was not pleasing to me, leads me out of the theatre into another room, where there is only a wrought iron bed.

This is when I realize that the surrounding black walls begin moving. People are actually stepping out from the walls into the room. There are four phantoms. Then the strobe lights begins to shine from everywhere.

One phantom hands me a vial with some liquid, instructing me to drink it. Not recognizing the smell or taste I shake my head no. The phantoms ignored me. One grabs my arms, while another wraps my legs around his neck. My crotch is nearly in his mouth.

Through my mask, I can tell that I am now being taken into another, much larger room. I know from what Sterling has told me, that I am being prepped for a main event. This becomes very real when I am strapped to a bed.

The only thing visible are men with bidding paddles, wearing leather jocks, exposing various sizes of cocks. Some stiff and some limp. My groomer explains to me that I am going to be the main dish for their eating frenzy. The men will be bidding on how fast they can make me cum and how often.

The stimulating oils that she is rubbing on my body will attract the men's sexual organs through smell, touch and taste. Minutes before I am about to be presented, I remember my SAFE word at the same time as my ankle bracelet begins to flash.

I am quickly cleaned off, and escorted to a cocktail lounge where I immediately order a Bombay martini. Definitely out of my element and so very appropriate for the moment.

When Sterling sees what I am drinking he becomes concerned.

"Hey, are you okay, babe? You are as pale as some of these ghosts walking around," he says, anxiously.

"Let's just say that I came way too close to being the 'blue light' special' for a group of hungry beasts. I really do not think that this will ever be my fantasy Sterling," I say as clearly as possible.

One of Sterling's favorite settings was similar to the one I just escaped. He would call it "Coming to the Races." In this case the audience would cheer on men, who would pay very large sums of money for the opportunity to make the female model cum with only his penis. The faster the better.

The winner would be given a percentage of the pot and receive a professional blow job. Many men and women enjoyed watching this event, but he had never heard of any elite member being recruited to be the model.

After an hour of finally regaining my senses, I was curious where these people came from. Apparently, they were traveling performers that are booked only for private events. They are paid very high wages and even have a union that assures them that their contract will be valid. All the performers are tested for venereal diseases, have letters of recommendations and health certificates. This underground business is exclusive and restricted to only elite members who pay exuberant amounts of money to become members. It was definitely not something that I enjoyed regularly, but it also fascinated me.

Other men always presumed they knew who I was , what I wanted and what I would do. Sterling never underestimated me. That was why I always returned to him.

After a few more voyeurism experiences, we were done for the evening. The talking holograms mounted on the walls, wished us a safe return home. Knowing that Sterling had participated in an orgy meant that I would be going home tonight.

Alex would be home in the morning and this made it much more clean and simple.

"Did you enjoy anything about the evening Gabby?" He asked once we were on the plane headed home.

"It was a unique evening. But honestly, this is not my gig. You are more than enough for me. And, I can always count on you to keep me excited," I answered, relieved to be going home.

The Limo ride to the Meta garage where my car was parked was a fast twenty minutes. As I kissed Sterling goodnight, he had one last thing to remind me.

"Do not forget to call me the moment you get home, Gabby. No excuses. Promise."

"Such a silly rule...but, yes, I promise darling. And thanks for a great Halloween Night my Lestat.

"I blew him a kiss goodbye, as I watched him drive away. Just as I reached for my keys, everything suddenly went BLACK...

CHAPTER 29

What you love, you empower.
What you fear you empower.
What you empower, you attract.
> Justin Woltering.

Gabby and Sterling
October 31, 2001

"Look at the shitter on that critter" Murray was intoxicated just looking at the tall black chic with legs exposed to her waist approaching The Bentley they were casing.

But, this broad, in her sexy cat costume walked directly to the elevator.

Murray's mind was talking out loud to his brother Calhoun. They had been waiting what seemed like hours in the parking garage for just the right moment to strike.

Halloween night brought a lot of people out to party and they planned to do a little "trick and treat' themselves. It was just a matter of picking the best car to steal.

That meant carefully selecting the easiest one to snag with the most potential for profit.

So far with their black robes and clown masks on, nobody even questioned why they were there.

"Plump and round and tight, isn't it nice? And that's the moon from the dark side. Wonder what her million dollar pussy looks like from spread eagle? Like caviar, no doubt," Murray said, almost salivating like a bloodhound.

He could hardly resist the urge to grab the bitch right there, but he knew that Calhoun would go ballistic, if he blew this caper.

"Murray, where the fuck did you come up with that 'shitter...critter crap?" Calhoun is barely audible.

"You can get into more shit than you can shake a stick at."

"I overheard this black dude, you know, the senior left tackle on our high school football team, the one that got recruited by Georgia Tech. He was talk'n bout some black chic on campus. That black bruiser musta been 6'4" 250 lbs. ' member him Cal?"

Calhoun rolled his eyes and poked his brother in the ribs, "You moron....that was 30 years ago. How can you remember shit like this, but can't remember when I tell you to meet somewhere in 10 minutes?"

Murray ignored Cal and just keeps talking,

"His name was Nicklaus Spineron . We called him Nick "Stickpin", cuz he could really stick it to those guys,"

White trash and blacks lived on the other side of the "tracks", which is code for living in the poor section of town. There was a lot of poverty and racial discrimination was alive and well. Sports and drugs were the equalizers.

Getting out of that environment was top priority. Some actually made it. Besides the intellectual, sports was the next route out. The smart ones knew this; Nick, was no exception His grey matter oozed with smarts.

Stickpin knew how to take advantage of his charm and charisma and , it paid off for him. Nick made it out of the hood.

After playing professional football for ten years with the Kansas City Chiefs, the Carolina Panthers and finally with the Miami Dolphins, Nick, returned to Savannah High School as the head football coach , for the Tigers football team .

Giving something back to his community, was as foreign to Calhoun and Murray as learning how to knit.

Murray just ignored Cal and kept on with his story.

"Well, anyway, Stickpin was talk'n smack with some of his bro's about getting in her panties....either way he did or wanted to. I 'member laugh'n so hard that Jake Chevalier asked me what was so funny. I only told Jake, aka as the snake , cuz he was dating some broad at the time. I thought he'd get a kick outta it."

"Whatever, you prick. Are you ever gonna shut that trap of yours? Get your fuckin' head out of your ass and focus those nasty eyes on the task at hand. Calhoun smacks Murray behind his head

"Your problem is that you don't know your ass from a hole in the ground. We're here to cop that Bentley parked 50 yards away. We need to grab it when nobody is around. Just like we planned it. Got it, now?"Calhoun continues.

Society labels losers like Calhoun early in life, "lazy fucks". Teachers use the term LBS, for students who have Lazy Butt Syndrome. They then become content with sliding by, which later leads to short cut survival tactics.

It did not take Calhoun long after dropping out of high school to fall in with some surly characters. His street smarts and chiseled upper body served him well in fights.

For Calhoun, his fighting style was a mirror of his lifestyle; punch your opponent with the left until they beg for the right. This introduced him to petty larceny 1A ,and home robberies 2A .

"Graduation " came one night when , in "desperation " Calhoun, put a gun to the head of a night manager.

Once that line was crossed, he ended up in front of a judge who immediately sentenced him to three years. Poor Cal.

"I don't care about any Halloween goody booty, no matter how much she looks like eye candy. We ain't mess'n with this cunt. She is high society. Well connected. I ain't gonna back to eating bologna sandwiches in the slammer because you can't keep your pecker in your pants," Calhoun made this crystal clear to his brother.

Murray doesn't want to admit it, but somewhere in his pea brain he knows Cal is the"Alpha" brother.

"I'm just too pig-headed to let him know that he is in charge," he acknowledges to himself.

And then, Murray's attention suddenly turns to the. gorgeous brunette, with loose long curls. He can feel his fingers stroking her hair, while finger fucking her pussy.

She is dressed like a porcelain doll, or something like that. Whatever. He could play some serious games with this "dolly".

"All right I'm ready, but not too steady," Murray admits out loud.

Calhoun ignores Murray, keeping his

one eye on the broad. She is waving good bye to someone in a Limo.

"Been snort'n powder up your nose again? I told you to quit that shit. It's gonna put you six feet under," Cal says.

"Yeah, yeah....Let's do this NOW! It's fuckin' cold out here," Murray spits back.

They both pull from their pants over sized vinyl gloves and pull them over their leather gloves. Murray can feel an erection building. No time to jack off.. No finger prints is priority number one.

Murray is always the driver. He might not be the sharpest knife in the drawer, but he can handle a car. When it comes to crime, these two are like trained pigs that are eager to eat the slop thrown to them.

But this time he sees Murray, almost like a flash of lightning, lunge toward the broad just as he hears the beeping sound go off on the Bentley.

Immediately Murray has the black silk sac over the girl's head and his hands around her neck.[Trouble with mice is you always kill them, Gabby thinks]

. Once the back door is open, Murray shoves Gabby into the back seat and then follows her. Slamming the door.

"What the fuck, Murray. You're the driver. Did you forget that already? You need to get the keys from her. NOW MURRAY!"

Murray,follows the orders. "If you value your life pretty lady, enough to see daybreak, hand me your keys! Give 'em up bitch," he demands.

In the dark under this black sack, it is Lennie, she sees in her mind. Lenny from Of Mice and Men. He panics and clamps his strong hands over her mouth to silence her. The more she struggles the tighter his grip becomes, and he shakes her until her body goes limp. Lennie has broken her neck..

I am somehow now Curly's wife. It is the scene when Lennie is going to kill her. It is playing right now in the back seat of my car.

"They're in my purse. See them? They should be on top of my wallet," I answer quickly.

I am hoping that maybe he will just take the money and car and let me go.

My cell phone is still in my pocket. If I can just get to it. But with this black sac over my eyes, I don't know what this fuck he might do if he catches me. I *There's a little black spot on the moon today, and that's my soul.* The reality is beginning to fade into my consciousness.

Is this the day I die? Karma has finally caught up for all I've been doing...*The woman is perfected...The dead body wears the smile of accomplishment,* Sylvia Plath.

Then I remember that Sterling is still waiting for me to call him. It is what he always asks me to do when she insists on driving herself home.

I will never complain how overprotective he is of me. . What a sick joke that is right now. If he doesn't hear from me he WILL CALL. I know he will.

Murray snatches the keys from Gabby's Versacci bag and tosses them up front to Cal.

"Hit it man. We gotta get outta here and fast!" Cal hears the panic in his brother's voice. Murray always gets nervous when plans change. This was supposed to be an easy heist.

"How are you planning to drive you Fuck up. From the back seat?" Calhoun is losing his cool.

"I can now tell that the other thug is the one with some brains. I wouldn't even be here if it was up to him. "Gabby silently thinks to herself.

"Not today Bro. Today is my time to taste some of that caviar between this bitches legs before I get off on her. You just follow my instructions to the warehouse and keep your eyes on the road." It feels good giving Cal orders for a change.

Gabby begins to move as far away as she can from this beast, trying to recall what she learned in herself defense class at Georgetown.

"Steady bro, this won't take long." Murray feels that he is now finally in control.

"Why the hell does Cal think that he can always tell me what to do? My pecker is getting stiff just smelling this cunt next to me." Murray whispers. He is determined to get his way this time.

And then, Gabby realizes he is putting her hand on his penis, as to prove his point.

When she pulls her hand away, she hears him remove something from his pants pocket that make a clicking sound.

Next he is slicing the silk bag over her head so that now she was eye to eye with her nemesis.

His most pronounced feature is his hooked nose situated between two empty eyes. The bushy eyebrows framed what looked like portals into hell. His face had black stubble. The same color as his slimy hair that reached his shoulders.

And when he smiled there were gaps, missing teeth and a stench that almost made her vomit.

"Know this sound sweetie? Ever heard it before?" Murray is having fun now.

"Oh yeah," I answered, trying to get him to keep his hands off of me.

"Used to play torture games with my ex just for kicks, you know. I was the one who suggested it. He dug it, like most REAL men do. " Gabby, said trying to sound calm.

My plan was to get him to relax just enough to distract him from using that knife on me. A jacked up male is predictable. All I needed was to keep him talking.

260

"When I was in grammar school, fifth grade I think, I used to intimidate the whimsy, wimpy girls. " Gabby said, getting her confidence back.

"I would get five, six quarters cupped in my hand and walk by 'em in class and shake 'em close to their ear. Just like you did with the knife. The sound terrified them. A switch blade and a rattler sound a lot alike, you know," I noticed the anaconda tattoo on his right arm and made a mental note to remember this.

"Oh, yeah, they do, now that you mention it," Murray was temporarily distracted like I was hoping.

"Knew this dude in high school, that used to do that before the state football game. Said it would calm his nerves. Jake was his name. Georgia boy, from Savannah. Had a little kink to him. I used to call him Jake the Snake, as a joke, you know," Murray was ranting.

I could smell his putrid breath; it must have been the road kill he lives on.

"Went out with this chick two years younger than him. We all wanted to bang her too. But Jake kept a tight hold on that pussy,"

Did I know this moron? And, does he know me? Thirty five years is a long time. He wouldn't remember me, but now I will never forget him. Should I let him know who I am? That might make things worse.

"What the hell is going on back there Murray? I need to get off this express way and you two are having a tea party back there,"Calhoun was getting fed up with this really quickly.

"You just keep drivin'. We back here, are just getting' to know each other, aren't we Gabby? " Murray is smiling with those dirty gap teeth.

Gabby is silent. Her breathing suddenly stops.

"Ya, babe, I read your driver's license. Now we can get on with our own business."

No. He has no idea who I am. Now, Murray was pulling me over as close as he could. I tried one final tactic before I knew it would be too late.

261

"Murray, don't you just want to take the car and my money and let me go? I mean you must have seen that Limo that dropped me off...That' s my very, very wealthy boyfriend and he will be checking on me real soon....and that might make Cal really pissed if you blow this caper. Just , saying," I tried to keep my voice steady.

"Well, the way I see it," His hands were stroking my inner thigh, and I could feel the sweat building on his fingers.

"You're like a bird in my hand and I just struck the daily double...making money and fucking you."

Right at that moment his hands ripped off my panties and my phone began to ring at the same time.

Chapter 30

"The more wild a creature is, the less sorrow it feels."

Gabby and Sterling
 October 31, 2001

"Thomas? Gabby should have called me by now. How long has it been since we dropped her off," Sterling asked worried.

Thomas looked at the digital clock and realized it had been nearly an hour. It typically only took Miss Gabby 30 minutes to get home, and there was no traffic tonight at 3am. Even all the bar hoppers were now home nursing their hangovers.

"Yes sir, she had plenty of time to make it home by now," Thomas replied.

Sterling was hoping that this was, one of Gabby's games. Like testing how high or how many rings of fire he is willing to jump through for her.

He thought that by now he knew her well enough; but tonight may have been just too much over the top for even her.

There actually was a point where he thought she was ready to participate in one of the orgies. Then an escort informed him that she was out of her comfort zone and he should consider ending the nights revelry.

What Gabby was never told , was that the anklet bracelet did more than track where she was. The lights would track her pulse rate. When the orange lights transmitted on the tracking key it was strongly advised that the guest be reunited with the host.

If the red light flashed, it was critical. The guests sometimes refused to use their "Safe" word, or it was too late by the time they realized what was happening. This device was more reliable.

Sterling reached inside his suit pocket and felt the key vibrating. The color was red.

"Thomas, can you use this key as a transporter, syncing it with our GPS? Apparently she still has it on, and unless she decided to microwave it, I am afraid she may be in trouble," Sterling was nervous, but remained calm, as always during any crises.

Sterling handed the key to Thomas and proceeded to call Gabby from his cell. Murray also heard the phone go off. It was programmed to play "Come on over Baby (All I Want is You)", by Christina Aguilera, whenever Sterling would call.

"What the fuck is that? Hand me that God Damn phone. Now Bitch. And no funny business," Murray demanded.

It was clear by now, that this pig was not happy being disrupted, but Gabby was hoping that it would make him just nervous enough to back off.

"If I don't answer that, my boyfriend will know something is very wrong, and then you can say bye bye to any money you were going to get for this pimp ride. Just think about that Murray. Calhoun is going to blame all of this on you," Gabby was talking loud enough for Calhoun to hear her.

"What is wrong with you Dick Head? No pussy is worth going back to the slammer. Answer that blasted phone, and let's split," Calhoun was now yelling at Murray.

"Make a right at the first stop after you get off the expressway Cal," Murray said, ignoring what Calhoun was saying.

Now Murray had to deal with me, his brother, and the phone. I was pretty sure that this pea brain could never micromanage or multi task, so I might just get a break.

"If you just give me the phone Murray I can help you out," I asked, softly.

Calling your aggressor by their first name was one of the basic strategies I recalled from my training at Georgetown.

It is supposed to mentally bond you , making it more un-likely that he will hurt you. I was just praying that I wasn't going to die over this ridiculous car that Alex insisted I have.

The phone stops and the the song begins again. Murray finally cannot take it any longer. "Hey...What the Fuck do you want?"

"Who is this? Where is Gabby?" Silence. Murray is breathing heavy, not sure what he should do.

"Cal...Cal ... What do you want me to tell this guy?"

"Hang up that fucking phone you fruit loop. What are you thinking?" Murray says.

Calhoun ignores his brother and is now back on the phone.

"You have the wrong number Asshole. No Gabby here. Hasta luego," And then I heard a click.

"Give me that phone Moron".

Murray finally obeys. And I watch Calhoun throw my phone out the window.

"Have you got the directions Thomas?"Sterling asks.

"Yes Boss. They are headed for the old warehouse that has been abandoned for ten years. We should be there in 5 minutes. Should I notify the cops, Sir?". Thomas waits for instructions.

Sterling hesitates. The chances that this publicity would go viral is not a pretty image, but he could not risk Gabby's life.

They also carried a 45 for protection, but even with the gun this might be too much for the two of them to handle.

"Yes, Thomas, better be safe and not take any chances". Sterling ordered.

Calhoun cruises to the back of the deserted building, kills the engine, and turns off the lights. He proceeds to take out of his backpack a car cover, that is meant to con-ceal this baby until Sam gets here for the delivery.

The plan is simple. Once Sam takes possession, he leaves the cash in an envelope at the local bank's safe deposit box. The account is always under the last name Yolo, which is an acronym for You Only Live Once.

Callahan always admired Sammy's smarts. Not like his dumb ass brother, Murray who might have screwed this all up because he can't keep his pecker where it belongs.

A Bentley 4509, like this baby, in mint condition, would net him about six grand, not bad for one nights work.

"Okay prick, take the broad past that open space," Calhoun was pointing to the wooded area about 100 feet away.

"You only have about ten minutes to play with this doll, and then we need to scram. Do you HEAR ME, Murray," Cal was once again in control.

Murray was searching through my wallet, and purse not paying attention. If there was anywhere nearby that I thought I could run and hide I would have taken the chance. But, without a phone, my odds were not good.

"And if she has any jewelry get that too, before you dump her," Cal continued.

The two thugs were eying each other until Murray finally said, "I KNOW...you don't need to remind me. I won't touch her and I'll bring back what I take off of her."

"This won't take long", Murray reassured him.

He grabs me by the hair and jerks my arm forward. I stumble over a wooden log, but somehow remain on my feet. Murray takes the switch blade out of his pocket again. *They made her a grave too cold and damp, for a soul so warm and true. Thomas Moore.*

"Please, just don't kill me. Remember what Cal said? I don't know why you are doing this, but I won't tell anyone, if that's what you are afraid of," Gabby is trying to remain calm.

Murray was ignoring me. I wonder if I should tell him about Jake? Or, maybe he knew the Blair name and would be afraid that Alex might go after them. If Sterling didn't get here soon I would have no choice but to try to escape, somehow.

"Do you even know who I am?" I said, finally,

"Do you really think I even give a shit who you are? To-night , you're my Ho and that's all that matters. Now shut the fuck up," Murray made it clear.

He teases my ear with the tip of his six inch blade. Dancing in front of me, I feel like I am about to be sacrificed for some ritual.

"You do as I say or you will wish that you were dead when I finish carving you up,"He continued.

And right then, I feel the blade cut just slightly near my ear lobe. He pulls up my dress. No panties. He pulled those off in the car.

He begins to taste the blood that he drew from my ear with his disgusting lizard tongue. I am standing, in the frosty cold October night with only a bra.

As Murray eases me down on the wet, muddy ground , I can feel my nipples get hard and the leaves on my stomach crackling. Then the sound of the branches , next to my head , begin to warn me when he shoves my face on top of some dead grass.

"You scream Bitch and my blade will carve your pretty face like a grotesque Jack O lantern," Murray refuses to stop talking.

That is when THE HOUNDS of BASKERVILLE , over-takes my panic. *I'm none other than the reincarnation of Hugo Baskerville, a profane and godless seventeenth centu-ry ancestor of The Baskerville Clan. No need to cry out; you go and I'll hurt you.*

I can hear Murray, trying to unwrap something which I can only think must be a rubber. But with his hand push-ing my back to the ground he is having a hard time manag-ing. I can feel his semen begin to roll off of my bare bottom.

"Okay baby, guess you are going to feel the Murray Ex-press first class, up your tight ass. All eight inches. Hope you are as clean as you seem. Don't want to catch any STD's," He says.

And then I finally feel nothing , but I hear moaning and grunting, like a squealing pig. That is when I allow my

267

mind to travel back in time when Jake and I were alone in the deserted farm loft.

He always made certain that when we made love it was what I wanted. I would be the one pleading with him to make me feel his entire shaft inside of me. Now I began to whimper with each thrust of that bastards cock.

I try to release the arch in my back praying that this deep penetration will finally lose its stamina. Then I hear Cal yelling at Murray and he eases to a stop, although still inside my ass.

"Douche Bag, we gotta get outta here NOW. I just shot her boyfriend. Hear those sirens? There for us. This broad is Gabriella Blair. Some high society dame. If you don't stop now Murray I'm leaving you to take the rap , no shittin. "Cal was serious.

Murray was like in a daze, refusing to stop until his pecker wouldn't go any deeper and I could feel his cum stinging inside.

Finally, Calhoun pulled him off me and the relief was like removing a torch from my anus. My head was pulled up and Murray's bugged eyes were staring at me like a demon from hell.

"We'll meet again, baby. I will track you down. I have the smell of your pussy tattooed on my brain," He then stuck his finger, that had traces of his semen, in my mouth.

"Don't you ever forget that taste Bitch. You were one tight ass fuck," As Calhoun kept dragging him away he kept yelling at me.

"Murray will show you what a real man can do with that pussy of yours."

"Shut your trap scum bucket. We don't want the bitch to remember us. Let's split NOW," Cal shouted.

As soon as I knew they were gone I started crawling through the mud. There was a far off sound of thunder, low and rumbling, not loud but, constant enough to smell the refreshing rain. I knew soon, that this rain would remove the traces of the animal that had just ravished my body.

My head is pounding. An inner explosion, approaching louder now with the whack-crack or flash of light I see.

I try to stand but instead I am unable to move. Green and yellow vomit spurts from my mouth and nose uncontrollably. At last, a warm blanket and two arms wrap around me, cradling my broken body and I hear an unfamiliar voice.

"M'am....I have an ambulance just steps away. "And the next thing that I realize is he is holding me in his arms and carrying me to safety. Someone in the ambulance is hooking me up to some tubes and washing my face off with a wet cloth.

"Sterling...Sterling Powers? Where is he? ...I have to know. "The words coming out of my mouth did not even sound like my voice.

There is an echo, and everything is in slow motion. Under the blanket I am, soaked, sticky, and, slimy.

"Please I have to know?" I ask again.

"All you need to know is that right now you are safe and Mr. Powers saved your life."

I began to cry uncontrollably, until the ambulance doors slam closed and the medication flowing through my veins finally force me , thankfully, to pass out.

Murray is driving top speed on the turnpike, headed towards Cincinnati anxious to find some all night diner that would serve him a chill dog and a cold beer.

"Still have those pantics Murray?"

Calhoun looked at him disgusted.

"God, you are gross! Can't believe that we have the same mother."

"Calhoun, you just can't stand it that I get all the pussy," Murray says.

Calhoun spits out the window.

"The only ones you ever get, you mother fucker are the ones you rape. One day you're go 'in to stick the wrong bitch and it will be all over. You just be pray'n that it ain't this Gabby Blair. She can lock your ass up forever," Calhoun responds.

Murray turns off the turnpike into a gravel road that leads to a rustic looking building with a neon sign flashing "The Dive. Welcomes you to Cincinnati ".

"I ain't worried about any , Abby, or Gabby Blair, Bro. I think she got her kicks out of me pounding her ass. Man am I starving. Sex and drugs does that to me every time."

CHAPTER 31

"Death does not stop love that guides you to my side; what may seem broken is only on hold. Look beyond the sunset."

Jake Chevalier 2000

A sweet smile flashes across her face, as we nearly collide in the narrow hallway, and for a brief moment it is Gabby's eyes that meet mine. Once again it is a time when life is less complicated, more meaningful.

Sitting on the commuter train, reading a review of the play Cats, the adaptation of TS Eliot's poems, I am overtaken by the scent of Shalimar, and it immediately jogs my memory back to the Tybee Lighthouse.

The sudden silence is deafening. Through the shadows I hear a noise and careless laughter, while watching the sun rise over the Atlantic Ocean.

The morning tide sets the day's pace. A young girl with a crooked smile is dancing on the foam. When the tide kisses her feet, I wrap an oversized towel around her. We move to a sheltered cove where unheard melodies, serenade only us.

It is here that I learn that the value of life depends on every moment spent wisely, and that [life is all memory, except for the present moment, that goes by you so quickly that you hardly catch it going]. Then it ends. And, once again I am someone that I barely recognize.

Days later, at my podium, I review my notes on Kubla Khan., when, from the corner of my eye, I am drawn to the young girl in seat 30C. She tilts her head at just the right angle. Her ponytail falls freely into a cascade of brown sugar, flowing past the middle of her back.

It takes me a moment to realize that this girl is not Gab-by. That image does not fade away easily. I am transported back to the sawdust loft, where the orange blossoms fill the air and I am safe in Gabby's embrace

All people dream, but not equally. Those who dream by night in the recess of their mind, wake in the morning to find that it was only vanity. But the dreamers of the day are dangerous people, for they dream with open eyes, and make them come true. DH Lawrence.

We never knew then, that our naive dream of spending eternity together would last no longer than that of a butter-fly's lifetime. My world is now spinning on a dime, desper-ately searching, yet finding nothing, until at last I realize that [whatever the imagination seized as beauty, must be truth, whether it exists or not.]

During the early years it was Isabella that taught me how to cope with everyday life, and limitations. But, later it was Gabby and her passion for literature that motivated me to return to college and earn my PHD.

My appreciation for Joyce, Eliot, Lawrence and so many other phenomenal writers lead me to share their dreams with those eager students. Time was no longer an obstacle. More importantly it also kept me emotionally, intellectually, connected to Gabby. Whenever I would teach a lesson , I thought of how Gabby would teach me.

To say now, that I ever stopped loving Gabby defies logic. There are times that I despise myself for never falling truly in love with Isabella. It disrespects the vows of our mar-riage to admit this.

There will be times that I recall, more often than I would like to admit, that New Year's Eve, 1967. The last and final time I saw Gabby.

There is no doubt in my mind that she was still mine. That Caden Cassidy, he was no more than a distraction. A substitute, a mere transition, that she felt she needed at the moment.

What we experienced, could never be dismissed as a mere high school crush. We both realized that, in our world there was no need for validation.

This love generated a mysterious flowing of breathless anguish; a distortion of excessive ingenuity that linked us together in the future through the dynamics of the past.

It did not matter that the day that I stepped on that live mine at Nam, my life ended. The last image I saw was Gabby's face; the first name I called out when I woke up in the hospital was Gabby.

For years I really believed that the shattered pieces floating in space, after the explosion, might settle, and reassemble, somehow, making my life normal again.

When that didn't happen, and our separation became real, was when I became dedicated to find some way back to Gabby. All that I was certain of was that there was no way that I could ever permanently leave her.

Then, I discovered, that I could keep up with her life over the years. It was fascinating. Like watching a wild animal react to natural changes in a new habitat.

When Caden left her in Georgetown and she eventually married Alex Blair, I was so tempted to tell her none of this is really going to matter.

Destiny guides our fortune more favorably than we could have expected. For neither good nor evil can last forever; and so it follows, that as evil has lasted a long time, good must now be close at hand. Don Quixote. That is why, on April 18, 1970, while in Lexington for a literature conference, I had the opportunity to once again see Gabby.

I overheard someone mention that Gabriella Girard and Alex Blair were being married late that afternoon. This wedding was considered to be the event of the year.

It did cross my mind, just briefly, to make a cameo appearance, of course at a distance, just to watch how Gabby would look as a bride.

To live vicariously, through Alex Blair and experience the moment that Gabby declares her eternal love, is almost too difficult to ignore.

Could she really make her marriage work, or would it be like mine; a convenient alternative? Maybe, in retrospect

It was better that I never saw that moment. But, I always knew whatever the vows were that she stayed that day, were never strong enough to break our bond.

It was soon after that close encounter, with Gabby, that my had become obsessed with the idea that she would just appear one day at my lecture room at Boston College.

She deserved to see the man I had become, in spite of Vietnam. *The great living experience of every man, is his adventure into the woman. All that is not himself, and from that one resultant, from that embrace, comes new action. DH Lawrence*

As the years kept passing, the urge to see Gabby became stronger. I turned to Molly for advice and updated information. Whenever I suggested that I might contact Gabby, Molly's reaction was always the same.

"If you love Gabby, Jake, as I believe you do, then you must permanently stay out of her life. You made your choice, right or wrong to be with Isabella. Gabby chose to move on with Alex. That chain reaction cannot now, after 35 years be changed. And, she is much too fragile for that. How could seeing her now improve anything? You cannot change the past Jake," Molly reminded me.

Suddenly a scene from The Great Gatsby novel, that I have taught many times surfaces. Jay Gatsby is disappointed that Daisy does not react as he expects after many years later. His friend, Nick Caraway warns him,

"I wouldn't ask too much of her. You can't repeat the past," But, Jay responds incredulously,

"Can't repeat the past? Well of course you can." And just like Jay, I looked around as if the past was lurking here in the shadow of our house, just out of reach, beyond my touch.

Gabby being fragile was a definite misnomer by Molly. That adjective would never apply to Gabby. She is the epitome of a steel magnolia and would be the first one to object at being considered fragile.

It is a common, underestimate of this lady, that is gross-ly exaggerated. *One must learn to love and go through a good deal of suffering to get to the journey that is always traveling towards the other soul.*

Am I now sorry that I ever married Isabella? Never. There was no real choice. What I was not expecting was how much time I spent over the years thinking of Gabby.

This June, after my yearly check up at the Vet's hospital, I was diagnosed with a mild case of Agent Orange, thirty years after returning home from Nam.

Agent Orange is the name given to a powerful mixture of chemicals that were used by the US Military forces during the Vietnam War to eliminate forest cover, and crops. Over 19 million gallons of herbicides, containing the chemical dioxin, was used between 1967-1972.

Only many years later, after the war was over, did any-one realize that exposure to the spray would cause serious health issues, including, tumors, birth defects, rashes, psychological symptoms, and cancer among US servicemen. *War, huh, yeah, what is it good for, Absolutely NOTHING*

Those of us who were sent to Germany when we were in-jured actually were informed about the side effects that we might experience. None of us knew to what extent that meant, nor did anyone else.

It was not brought to the public's attention until 1979, when a class action suit was filed on behalf of 2.4 million Veterans. Naturally, as bureaucracy is always slow to rem-edy the situation with money, I was in a holding pattern.

There was nothing that the Doc could tell me, except that he would treat the symptoms as they developed. *War means tears to thousands of mother's eyes when their sons go to fight and lose their lives.*

Then, first came the rash, covering my entire back with raised hive like splotches that would remain for five years. Later I was told that this rash was actually Chloracne; Its cause is prolonged exposure to herbicides.

For some odd reason, the novel, Clockwork Orange kept popping into my mind. *It's funny how the colors of the real*

world only seem real when you watch them on a screen. An-
thony Burgess.

Time was not my friend. Every day some new symptom was ranging in my body. I was just not always aware of it. I find it Ironic, how ugly things are always given pretty names, as to reduce the nasty images conjured by the mind.

Agent Orange was no exception. There were other colors more appealing, such as Agent Purple, Agent Green, often only whispered about.

It was that first mention of Agent Orange, while in Germany, that I made the decision to never have children. When I explained this to Isabella about the chances of our children having no limbs, spins bifida, cleft pallet, or worse yet, she understood but was not happy about it.

"That's okay, Jake, really, we can always adopt...I mean later, when we are settled, and things become more normal," Isabella resolved.

What she did not want to face, was the reality that nothing would ever be NORMAL again; at least the normal that I was familiar with. I could tolerate not having Gabby, because I would be the martyr if I needed to be, but sharing a child with Isabella under any circumstances would be impossible. That would involve another innocent life being exposed to my own depression.

Naturally, no politician would take any credit for committing herbicidal genesis over so many victims on both sides of the war.

After such knowledge, what forgiveness is possible, when forgetting is impossible. Bitten by flies..., my house is a decayed house. In depraved May, dogwood and chestnut, flowering Judas, to be eaten, to be divided, to be drunk. History has many cunning passages, contrived corridors, and issues; deceiver a with whimpering ambitions, guides us by vanities. TS Eliot.

The time was now to plan for the end. I knew exactly what I needed to do, while I was still mentally and physically capable. First my will would be prepared by my good college friend Andrew Young.

I had shared my deepest secrets and desires with him, so I knew that he would respect and honor my last wishes.

All of my financial assets, of course, would go to Isabella. My cremated ashes, were to be distributed into the ocean in front of the Tybee Lighthouse.

At my memorial service, Isabella would return the cardboard box, to Gabby. It was the original one she gave me thirty-five years ago, the last time I saw her, at Georgetown.

I knew that this would not be an easy meeting for both, Gabby and Isabella. However, what I was counting on, is that both would respect my final wishes.

Andrew, appropriately began to call it the "Death Box", which at first I found disturbing but later thought quite accurate. Andrew would first, make certain that Gabby knew about the service. I was certain that she would attend.

Lastly, Isabella would accompany me to several European destinations. It would require her to allow me the freedom to discreetly carry out my mission without questioning or probing.

After living with Isabella for so many years, we both understood that there were some topics left unspoken; the Vietnam war and Gabby Girard. I agreed not to express my feelings about Gabby and she agreed not to ask. With all this settled, I was now ready for the next stage.

Love never dies a natural death. It dies because we know not how to replenish the source. It dies of blindness, errors, and betrayals. It dies of illness and wounds. It dies of witherness, of weariness, of tarnishings.

The entire purpose for going to Europe was to reunite with Gabby. Well, of course, not physically, but my elaborate plan would allow her to realize that I never forgot her, or stopped loving her.

Strategically, I began to map out where I would be sending Gabby, and who I would illicit to provide her with my tokens and messages. This was not an easy task. It would be difficult to convince strangers of my intentions, without sounding demented.

But, then again, maybe I was a little crazy to imagine that this intricate scavenger hunt would actually work. For me it would be a dress rehearsal, since I would not be there for the "opening night" premiere.

The first stop was a no brainier; Dublin, Ireland of course. It was where I was first introduced to Stephen Daedalus. We shared an epiphany that changed our lives.

That moment, in the Savannah High School library, is when I realized for the first time that I was in love with Gabby.

There were times that we spoke about traveling to Ireland for our honeymoon. Blackrock Castle, just south of Dundalk would be the perfect setting. I booked on line, a cottage steps from the beach.

Once, Isabella and I were settled in our hotel room in Dublin, I convinced her to take a tour to Belfast. She hesitated at first, worried about leaving me on my own in a foreign country, but I assured her that I would be fine and that I wanted her to enjoy herself.

That evening we walked across the street to a pub called The Brazen Head. It is the oldest pub in Dublin, dating back to 1198. Literary giants such, as James Joyce and Jonathan Swift, just to mention a few were regulars here.

In more modern times Van Morrison and Hot House Flowers used to enjoy sharing ideas over a pint or two.

Conveniently, Isabella and I met some friendly tourists who were signed up for the same tour to Belfast. It was after two in the morning when we all strolled, or more like crawled, back to our hotel.

By the next morning Isabella was already gone. Her note was simply, "Do whatever you must do, but remember I too love you. Isabella".

For a brief moment I wondered if she somehow figured out what I was up to. But, no, there was no possibility that she could know the real purpose of my trip. Only one other human being, Andrew Young was privy to that information, and I literally trusted him with my life.

In truth, it was the sense of immortality that lead me to believe that Ode to a Grecian Urn had captured the paradoxical moment when the imperfection of beauty is realized. It is a beauty created by men who have an obsessive need to control their destiny.

Once this revelation became evident, not unlike the epiphany, that I shared with Joyce, there was only one thing left that I needed to achieve before my final breath.

I had traveled to the edge of knowledge and learned that my eternal and abnormal craving to love and be loved was the only thing left in life. I needed to assure myself that my desire was not in vain. Gabby would reassure me that my dreams are legitimately a result of my thoughts.

CHAPTER 32

How many loved your moments of glad
Grace, and loved your beauty with love false or true...But
only one man loved the pilgrim soul in you, and loved the
sorrows of your changing face.

- William Butler Yeats

Jake, June 2000

Inside my head there is sometimes a place that I escape to,
in a cloud that floats above the world. There I am able to
take any shape that I want. Arriving at Inchydoney Island
had a similar effect. It convinced me that the world's beauty does not need to be duplicated in a photograph or even a
painting.

Life becomes at this point your own palette, where a so-
liloquy can express the emotion in fewer words and person-
ify the spiritual need beyond a literal translation.

I now was confident that when Gabby arrived here she
too would feel this intensity. It would be the perfect beginning to a perfect ending.

My first priority, at the moment was locating the owner
of the beach house. As it turned out, Tom O'Leary was also
the proprietor of the Claddagh Pub which everyone knew.

Several friendly neighbors tried to give me directions but
their heavy brogue accent was to difficult for me to follow.

That was when I noticed that tacked to the front door of
the beach house was, a pencil written note with an illustration of a stick man.

I presumed that the stick man was me, since it was
missing one leg. I did share with Tom that I had a prosthetic leg..

The map included a winding road that lead past a bakery, labeled Mulvaney's, Tom had painted a postage stamp to designate the local post office, as a land market, just, in case I didn't understand his primitive drawing.

Once at the PO and across the cobblestone road, I was at my final destination, the Claddagh Pub.

I found it endearing that thr note was written on the same embossed stationary as my confirmation letter. Tom was as careful to impress as I was in my planning.

Everything that I was arranging must include significant meaning or purpose that Gabby would recognize. Not an easy task since I had not laid eyes on her for nearly thirty three years..

When searching for the ideal location, in Ireland, my first consideration was Gabby's comfort. If I thought about this too often, it seemed even a little macabre to me. I mean let's face it, when she gets here I will already be dead.

Nevertheless, it was imperative that although this was my "death wish" in reality, my objective was to make her understand that it really was my living will, designed exclusively for her.

When Tom O'Leary's beach house was advertised with the Claddagh illustration, I knew that this would be "our" perfect location to initiate this pilgrimage.

Most people will recognize the Claddagh ring if they see it, but are not acquainted with its romantic story. Hundreds of years ago, in the quaint fishing village of Claddagh, pronounced, [Klah-duh], a young man, Richard Joyce was enslaved by the Algerian Corsairs around 1675.

He was sold to a Moorish goldsmith where he learned the craft. After fourteen years, King William III sent an envoy demanding the release of all British subjects. Richard was reunited with his fiancé, who had waited for him all those years.

He presented her with a uniquely designed gold ring that included a heart in the center, representing his love, with a crown, symbolizing loyalty, surrounded by joined hands indicating friendship.

With Tom's note in my hand, I began the short trek up the dirt road right, outside the cottage gate. I must have looked extremely strange slowly walking with crutches, wearing shorts that exposed my left prosthetic leg.

At home I became accustomed to walking around without anyone noticing, but here I became a little more self-conscious when I passed a shepherd with his flock. He stopped to ask me if I could manage on my own or if he should ask a neighbor for use of his horse and wagon.

I assured him that I could manage, even though I found the road very uneven. Once I reached the Pub, inside it was quite dark, although there were windows facing the outside. Behind the bar stood a tall, sandy haired man with gray highlights and a full beard.

A toothpick was dangling from his mouth while he was talking to a customer sitting on the other side.

The rather loud patron. was complaining about how the summer tourists, from London, in particular, were too picky about everything.

"Excuse me, but I am looking for Tom 'O'Leary?" I interrupted.

Both of the men stared at me as I were an alien here to predict the Armageddon. As I looked around, all the people seated, stopped chatting and just stared.

I approached the bar and extended my hand, "I am sorry. I should have introduced myself. I am Jake Chevalier.I am renting one of the beach houses down the road?" I said, calmly.

The man behind the bar suddenly came out of his trance.

"Yeah....yeah, yeah.... I'm Tom. Welcome to Ireland Jake. Sit yourself down and let me pour you a Guinness pint. On the house, best in the world."

Before I could decline his generous offer, Tom was handing me the tall foaming warm beer. Then he reached under the bar for what appeared to be a cow bell. Tom then began to ring it, getting everyone's attention.

Let us all rise our pints to Jake, our new neighbor, who travelled here from the U S of A on a secret mission". Tom shouted.

I looked at him with a confused smile. Did I ever tell him why I was here? Maybe, but I don't recall now. We clinked our glasses and I heard a loud roar from the rest of the patrons. There was a sense of relief, that I was among friends. Later, that would be critical, when the time came.

A few days later, I decided that the time had come for me to reveal the details of my Gabby Odyssey, as I was now referring to it. At first, Tom was puzzled at why I had requested him to be my liaison.

After several long evenings and many pints, along with a few shots of Irish Whiskey, I was able to explain that my love for Gabby, had extended beyond, thirty years. Tom then, agreed to be my messenger.

"All I can surmise, my new friend Jake Chevalier, is that you are a hopeless romantic, with an ancient Irish soul. I must admit that I am anxious to meet this Siren of yours. She must be something special if you are determined to follow through with your plans. ". Tom said one afternoon.

"Oh, let me assure you, Tom I do intend to accomplish all that I have shared with you. It is the only way that I could leave this earth in peace," I replied.

Now, I just did not know, exactly how long it would take for Gabby to begin this voyage after my death.

"I would like to share a toast with you Jake and my pledge to carry out your wishes," Tom said.

We lifted our glasses one last time, since I would be leaving for Dublin in the morning to meet Isabella.

"May you have the hindsight, my dear friend Jake, to know where you've been; the foresight to see where you are going and the insight to know when you have gone too far," Tom stated.

I shook hands and embraced my new friend before parting.

"I wish I had that blessing many years ago, Mate. I would be here with Gabby celebrating our anniversary, instead of planning my wake."

My last evening in Inchydoney was one of reflection. Everywhere I went, my mind kept repeating, *that I cannot die without you knowing ,that my creed. Is love and you are it's only tenet]*.

Every path I walked on lead me to the same conclusion. The peace that I was now feeling, gave me the energy I needed to continue.

I was beginning to accept that even this short time I had left on earth, was more important ,than ever before.

CHAPTER 33

God, but life is loneliness, despite all the opiates, despite all
the shrill tinsel gaiety of "parties" with no purpose, despite
the false grinning faces we all wear. And when at last you
find someone to whom you feel you can pour out your soul,
you stop in shock at the words you utter...
                    - Sylvia Plath

GabbyFebruary, 2003

Life, as I knew it, would never be the same. Sterling recov-
ered from the physical scars of that horrendous night, but
there was something very different about his laize fair attitude.

I don't believe that he ever frequented the erotica clubs
again. If so, he never asked me to join him.

We continued to be distant friends. I know that he felt
responsible for the outcome of that night, regardless of how
many times I tried to convince him otherwise.

"I promised you Gabby, on that first night we met, that I
would keep you safe, and I failed at that. I should have insisted you come home with me. At the very least, I should
have waited to make certain you were in your car before
leaving." Sterling said often.

He refused to listen to anything that I tried to tell him.

"You risked your life for me. If you had never showed up,
those bastards would have killed me." And that I had no
doubts about.

What terrified me the most, was the threat that Murray
would find me, and the hell he put me through would continue. Alex insisted that I attend regular therapy to help my
panic attacks.

For months after the assault, I refused to leave the house. I became a self-imposed hermit. Thankfully, Alex kept his distance, allowing me the space I required to rehabilitate.

It was on the second anniversary of Jake's passing that I decided it was time to shed myself of all the old "baggage" that was weighing me down. That was when I came across the box that Isabella had given me at Jake's Eulogy.

I had buried it in my closet for two years, avoiding the memories that I knew would stir within me. When I mentioned this to my psychiatrist, she suggested that now was the time to allow myself a trip back to memory lane.

The plan was one last time, to rekindle memories and then throw away what physically and emotionally was preventing me from moving forward.

I placed the box, still wrapped with duct tape, on my bed, and took a deep breath as I began to dissect the outer binding with my sharp scissors.

I didn't care if I mutilated the box. It almost gave me pleasure as I saw it collapse, revealing the familiar inner contents Inside, was all the expected treasures that at one time were priceless to me.

There was Jake 's Letterman Jacket from Savannah High School lying on top. The next layer revealed his class ring, a few photos from Tybee beach, my nearly empty bottle of Shalimar, all the letters I wrote Jake while in Vietnam, and all of his letters to me.

Thus far, nothing new and everything that I expected, until I got to the bottom of the box. There I saw a bubble wrapped leather bound book. Again I used the scissors to open this last mystery.

Inside, was a hollow case holding a DVD and a sealed envelope. Immediately I recognized Jake's handwriting. I put it down, my hand was beginning to tremble as I ran my fingers over the envelope: "To My Gabby". I decided to wait before I went any further.

What could he possibly tell me now? Did I really even want to know?

Reluctantly, I walked downstairs and poured myself a chilled glass of wine. I began to reflect carefully on what I was about to open. *Would it be my Pandora 's box?*

If I never opened it how would my life be different? Was it even too late now? And then the answers became easy. Jake would never do anything to hurt me. After all these years he was the only man in my life that I trusted undeniably.

If Jake wanted me to have this last "gift" I would not disappoint him. In reality, I now knew that he never really left me. He has been with me in some form my entire life. *When I was with Caden my mind would wander off to Jake.*

When Alex asked me to marry him it was my way of accepting rejection from Jake. At the time, I thought it was the answer to moving on. But, all I was doing was hovering in a stand by pattern that lead me to Sterling.

That attraction to Sterling was always his mystic. From our very first meeting, our future together was clearly a foreshadowing of our future relationship.

I can still hear him saying,

"If you don't stop calling me Mr. Powers, Gabby, I will have to spank that inviting rump of yours."

"Are you trying to test me, Mr. Powers? Because it takes a lot more than just a spanking to keep me in line," I replied

Once that volley began the rest became history. Sterling was going to be the one to rid me of anymore "Jake baggage".

The fantasy enterprises I was introduced to aroused not only my inner sexual senses but also removed the fear I had about the unknown. Not even facing the **Death Box** now could frighten me.

When Murray was raping me, my mind was on Jake and how he would have wasted that piece of shit. Even in death, I was pretty sure that somehow he would find a way to revenge this vile act.

Upstairs, I walked to the bedroom door and locked it, even though I knew that I had privacy. I did not want to be disturbed. I then settled on my chaise lounge first, and then read Jake's note.

"My dearest Gabby,

By this time, you know that I am no longer of this earth and Isabella has fulfilled one of my last requests, delivering to you **The Death** Box. I will explain all of this when you decide to watch the video that I have carefully prepared. Please do not wait too long. I know that you could never forget "us" any more than I could.

Love, Jake

Simple, straight and to the point. That was always what I loved about him. Okay I am now prepared to watch the video. At least I hope that I am.

I insert the DVD, adjust the volume and wait. After a few moments there he is. Older, and looking tired but still with that dimpled smile, eyes that looked deep into my soul and looking very much alive.

"Hi Gabby. I wish that I could be there to deliver this message to you in person, but then the irony is that I would not need to if I was still alive, would I? Okay, let's cut to the chase. Without spending a lot of time here is what I want you to do as soon as it is reasonable.

Contact my very close friend and attorney, Andrew Young. His phone number is listed at the end of this video. He will explain everything in detail. As I alluded to in my note I never, ever, forgot about you. And over time I never lost track of where you were and what you were doing.

That is, of course less important now. But, you must promise me you will call Andrew. He is waiting, and has been instructed not to bother you until YOU call him. Oh, and one more thing Gabby. I was a professor of English Literature at Boston College for the last 20 years. I wish that we could have shared how much I learned to enjoy literature because of you, but maybe you will eventually understand this.

288

Well, I guess this is all I can say for now, except that Andrew was the one to name the box you gave me, appropriately I will add, **The Death Box.** He said it was because from what he now knew about me, it seemed like my world died when I received that box. And he was right. But, now that I have you back, in theory at least, I am ready to face death without any more regrets.

I only hope that at the end Gabby, you will know how much I love you, now and for eternity."

And then the video ended.

I had been in tears the entire time but as soon as I allowed everything to sink in, I reran the tape and jotted down Andrew's phone number. *Jake, a professor and of all subjects, English. Oh how I wish I would have known that earlier. I was soon about to experience a new world even more exciting than anything Sterling could have ever imagined.*

The next morning, I was on the phone to Andrew Young who was surprised and impressed that I had finally called.

"I must say, Gabby...may I call you that Mrs. Blair?"

"Yes, absolutely. Please call me Gabby. I am sorry that it has taken nearly two years for me to have responded to Jake's request, but, honestly I had no idea until yesterday that there was anything in **The Death Box** except for what I had given Jake years ago.

Once I watched the video last night I knew that I had to call you immediately."

"And, I am so glad you did. Would it be possible for us to meet tomorrow? Maybe for lunch? This will not take long for the initial meeting. Everything else we can correspond by email".

I was rather confused about the suggestion of any future meetings, but, decided all would be clarified shortly. Andrew agreed to fly in from New York and meet me at The Hurstbourne Country Club at 1:00 the next day. *It was the longest night of my life.*

CHAPTER 34

All people have dreams, but not equally. Those who dream by night, in the dusty access of their mind, wake in the morning, to find that it was vanity. But, the dreamers of the day are dangerous people, for they dream their dreams with open eyes, and make them come true.   -
D.H. Lawrence

Gabby, March 2003

"Jake was a dreamer, Gabby. A romantic; an unbelievable dreamer. And, I feel fortunate to finally meet the woman that he was hopelessly in love with," Andrew Young extended his hand out to greet me.

He had an inviting smile that immediately made me relax. His handshake was firm, but smooth as velvet.

"I appreciate you taking the time to fly out to meet with me, Mr. Young," I said.

We both took our seats, and I tried not to seem anxious about what I was soon to discover.

Andrew Young was about the same age as Jake would have been. He had sandy blonde hair slightly tinted with gray and very dark blue eyes, that reminded me of marbles. Although impeccably dressed and very confident there was something about him that appeared restless.

"Jake mentioned in his letter that you were friends for many years but how did you two meet?" Our drinks had just arrived, and I was beginning to feel more comfortable with the situation.

Since the rape, less than six months ago, meeting strangers always made me nervous. Typically, I would not even leave the house alone. Today I made an exception.

"Jake and I met at Notre Dame. He was an English Lit. Major and I was pre law. We were both huge football fanatics and that was the start of a thirty year friendship."

I wasn't really surprised. Jake had a way of making friends with everyone. What was confusing was his relationship with Isabella.

"You must be wondering how I could be meeting with you if I also knew Isabella?"

Now, I was worried that I was being too obvious. It wasn't that I blamed Isabella any more, or that I was even still jealous. It was just painful.

"Was I that transparent about my feelings?" Andrew was smiling, as if he already knew me well.

"Damian, my partner, and I spent many wonderful times with Jake and Isabella. But let me assure you Gabby that I knew very well from the time I met Jake that you were always on his mind. I learned to separate those feelings like he did. Isabella has no knowledge of what Jake has left you"

"But, it was Isabella that delivered the **Death Box.** She had to have some idea what it contained?"I said, knowing that if it had been me I would definitely have snooped around.

"Let me assure you Gabby. That box was in my possession after Jake created the video, at all times . Isabella chose to hand you the box as her gesture for closure," Andrew said without taking his eyes off of me.

I was impressed that Jake embraced Andrew's life choice and how much he trusted him with his final arrangements.

The Bloody Mary I was drinking finally began to give me the courage to confront some of my past demons.

"Okay then, I am ready to hear what Jake wants me to do".

I watched Andrew pull out a rather cumbersome expandable folder with a handful of legal documents.

"These are Jake's last and final wishes, that he hopes you will follow for him. It will involve traveling abroad for about one month by yourself, but I can assure you that you will never be truly alone. There will always be companions to guide you and help you through the journey," Andrew hesitated for a moment to make certain that I was comprehending what he was saying.

"I know that this is a lot for you to digest at once Gabby, so if you want me to stop and go back at any time just tell me,"

It wasn't that I was not understanding, I wasn't sure if I could do this. And why did he want me to do this?

"At each destination, you will be provided with additional directions. Oh, and most importantly, all expenses are paid. You just need to allow twenty four hours in advance for me to make the necessary arrangements".

It was taking me some time to react to what I was hearing. *How did Jake think that I could explain to Alex that I was going to go to Europe for a month on a treasure hunt that my dead ex-boyfriend requested as his final wish?*

"Are you alright Gabby? I know that this is a lot to accept but once you get started it will all make sense. I promise you."

Andrew was holding my hand trying to assure me that this was really happening. For some reason this time his touch was much more comforting. It was like Jake had used Andrew to channel his spirit for just a moment so that he could feel my hand one last time. Whatever it was, I was no longer worried about Alex, or what other obstacles I might encounter.

When I arrived home I called Dr. Perkins, the psychologist that I have been seeing since the Halloween catastrophe. I told her all that had just happened and my meeting with Andrew.

"And Gabby, how does all of this make you feel? Do you think that you are emotionally stable enough to take a trip around the world?"

I thought that was an odd question. I was hoping that she would be able to answer that for me.

"As I see it I really do not have a choice. I have kept everyone waiting almost two years already. I think it is time now to listen to my heart and fulfill Jake's wishes."

"I just want to remind you Gabby that you always have choices, and if you believe things are getting too much when you are on this trip let me know. We will get you home. If Jake and you really have a bond that goes beyond the grave, he would want you to be safe. Remember he never knew the hell that you are recovering from."

I wanted to say that Jake does know what I have been experiencing and that is why he wants me to leave here. But I didn't want her to think I was any crazier than she already must think I am.

My next mission was to convince Alex that this was something that I must do, and by myself. Since he never had any objections when I spent all those months with Sterling, I presumed he would not have a problem with a dead man. I was wrong.

"Are you serious Gabby? How do you think it will be interpreted by our friends and even the media if anything odd happens? Not to mention if you like flip out in another country. I just think that it is a very bad idea."

I wasn't even sure if he had been listening completely to what I was saying. He was busy straightening his tie, checking messages on his phone and just about anything but listening.

"Did you even hear what I was saying? I really wasn't asking your permission Alex. I was giving you the courtesy of telling you that I would be gone for about four weeks."

"Whatever Gabby. You always have done what you wanted. Drop me a postcard now and then. You know I will be here when you get home."

As I heard the door slam behind him, I looked around the empty room. I was not angry, or upset. It was difficult to be specific about the emotional roller coaster that I have been on for so long. I put both my hands in the air and declared "let the games begin."

Chapter 35

Come away, O human child
To the waters and the wild
With a faery, hand in hand
For the world's more full of weeping
Than you can understand.
- Miguel Cervantes

Gabby, April 2003

True to his word, Andrew Young had emailed my itinerary the next day.

Cheers Gabriella,

I have included your airline tickets with a schedule, along with any further details that Jake requested. Please advise me as soon as your departure date is finalized. All funds are available to you at any time, as well as credit cards and travelers checks.

The only real restriction is that you travel independently, just as we discussed. I have also provided my personal phone number. I will be available to you 24 hours. On line you will see specific details.

Andrew Young

I clicked the attached file. I was curious to find out where Jake was planning to send me. The form popped up and the list appeared in chronological order:

Dublin Ireland. After your first night a hired car will pick you up and deliver you to a most magical island, known as Inchydoney.

Mr. O'Leary will be there to meet you at the beach house. He is also the owner of The Claddagh Pub, where you will find a very warm and friendly group. An added benefit is the superior Irish Coffee and outstanding selection of ales.

Further details will be given upon your arrival. Your stay, unfortunately, is only 4 days. I wish that it was longer but I wasn't sure how much time you could spare. As you will notice on the agenda, it is quite busy. So, enjoy the peace and solitude while you are in Ireland.

Andrew was not kidding about the extent of this trip. Jake had me traveling a total of twenty two days. I decided that July, although busy with tourists, would be the most convenient time for me.

After Ireland, I would fly to Paris for four days. Next I would travel to Edinburgh, Scotland for another four days. My journey would continue to Wales, and eventually London for five days. My final destination would be various cities in Italy, concluding in Venice.

It didn't take me long to realize that all these countries were ones that we had talked about and dreamed of sharing together when we were younger.

But, twenty two days of traveling through Europe, by myself now, at fifty-three years old could be both exhilarating and exhausting. I was hoping that it would be something that I could accomplish.

I found it fascinating that in all the years that Alex and I had been married, we never traveled to these countries. Oh, traveling was a part of our life, but mostly for business, or charity functions. Never the way that I had imagined it would be with Jake.

I had no idea what to expect but what I did know, from what Andrew shared with me, was that Jake spent many hours of planning, in spite of physical pain, this agenda. It was my obligation to follow through with his request.

It really did not matter to Jake if the entire world thought this was insane. By this time, in our lives, we were beyond defending our actions or explaining our intentions.

The direct flight on Virgin Airlines, from New York was extraordinary, from check in to landing. As soon as I arrived at La Guardia, a representative from Virgin was there to escort me to the VIP lounge.

When I traveled with Alex, we always used the executive lounge but nothing could compare to this one, that included not only a private bar and complimentary food, but also showers, hairstylists, massage rooms, and tanning booths.

Thirty minutes prior to regular boarding, an airline representative, took the five of us, who were flying first class, to our seats.

We each had our own private attendant and the leather reclining seats transformed into full length beds. Andrew had mentioned that Jake was a professor but this type of luxury was more on the celebrity grid.

After a very relaxing sleep, ninety minutes before landing, the flight attendant woke me up.

"I thought you might enjoy a spot of tea while watching the morning sun rise above Dublin," She said.

It was a very distinct Irish accent but her English was impeccable. I stretched my arms and shook my head trying to adjust my mind to where I was.

Then, I looked out the tiny porthole window to see the valley of ancient death. The land that Queen Maeve, infamous for her Celtic beauty and sexual prowess reigned at one time.

A tranquil restoration begins in my heart before traveling to my mind. Is it irony or fate that I will soon be walking on the land Caden came from? Jake could never have anticipated this.

Regardless how I tried, it was impossible to ignore Caden's presence. He was born in Dublin, and yet, I feel that to think of him now, is a disgraces to Jake's memory.

The three months that Caden and I spent together, never even came close to how Jake and I felt about each other for three years. . This journey is a tribute to that bond.

Once I accepted that Jake was dead, it was easier for me to understand why he left me. But, Caden? Caden had no reason to react with such hostility and jealousy. His irrational behavior led me to Alex.

Perhaps, that was how it should be now. Alex and I, Caden with Kaitlin; everybody neatly in a relationship that works best.

I continued to let the warm tea redirect me to the reason I was here. I could see miles of emerald green grass to one side and the powerful Irish Sea on the other. Just as Maeve is the goddess of intoxicating power, it is a thin line between love and hate; sex and violence. I sensed that like a precarious house of cards my serendipitous journey was about to begin.

The sun rising at a distance appeared even more gentle; more poetic. The sunbeams we're inviting us to come live the dream, sing the songs, listen to the tales, drink the nectar.

Internally, I was ready to wave goodbye to yesterday's melancholy melodies, and allow the surroundings to resurrect my soul.

"To your left is the Cliffs of Moher. A great natural attraction that you can enjoy right here in the comfort of your own seat".

It was the flight attendant, once again making certain that I would not miss anything of interest.

Instinctively, I reached across my seat to share something, when I realized that I was all alone. Yet, Internally I felt Jake's presence with me. I could hear him whispering,

"Gabby I will never leave you Listen to your heart. It speaks our language."

"We will be landing in thirty minutes Ma'am. Is there anything else that I can do for you?" The attendant asked cordially.

Her voice brought me back to reality. But as soon as I stepped off the plane I knew my world would never be the same again.

At the gate, a driver was holding up a sign that read," Gabriella Girard". It took me a moment to realize that this was me; at least it was me a long time ago.

"I am Gabriella Girard" I answered, quickly.

"Excellent. My name is Sean, and I will be taking you to The Shelbourne, Miss. Don't worry about your luggage, it is being cared for along with your entry into the country. "

"But, I haven't even cleared customs yet," I said, confused.

The more I objected, the more Sean insisted that, "No need to worry. All has been handled."

Before I could say anything further, I found myself sitting in a black Cadillac, taking deep breaths and praying that I would not regret this after all. Although, my eyes were beginning to succumb to the time change, I refused to ignore my first sights of Ireland at ground level.

"Sean, would you please point out to me ALL the touristy attractions, regardless how blasé it may seem. I am excited to see as much as I can, even if it means only from this car."

I knew that I would only be here overnight, but I was hoping that I could coerce Sean into at least taking me to see The Book of Kells which are on display at the old library at Trinity College.

It was of course something I had to see. It is believed to have been created in circa 800. The four Gospels of the New Testament, is one of the finest preserved examples of Insular Art.

The extravagant and complex illustrations, include human figures blended with mythical animals and interlaced with Celtic knots and folklore.

"Miss Gabby, I would be honored to be your tour guide, like I was for Mr. Jake. He has left specific instructions, with footnotes that you could make any changes to his itinerary, Sean explained.

As always, Jake knew me well enough, even now, to understand that I would be totally immersed in this culture.

"This is what Jake asked me to give you once we arrived at the hotel," Sean passed me a small envelope with my initials GG embossed in gold. I decided to put it away in my purse until I was alone just in case I could not control my emotions.

"Coming up on your right, next to your hotel is St. Stephen's Green, twenty-two acres of park," Sean pointed out.

Once again, Caden was trespassing in my thoughts. No wonder, he was so comfortable at Central Park, St Stephen's Green was a mini replica.

Sean was continuing with his narrative as I returned mentally to my present attention.

"In 1916, it was the site of the historical Easter Rising. Two hundred and fifty insurgents took over the Green and established road blocks. It was an attempt by a few rebels to demand freedom from the British Crown.

Hoping that the United Kingdom would not react as quickly, the lenders had hoped to gain public support. However, that was not the case.

The British army took over the Shelbourne Hotel, right where you will be staying Gabby, and they were able to stop the rebellion in six
days. "

As we pulled up to the Hotel valet, Sean added one more note to his narration.

"When you get to your room, Miss Gabby, note the ducks in the pond outside your window. During the rebellion, both sides cased fire long enough for the groundskeeper to feed the local ducks," Sean winked.

I thanked him for his historical story and for his company during the drive from the airport. As I began to approach the front desk to check in, a timely quote from Samuel Beckett enters my mind. "We are all born mad. Some remain so."

Was this experience going to allow me closure, or will I continue to make connections to those times in my life that seemed to constantly overlap?

"Miss Gabriella Girard?" I heard again my ancient name being brought to life with a lovely Irish accent.

"Yes, that is me." And once again I was being lead to a new chapter of a very old story that refuses to end. In hindsight, I already know the ending before it begins but, that will not affect what I must now do.

CHAPTER 36

Poetry is what we do to break bread with the dead.
> - Sean Heaney

Gabby, July, 2003

"Eat breakfast, like a king, lunch like a prince, and dinner like a pauper, " was more like a lifestyle than an old Irish motto. The menu I was looking at this morning tempted me to start the day off with a traditional Irish breakfast, which included: loin bacon, or rashers, local sausage links, black and white pudding, and fried eggs, mushrooms, tomatoes, and haggis.

"Top of the morning to you Miss Gabby."

Sean, was dressed in a very official Limo outfit, with a fisherman's hat.

"You look quite impressive, Sean. Is all this finery for me? Pease join me for some tea and advise on all this food," I said.

Sean didn't even need to look at the menu. He seemed to know that he should steer me clear of the black and white pudding.

"You do know of course, that pudding is much different here than in the states, right?" Sean warned.

I looked at him skeptically. "How different do you mean?"

"I mean it is prepared from a particular type of sausage, made of pork meat, oats, spices and pork blood," Sean continued.

"Really? Pork blood? .... uh, I think I will pass on that. And what about haggis? I have no idea what that is either," I confessed.

"Oh, that is a real delicacy ...it is a savory pudding using sheep heart, liver, lungs, minced with onions, oat meal, suet and spices."

I was beginning to think that I should just stick to the familiar foods that I recognized.

"Seriously, Sean? Or are you just trying to freak me out?" I asked, doubting.

"Not sure what 'freaking ' out means, but I do love both haggis and puddings for breakfast."

After settling on some oatmeal, fresh fruit, juice, Irish soda bread with homemade preserves, it was time to discuss our day.

"Jake suggested that I see the Book of Kells at Trinity college, Martello Tower of Sandy cove, David Byrnes Pub and 7 Eccles St. "

Sean was enjoying his breakfast and tea, but nodded that he agreed with that list.

"That will be a full morning and will get you to the beach just about sunset. A great time to arrive. I will just give Tom a call so he won't need to wait at the cottage all day, "Sean replied.

Our first stop was Trinity College, founded in 1592 by Queen Elizabeth. I was fascinated how it was located in the center of Dublin, offering a unique sense of experiencing the past and present like a literary meridian line.

After viewing The Book of Kells we began to explore the university that contributed to the intellect of such great writers as, Jonathan Swift, Samuel Beckett, and James Joyce. A living tribute to those who were currently searching for answers to the same questions as I was.

When Jonathan Swift challenges man's ability to reason in his satirical essay "A Modest Proposal", he offers human babies to be raised like cattle to solve Ireland's famine. No more absurd than man's continued inhumanity today.

Samuel Beckett called James Joyce a synthesizer because of his ability to use Greek Tragedy to interpret modern dilemmas. While Beckett analyzes human motivation as we observe, two very confused men searching for Godot.

As Sean and I explored the various tributes to some of Trinity College's most famous Alums, I moved to a bench under a shady tree and reached for the embossed note Sean gave me yesterday, from Jake. When I was certain I was alone, I reread his words, aloud.

Dearest Gabby,

When I was at Trinity College, I was reminded that the masters of the world are those who have discovered that "Waiting for Godot" is a play that strives above all else to avoid definition. I have, nevertheless, come to the conclusion that this is what my life has been. You are the only one that has any chance of understanding. So, I am now leaving you with the first clue to what I hope will be the universal truth that we were both in search of. Please read this carefully, and often during your trip.

My undying love,
Jake

The short essay that he is referring to was not a new study of Symbolist Drama, but considering that my current life was moving in that direction, a new definition of life imitating art was right on target. So, I decided to read it once more:
"Static Drama" written by, Remy Gourmont, 1895 Hidden in mist somewhere there is an island, and on that island, there is a castle, and in that castle, there is a great room lit by a little lamp. And in that room people are waiting for someone to open the door, waiting for their lamp to go out, waiting for FEAR and DEATH.

They talk. Yes, they speak words that shatter the silence of the moment. And then they listen again, leaving their sentences unfinished, their gestures uncomplicated. They are listening. They are waiting. Will she come perhaps, or won't she?

Yes, she will come, she always comes. But it is late, and she will not come perhaps until tomorrow. The people collected under that little lamp, in that great room, nevertheless, begun to smile; they still have hope. Then there is a knock-a 'knock' and that is all there is: And it is Life Complete, All of Life.

I folded both the essay and the note, returning it to my purse.

"I think I'm ready to move on Sean. Can we go to 7 Eccles St. next, and then just a quick stop at David Byrne's Pub before heading out to Martello Towers of Sandy cove?" I said, excited to get started.

"That's a plan. Especially stopping at the pub. You're already fitting in Miss Gabby. Pretty soon I will be calling you Lassie Gabby," Sean, said tipping his hat.

We both headed toward the limo, feeling like whatever Jake wanted us to accomplish, so far we have fulfilled. I was beginning to feel a weight being lifted, as if each day was bringing me closer to some lost recognition of a truth revealed.

James Joyce writes in **Ulysses**, that, "every life is in many days, day after day. We walk through ourselves, meeting robbers, ghosts, giants, old men, young men, wives, brothers-in-love. But always meeting ourselves."

This is why, when the literature I read no longer remains fiction, and my life becomes layered with the chemical emotions created by authors that span history, it is becomes more than a temporary journey that I share, it is a connection that suspends time. The world is no longer a mere stage, it is a looking glass into the past and future using the same lens.

And because of this, I find that I no longer need the 3.5 mile walk in Dublin, that attempts to condense Joyce's iconic novel, **Ulysses**, into an abridged version. Only Joyce (and perhaps Virginia Wolfe) could pull off a one-day pilgrimage through the eyes of his character, Leopold Bloom.

I already know how Bloom is consumed with irrelevant matters, like his weight, and the weight of all bodies including falling bodies in particular.

I had resolved, that stopping at Dave Byrne's Pub would be a more honest tribute to Joyce. Situated on 21 Duke Street, it is considered the most frequented literary pub in Ireland.

Both Sean and I order the now famous Gorgonzola cheese sandwich and s glass of burgundy wine that Leopold had at his visit.

I admire the art nouveau ceiling light above the curved marble bar, and notice the Joycean Dublin mural painted by Liam Proud, depicting David Byrnes himself surveying his famous bar. The decor remains authentic, original pre Second World War. Another place where time remains still.

We do not stay long, but just long enough to admire how the ambience has retained the images that Joyce described eighty-one years ago.

Sean begins to prep me for the Martello Towers of Sandy Cove, which has sentimental roots for both Jake and me.

"Martello Towers can be found all around the coast of Ireland. They were built by the British in the early 19th century to defend against the Napoleonic invasion. As you know, the particular one in Sandy Cove is the setting for A Portrait of an Artist of a Young Man. It has also been converted to a Joyce museum. "

I continued to listen silently while staring out of the dark tinted windows. I was about to approach the literary site where Jake and Stephen Daedalus learned that an appreciation for beauty can be truly good.

For us, the human spirit of our lives, were dramatically changed in a few seconds of epiphany, forever.

Sean was parking the car near the tower when I instructed him to drive as close to the beach as possible.

"Of course, Miss Gabby, but don't you care to see the museum first? There are some fascinating artifacts that I am sure you would appreciate," Sean insisted.

I ignored for the moment any outside interruptions. As I exited the car I removed my shoes and started to walk on the sandy beach.

"Not too close to the water.... the waves can be unpredictable, Miss, during this time of the year," I heard Sean yelling behind me.

I continued walking. *My "memory " mind watching a young girl standing midstream in front of me with her head bent, gazing out to the sea. Her skirts were tucked around her waist and her toes are playing with the sea foam. As she looks up, and directly at me, I recognize her face. The long chestnut hair being windblown, the freckle kisses on her nose and then the green eyes stare into mine, and suddenly my knees begin to shake, and I feel like I am going to collapse, until two arms wrap me in a wool jacket and catch me from falling.*

"Gabby! My God, are you alright? You look as white as a parchment sheet". Sean asks, genuinely concerned.

I regained my balance and assure Sean that I was fine. *But, as we walked back to the car, I turned around for just a moment as the girl waved goodbye. It was then that I realized that she was me.*

CHAPTER 37

He had ceased to live within himself; She was his life. The ocean to the river of his thoughts. Which terminated all; He had no breath, no being, but in hers; She was his voice.
-The Dream, Lord Byron

Gabby, July, 2003

Like an interrupted dream that is left unfinished, my drive to Inchydoney Island challenged me to understand a reality that was forever evolving.

Outside was a world of green that must be experienced to be understood. It was as if an artist carefully chose an analogous color scheme that included various shades of yellow, reds and purples to create the necessary warmth and coolness that encourages harmony to exist.

When Sean pulled up to the small white cottage that was surrounded by sand, I felt like I was coming home. A sentimental awakening where I could sense that Jake had not only been here but was still here at this moment.

"Welcome, Miss Gabby to Inchydoney. We painted the sky for your arrival," He was pointing at the horizon where the sun was beginning to quickly slip away leaving traces of incredible pinks, raspberry, and lavender, streaks that resembled ribbons of ice gleaming with just a hint of sparkling silver dust. And at a distance I noticed a Lighthouse, a charming unexpected addition to an already perfect landscape.

"My name is Tom O'Leary. You have no idea how thrilled I am to finally meet you. After spending some time with your, Jake...you don't mind me referring to him that way does you? "he asked, politely.

I assure him by nodding my head, encouraging Tom to continue. I am fascinated with not only what he is saying but with his genuine enthusiasm as he leads me into the cottage.

Inside the courtyard, I noticed a bicycle. That would come in handy, I thought to myself. Am sure it will be my primary mode of transportation.

The home interior was simply decorated, with wicker baskets lined in fresh cut flowers that invitingly filled the room with the aroma of fresh lavender.

As we walked up the stairs, Tom revealed my bedroom for the next few days. As I approached the four poster bed my fingertips lightly touched the comforter.

"Is this where Jake slept, when he was here?" I asked, staring out the bay window at the powerful Irish Sea.

"Oh, yes, of course. Mr. Jake was very specific that this room be your room as well," Tom answered.

It would be the first time that we shared a bed together, even though, ironically he is dead.

Tom, then pulled out a card from his pocket, it had the same embossed initials stamped in gold GG, as the one I was given earlier, from Sean at Dublin.

"Jake requested that I personally deliver this to you as soon as you were ready to settle down. I am so pleased that I now can finally fulfill my obligation," Tom, said gently.

It was clear that Tom was relieved, that whatever this mystery was, it was at last coming to its conception.

As I took the note, from Tom I had to ask," How well did you and Jake get to know one another?"

Tom, was placing my luggage in the closet for me, when he turned and held my hand in his gently.

"Jake made many friends here, in a very short time. He was an old soul, with an Irish charm that invited everyone he met to celebrate his amazing life. We, Irish admire those who are dedicated to love and there has never been a man more loyal to love than Jake," Tom said sincerely.

Now I knew that Tom had fallen into Jake's charm like most people that met him. This charisma was a gift that made him capable of achieving anything that he wanted to.

I never truly knew this Jake, but I didn't need to. He was the kind of man that could only grow larger than the shadow that he left behind.

"There is a shepherd's pie in the fridge and a bottle of wine if you get hungry. May God hold you in the palm of his hand, until we meet again, sweet Gabby," Tom said.

"Oh, thank you Tom, for all that you have done for me and Jake. I look forward to seeing you tomorrow," I said, with relief that I was finally here.

When I heard the downstairs door close I laid across the bed, fully clothed, forgetting about the note in my hand.

As I shut my eyes to the monochromatic past a cinematic light replaces the day. *Sleep hath its own world, a boundary between the things, misnamed Death and existence*

The image of my Tybee Lighthouse appears in a noir photo with a plastic multicolored overlay, producing a beckoning image inviting me to enter.

A wide realm of wild reality that the mind can make, and create substance and people, even planets of its own , with beings brighter than they have ever been. A breadth to forms which can outlive all flesh.

As I enter, this foreign state, not certain why, I do believe, like J R Tolkien, that not all of those that wander are lost.

I am not lost. I have finally found my way back from a very dark road, to here, where dreams in their development have breath, and tears, and tortures, and the touch of Joy.

A short distance, up the spiral staircase, I have a glimpse of Jake, like spirits of the past, they speak of the future; they have power- the tyranny of pleasure and of pain

In slow motion, my legs feel like they are weighted down with lead, I get closer and closer. When they leave, a weight, upon our waking thoughts remains. They make us what we were not, and shake us with the vision that's gone by. Is not the past all shadow?

Beneath my feet, I feel hay spread all around the bare ground, I recall a vision which I dreamed Perchance in sleep. A slumbering thought, is capable of years, and curdles a long time into one hour.

Until the orange blossom scent is not enough to stop the annoying ringing in my ears.At last I realize it is my cell phone, next to my head. I answer it, still not certain what is real and what is not.

"Gabby? Gabby? ....."

I hear my name, being called in my ear and then look at my watch that displays both Irish time and Kentucky time. That is when I recognize Alex's voice.

"Oh Alex, I am soooo sorry. Everything is moving just so fast and with the time change, well I know none of this is a good excuse. I should have called you, but I guess all I can say is I am sorry and hope you will forgive me?" My apology is only half sincere.

I waited a few seconds and then Alex finally answered.

"You had me with, "Oh, Alex". I just wanted to know that you were safe and not overdoing anything. Please just promise me that you will be careful over there?" Alex said, sounding like he was on another planet.

"You don't need to worry about me Alex. I have a great support system here,"I reassured him.

Reluctantly, I could hear him say, "Okay, I am trusting that you know what is best. Have a good time and remember that I love you," He said, almost out of obligation.

"24-7 babe. Alex? " And before I could add that I missed him I heard the phone click. It was probably best. I was losing my talent for lying.

When the sunshine crept in through the sheer curtains, I was stunned to realize that it was 6 AM. The card from Jake, still lay unopened on the bed.

I decided to take a fast shower, and change into a comfortable T-shirt and my favorite pair of jeans. The beach was my first priority after I brewed a cup of tea to take with me on my walk. The letter would have to wait until I returned.

Once on the boardwalk, that lead me to a beach path, I marveled at the sweeping views of the Cooley Mountains, and the wading birds along the inter-tidal marshes.

This invited a pleasant contrast to the nervous movement that I found in Dublin.

At a distance, near the tide, I could see people kite surfing and sail boarding. But, other than that I was alone. As I started to walk toward the cliffs and Lighthouse a beautiful golden retriever was skimming the surf in search for what I presumed must be a stick someone had thrown for her.

As I stopped to watch, she saw me and with her dripping wet coat, that resembled a melted piece of caramel candy, she proudly showed me the fish between her teeth. I bent down to pet her.

Her eyes were sparkling brown, like the Milky Way flying by.

"Karma, are you showing off again to the ladies?" I recognized that voice.

It was Tom, standing behind her.

"Did you sleep well Gabby? I was going to ring you but thought best you sleep as much as possible. With the time change and traveling yesterday," He said.

I debated whether to let Tom know about my rather odd dream, and at last decided against it. I did share with him, that I was still confused why Jake was so determined to spend all of his last days negotiating this trip.

"Tom, I do not know if you knew that the last time I saw Jake alive was thirty five years ago. And, that our parting was not a pleasant one. So, you see Jake never was mine for very long. There was a time, very long ago when...." I couldn't finish, before

Tom abruptly stopped me from completing my thought.

"Oh, but you are so very mistaken Gabby. True love is never measured by time. True love has no time limits or restrictions. Jake did this to show you that he never left you, not even now," Tom said with passion.

It must have appeared that I was an unwilling believer, but I was still processing logically and what I was learning, required me to think in unchartered territories.

I know how confused you must be, but you also must trust and appreciate this design that was tailor fit for you. Trust me when I tell you that the outcome will make you feel exhilarated, and most importantly relieved," Tom emphasized.

 Perhaps, that is exactly why I felt that I must complete this journey. Closure would be the only way I could at least spend my final years in peace.

"I am praying Tom, that it will do all that. " I answered at last.

Inside of his coat pocket, Ton revealed a box wrapped in brown butcher paper with a blue Tiffany ribbon tied in a bow.

"Here in Ireland Gabby, we have a saying that goes like this: The mystery of love is greater than the mystery of death. And I do believe you will soon agree. Hopefully, this token will begin to give you clarity," He said.

Before I could respond, both Tom and Karma were out of sight.

Heading back to the cottage, the late morning mist was hanging like a conspicuous cloud that was sneaking down to the earth. I noticed smoke coming from my chimney, inviting me to enter.

As I got closer, the smell of sizzling bacon, and freshly baked bread, immediately made me forget about any conflicts that might be stirring in my brain. While I was out, it was like leprechauns, or maybe fairies, had prepared a wonderful feast.

After eating, my attention turned to the brown paper wrapped box. The small card on the outside merely said Tiffany. I could only presume that Jake was having fun with the two opposite images, the butcher paper and Tiffany Blue ribbon and card. When I opened the card it said:

"You have always been the 'classic beauty' that held my coarse life together, my Tiffany, my energy, my ALL. My Gabby Golightly," Jake.

Of course. Breakfast at Tiffany's. So many years ago, but these words were intense, tender, and not from the man I used to know.

Jake had become the man I never knew, but somehow still the man who knew me better than I knew myself. I had to wonder if this change was somehow due to Isabella.

As I unwrapped the package, I noticed that even the tape had yellowed from age. Once opened the front cover of a leather journal had a brass engraved plate that read, "Love is the emblem of eternity; it compounds all memory of a beginning, all fear of an end".

Madam de Stael

Below this quote was another handwritten inscription:

To my Gabriella Girard
August 20, 2000

The two things that struck me at once was, that Jake continued to call me by my maiden name, even though he knew I was married; and the date. August 20 was the day we met in 1963. I knew that both of these details were significant. It was not a coincidence that Jake chose that date to be here, thirty-seven years later.

Once I opened the journal, I realized that most of the pages were written. I continued to read the first page:

"This journal can only begin to make you understand, what my life has been without you all of these years. I do not regret the ultimate paths that we both took, but I am sorry that I never respected your maturity, logic and intelligence.

Without sounding redundant, I must hope that somehow, by the end of this odyssey, you will have at least a sense of what I discovered about the intensity of our lives.

My objective for you to travel, with me metaphorically, through Europe, is more than a sentimental one. Crossing the time lines, surrounding you in countries that hold answers to so many ancient questions, regarding life, love, and yes, even death. I am optimistic that you will discover, as I did, some amazing answers.

I have come to believe, my dearest Gabby, that now as I face the ultimate time destroyer, known as DEATH, that to love as we have, holds a special power that opens other time vaults, making love truly eternal.

You may, of course, look through this journal at any time, since I have prepared it for YOU. However, it would be wise to follow the instructions outlined, to benefit most from the experience.

Do not be surprised if you feel my hand caress your face, or you feel a kiss on your forehead unexpectedly. I may even whisper in your ear or play with your hair, because I am forever with you.

You already know by now, how much Ireland means to me. From the first Joyce epiphany to our first night together at Tybee Lighthouse, there was nothing more powerful that influenced my life.

I want you to feel that spirit, breathe the air. It will remove all the sorrow and pain that you have. There is a balance here that will follow you forever, and I had to share it with you.

JAKE

Attached to the journal was a silver bracelet, with a Claddagh ring, symbolizing eternal life.

"Wear this when you can, keep it close when you can't, and never turn your back on the inevitable."

315

I put the bracelet on, and turned the journal page. I recognized part of a poem by Lord Byron that has been fading in and out of my brain since I arrived. Was it perchance that Jake included additional lines here?

How could he ever know that Byron's words would evoke so much emotions within me? I began to read it aloud:

The Lady of his love; --Oh! She was changed, as by the sickness of the soul; her mind
Had wondered from its dwelling, and her eyes, they had not their own luster...but the look, which is not of this earth.... We're combinations of disjointed things....and this the world calls frenzy; but the wise have a far deep was madness---And the glance of melancholy is a fearful gift; What is but a telescope of truth? Which strips the distance of its fantasies, and brings life in utter nakedness, Making the cold reality too real!"

I wanted to read on, but should I follow what Jake said or my own instincts. I turned the page.

"Now, how did I know that you would NEVER follow my instructions, Gabby?" I could almost hear his voice mocking me.

I began to laugh, like when he played some crazy prank on me at the beach.

"If you do insist on reading on, just know that it will not give you the answers that you want. It is the actual experience that will be your guide. So, sweetheart, just try to trust me one last time, and go with the plan."

This was actually beginning to be fun and I wasn't even feeling alone.

Most of my remaining days I spent walking the beach, riding my bike to the village and joining Tom at the Pub for conversation and storytelling .

When I was at home in the evening, I decided to add my own thoughts and comments to Jake's reflections. It was a way that I could establish a connection that might appear unconventional but, therapeutic.

Dear Jake,

In Dublin, in front of the Writer's Museum at Parnell Square,then the Georgian architecture was what first held my attention. And the trees in Stephen's Green were "fragrant of rain and the rain sodden earth gave forth it's mortal odor".

It was uncanny how Joyce was able to describe such simple experiences with profound enlightenment. Very much like you.

I put down my pen, closed the journal and for the first time, I felt like I was moving in the right direction.

CHAPTER 38

"My dreams were all my own; I accounted to them for nobody; they were my refuge when annoyed--My dearest
pleasure when free."-Mary Shelley

Gabby, July, 2003

My final days in Inchydoney were spent either walking on
the beach or, enjoying afternoon tea with Maggie, the owner of the local bakery, Queen of Tarts. It was hard to say
how old Maggie was, since everyone looked like they
stepped out of the fictional musical **Brigadoon.**

Like a mythical village, the locals all appeared to be
locked in a time warp. It was a comfortable, layback existence that beckoned me to stay.

In the original**, Brigadoon**, Tommy, the intruder from the
modern world, falls in love with Fiona, a resident of Brigadoon. He, at last decides to remain with her in this enchanted land, that only appears once every two hundred
years to the outside world.

It would be easy for me to remain in this Irish "Brigadoon
" if it wasn't for my promise to follow Jake's plan. Had we
both come her together, when we were young, I know we
would never have left. It was wise for him to choose this as
my first destination and not the last.

"So dearie, tell me proper, where has Jake sent you next?
We here in the village have been waiting several years to
find out how this mystery will end."

"Paris, Maggie, and honestly, I would rather remain here
with you."

The thought of moving forward, once again, just as I was
beginning to feel at ease, was not appealing.

"You know, Maggie, I wish that I could stay longer, but from what I have gathered so far, once this plan is put into gear it must keep moving until it ends."

"We Irish, always say that 'may the saddest day of your future, be no worse than the happiest day of your past."

"Thank you Maggie. You Irish are wise people. I will never forget you." And with a quick kiss on her cheek, my farewells were beginning.

Saying goodbye to Thomas was the most difficult. He was my "straw man" on this journey.

"In Paris, Gabby you will learn even more about Jake and I just know that with each day the answers to all of your questions will be revealed," Tom said, reassuringly.

I knew that I would miss the warmth of Tom's wise words as well as his strong shoulders that I often cried on.

Karma looked at me with longing eyes as I reached around her neck for one last hug. I bent down and whispered in her ear,

"I am looking forward to you sending me all those positive vibes, that I know you have been planning for me, my love." I felt her head nuzzle beneath my arm.

That evening, I returned early from the Pub. My bags packed, it was time to turn to Jake's journal.

I noticed that on the next page there was an entry titled "Leaving Inchydoney."

"I know exactly how you feel right now Gabby, but each day only gets better. I will give you a little foreshadowing that I think will make you smile. In Paris, you will be met at the airport by Molly. I have made arrangements for you to stay with her the next 4 days.

My time in Paris had to include your childhood friend to make this part of the journey as comfortable for you as possible. That is all that I am sharing now, but that should put your mind at ease."

Love J

Of course, Molly. In all of the excitement and stress it just slipped my mind completely that Molly was living in Paris. But, that Jake actually spent his time with her there, alone, seemed very odd.

We were naturally all friends in high school, and he knew how important she meant to me, but that was thirty-five years ago. How did he even know where she lived?

And, why didn't Molly ever tell me about all of this? I guess those are some of my unanswered questions that will soon become clear.

Sean was on time, as always, to take me to the Dublin airport the next morning. Since this was only a ninety-minute direct flight, I was traveling in coach.

The gentleman seated next to me was flying back home to Paris. He asked me if I had ever been to "the city of lights" before.

"No, I have not. But I have a good friend who lives there and I am excited to learn as much as I can about your exceptional country," I said, excited.

I was not going to divulge my true reason for visiting Paris to a complete stranger that would consider me just another crazy American.

"Well then, let me introduce myself to you, Madam. I am Pierre Marcel. And I will share with you a very interesting fact about my beloved Paris."

He took my hand and kissed it gently.

"And, who do I have the pleasure to be sitting next to?" He asked politely.

"I am Gabriella Girard, and I am from Savannah, Georgia."

I wasn't sure why I didn't give Pierre my married name, or that I lived in Kentucky, but maybe it had something to do with the last few days when I was beginning to feel like my old self again.

"Magnifique! You too are French, no?"

I had never thought about being French. We never really discussed it at home. I knew that my mother's mother was

Russian, but my dad's familywere all deceased and he rarely spoke about them.

" I suppose maybe I have some French ancestors, but I cannot be sure."

Pierre winked at me, and I noticed that when he smiled he had dimples that just for a moment reminded me of Jake.

"My Cheri, in France your name means Angel of God. There is no doubt that you have French running through your blood." Pierre said in a very thick accent.

Thankfully Pierre was being very kind to this older woman, traveling alone, and it was comforting to hear him share his stories.

"Please Pierre, tell me about Paris. Why is it called The City of Lights? " I truly wanted to know., I, of course, like most people thought it must be because of all the city lights, but that just seemed too obvious.

" In the evening the city does light up more than two hundred ninety buildings. But, there is more than this fact. My city was the birthplace of The Age of Enlightenment, then known as 'La Ville-Lumiete'.

In addition, Paris was one of the few cities in Europe to have outside lighting, allowing people to walk late in the evening. It later became known as the City of Romance because lovers would seek each other on the famous lit Seine River."

Would I be finding Jake somewhere here in Paris? Or maybe him bringing me to this city of Enlightenment would somehow be where I intellectually would be able to sort out my many conflicting feelings? I was now, more anxious than ever, to find out more about the magic that this city had to offer.

"Thank you Pierre. I now am a more informed tourist. I will definitely be looking forward to my evening strolls on the Seine,"I said.

As the plane circled the city in preparation for its final decent, Pierre handed me a card.

"Madam Gabriella, here is the name of my art gallery. If you are in the vicinity, please stop by and let me know how you find my city. We can toast with a glass of champagne to the future," He replied.

Once off the plane, I never saw Pierre again. Going through customs and retrieving my luggage was more difficult this time, until I spotted Molly running toward me. Her long strawberry blonde hair flying all around she grabbed me with both arms and held me close for several minutes.

"Oh my gosh Gabby....I can't believe you are finally here," Molly said.

The last time we were together was at my wedding thirty three years ago. We were both so very young and our futures were moving in different directions.

But, we never lost contact with one another. At least once a month we would phone or text.

"Why didn't you ever tell me about all of this Molly? I would have come sooner?"

Molly looked right through me like she always was able to do.

"Do not even give me any attitude missy...why did it take Jake dying for you to come out here? And, I was sworn to keep the secret about this entire adventure. Do you really think that I would lie to a dying man? "Molly insisted.

I knew she was right. And quickly apologized. I could never stay mad at Molly for very long.

"The two of us are going to have the time of our lives, girlfriend. But let's get you settled at my place first. "Molly said, grabbing one of my duffle bags.

Being with Molly after all these years made me feel like I was back home in Savannah. If there was anything that I regretted it was that I waited this long to get here.

Once in the car, our ride from the airport was historical. From every angle I could see parts of the Eiffel Tower majestically reaching for the clouds.

"MI Cheri, you look amazing. Not any older than on your wedding day. Forgive me for not telling you, but Jake wanted to see you many times and I convinced him that you both moved on and nothing good would come from him contacting you now,"

I was listening but my focus was on the beautiful architecture that I had only read about. The Basilica of St. Denis, where every monarch was buried until the French Revolution; the Place de la Concorde, where Louis the XVI, and many others were executed during the French Revolt; and of course the Arc de Triumph, an iconic Parisian landmark.

"You know Gabby, he could have hired a guide and left me out of this entirely, but he knows how special you are to me. He wanted this to be perfect for you," Molly continued.

Finally, I now turned my attention toward Molly, who was obviously concerned that I was still upset with her.

"I know Molly that you could not share this with me. I would have done the same for you. But, do you at least know what the plan here is? Or is that a secret as well?" I asked.

Molly seemed to ignore me as she began turning down a quaint boulevard near the Champs Elysees.

"We are almost there. Let's get home and settled first and then we will talk, okay? "Maggie pleaded.

I had to admit that patience was never a virtue that I could claim. As we parked and walked up the first flight of stairs to a rather large flat with a bay window that faced the colonnade and Seine River, I was not surprised at how artistic everything was.

Molly had the eye for the unusual and it was obvious by the paintings on the walls to the sheepskin rug and the red leather couch.

"I have prepared the same room for you that Jake stayed in. He insisted that you sleep here," She said.

I was beginning to see a pattern that he was creating. For whatever reason, he felt that sharing the same bed would bring us closer, even now.

The bedroom was small, but comfortable with an airy feeling. The wall to ceiling window created a frame for the view of the Seine from another angle. As I walked closer I could see that there was also a bistro on the corner that looked exactly like the painting over the bed.

"Is this one of yours Molly? "I asked, admiring the details.

From behind, Molly a short lady with jet black hair piled on the top of her head with a bun and a black enameled hair clip in the shape of a butterfly, replied.

"That would actually be one of my pastels. " she said, proudly.

She reached around Molly and gave me a gentle, almost light hug.

"Gabby, meet Gigi, my partner for the last ten years," Molly was holding her hand.

I don't know why I was shocked. Molly never had a boyfriend since I've known her. But, she also never appeared to be Gay, whatever that might mean.

"You are just filled with surprises aren't you Molly? Glad to finally meet you Gigi. "I said warmly.

"Well, Gabby you have to admit that this is not something that you just text your best friend, and your life has been so complicated, I just thought it would be easier if you met Gigi in person."

There is no doubt that my life has been a very strange mess. That is one of the reasons why Jake's proposal came at a perfect time.

"I am of course thrilled to meet you Gigi. Molly deserves someone who loves her and can tolerate all of her idiosyncrasies," I added, winking.

Molly walked over and gave me a slight hip bump. "You should talk, Gabby. Your here because at least one man couldn't ever forget you his entire life. How strange can that be?" Molly half teased with me.

We all broke out in laughter and decided it was time to open a bottle of French wine and review what my plan would be.

"The only request that Jake made me promise was that I would let his contact know that you had arrived. From that point on, he said all would happen naturally."

Naturally was an odd choice of words. There is nothing natural about any of this.

"It is like I expect at the end of the trip, Molly, that Jake will meet me at the airport and we will fly away together. And I know THAT isn't going to happen."

Molly was staring at me with her huge, brown almond shaped eyes, and took a sip of her wine methodically.

"You have to live for this moment only Gabby. Just stop forecasting, foreshadowing, and predicting. Enjoy this moment. It will never come again. "Molly's wise words were priceless.

She was holding Gigi's hand as if that message was for both of us. We finished the wine and I was told that we were going to meet a few other people for supper at a near-by cafe.

The next morning, after a croissant and cappuccino we began our short walk to the Louvre and Notre Dame Cathedral. Every day was a new attraction, and nothing ever strange happened. No, gifts delivered. No notes from strangers. This was beginning to seem like a normal vacation.

On the last day Molly got me up a little later. We had spent the previous evening at a jazz bar until wee hours of the morning and all of us looked forward to sleeping late.

"Okay, sleepy head, " I heard her tapping at my door. "We are going to the Eiffel Tower today and need to be there by noon. Our tickets just arrived by a bike courier. "Molly said, holding them up for me to see.

It took me less than thirty minutes to be up and ready. I could not imagine leaving Paris without seeing the Eiffel Tower. Molly decided that walking during this time of the day would be better than driving.

Along the side streets we stopped at a souvenir shop to browse since we were quite early for our tour. While I waited outside for Molly, who was buying me a flashing Eiffel Tower replica to take home, I noticed the small art gallery.

In the window on a small canvas was an oil painting of a young surfer holding the hand of his girlfriend. As I looked closer, in the background was a Lighthouse.

But, it wasn't just any Lighthouse. On the door it read Tybee Lighthouse. Then I looked at the couple once more. On the sand the initials J Loves G stood out.

When Molly finally came out I pulled her over to the window. " Look at this picture, Molly. What do you see? "I asked, bewildered.

"Okay. And what about it? "Molly's response was not what I expected.

"Doesn't it look familiar to you? "I asked.

And that is when she began to gently push me into the gallery. "Yes, it does look familiar. Because it was me who painted it,"Molly revealed.

"What? How could you ...I mean why would...."

"Because, Jake commissioned me to do this for you."

And then I saw Pierre walk over from the back of the studio. " Bonjour, Madam Gabby, so we meet again." Both he and Molly were smiling as if they had just pulled off the best caper of their lives.

"I mean I don't exactly understand. Did you know Jake, Pierre? And was it planned that you would be seated next to me on the plane?"

"Yes and yes. Molly introduced me to Jake when he was here. This studio belongs to us. Gigi is my sister. I hope you will not be angry with me," He asked, shyly.

"I could never be angry about this. I just cannot believe that so much effort was put into all of this for me. Molly, this painting is a masterpiece. But, you know I cannot take it with me home. It would be impossible to explain to Alex." But, I knew It would be difficult to leave this behind.

"We did take that into account. I took a picture for the journal and will keep this in the gallery for you. Just let me know when you will want it and I will ship it to you. "Molly said.

We both said goodbye to Pierre and continued to the Eiffel Tower. We grabbed a table outside, waiting for the tour guide to arrive. The plan was to have lunch at Nemo's on the second floor of the Eiffel Tower after the tour.

From nowhere, in particular, loud music could be heard and on a make shift stage in front of the Tower a young man grabbed the hand of his girlfriend and fell to one knee.

The crowd was beginning to cheer in all languages. But this couple had microphones on and were speaking English.

The young man looked into the girl's eyes and said very clearly " Gabby, for now and eternity, will you be my wife?"

Then I knew that this was Jake at work again. The young girl looked totally surprised but by this time we all realized this was a staged engagement.

"Of course Jake I will marry you. But let me see the ring first."

The crowd went wild. And then the actors came to our table and said, "You are Gabby, oui?" I was speechless, but Molly answered for me. "Yes, this is Gabby," She was pointing directly at me.

"We hope that you enjoyed our little skit. Monsieur Jake asked us to perform it for you. He said you would understand."

I reached out to thank them, when the Gabby persona removed the ring from her finger and placed it on mine. I noticed it was not an engagement ring but an infinity ring. The music began once more and the crowds continued to cheer. I was speechless. What possibly could come next.

"Do you think we can just skip lunch Molly? I just want to go back and read what Jake wrote about this in the journal," I said, holding back tears

"Of course, Honey. I think that is a great idea," Molly replied.

Back in the apartment I realized that I hadn't called Alex since I arrived. But this was not the right time. After staring at my ring for what seemed forever, I opened the journal:

Welcome back Gabby.

It took you a little time to get to this part didn't it? I hope the skit did not upset you. I had to include the marriage proposal, even if it was by proxy. I promised to marry you all those years ago in Savannah, in the barn. Remember, it was going to be official at the Eiffel Tower?

I know you remember this. The ring is my promise to love you beyond the vows "until death does us part." Nothing, especially death, or time will stop me from that love. The ring is only a symbol, but I hope you will at least keep it and wear it when possible when you get home.

Love, Jake

This would be something that I could never share with Alex. Processing it for me was even difficult. But, at the moment the ring was finally where it was meant to be. I would continue to wear the ring until I landed in Kentucky. Then I would need to decide how to live with what I was now dealing with.

CHAPTER 39

"Life is divided into three terms--That which was, which is, and which will be. Let us learn from the past to profit, by the present, and from the present to live better in the future." --William Wordsworth

Gabby July, 2003

Once I arrived in Great Britain the train became my mode of transportation and my serene retreat. This is where I was able to daydream when I wanted to and digest each new experience when I needed to.

The journal that Jake gave me became my daily devotional. Whenever I began to feel lonely I would read the passages, that were sometimes insightful quotes or enigmatic reflections.

He included several pencil drawings. Some that were portraits of me over the years. It was clearly his way of imaging how I grew older.

Sometimes there would be snapshots of Savannah, or Boston and Notre Dame University. Never any pictures with Isabella.

I was curious why Jake and Isabella never had children. Was it an intentional decision, or a medical issue? At this point it really didn't matter. Although there were also sketches of young children in the journal.

Did Jake ever imagine what our children would have looked like? Escaping into Jake's world, was both painful and delightful. And sometimes, it was just curious.

I continued reading, eager to discover new insights that Jake would share with me.

"I so wish that I could see your expression when you walked into the garden where Keats wrote 'Ode to a Nightingale'. It was Wentworth Place where he fell in love with Fanny Browne. "

Jake wrote.

"She was his truth like you are mine. Because of her, Keats was able to bring Endymion to life, fulfilling his every desire; symbolizing beauty, reconciling reality with his poetic quest. I am including here, some of my most favorite lines from that poem, primarily, because it reinforces what you shared with me in "'Ode on a Grecian Urn'". *A thing of beauty is a joy forever, its loveliness increases; it will never pass into nothingness...* '

Endymion, who fell in love with the moon goddess Selene, was given a destiny choice by Zeus. Wisely he chose immortality and to live in eternal slumber. Laid to rest at the cave at Karian Mount Latmos, his lover the moon would visit him each evening. Sleeping where I have slept, I know you have felt my spirit.

Never doubt the power of my love for you."

Jake

Recalling now, how Isabella was instructed to spread his ashes at Tybee beach, made the obvious even more relevant.

Jake was determined to suspend his death, daring to continue to live through words and images. His goal was to remain a powerful part of my life.

Continuing on to Stratford -upon- Avon, by train, I listened to a collection of sonnets that Jake selected. They began with innocent, young love concluding with a celebration of commitment and adoration.

The enduring, reoccurring theme of faithfulness, as well as, exploring the sadness of loss was so powerful that I was moved between joy and grief blended together as one.

"Love is not Love which alters when it alteration finds, or bends with the remover to remove.... Loves not Times fool. Love alters not with his brief hours, and weeks...if this be error and upon me proved, I never writ, nor no man ever loved." Sonnet 116.

At the end of the Sonnet Readings, Jake annotated these in the journal with his own personal reflections and memories that he now shared, with me.

It was documented like a scholarly thesis, defending his position. He dedicated Sonnet 116 to me for that purpose.

Back on the train, once again, my next stop was Chested Wales. An hour train ride from Bath. There I would find the remains of Tintern Abby, immortalized by William Wordsworth. This was my next destination.

I opened the journal to the section marked, Wales. From what he wrote it was clear that he wanted me to experience more than just the poetic words. It was this fascinating setting that inspired Wordsworth.

From, the train windows I was captured by the rugged coastline. Boarded by England to the east and the Irish Sea to the north and west, Wales retained a distinct original ambiance. I was certain that Jake's fascination with Wales was more than merely Wordsworth's legendary poem set at Tintern Abbey.

The Eisteddfod tradition, celebrating literature and music, was a festival that originated in the 12th century, and continues to attract competitive artists and musicians throughout Europe today.

As I approach, however, the remains of Tintern Abby I can hear the wind echoing the words,

"Where I stand, not only with the sense of present pleasure, but with pleasing thoughts, that in this moment there is Life and food for future years..." William Wordsworth.

I am now reminded that we too, just like this Abby, can continue to communicate through, poetry, music, and art. Once again, I open Jake's journal.

Gabby, darling,

By now, I hope that you are learning that we are sharing more together at this time than we were ever able to while I was alive. Experiencing "sameness" connects us forever. You will read through the journal and I will come to life in your mind.

Love,

Your, Jake

It was becoming much easier to understand what he was saying. And there were many times, that I would wake up at night and feel Jake's presence. It also explained the reason why I would be distracted by thoughts of Jake without control.

But, I was not yet convinced that this was what I wanted. Did Jake really expect me now to fall in love with him all over again?

Even if I admit that I never stopped loving him, I was able to accept his decision. Venice was supposed to be where everything would be revealed.

Venice, I was promised, would provide me with my most direct message from Jake. Had he discovered a way to transport me to another world? The true world of reality? Or would it be the world of the absurd?

Regardless of the outcome, I would return to Kentucky with a deeper understanding of who Jake really was.

Whereas, Paris is known as the city of lights, Venice is often called the land of love. Not until you arrive to the canals does the ambiance become clear. Senora Sophia was dutifully waiting for me at the water taxi.

After a brief introduction, she gave the driver instructions to the exclusive, five star, Belmond Cipriani. It was impossible for me to calculate the cost of this trip, but arriving at the Belmond there was no doubt that Jake had left the best for last.

Sophia was telling me that this four hundred fifty year-old hotel, located on the canal front, had glorious views of the city from every direction.

Once in the palatial lobby, the multifaceted bedeviled windows, sparking chandeliers, original ceiling frescoes, oak parquet floors, surrounded by Murano glassware, brought a new appreciation of elegance.

From the reception hall I could see the sweeping stair-case that leads guests to a library, and canal terrace with private gardens. Years ago, when Caden took me to the Waldorf Astoria in New York, and even the spectacular Seelbach ,where my wedding reception was held, neither could even come close to the Belmond Ciprini.

"Two years ago, when I had the pleasure to meet with Jake, he outlined his objectives, and I immediately brought him here to the Belmond for his approval. We sat, right here," Sophia said.

She motioned me to take a chair at the same table, and ordered several Bellini cocktails.

"He told me his story and his love for you all these years. And I could not stop crying," Sophia continued her story.

As I sat with Sophia, I felt that now, finally Jake's testi-monial to her had been validated with my presence. I still could not believe that all of this had been so thoughtfully planned for me.

"The irony here, Sophia, is that all of this spectacle was unnecessary; I already knew that Jake loved me, and he knew that I loved him. What was he trying to prove? I also understood, finally, that he made the only choice he could at the moment."

Sophia looked at me perplexed.

"Have you not understood yet, Gabby, that this is not just a declaration of love; This is Jake's legacy, his tribute. Everywhere he has sent you, and everything that he planned was a celebration of his life that he needed to share with you, and you alone. Maybe Anniversary would be a more appropriate term? If he was here, right now, there would be no hesitations. It would be perfectly natural.

This final stop is where you will finally embrace the magic of Venice and fall in love with Jake again, once more," Sophia had pleaded Jake's case like a seasoned attorney.

At last, someone was able to say precisely what was happening, although it did seem very bizarre.

"Well, maybe you have made a logical point, except for the little matter that we were both married to different people. That makes this more complicated. And of course, Jake is dead," I finally was being sensible.

Sophia gave me a look that reflected both annoyance and frustration.

"Marriage, Gabby is a contract, most often a practical arrangement. That is why in Europe, Mistresses are not only accepted but, acknowledged. Jake understood that his marriage would never prevent him from continuing to love you, and that is what he wants to celebrate."

Sophia made sense but I was still confused.

"But what we shared was such a short time, and we were both so very young," I added.

"Oh, but Gabby that is not true. Even apart, what you shared with others was not enough to turn your back on the opportunity to allow Jake back into your life. When you are able to admit this and embrace it your life will be complete," Sophia made her closing statement.

What was amazing to me, was how all of these strangers accepted what Jake was doing without hesitation, and I, the object of is affection, was bewildered.

Perhaps the answer was the enormity of this truth that Jake was determined to prove. What I decided now, was to no longer question or doubt his motives. It was time to give him complete control.

On the terrace, outside of my suite, with Venice at my feet, I sat down and turned to Jake's journal entry for Venice. "Well, I never doubted that you would finally make it here, and what a grand time you will have. Breathe the air, take a gondola ride, visit Harry's Bar, Hemingway's old haunt, and listen to an opera in Italian, even if you cannot understand it. Take time to reflect on all that we shared in the past and in the last few days.

On your last night here you will attend a masquerade ball. Why masquerade you might be asking? Because this is the Carnival capital of the world, and there is nowhere that knows how to celebrate like Venice. I will be looking forward to your reaction. Remember to record everything in our journal. Enjoy, but it my love!"

Jake

The last masquerade ball I attended was at Georgetown and I met Caden. Was I ever in love with him? At the time I thought I was. The same amount of time, to the day, that I last saw Jake. Why was Caden, from nowhere trespassing on my thoughts?

If Jake was correct about eternity then, I could never have loved anybody but him.

And where does Alex fit into this paradox? When I left Kentucky, he reminded me that our 32 years of marriage was the foundation that allowed him to accept my decision to travel through Europe without him.

Naturally, he knew nothing about Sterling, or maybe he did. Regardless, I never allowed him to know that every once and a while both Caden and Jake surfaced in my deepest thoughts. Like aftershocks or tremors, they would eventually pass without leaving a destructive mess.

What was on my mind now was THIS masquerade party. In Venice the Carnival tradition is well known for the variety of distinctive masks. Guests attend, wearing elaborate costumes. This yearly event, ends on the first night of Christian Lent, forty days before Easter, known as Shrove Tuesday, or Mardi Gras.

New Orleans was not far from Savannah, about a nine-and-a-half-hour drive. One year, Molly, Jake, and I, along with about forty other high school students talked our parents into allowing us to go there on a church sponsored help mission.

They never connected the dots that after the mission trip was Mardi Gras. It was a wild time and my first experience with uncontrollable crowds. It was not anything that I wanted to experience again.

New Orleans was also where the worst experience of my life occurred .Not only the Halloween Orgy Party, but the rape that followed .

It was also time to purge myself from all the horrors that were living in my closet.

In 1162, Sophia told me, that the Venetian people were so excited about their victory from Patriarch de Aquiline, that they danced and made revelry in Saint Marc's Square. After a long absence, in 1979 it was resurrected once again, primarily to attract tourists, by the Italian government.

The masquerade party that I was to attend was not during the official Carnival. It was a celebration of a spirit set free, that I found to be a very appropriate title. She would not elaborate on whose spirit we were honoring, but since Jake planned it, I presumed it would be his spirit.

My gown was delivered to my room the evening before the event. Sophia had warned me that it was very difficult to wear and that she would assist me with the corset and any other adjustments. She insisted on a dress rehearsal, and I was thankful that I had agreed to it.

My first reaction was that it was just a dress and nothing could be that difficult to put on. I was very wrong. Once the dress arrived there were so many rhinestones on the brocade fabric that I was not sure if I would be able to move.

And then there was the hoop under the gown. I had to learn how to walk and sit without the dress turning upside down. Somehow, hours later, it was manageable.

Sophia looked at me in costume and said, "Now you understand why a dress rehearsal was necessary, no?" She smiled.

"Yes I do, and I hope I never, ever have to do this again. This took longer than it did when I had to put my wedding dress on."

"But, oh my darling Gabby, this is not just any dress. It is a Versace Carnival gown. One of a kind. You look absolutely regal," Sophia said, admiringly.

As I looked at myself in the full length mirror, I too was impressed at how beautiful this gown was. I was no longer the shy fourteen-year-old girl that Jake fell in love with. But, if Jake was here now looking at me that is the girl he would remember.

"There is little doubt that you will be the center of attention tonight in that dress, Gabby," Sophia said.

"Oh but I do not want to be the center of attention, Sophia. You will be there, won't you?" My voice could not hide the panic that was now overtaking me.

" Oui, of course I will be there, and of course your escort will always be by your side. Please do not worry about anything now". Sophia was trying to calm my nerves.

Finally, the time had come, and Sophia answered the door. Once inside, the gentleman wearing a dark tuxedo and ornate mask resembled a Phoenix, bowed and took my hand.

Sophia placed my mask properly on my face. It resembled an ornate dove. Nothing was said until we got on the elevator. Then I suddenly recognized the deep voice and I knew that I had no reason to worry.

CHAPTER 40

Sometimes the most profound awakenings come wrapped in the most silent of moments.

-Stephen Crane

Gabby, July, 2003

"I know Gabriella that I am not what you expected. I wish That I was, if only for this evening," Immediately I recognized Andrew's voice.

All I was feeling at the moment was peace. No longer was I dwelling on what would happen next or if I was prepared for it. Jake had somehow pulled off the most unbelievable wake in history.

"But, for tonight I will attempt to do my very best to be the closest emissary to Jake as possible," Andrew said while bowing in front of me.

At that moment the elevator opened and we were entering the grand ballroom. Andrew was holding my gloved hand, and was guiding me through the room, stopping to introduce me to people who had come from all over the world to celebrate Jake's life and accomplishments.

Andrew explained to me that Jake was not only a Literature Professor, he was also a humanitarian that spent most of his free time providing hope to so many different charities. Not only with financial support but by opening schools in the Vietnam jungles, and supporting veterans when they returned from combat.

All those people are here tonight, "And, all those people know you," Andrew said as a matter of fact.

"But that is impossible, Andrew. I cannot believe that Jake just left Isabella out of all this. She was his wife, not me," I said.

"Isabella and Jake had a mutual understanding. She would never interfere or ask questions about Jake's commitments. I know it must sound like a strange relationship, but they respected each other and I do believe there was some love between them, although nothing like the passion he had for you," Andrew answered.

This was a lot for me to accept. But, tonight was not the time to figure out what my role was. Tonight we were all here celebrating our love and compassion for a remarkable man.

As the evening began to wind down and a few of us remained to see the sunrise over the canals, Andrew pulled me away to a private room off the balcony.

"I hope that these last few weeks refreshed your memory of Jake and introduced you to the remarkable man he became," Andrew said.

"This has been more than I could ever imagine in my wildest dreams. It also made me realize that we do belong together, in some way forever. Not quite sure how that will happen, but I know now that it will," I replied.

Andrew walked over to a locked cabinet and retrieved another leather bound book that matched the journal that Paul had given me in Ireland.

"This is Jake's final gift to you Gabby. He instructed me to ask you to complete the journal reading before you return home to Kentucky. I will never forget you. Please keep in touch with me. You are also my link to Jake," Andrew tried to hold back his tears.

We embraced for a long time before Sophia came in and suggested that we all get some rest before our departure the following day.

The last journal message from Jake was about to reveal his final thoughts to me. I knew that they would be profound and emotional. I would plan to read it with a clear and open mind before I boarded the plane home. Nothing could prepare me for this mind exploding revelation.

TELL me not in mournful numbers,
 Life is but any empty dream! --
For the soul is dead that slumbered,
And things are not what they seem.
Life is real! Life is earnest!
And the grave is not its goal;
Dust thou art, to dust returnest,
Was not spoken of the soul.
                    - Henry Wadsworth Longfellow

Gabby July, 2003

The time had finally arrived to read what Jake had shared with me in tonight's journal, regardless how painful it may be.

January, 5 2001

Dear Gabby,

My days on earth are now limited. I am struggling to stay awake more than 30 minutes at a time. It is crucial that I complete this entry before I pass on. So, I ask you to bear with me, if I appear to fade in and out of consciousness.

Our universe is so finite Gabby, that it is home to infinite parallel universes that are arranged like a deck of cards that when shuffled eventually will repeat itself. It is what many philosophers refer to as the hidden reality.

Without getting into such a deep discussion that you will be lost in theory, just imagine that there are really small strings so finite that they are invisible to the human eye but they do exist.

What this means to us is that it is possible that I am going to be floating on those wires so close to you, that you will sense my presence, but not with all your tactile facilities

Since we cannot control which senses will be accepted at any given time, you must be open to all at all times. In order to prepare you for this, I have written in this journal, that you received tonight, as many ways I could imagine that I will contact you. Whenever you think in your mind that I am with you, I will be. It is that accurate.

I know that this is a lot for you to accept by faith, but I also know that what we share is so strong that we can no longer control the infinite future. It is NOW. Sophia gave you a small glimpse of why we are able to connect beyond death. I will attempt to provide you with another piece to the puzzle. Think of your life as a motion picture, with many clips.

Which ones do you remember and want to repeat and extend? Those are the ones that we shared together. The rest of our life is just background that we edit when we can. Does that make more sense to you? It will I promise you.

All the "snapshots that you have accumulated these last weeks are powerful, because I was also there, just on a different string at a different time.

When you replay it in your sleep it will be with me. Eventually you will be able to control this when you are awake. I will help guide you directly to me.

Now it is time to allow all of this to register and become familiar to you. Do not push yourself or worry about failing. It is as normal as the nature of living, only beyond human restrictions. I am anxiously, yet patiently waiting for you to join me.

Love, Jake

Could this really happen? And, more importantly did I want it to happen?

CHAPTER 41

"The late age of the world's experience had bred in them all, all men and all women, a well of tears. Tears and sorrows; courage and endurance; a perfectly upright and stoical bearing."   - Virginia Wolfe

Gabby and Caden January, 2005

Sometimes, I think that my parents must have been Leopold Bloom and Clarissa Dalloway. Or maybe James Joyce and Virginia Wolfe just somehow knew exactly what I was thinking.

Returning from Europe, I was hoping that my life would finally become normal and the literary flashbacks would finally subside. Unfortunately, not only did they not disappear, my mind now was also obsessed with the ideas that Jake had planted.

My garden, was now being nurtured with his journal entries. I read them daily, like devotionals and often more than once.

There was at first some concern how this obsessionI was effecting my marriage. It was becoming more difficult, now to assess how Alex felt about me.

When I arrived home from my journey, it sometimes seemed like he was patiently waiting for me to reveal some deep secret.

Other times it was more like he didn't care at all. *Realistically, I had no idea how I could explain to anyone that I was still in love with my dead boyfriend; and by the way we were both married to other people for nearly thirty-five years. How bizarre is that?*

As for Alex and I? Not much had really changed. He continued to travel throughout the country speaking at medical conventions, being recognized as one of the top cardiologists in the world.

I sometimes found humor in the fact that he was an expert at mending so many hearts, but mine was slowly dying.

The horse ranch was now being entirely managed by the Blair Conservatory providing Alex with a yearly financial report that seemed to thrive despite that Winston had been deceased for several years.

The lavish parties that always started during the Kentucky Derby week and went through the winter holidays, were no longer part of our lives.

Occasionally I would still volunteer at the local food banks and hospital wards, but I stayed clear of any committees or country club lunches.

I had heard that Sterling was spending most of his time at the Bahamas or the Mexican Riviera. There were days that I was tempted to call him just to talk casually, but I knew that would result in something ugly and I could not handle another emotional conflict.

Maybe out of boredom or just a need to escape the powerful forces that drew me into a mournful abyss, I became, like those moths that are drawn to flames.

I felt myself moving into Clarissa Dalloway's world. My brain, layered in gauze became lost in an expected obligatory persona] and shallow existence, like those people who insist on buying saccharine greeting cards with hypocritical messages.

There were times, like Clarissa, that I attempted to balance my internal life with a hostile external world. The result was me being swallowed by an earthquake.

Constantly overlaying the past with the present, I continued with this facade convincing myself that all this was preparing me to finally join Jake on his infinity path There *was a perpetual sense... of being out to sea and alone, I al-*

ways had the feeling that it was very, very dangerous to live even one day.

That was when premonition or instinct became a game of possibilities. A warning, a red flag, cautioning me that my life was becoming sedentary. This routine, formally known as the decorum of marriage dictated who and what completed me.

Not unlike the phantom sensation that Jake must have felt when his leg was amputated, I sometimes would recall what my life was like before I danced with the devil and settled for wealth and security.

Clarissa Dalloway, reassured me that suicide was not a sound option of escape. So like a heroine, from a novel, I summoned my doppelgänger to assist me in successfully completing my obligatory role.

What contributed to this feeling was ,always being referred to as Alex's wife was suffocating. There were times that I believed that I was being groomed to be a Stepford Wife.

The determination and passion that I felt at twenty, encouraged me to fight windmills, chase fireflies, and taste snowflakes on my tongue, was no longer in me. The pulse of life, had somehow began to challenge all my choices.

At first, grief and sorrow is sometimes mistaken for weakness, when in fact it is really a rational expression that allows you to move forward. It is disturbing to witness, yet a logical reaction that leads to purging.

All of this consumed my mind when Molly and I spoke during our monthly chat. Out of nowhere, and unexpectedly, Molly began by asking.

"Gabby, do you ever think about Caden after all these years? I mean now that Jake is dead; did that also stir up some memories of Caden?" She carefully inquired.

I had not shared with anyone that Jake did not consider himself "really" dead. What I was learning from reading his massive journals, was that he expected us to be reunited.

After a few awkward moments of silence, I tried to answer without sounding defensive.

"Why would you ever bring up Caden's name? I mean my relationship with Jake could never be compared to Caden. You of all people know this, Molly," My voice was tense.

"Okay Gabby, chill. I also know that for the three months you two were together, you THOUGHT that you were in love. I mean, come on, you two were moving in together when everything just exploded," Molly never did back down.

Just being reminded about that night made me feel vulnerable. I had spent years working on insulating layers of protection to prevent any further damage. I was not ready to test how well it was working.

I could not deny that there were times when a certain song would come on the radio, or during the lighting of the Christmas tree in Rockefeller Plaza, or when I heard that Aunt Selena had died, that my mind didn't flashback to Caden.

This is when it is consoling to believe, that at least death was predictable. I admired how Jake in spite of knowing that he was dying, continued to keep our love alive.

"Well, I was trying to be subtle about this, but I should know better with you Gabby. " Molly continued.

"Just get to the point Molly. We have been the closest friends for over four decades. Tell me whatever it is," I was now insisting.

"Caden has asked me for your phone number so that he may text you and ask you to forgive him for his actions," Molly said bluntly.

I was trying to digest what Molly was saying. Caden had asked my best friend in the world to intervene on his behalf and she agreed. Over thirty-five years had passed since the last time we saw each other.

The exact same amount of time that Jake and I said our last words. Actually Caden and I never did say good bye; he just disappeared. These days the term is "ghosted".

In this new century, which I am still adapting to, the term "ghosted" refers to someone who suddenly leaves without an explanation or clue to where they have gone.

I may have eventually figured out why and where Caden went, but, I still felt "ghosted" in 1967.

Just hearing Caden's name again made me relive that awful night. The image of an unsuspecting moth being attracted to the mesmerizing flame of a candle made me nervous.

Moths do this because they confuse any light with the moon, which ironically is a safe object for the moth since they can never reach it.

That distance assures them that they can fixate, and even fantasize from afar without risking death. Now, Molly was luring me to a light that I knew would result in a death spiral if I continued to pursue it.

Then again, an inner voice was whispering, maybe I will be that exceptional moth that flies curiously near, but avoids the heat from the flame. Would it be possible to keep my safe distance from Caden?

"I did tell you that he is married and has twin boys, didn't I"? Molly kept talking.

All that was registering in my mind, but at the moment the question was, how would I put my life on pause, while I figured out what all of this meant.

If I agreed to this arrangement it would be on my terms. Texting is actually an excellent way to avoid any emotional expression. I would limit the texting to just the facts.

I would listen politely to his apology, and it would be over. Not like the whirlwind closure that Jake insisted on. It would be an exquisite moment; Caden admitting he was wrong and I forgiving him. Finis, the end and my world would once again be turned right side up.

"Say a prayer for me Molly, I may have lost my mind but give Caden my personal cell number with the very specific condition that there will be no calls, only texting. "I said.

"That is a very mature and wise decision My Cheri. This is what you both need. Enough time has passed, and you both have established lives, why not be friends? I will let him know today. " Molly seemed pleased.

347

I wasn't convinced that we would ever be friends, but not being enemies would be a good start.

Considering that Molly was in Paris and six hours ahead of both, Caden and me, I was confident that I would not hear from Caden for a few days.

That would allow me plenty of time to be prepared and make the appropriate mental adjustments. I did not want to dwell on this for very long. Just do it and get it over with.

I knew how Molly was with her Pollyanna attitude toward life, but if we could simply make amends I would consider that a major accomplishment.

The longer the anticipation, the worse the thought of texting with Caden became. Those powerful feelings that I once had when we were together, gave me chills, and sharp pangs in my stomach.

Eating away at my heart, I was remembering how Caden made me feel, when my brain took second place, and I could learn to live without logic but I could not live for a long time without him. My world stopped when we parted, so many years ago.

Caden January, 2005
Twenty-four hours later

The moment I received Molly's text informing me that Gabby had agreed to let me text her, I began to scrutinize what would be the best approach. I had heard that Jake had passed away a few years ago, and Molly filled me in on the European pilgrimage that he sent Gabby on.

I always thought that Jake was a little over the edge. What did he think he was going to accomplish by that extravagant trip now that he was dead? Did he think that would make Gabby forget that he left her for another woman?

Well, anyway, I guess the point is if Gabby can forgive Jake, then I have a real chance that she might....NO damn it, she has to forgive me. All that I am going to do is ask her to briefly let me back into her life.

My memory of her was that she was beautiful and amazingly bright. Lately I found myself dreaming about her at night and fantasizing about her during the day. And this was NOT just recently.

My life with Kaitlyn was normal. After the twin boys were born, the focus was mostly on them. At the beginning of our marriage I tried desperately not to compare her to Gabby.

Physically, they were polar opposites.

Kaitlyn was tall with long sensuous legs, blond silky hair and brown eyes. From the moment we met, I admired how confident she was; always the one in control.This arrangement worked well for us.

When I returned home to Savannah, I was lost, I had no direction. Kaitlyn was my anchor and she kept me grounded.

But, it was never enough. For a while I convinced myself that the world had no real purpose: no real meaning.

There were times that I would look at the ring that Selena gave to me, the day I left Georgetown. Nobody knew about that ring, and I kept it in a secret place.

Recently I took the ring out and Gabby's face flashed through my mind, like a leaf floating through a rush of air, with no direction, in wild circles, yet somehow always in control.

I soon found myself fascinated by a sunbeam reflecting off a blade of grass, as if it was normal, a reasonable thing for the sun to do. That was when I realized I had to see Gabby again.

CHAPTER 42

I can only note that the past is beautiful because one ever releases an emotion at the time. Later it expands, thus we don't have complete emotions about the present, only the past. - Virginia Wolfe

Caden 2008

In 1992, twenty-two-year-old test engineer, Neil Papworth from the United Kingdom sent an SMS message, "Merry Christmas" on his Vodafone to Richard Jarvis, who was at a party in Newberry, Berkshire.

This event had been pre planned to celebrate this technology break through. It was not until 2008 that text messaging became the norm. This new phenomenon changed how relationships would evolve forever.

For our generation, known as the Baby Boomers, it would become more than simply an entertaining device. It allowed the past to connect to the present and ultimately change the future.

It was this fragile past, like a spider's web, that delicately attaches all four corners, that kept me waiting for the final approach. Timing would be everything.

The importance of demonstrating just the right amount of vulnerability, to Gabby was my first goal. When Molly described Gabby' s recent life as lethargic, I knew that now was when things could change.

I can testify that once your life loses that stamina to take chances, it leads to a dull, callous and indifferent state of being. I am definitely proof of this.

Lately, with my mind being more preoccupied with Gabby, than ever before, I was convinced that the remaining years of our lives were destined to be together in some form. Making Gabby realize this, may be more difficult. Thirty eight years it has taken me to understand the enormity of my error. Now I must make Gabby understand, that it is not too late to rectify this problem.

There will be no peace of mind, no harmonious life, without her forgiveness. Now, is when I must ask her forgiveness.

Avoiding this truth for nearly four decades was an easy way to escape. Until recently, I did not have the necessary strength to accept my actions.

Today, there is a semitransparent light that reflects my honesty in a mirror, that I cannot avoid. This closure will set me free.

Once I began to accept that Jake's shadow was only a phantom, a new clarity became visible. In the past, it was easy for me to blame Gabby. I had convinced myself that she could never truly love me as she did Jake. Then I came to the realization, that the entire time, I was the one creating those obstacles.

That fateful New Year's Eve can never be entirely erased, but it can be modified. I knew that. And, it all started when Molly, brilliantly suggested that I try texting Gabby. Naturally it made sense. It was a less threatening way to communicate.

This would also allow Gabby complete control. She could decide how long and how much she is willing to reveal to me, without a commitment. And, Gabby can erase all memory of what was said.

Eventually, I am hoping, in time, it will be more relaxed. This turtle may be older, but I intend to use the same moves that won her heart the first time; allowing her to set the pace.

Of course, without seeming too forward, my objective is to make Gabby feel completely at ease in in a nonthreatening environment.

I know that there still exists a little spark of fire in her heart for me. I am counting on cyberspace to carry my vibes to her. The intensity that, I feel is not in vain.

It is the delving and dissecting my approach that is causing me sleepless nights. Trying to conjure the perfect words that will express, only what my heart can feel, is mind blowing.

Finally, on one early morning vigil when I slip out of bed, careful not to wake Kaitlin, my memory begins to flashback to Gabby in my arms in the middle of the night. Before, I would brush aside those past thoughts, claiming that it was nothing more than a normal reaction, to a bad dream.

This particular morning, was going to be different. The tile floor in the kitchen, was exceptionally cold. In the window, facing the street, I could see a young couple saying goodbye.

I imagined that it would be the way Gabby would kiss me. Long kisses, with her tongue tempting me to stay. Their embrace seemed indefinite. Neither wanted to be the first to move away.

At last, the couple parted. it was over. It would be just enough to keep them satisfied until they reunited once again that evening. What I felt now, was more than a frigid morning, it was a frigid marriage.

Now my mind allows Gabby's vision to visit me. In the past, I brushed aside those urges to succumb. I resolved they must be an exaggerated memory. But now, I no longer fear how I will react.

My adrenaline is unleashed, flowing with sexual desires that had been dormant for years. Now that I know that Gabby will be somewhat receptive, it is my move.

Today, everything is about to change. My strategy is carefully planned. I will go to the bar as usual. Devon, the manager, and Brandy, the bartender, will not arrive earlier than ten AM. That allows me a good two hours in my office to text Gabby in private.

Plenty of time to get my thoughts in order. I am thankful that at least I don't have to deal with a time change like when I texted Molly.

But, when would it be the best time to get Gabby's immediate attention? Eight thirty this morning just sounds like a good time. No more excuses.

I check my cell phone. Exactly eight thirty.

C: Thank you Gabby for allowing me to text you. I know that it has been many years. Too many years. But I have always wanted to say that I am sorry for leaving you the way I did. Without giving you lame excuses, I am asking your forgiveness. It would mean a lot to me.

(Send).

I never even stopped to read what I wrote. It was now up to her to respond.

Three hours had passed. No response. Finally, at 11:30, just when the lunch hour was starting, I decided to go to the front, but kept my phone on vibrate.

"Hey, boss.... didn't even realize you were here. I added the potato skins and fried pickles to the menu along with the potato soup you wanted," Devon said.

He was always trying new ideas. Once we realized, that for some reason, Thursday afternoons The Molly was a popular hangout spot, Devon went to work on expanding the menu.

"And, Brandy signed for the delivery this morning for the Guinness. So it looks like we are ready to rock and roll," Devon added.

Both Brandy and Devon have been with me since I opened The Molly over thirty years ago. Devon is about 6'5" and weighs nearly 300 Lbs.; all solid muscle.

Even at 55 years old the man is in better shape than men decades younger. Devon also becomes an asset whenever someone just has too much ale and chooses to start a rumble

Devon and I are as close as brothers, but I never confided to anyone about Gabby.

And, then it happens I can feel the cell vibrating in my upper pocket, close to my heart.

"Great Devon. I will be in the office recording the receipts from last night. If you need anything, come fetch me."

I close the door behind, sit down at my desk chair and just stare at the cell phone.

Finally, I enter my pass code and notice that my message notification is on. I click to open.

G: I am rather confused about what you feel you need to apologize for after so many yeas Forty one years is a very long time for anyone to stay angry, even me.

I checked the time recorded when it was sent. Five minutes ago. I am hoping that she is anxiously waiting for me to respond. I decide to appeal to her love of literature .

C: A quote by DH Lawrence, whom I recall was a favorite of yours,should explain it better than I can. "One must learn and go through a good deal of suffering to get to it, and the
journey is always toward the other soul." Can we please just be friends?

I just want to know how you are. No. pressure. No demands. What harm is

there in that?
(Send)

This time it took longer to get a reply.

As soon as his text came across, Gabby began to feel his presence. But, logically she knew that it was impossible. These are only words being transmitted through the air, but it was Caden on the other end.

As much as her mind was begging her to say goodbye, it was her heart that wanted to come out to play and have some fun.

Her first instinct was to make him sweat a little and not respond immediately, but if she was going to continue with this charade there would be plenty of time in the future for that.

G: Okay Caden, I'll play with you for.awhile, at least until I become bored.

This seems like safe turf. But, the real test will be who gives up first with the texting.

(Send)

Almost as fast as she pushed the send button, he responded.

C: You know Gabby that I will win that test. I remember how much you hate losing. My life is so boring and mundane that my texting is where my imagination will find a proper home. If you want entertainment Gabby, you found the right person for that. Game on!

(Send)

Gabby 2008-2010

This turned out to be perfect. We had agreed to respond to each other's text as soon as possible, with a mutual understanding that both of our spouses may cause occasional delays. We also would inform each other of any temporary interruptions, due to social commitments. Failure to do this would declare a winner by default.

For me, it was the perfect solution to my miserable life. Without Sterling around, I had little to keep me amused. But, nothing could make me return to that life. What Caden had introduced was interesting.

Naturally our spouses would never know, even though this was entirely harmless. What neither of us never expected was that this texting courtship, would build a bridge that connected two lovers in a cyber affair.

This may have been unconventional. It was definitely unchartered. But, neither of us could call it off.

We went through various stages of intense love, hate, jealousy, sex, and even death without ever having any physical interaction. This was real. More real than anything that I had ever encountered.

Trying to reconcile what Jake claimed was an indefinite tie to one another and Caden's pursuit of what he insisted was our destiny, was difficult for me to comprehend.

What made all of this complicated involved justifying why my emotions for both of these men was still relevant.

The texts that I have chosen to include in my journal,demonstrates my struggle as well as my, moments of unparalleled joy.

Caden and I continued this clandestine affair for two years. If I had not documented some of the texts, I would never believe that this actually happened.

The only other person that was aware of this relationship was my Psychologist, who encouraged me to share them with her. She claimed that the texts were a form of catharsis that could help me resolve the cauldron that was boiling inside of me.

Eventually, Caden and I conceded that texting would only serve part of our needs. An occasional phone call, later became a natural part of both of our daily routine.

Reject me not if I should say to you I do forget the sound of your voice, yet when the apple-blossom opens wide and the cherry blossom trees be in bloom, I see your gentle face through the mist, and long to lift you in my aching arms.

I sit and weep for very pain of you. Tossing through troubled nights, I fling myself at the doors of sleep; dreaming your yielded mouth is given to mine.

If there was a resolution, I had not discovered it yet.

CHAPTER 43

Words are but the vague shadows of the volumes we mean. Little audible links, they are, chaining together great inaudible feelings and purpose. - Theodore Dreiser

Gabby and Caden
2008-10

As the texting with Caden evolved it became a canvas of abstract nuances that never seemed to end. It was during these times of doubt that I questioned even continuing with this futile attempt to rekindle a friendship.
Then Caden would remind me that there are important times in life when no purpose becomes the very essence in life.

C. "Why do we admire an English rose garden, Gabby? So that it will reveal the secrets of the world? I think not. People are drawn to these gardens because it offers them an escape from the nonsensical annoyances of a corrupt world."

This was not the wild spirited Caden that I knew at Georgetown. There was a more sensitive, subtle, polish to the way he would express important philosophical ideas. It was unexpected and I was not sure how to react.
    While time had made me more cynical and less idealistic, Caden appeared almost romantic. I was not yet certain how to deal with this man, that I barely knew.

Our texting revealed so much more than either of us anticipated. Ironically, our new relationship was similar to designing an English rose garden.

It required an aesthetic approach that exposes various moods. It is the epitome of contradiction. To many it is a romantic interlude with rose climbing walls, intertwining with honeysuckle and ivy, sometimes winding wildly around the nearest pergolas located often in deserted abandoned paths.

Was I was willing to continue to explore how deep this rose garden would go and how would I be able to nurture and cultivate it?

I was still being haunted by Jake's memory and being loyal to whatever was left of my marriage. Certainly not everyone had to deal with these issues. Was I just setting myself up for more complications?

Whatever it was about Caden, at least for the moment, he was fulfilling a desperate need. One that not even Molly could fill. I just needed to make certain that we kept our distance not allowing any temptation to turn our "garden" into an abandoned desert with nothing but weeds.

It was astonishing how the texting, although awkward at times, also revealed inner feelings fairly accurately. There was at one point, during the holiday season that, became especially difficult for me.

We were both busy with family obligations, parties; days filled, at times, with hypocritical joy, and confusion. The nearer that we got to the New Year the closer I began to walk away from this fantasy affair.

C: It is almost time to say goodbye
to another year, Gabby. Did you open the Christmas gift I sent you?
(Send)

G: No.
C: Okay. What is wrong?

G: Nothing.

C: Don't lie to me. I can always tell
if there Is something bothering you.

And the uncanny thing about that comment was that he
was right. Nobody else, not even Jake could read me that
well.

G: Just feeling a little depressed. How could you tell
there was? anything wrong?

C: I can tell by the way you text. I
am always in tune with how you text. It is not too much
different from when we were physically together. Talk to
me
   girlfriend.

G: It's just so hard during this time of the year, with all
the Christmas songs, and cheerful people holding hands. I
just
   remember New York during that time when we were....
there.

C: Just say it Gabby, when we were together and in love.
It is a difficult time for a lot of people. But you must now
know how much I still love you.

It was the first time that Caden had texted those words to
me. I knew that this was more than friendship, but seeing
"I love you" on the screen was much more powerful.

G: I know all the natural reactions point us to that direction, but we both have
other commitments. All of this
just makes me question where all of this texting is going to
get us. Even when you make me angry, I still love you too.

There I said it. Admitting that I loved Caden was more for me than for him. I was not sure how I would reconcile loving three men, one who is dead, one whom I may never see again, and one I vowed to love, in the name of God, until death do us part.

C: Gabby, it took me over forty-one years to find you. There was a time, and I know that you remember, when together we made the world go around.I will never let you go again. We will be together, at last if it takes forever then I will wait forever.
(Send)

G: The most difficult part is not being physically with you. There are times that I cannot imagine the remainder of my life without your touch. I remember how it feels to have you inside of me and now I only feel empty.
(Send)

C: Okay. I know that feeling. If we can get on the phone privately, I have an Idea that might help both of us.
(Send)

G: Have you discovered some miracle that allows you to penetrate me while we text, because that Is what I need.
I get wet just hearing your voice
sometimes.
(Send)

C:You have to understand Gabby that I'm not that viral man anymore. But,what I can do is love you the way no man has EVER loved you including
Mr. Jake Chevalier.
(Send)

That text made Gabby pause. Caden never mentioned Jake ever before. Was it even possible that anyone else could love her, more than Jake did? More importantly, the question was, could she ever love anyone else the same as she did Jake?

"Absolutely you can Gabby. That was one of the reasons why I encouraged you to go on that trip that Jake arranged for you. And, those journals he wrote, have insights that he may not have even known," Dr. Mason explained.

" But, Dr. Mason, Jake was dedicated to loving me forever. He spent the last year of his life trying to prove that we belonged together eternally.

Now, I have allowed another person, from my past, into my pathetic life, and he claims that we are destined to be together. And, did I fail to mention that we are both married?" I said, totally frustrated.

"My darling Gabby...it is YOU, that determines your destiny not fate. Even if you accept that Jake loved you,

And, EVEN if you believe that he has found a way, beyond the grave, to claim you as his, you must decide, is that what you want?" Dr. Mason replied.

For the very first time, I was beginning to understand that *the song about myself, I sing is full, sad and my own distress. It reveals the hardships I have had to suffer, present and past but never more than now* (Walt Whitman)

If what Dr. Mason was telling me was true, then my entire life I have allowed men to manipulate me. Starting with Jake. I never questioned his motives. Later, when I did begin to independently make choices, they were either wrong, or too late.

Ironically, Sterling, the only man I never really loved, was the one I felt most comfortable with and less threatened by.

When I shared this information with Dr. Mason, she seemed pleased.

"Finally, Gabby...I believe we are making some progress. Identifying the source of the problem is the first major step to recovery," She added.

361

Recalling those recent sessions with Dr. Mason, I eventually texted Caden back.

G: I can be alone tonight at 8 pm. Will that work for you? This sounds a little kinky but fun.
(Send)

C: I will make it work for us. We are going to have simulated sex, Gabby, on the phone. Will you try it?
(Send)

G: I am willing to give it a try, but you will need to be patient with me. I haven't had sex for a while.
(Send)

C: Great. I have never done this
before either, but I will do my best baby. Just imagine how we were once together, and the rest will come naturally. It is amazing
how the mind works.
(Send)

It is difficult to explain how that night changed our relationship. What happened was beyond my expectations. When Caden whispered in my ear, a play by play, of every move he was making on my body, I closed my eyes and could FEEL, not just HEAR him.

His hands, gently stroking my breasts and his mouth sucking my nipples, made them hard. My pussy began to pulsate. It may be my hand touching and spreading my legs apart to let him enter, but it was his cock that plunged deep inside of me, as if he was there.

It was real enough that I knew I belonged with him. When we were done and both of us were breathing normal again there was no doubt that we had crossed the line to a new and very special relationship. A relationship that nobody else would ever understand.

" Are you feeling the same as I am right now, Gabby? How did we pull that off?" Caden said finally.

I was convinced that whatever just happened was so powerful that nothing would ever pull us apart again.

We had, together recreated the exact emotions that we both shared the first time we made love at Aunt Selena's home forty-two years ago.

"You are a genius Caden. I do not know how we did this but I want to do it again, and real soon, babe," I said, still breathing hard.

This was the beginning of our new extended relationship Even time was no longer an enemy.

However, exhilarating it was, I also was extremely frightened. What would happen next? And how long would it take?

As the winter months began to suggest family holidays, Caden and I began to drift slightly apart. During this entire time, we decided never to allow our relationship to interfere with family obligations.

In addition, we agreed that no gifts between us would ever be exchanged. Caden was the first one to break that rule.

C: I am sending you a very important gift that I don't want you to open until New Year's Eve. Will you promise me this Gabby?
(Send)

G. Caden, you are breaking the rules.
Remember, NO GIFTS.
(Send)

C. Okay then.....it isn't a gift. It is on loan. And once we are together again, you can return it to me.
(Send)

It was impossible to change Caden's mind. Once he made a decision, he was determined to play it out. I just asked him to be careful sending it to me, and that it should not be anything expensive.

"Gabby, sweetheart, nobody will ever know this is from me, but you. And, I trust you will keep it safe until the day we meet again," Caden said.

Our phone calls were beginning to become more regular and longer. Most of the time, we discussed everyday events, shared our opinions about everything and supported each other's decisions.

There were legitimate times that the interaction with Caden was more therapeutic than my sessions with Dr. Mason.

Finally, on New Year's Eve, the highly anticipated gift from Caden arrived.

It was cleverly wrapped in butch paper with no return address. The postal stamp was from Tennessee, which even confused me at first sight.

Alex was out playing racket ball at the country club with a group, that later we would celebrate ringing in the New Year with at some exclusive soirée. I continued to accompany him to these events, making it, clear, however, that we would live our lives as separately and civilized as possible.

Therefore, Alex had no need to know anything about this "mysterious" gift from Tennessee. Soon the butcher paper was off and the incriminating packaging would be permanently discarded.

As I carefully unwrapped the butcher paper, it revealed a framed LP album cover. As I examined it closer I noticed that it was a Beatle's album. **Abbey Road.**

A closer inspection, revealed that there was a G above the title. It no longer had the red X crossing it out. That is when I noticed the inscription at the bottom with George Harrison's signature.

I opened the card that simply read.

"Thanks for allowing me back in. Your G will always be on MY Abbey Road".

PS. Google the lyrics to "Something" if you don't remember them.

Love, C

Then I remembered Caden telling me the story about the day George Harrison wandered into The Molly.

It was around 1974, a few years after the Beatles broke up, when George Harrison and North American Friends Tour came to Atlanta.

Unannounced and with no entourage, George Harrison and one other man, perhaps a body guard, came into The Molly.

They told Devon that they were both homesick for some authentic Ale, and concluded that The Molly, having an Irish name and all, must be the right place.

When Caden came in a few moments later, he knew immediately that it was the famous George Harrison, but did not want him to be mobbed by other clients.

Once behind the bar, Caden told Devon to check on the customers at the tables and then take a break.

"Mind if I ask you, why is there a "G" written on that Abbey Road album cover, and why is it crossed out?" Mr. Harrison asked Caden.

It was the very first time that ANYONE had ever asked.

Caden proceeded to give the abridged version of how Gabby and he parted. He even admitted that he used a sledge hammer on the record. Something that he no longer was proud of.

"Just curious, Man... what would be your favorite song on that album?" Harrison continued to ask questions.

"Well, that is difficult. "Something" means the most to me, but it is also the most painful to listen to," Caden said, hoping that he didn't think he was patronizing him, since George Harrison wrote and sang that song.

"Would you mind, if I could see that album for a sec.?"

George Harrison was sitting in MY BAR, asking ME, if he could see HIS album. There was something just so unreal about this scenario. I reached behind the whiskey bottles, which had a story of their own. I would save that for another time. I handed him the album.

"Johnny...you still have that sharpie that I gave you when I got off stage last night?" Harrison was examining the album carefully.

"Sure do, boss...here it is."

Without saying anything else, George Harrison only asked me one thing....my name. Then he wrote on the album, "Never stop searching for that 'G' Caden, my friend.

Listen to 'Something' it will be in your soul," Signed, George Harrison, 1974.

Maybe....Just maybe, that time is NOW.

Chapter 44

Capture those moments of happiness like you would a shooting star or the sighting of a comet. If you blink it will surely disappear. - Gabriella Girard

Gabby. 2010

I was coming to the conclusion that marriage to Alex now was nothing more than an extended contract that neither of us wanted to take the time to break but also not renew. We were in limbo. The first circle of Dante's Hell. There was no doubt that both of us would see more of that Inferno.

When we were together, the primary objective was to discuss what each of us had been doing while we were apart. Like a current event update. FLASH: *Alex Blair, shot an amazing 80 on the Augusta Golf Course, while his wife, Gabby scored a 100%while having phone sex with her lover.!*

When we were both home it was expected that we would have breakfast every morning. Martha, our live in housekeeper would make certain that our food was always available with a pot of tea for me and a pot of coffee for Alex on the veranda daily.

It was as predictable as our daily conversations. This, I soon realized, would be Alex's compromise to my complaint that we no longer spent any quality time together. And this only came after my psychologist insisted that Alex be present at least during some of our sessions.

"It just makes no sense to me Gabby why I have to attend ANY therapy meetings with you. I am extremely busy attempting to provide YOU with all the luxuries that you want and, by the way, that I agree you deserve," Was always Alex' answer.

Alex had become a carbon copy of his father, Winston. Any traces of Eleanor were buried with her.

"Alex, I have never been a high maintenance wife, and you know this. I would have been very happy as a college professor. It was you and your family that insisted that I spend my time as a 'Goodwill Ambassador 'to the Blair Estate." I was nearly in tears, and my anger was becoming more difficult to subdue.

This constant self -sacrificing exaggeration was just one example of why our pathetic marriage needed counseling.

"Yes, I know Gabby, it is all me. Your life has been so terrible here. So bad that you needed to take a month off to chase after some ridiculous whim that a dead ex-boyfriend arranged for you. And, by the way you never heard me complain about that did you?"

Alex' s voice was never loud, even when we argued. It was always the same tone, condescending. I was curious if this was the same approach that he took with his patients. Alex had only one emotional level, insipid.

I was now at the point where our arguments were so futile, that nothing ever was accomplished. The result was an empty, shallow echo of angry words meaning nothing. Past experience taught me that it would only result in my own misery.

What I needed to determine, was why did I continue to stay in this arrangement.

Turning to Caden eased the pain. He became more than my sounding board. in many ways he was my refuge. Alex never even knew Caden existed.

. The only two people that knew about Caden and I, were Molly and Laura, my Psychologist. I trusted Molly with my life and Laura was bound by her client privacy oath.

"Gabby, have you ever considered that the reason you are attracted to Caden is due to a desire to escape from Alex? And, since he is married, unwilling to leave his wife, it makes the situation fairly safe for you both."

Laura had brought this up before.

I had thought about that scenario. The other motivation that I may have is to hurt Caden like he did me when he left. But, in fact what I was more fearful of accepting was that I truly was in love with him.

If that were true, how could I explain my inability to accept Jake's death. I could not find the release button that would allow me to move forward. In my mind I concluded that if I made no choices everything would remain the same.

Dr Laura however, unpleasantly pointed out to me that change would occur whether I made choices or not.

"Unfortunately, Gabby we do not have the ability to control our fate by deciding to remain neutral. If you do not make choices someone else, ultimately will make choices that effect you. Therefore, it is always a better strategy if you have some input in the direction you want to go in," She reminded me.

Dr. Laura was convinced that most of my indecisiveness was a result of the rape I was still trying to erase from my memory.

"Once you can accept that you were a helpless victim, Gabby, you will be able to make decisions much easier. You are still experiencing what is known as Rape Trauma Syndrome. In lay man's terms it is the inability to forgive yourself for something you had no control over. That is why rape is so much more than a violent physical act. The emotional scars can last a lifetime. "She said.

My weekly therapy sessions allowed me to release my frustrations with Alex, my loneliness for Jake, and my confusion about Caden, but they did not bring me any closer to the answers that I was searching for.

"And unfortunately, Gabby all that I can do is help you to discover a method that will bring you at least to the state of balance. Once you reach that level you will be able to determine the consequences of your choices," Dr. Laura repeated.

That was my dilemma. Throughout my life I had made decisions without balance. Now that I was approaching the end of my life it was crucial that I do not make those same errors.

"Have you ever told Caden what happened to you that Halloween night? Does Alex know about you and Sterling? Do you even know why you were with Sterling? Or for that matter, why you married Alex?" She asked all at once.

Wow! That was a lot of questions to digest in one session.

"Did you just somehow change to the Mad Hatter, Laura? All of a sudden I have a tremendous migraine headache," Was all I could say.

Dr. Laura just smiled, saying nothing but letting me know that she was in charge.

"I want you to understand without a doubt, Gabby, that until you can be honest with yourself about these issues, the other answers you have are inconsequential. Do you understand what I am saying?"

It was the first time in two years that I left her office knowing what direction that I must take. There would be no right or wrong answers or choices, just many hours of meditation and introspection.

When I woke up the next morning there were snowflakes staring at me through my bedroom bay window. Alex was on a golf excursion to St. Andrews in Scotland for the week, and although the winter months here in Kentucky can be depressing, today I looked forward to spending some idle hours just sipping tea, allowing my mind to absorb the slow silence of shapeless air.

"Good morning, Gabriella. I have brought you a pot of chamomile lavender tea, and blueberry scones, on this frosty morning," Martha said.

Along with the breakfast tray, Martha fluffed my bed pillows and started the fireplace in what appeared like one continuous motion. Sometimes her movements were as precise as a ballet dancer, gliding through the room with ethereal grace.

"Thank you, Martha You are an angel that reads my mind. This morning I plan to stay in my room for a while just thankful I do not need to be going anywhere in this dreadful snow."

"Yes, Ma'am, I too am grateful to be indoors today. Enjoy your peaceful moments". She said quietly.

Even, Martha had noticed how strained my relationship with Alex had been lately. I had been waiting anxiously for this golf outing, hoping by the time he returned I had some definitive answers.

One thing was certain, Laura was right, if I did not make a choice someone else would. Change was inevitable.

There is something very nurturing in sipping hot tea while staring at the delicate snow transforming all the outdoor colors into one world surrounded by white. On the tree branches that touch my window I watch a busy squirrel trying to hide some treasure inside a hollow stump. Thus far, there was only a small amount of dusting on his fur.

Once the squirrel left, a red breasted robin instinctively flies to the same spot, removes the object with its beak and flies away. Probably following the squirrel, who is busy stashing away acorns.

The squirrel has no idea that the robin is stealing his rations. Only the snow owl at the very top of the tree, like a guru, is aware of this unfolding tragic drama.

Now if I could only determine if I was the squirrel, the Robin or the owl, my life would be simplified. *If you build castles in the air, your work not need be lost; that is where they should be. Now put the foundation under them.* you (Henry David Thoreau)

What I needed to learn from Thoreau, is that what I look at, is not as important, as what I see. *As a single footstep does not make a path on the earth, so a single thought will not make a pathway in the mind. To make a deep mental path, we must think over and over the kinds of thoughts we wish to dominate our lives.*

Just when all of this philosophical data was beginning to process mentally, my cell began to vibrate. It was Caden.

C: I know that it is early, but I MUST talk to
you. Find a private place where we can talk on the phone.
It is extremely important.
(Send)

G: Yes. It is alright to phone. Alex is in Scotland on a golfing trip. This sounds serious. Did Kaitlyn find out that you have been texting me?
(Send)

C: No, nothing like that. I just need to call you NOW.
(Send)

If Kaitlyn had not found out about us I could not imagine what had happened.
What I was soon to discover was what Dr. Laura had warned me about for many years.
"He who controls the past controls the future. He who controls the present controls the past" (George Orwell)

CHAPTER 45

Security is mostly a superstition. It does not exist in nature, nor do the children of men, as a whole experience it. Avoiding danger is no safer in the long run than outright exposure. Life is either a daring adventure or nothing. -Helen Keller

Caden 2010

Gabby never did share with me any of the details about the rape or her relationship with Sterling Powers. That all came much later. My first reaction was incredible pain and helplessness.
Being so far apart there was nothing that I could do to help her overcome that nightmare.
And then, it happened. Call it fate or Karma or just old Irish luck, when Calhoun and Murray slithered into The Molly I knew what I had to do.

Everything that night was coincidence. Normally I take Sunday nights off to spend with Kaitlyn. It was the way I eased my conscience for spending nearly every day thinking and texting Gabby. A small sacrifice to pay for my guilty indulgence.

But, Brandy had asked for the evening off and usually after 10pm on Sunday there is only the small group of bar flies that hang around. Devon and I also get to catch up with what is happening, which is usually no more than what bowling team is dominating the local league in Savannah. Tonight, would be a little different.

"Hey, boss. Remember me telling you about those two cons that were here last week. I think their names are Murray and Calhoun? " Devon said.

I was drying some of the glasses that were left over from the earlier shift.

"Oh, yeah I remember. You thought that they went to high school with me? Did you ever figure that out?" I asked.

Devon walked over to the other side of the bar and leaned in so that he could not be heard.

"Well, no I could not place them. But, that greasy monkey, the one that goes by Murray....he was flapping his gums about some chick up in Kentucky that he fucked," Devon sounded irritated.

"So, what is so unusual about that, Devon. Guys come in here all the time bragging about the girls they bang. You know this is a bar? Alcohol and sex, just seem to go together. " I reminded him.

Devon seemed like he was holding something back. Something he was afraid to tell me,

"Well, it's more than just that, Caden. You, know that girl you went to school with that you were almost engaged to in Georgetown?" Devon whispered.

"Yeah, Gabby Girard. What does she have to do with those goons."

I had told Devon about Gabby and me but never shared with him that we were now texting.

"Well, boss I don't know if it is the same chic, but that's the ladies name that he was talking about."

I almost dropped the glass in my hands.

"That just can't be the same girl, Devon
. There is no way in hell that my... I mean Gabby be with a dirt bag like that," I said emphatically.

It was not even a possibility. But then Devon came in with the clincher.

"No Caden, you don't understand. This pig was bragging about RAPING her. And he kept telling his brother how he pleased her better than that high school football jock Jake Chavalier .

That was when Devon noticed my cool face change to white with anger.

"Are you sure about that Devon."

"You know it man.... Why would I make up a thing like that?"

"Next time they are in here, if they are, you let me know Devon, no matter what time of the day. Understand?"

My voice was getting louder as I emphasized what I wanted.

"Oh you won't have to wait very long Boss. They are at that corner booth."

The blood in my veins began to heat up. I was going to get down to this right now.

"Caden, don't do anything dumb now. I mean let's be smart and call the cops. Okay?" Devon said, holding me back.

It was too late for logic. I was at the booth.

"Hey, guys? I remember you two from high school, and I think we did some snorting together years ago. You mates are from Savannah High? I am the owner of the Molly and wanted to personally come by to let you know these drinks are on the house."

I pulled out a chair and took a seat. Devon was right behind me.

"Well, now that's mighty nice of you. This is almost like homecoming. I was just telling your friend behind you that about a few years ago we ran into another Savannah graduate."

Calhoun, was jabbing Murray in the ribs to shut up.

"Don't believe anything Murray says. His mouth is always flapping. He makes no sense," Calhoun said.

I was clenching my fist trying to control every fiber in my body from laying this moron right here, right now.

"Well, yeah I was sharing with Devon here, the last time that I finally got some grade A pussy from that bitch Gabby She was always going out with Jake Chavaliar. And man was that pussy worth all the fighting she put up. "Murray said between chugging his beer.

That was all I could tolerate, and Devon knew it. I reached across the booth and by the neck lifted Murray up above the table and dragged him outside to the alley.

Calhoun was out the front door almost as fast as we were in the back of the bar.

"Man....what the hell... I mean I was just saying what a sweet piece of ass she..." Murray couldn't shut up.

He was tripping over his own feet, losing balance when my first punch landed on his jaw. After that it took Devon and another police officer to pull me off of him. I know that I had the ability to kill him right there.

Once Murray was in the police car, handcuffed and bleeding profusely, I asked Devon how the police got there so fast.

"As soon as you headed toward the booth I called them. I wasn't going to take any chances of you killing him, and I wasn't sure that even I could stop you.," Devon admitted.

I nodded and wiped off the blood from my hands and face.

"Thanks Devon, that was a good call. And you are right. That was a dead man walking. "I said.

My next step was going to text Gabby Bu, then my cell began to ring. I recognized it was Molly from Paris. By this time, it was 6AM where she was. An odd time to call.

"Merci, may I please speak to Caden?"

I did not recognize the voice on the other end.

"Yes, this is Caden. Whom am I speaking to?"

After a few seconds I could hear the woman begin to sob.

"This is, Gigi, Molly's partner...I mean wife. Something horrible has happened. Molly is dead. An explosion at the cafe. I have not been able to even see her body yet. There is an investigation. But, your number is the only one I could find. I need to let Gabby know but..."

Her sobs were so loud now and her accent made it difficult to understand. But, I did understand clearly that Molly was dead. Then the phone was silent.

I would get all the details before I phoned Gabby. Hopefully she would not here it from anyone else first.

CHAPTER 46

The boundaries of life and death are at best shadowed and vague. Who shall say when one ends and the other begins?
– Edgar Allen Poe.

Gabby and Caden
March, 2010

Molly is dead. Murray is in jail, taking a plea bargain to avoid trial. Alex decided to extend his golf trip for another week and is now in Spain. Maybe chasing the Senoritas, or perhaps being chased by the Bulls in Paloma. I really don't care.

Dr. Laura is more than a psychologist. I think she is a witch doctor or a pseudo fortune teller. Only two days ago in her office she was warning me about how changes happen and we have no control over them.

Well, now I am truly a believer.

I once read an article that described how death by falling into a black hole in space might feel. There would be no feeling of force, because you would be weightless. The gravity of your two feet would be accelerating faster because of the proximity of them to the black hole's center.

The weaker force of gravity toward the head would move slower resulting in what is referred to as a tidal force. During the inquisition, the preferred method of torture was either quartering or racking. Death by black hole is so much worse,

From the moment that I heard Caden say that Molly was dead, to this very moment, I felt like the insides of my body were being shredded, my head ripped apart and everything else extruded, like toothpaste squeezed from a tube.

Two days later, only because I am sure Caden thought It was too much for me to handle, he told me that Murray was locked up and that I would not ever need to worry about him again. Trying to be sensitive he said,

"You know Gabby, if you later feel like talking to me about Murray I will always be here for you. I just want you to know that."

Caden may have had good intentions, but I had talked about everything to Doctor Laura, for so many hours that it was just now too much..

It had been years now and all I wanted to do was move on. I did not want to talk to Caden, or Alex, or Dr. Laura. Maybe in time I could have shared my feelings with Molly, but now that would never happen.

I could not convince anyone that talking about this made me relive it. Whenever I felt overwhelmed I would open Jake's journal and then share only with him my turmoil.

To discuss with Caden the details of the rape, would lead me to explaining my affair with Sterling and while I was at it, I might as well let him that Jake believed that we were destined for eternity. *No wonder I am seeing a psychologist every week.*

At this moment, my only priority was how I would manage enough courage to return to Savannah after forty-five years.

Not only would I need to face Caden, and very likely, Kaitlyn, at the funeral, but also the ghosts that I knew would join me at Tybee Beach. It would be impossible not to visit the site that Jake's ashes were spread.

Damn it Molly. Why did you have to die now? I need you more than ever. There is nobody else that could convince me to return to Savannah, and you are dead. Is this the reason you insisted that Gigi bring you home?

When I shared with Dr. Laura my anxiety of returning to Savannah, she advised me to arrive only one day prior to the funeral and leave one day after. That is a total of three days. Still too long for my comfort.

"Are you sure you don't want me to pick you up from the airport Gabby? I mean if you are worried about Kaitlyn, she has no idea about you. I am just concerned that this is all too much for you to handle, now by yourself," Caden asked.

Without sounding sarcastic I tried my best to be sincere.

"It is very sweet and thoughtful of you, Caden, but, I have learned to deal with these sudden partings over the years. I will be fine. " I said.

The allusion to our fateful New Year's Eve, did not go unnoticed by Caden.

"Will you ever let that go Gabby? If you want blood from me to prove that I am sorry, just tell me, how much and where you want me to send it?" Caden answered obviously irritated .

"I really don't want to argue about this now. I have too many other things to absorb at the moment," I replied. Ending the conversation.

The real truth was; I did not know how I would react to meeting with Caden after so many years. Texting and phone calls are one thing but face to face interaction is entirely different.

I knew that he was looking forward to this perfect opportunity for us to reunite, but Dr. Laura cautioned me, not to allow myself to be alone with Caden.

"Gabby, you must realize how vulnerable you are right now. This is not the time to add another problem to what you have on your plate. Please consider carefully how damaging this all could be," The doctor warned.

Convincing Caden that I could not see him alone, would be difficult. Making him understand would be impossible .

"Are you serious, Gabby? This is what we have been waiting for. The moment alone together that we both want," He said.

"I don't consider Molly's death a convenient time to try and reunite. My mind is only on her at this moment, as it should be," I responded annoyed, and Caden could tell.

"Okay, Gabby. I understand. But, at least stay a few days after the funeral. Neither of us know when this time will come again," Caden said, clearly disappointed.

"Caden I promise that as soon as I arrive I will text you. I am going to the viewing first and then maybe a few days after the funeral we can meet.

There will be an opportunity, at least for us to, have a drink together," I said, not revealing that I would be on the first flight home the next day.

Reluctantly, I could tell by the tone of his voice that this was not what he expected.

"Alright Gabby, I will let you call the shots, just don't shoot me in the foot while you are deciding," He said before hanging up.

I had booked three nights at the Desta Beach hotel at Tybee Beach. It was only five miles from Savannah. Close enough for the funeral and far enough away from any temptations. It was early March so the hotel was relatively empty as compared to Spring Break or summer.

Once I checked in, the first thing I did was walk to the balcony and search for my lighthouse. There it was, all in its splendor.

At one time it was the source that lead sailors to safety. For me it was where I discovered who I was.

During my worst nightmares, I would find my refuge in that tower. I had brought Jake's journals with me for comfort, but now that I was actually here, I was certain that he was with me.

The viewing hours at the funeral home were until ten pm. I presumed this was done to accommodate those visitors commuting, like me. Molly had people from all over the world sending condolences.

At the moment all I wanted was to change into my comfy jeans. I had intentionally packed the Eiffel Tower sweatshirt that Molly insisted that I have as a reminder of our visit. That was now over six years ago. Oh, how I wish I would have spent more time with her then.

I checked my watch and realized that if I left for the beach right now I could catch the sun dipping into the ocean.

Before I wandered too far I remembered my promise to text Caden, letting him know that I had arrived. Deliberately, I decided to avoid telling him where I was staying.

When he didn't respond to my text, I assumed he was busy at the bar. Normally he will text me back immediately, even just a few words assuring me that he is there.

I was now ready for Tybee beach. in the spring it is still cold, but not anything like Louisville. I grabbed my sweatshirt, my hotel key and cell phone. Before visiting Molly, I needed to be on the beach. With any luck the setting sun would give me the strength that I needed to accept this loss without agonizing over it any longer.

As soon as I stepped foot on the sand I could feel the comfort I was searching for. The sand was still warm in spots where the sun had found a place to rest.

After a few steps my shoes were off and in my hand. The fire pits that we used in high school, located right where the boardwalk ends had been removed.

A slight wind blew my hair behind my ears and I almost could feel Jake's arms reaching around my waist from behind, whispering the tune from Moon River gently in my ear.

As I moved closer to the ocean I found a rock formation far enough from the waves, for my shoes and phone to be safe.

I then began searching for seashells. This was my therapeutic way to deal with a crisis. I would imagine myself discovering ancient secrets from the sea. All the shapes are different and all of them have their own story to tell.

The foam off the waves, resemble gentle fingers concealing billions of creatures beneath the invisible surface. A peaceful interaction occurs beyond our comprehension.

And then the sun begins to sink into the deep ocean; where all the past, present and future comes together. The afterglow remains. There are visible tear drops that once touched my cheeks, promising that a butterfly will return to heal the hearts broken pieces.

It is in our dreams where freedom lives. There is something demoralizing when you imagine that life only takes on the forms that you allow it to take. *Its like watching Paris from an express caboose heading in the opposite direction . Every second the city gets smaller, and smaller, and only you feel it's really you getting smaller and lonelier, rushing away from all and lonelier rushing away from all those lights and excitement at about a million miles an hour.*

Then I overheard, Life ask Death,

"Why do people love me but hate you?"

Death responded,

"Because you are a beautiful lie, and I
 am a painful truth."

CHAPTER 47

It is the secret of the world that all things subsist and do not die, but retire a little from sight and afterwords return again.
Ralph Waldo Emerson

Caden, 2010

When Gabby did not answer my text that night or the next morning I became terribly concerned and not sure how to react. At this point I was just hoping that she would be at the memorial service in the morning.

"Gigi, have you seen or heard from Gabby? She texted me that she had arrived but, then nothing. I am getting concerned,"Caden asked as soon as he arrived at the chapel.

"I was going to ask you the same question. We were supposed to meet at the viewing last night. When she didn't show, I just presumed she had arrived too late or that she came earlier," Gigi answered.

"No. Gigi that is not like Gabby. She would never just leave you hanging, especially not now, knowing all the grief that you are experiencing," Caden said, worried.

There was no time to make any rash decisions. The service was about to begin in thirty minutes. We both agreed that it was the stress making us over react.

During the service there were over five hundred people and it was impossible to search for Gabby among those numbers

But, when Gigi's brother had to remove Gabby's name from the speakers, I knew there was a real problem.

Immediately after the service I notified the Savannah police department about her absences from the funeral. They informed me that they needed to wait forty-eight hours before making any official decision or filing a missing person's report.

They did take down all the information that I provided to them. Apparently, Gigi did have the name of the hotel at Tybee Beach where Gabby was staying. But for the time being there was nothing that either one of us could do, but wait.

It was difficult to explain to Kaitlyn why I was overly concerned. She knew nothing about Gabby and me. I tried to justify my concern by telling her that Gabby was Molly's best friend and we were all friends in high school.

The next forty-eight hours I spent most of my time at the bar, trying to keep busy and avoid thinking about Gabby. It was impossible. Then on Tuesday morning, while I was busy with inventory, in the back storage area, Devon escorted two police officer's in

"Mr. Caden Cassidy? Is that correct?"

I was startled to see them standing in front of me, but more than that I was afraid of what they might tell me.

"Yes, sir, that is me. Do you have any updated information on Gabriella Girard...I mean Blair?" Caden asked.

"We were hoping that you perhaps could fill us in on how you know Mrs. Blair. What was your relationship to her?" One officer asked.

I hesitated, not certain where these questions were leading to.

"We knew each other from Georgetown. Oh, and yes we both graduated from Savannah High School the same year. I mean...I don't know what else I can tell you," Caden said.

The officers were both writing down what seemed like a lot of information, much more than I was giving them.

"Please, just tell me, is she okay? I am out of my mind worrying about her," Caden said, adding, "like everyone else is here in Savannah."

"Sounds to me like more than a casual friendship, Mr. Cassidy," Officer Gilbert said.

Caden noticed the name on his badge.

"Mr. Cassidy, all we can tell you at this time is that we are in the process of an investigation. Mrs. Blair was last seen headed to the beach three days ago by a maintenance man working on the exterior of the hotel. We found on the beach her tennis shoes, sweatshirt, and cell phone.

Your number was the last one she called. Do you remember speaking to her on Friday evening? " The other officer asked.

My mind was still trying to accept that this was an ongoing investigation. What did that mean?

"Mr. Cassidy? Did you speak to Mrs. Blair two days ago? Yes, or No". Officer Gilbert was now much more aggressive .

"Oh, I'm sorry Sargent, no. I never spoke to her. I just got a text message," Caden replied.

The officer asking me most of the questions, stopped writing and handed me a card with his name and number.

"If you should remember anything that you might think will help us find Mrs. Blair or if she contacts you, please let us know ASAP," The officer added.

"Yes, sir I definitely will let you know if I hear anything," I said, softly.

As soon as both of the officers had walked away I collapsed into the chair next to the desk. I had no idea what was going on. Then my cell phone rang. At first I thought it was in my head, but it would not stop.

"Hello?" There was no answer. That is when I realized it was not the phone, but the text notification. On the screen were the words I never expected to see again:

"Text me when you can. Love, Gabby," The number included was different from her cell phone.

Where the hell are you Gabby?

ABOUT THE AUTHOR

Eleanor Tremayne is often asked if the characters she creates are based on her own personal life. "Most of the time that is where I begin to shape my characters, however, the final personality is a unique blend of reality and fantasy."

Like her heroine, Eleanor Tremayne was born in 1949, graduated from high school in 1967, and was briefly in love with someone similar to Jake Chevalier. In "Destiny Revisited," Eleanor's objective was to create a nostalgic 1960s atmosphere to demonstrate how powerful the past can influence the future. Literature, music, and art is the foundation of Mrs. Tremayne's life and writing is her passion. However, after obtaining a Masters Degree in Literature, teaching became a more realistic alternative. "Destiny Revisited" is Eleanor Tremayne's philosophical and psychological study of the heroine's attempt to understand the impact literature has had in her relationships.

She is currently writing her second novel, "Seven Days in Lebanon," a work in progress about her Grandmother's terrifying escape from St. Petersburg, Russia during the Communist Revolution, her marriage to the last Khan of Kiva, her dedication to surviving family and the amazing legacy she leaves behind. After completing her debut novel in May 2017, Eleanor looks forward to sharing many future stories with her readers.